THE AFFAIRS OF FLAVIE

(LES HÉRITIERS EUFFE)

BY GABRIEL CHEVALLIER

TRANSLATED FROM THE FRENCH BY JOCELYN GODEFROI

DOUBLEDAY & COMPANY, INC., GARDEN CITY, N. Y. 1949

CONTENTS

1. A VASE IN FLIGHT Beneath a gentle sky, as vast and azure as the blue immensity of a Far Eastern sea, with bright clouds for all the world like airships and drawing away in hasty flight towards the south, leaving untrammelled space for a whole pageantry of shrill and joy-filled birds, the month of May, all unawares, was performing miracles of splendour. In the streets the perfume of lilac and white carnations was hovering, and mingled with the odour of women loosely clad, their skin a trifle damp beneath their garments of georgette. People were feeling suddenly dazed, their minds filled with vague hopes, while their bodies, relieved of winter covering, revelled joyously in a newborn freedom, pervaded by little warm and titillating thrills. With this sudden burgeoning of spring, the earth was reaching its annual crisis of puberty, whose thrills and stirrings extend to all that lives and breathes.

Having become a trifle listless and enervated by the amalgam of sounds in the air and in the festive street below, Flavie Lacail was busy at her window decorating with lilac the finest vase in her apartment, a heavy piece of stoneware which had been a present to her some years before. She attached great value to this vase, having seen others almost similar to it in the shopwindow of a dealer in *objets* d'art who was believed to be purveyor to ladies of the highest standing in the town. With these ladies Flavie Lacail had no connection whatsoever, neither by education, birth, nor the profession of her husband, Félix Lacail, an entirely undistinguished employee in the prefect's office. Nevertheless she was by no means unassuming, prided herself particularly on her knowledge of the world of fashion and good manners, and felt that her competence entitled her to some far less humble existence than her own. She had believed herself to be well versed in the manners and customs of the best society ever since American films had formed her taste in rich interiors and luxury in general and taught her how to loll back on the cushions of cars with folding hoods and the dimensions of a railway engine.

These same films had given her a taste for a certain irresistible masculine type derived from those juvenile leads, as fearless as they are warm-hearted—and handsome, needless to say—whom you never meet but on the screen, and who have a way entirely their own, so airy and detached is it at moments of the utmost pathos and of sentiment, of tapping their cigarettes on the case to shake down the tobacco; so touching a way of saying "Darling!" that it wrings your heart as though his hand had been used to do it. . . . Whenever she chanced to be thinking restlessly of certain things, Flavie Lacail chose her imaginary adorers from among the most seductive and wavy-haired that Hollywood could produce. It must be added that these mental meanderings had no sequel in concrete fact, the young woman failing to meet that ideal partner to whom she was dedicating her imaginary embraces. The situation of the winsome Flavie in matters of the heart had been static for a long while past—static and requiring to be filled. For in the hidden recess of her mind she was reserving a place for a possible adventure—a magnificent adventure which time, passing all too quickly, was bidding to come forth and show itself without undue delay.

Whilst vaguely awaiting this unlikely event, Flavie Lacail had to rest content with those fleeting tributes snatched, so to speak, on the wing, which the street does not customarily award to every woman rather more than tolerably good-looking. But these transient admirers she felt she could not trust. What she wanted was seduction with the maximum of security, in surroundings where everything would be known about everybody. Her physical make-up was such as to give her a strong preference for youth, a taste which greatly increased any risk she might run: to trust one's self to the tender mercies of some young popinjay is no light undertaking for a woman with an establishment of her own and a wholesome fear of domestic upheavals. As for Félix Lacail, there was nothing to be said about him—a devastating nonentity. He was a dull, average sort of husband, with whom some years of life shared in common had done nothing but reveal his entire insignificance. Still (as there was nothing better to be had) he was a husband, a sort of handrail to hang onto, a poor sample of a bay to give the vessel shelter. But the heart could only remain untouched by such a man. And Flavie Lacail, on that lovely May morning, was feeling more plagued than ever by her heart. . . .

It was most certainly rash on her part to go to the window to arrange her flowers, and this prudent woman ordinarily took great care not to place the vase too near the empty space below. But everything that morning seemed so fresh, so new; there was such encouragement, such life and colour in all that could be seen outside, all the way to the smil-

2

ing mountains which appeared in the background at intervals along the street; it was all so conducive to happiness that for once in her life Flavie Lacail was neglecting those housewifely precautions which make it quite certain that objects will last forever; though in a general way she was keeping an eye on the safety of the vase, which was very heavy at the base, and the danger of its being upset was thereby lessened.

Having finished arranging her flowers, and being suddenly overcome by a strange feeling of inertia and slackness—a thing which had rarely if ever happened to this sane and well-balanced woman—Flavie could not tear herself away from the fascinating splendour of the heavens above and the concert of unseen flutes with which the air was quivering and alive. So she stayed at her window, leaning out a little, daydreaming. Almost unconsciously she kept rubbing each leg, bare beneath her morning wrap, against the other, enjoying its soft texture so slighted and misprized, and deprived of any tribute worth having, of caresses as sweet and gentle as the hand that lightly plucks at harp strings. . . . Indeed, Flavie herself was feeling like a harp all ready to vibrate and thrill. She was thirty, an age of rich, full-bodied charms; she was like a fruit that is full of pulp and has reached the right moment for plucking. Alongside her the lilac filled the air with its lovely scent. It was a little before ten o'clock in the morning.

This was the moment at which her visitor of ill omen made his way into the room; it was Pamphile Garambois, whom the servant, knowing him to be a friend, had admitted without even announcing him.

The new arrival was himself carrying a bunch of flowers, and his rather unpleasing countenance was lit up with a joyful expression which he had assumed for the occasion. He was getting ready to smile politely, when he was rooted to the spot by the wholly unexpected sight which met his eyes—a sight which might perhaps prove favourable to his designs, was certainly suggestive, and which, so far as he himself was concerned, was indeed enough to send him crazy. His manner underwent an instant change. His features and expression became those of a moon-struck person, and his gestures grew feverish, betraying the inner conflict of a man suddenly faced with a decision vital to his happiness for the remainder of his life.

Is it not reasonable to suppose that one may love without expressing one's feelings for six long years, and with undiminished, nay, increasing fervour? That such a love as this, conceived by a man whose shyness acts as a restraint upon desire—which may perhaps expend itself in wild outbreaks when he is far from his beloved—that a love like this may gain added strength as time goes on? And if this be true, should we not ex-

3

pect a passion of this nature, having now become explosive, to end by despising all accepted standards of good behaviour and self-restraint, and even trampling them madly underfoot, and to burst forth with violence from having been held too long in check?

For six years past Pamphile Garambois had been madly in love with the wife of his friend Félix Lacail, and for six years the image of Flavie had been haunting the old bachelor's life of solitude and gloom. For six years he had been snatching at any and every excuse for another sight of the charming creature, telling himself each time that he was now going to declare his love to this misunderstood and forsaken lady, upon whom Félix's neglect must inevitably sooner or later force some moral lapse, and that he, Pamphile, would not be the beneficiary unless he took the bull by the horns in good time. And for six years past he had kept silence. There were days when it made him ill. And now at last he put out a feeler:

"I'm very fond of you, you know, Flavie!"

Seemingly quite unmoved, she replied, as though it were a question which had already been settled for good:

"And I am very fond of you too, my old Pampan. And Félix is very fond of you. And so is everybody."

Anger, refusal, extreme indignation—any of these would have been less discouraging! In actual fact Flavie was feeling something like hatred for Pamphile Garambois, whose passion, which for a long time had been fairly obvious, did not flatter her. It was a caricature, and a grotesque one at that, of that passion of which she had just been dreaming. And the presence of this ridiculous wooer might be keeping other men at a distance who would have been more to her liking. But Félix Lacail could not do without his old Garambois, who himself could not do without Flavie; and the husband and wife were even slightly in debt to the bachelor. Flavie wished to remain in entire ignorance of this matter, which was supposed to be dealt with unbeknown to her and which was really not a woman's concern.

And thus it was that on this May morning, urged on by a spring which was now bursting forth in final splendour, Pamphile Garambois, bearing a large nosegay of flowers—by which he was no less hampered than by his own heart—was coming to wish Flavie many happy returns of the day, in the absence of Félix, whom he knew to be at his office. On the way there he had thought out some bold and pleasing projects, the same indeed as those he had been devising for six years past, forgetting that, during those same years, however impetuous or strong his feelings may have been, the mere sight of his fair lady had always made him speechless.

4

And so it was that no sooner had he reached the landing on the fourth floor than Pamphile felt his courage ebbing, as toothache may sometimes vanish at the dentist's door. He was like those too sensitive lovers for whom a single fiasco will mean a fiasco every time, because their approach to love is made in a doubting mood which can only harm their cause, and with a lack of straightforwardness and simplicity. But all this was altered when his eyes fell upon Flavie that morning.

It must be made clear at what angle this faithful admirer, stricken dumb by a sudden access of feeling, and fearing lest he be heard and thus disturb so charming a picture, first caught sight of the young woman in the unstudied pose of one who thinks she is alone. It was from behind, with hollowed back, that Pamphile's blazing eyes devoured her, she being lost in reverie and having no suspicion of any presence other than her own. For a shy and timid lover, who had never dared to gaze at the beloved at his ease, the posture of his idol was thrilling to the last degree, with that soft and careless freedom which gave such prominence to the lovely symmetries of a rich and splendid frame, whose firm and shapely outlines her thirtieth year had finally secured. Flavie was perhaps inclined to plumpness. A passing fashion has brought this term into disrepute, while formerly it enjoyed an almost universal esteem. But despite that fashion, the qualities which that term evokes are never lacking in fervent admirers, especially among tall thin men, as Pamphile was. The law of opposites, which is so largely responsible for the continuance of a reign of harmony in this world of ours, as also for the beauty of its many races, inspired him with an irresistible fondness for lovely masses smooth and round and with a horror of angular creatures with flat chests and curves of meagre design. Firm and abundant masses were the very things which Flavie could display, and he himself could admire beneath the transparence of her morning wrap. And they moreover were given life by a slight swaying of her hips, since Flavie was gently rubbing her legs each against the other.

A thing which usually hampered any amorous attempt on the part of Pamphile Garambois was to feel the admirable Flavie's haughty gaze aimed steadily at him—a look which was not only penetrating but also chaste, an effective check on any misplaced avowal and which made him blush. And now, for the first time in six years, he was catching the young woman unawares in auspicious solitude, and lightly clad in a way no less auspicious, with himself unembarrassed by that look of hers. It was an exceptional opportunity, an outstanding moment. And everything outside, the scents and colours, the sunlight and song, held promise of kindness and of ways made smooth, of the final attainment of all he craved. . . .

5

Already immensely relieved at the idea of not having to say a single word, Pamphile Garambois was spurred into hasty action by a fear lest Flavie should suddenly turn round and completely overwhelm him with those fine eyes of hers. But she was not looking at him, and he must take advantage of this. Here was the one opportunity of his life, the finest piece of good fortune that had ever fallen to his lot.

An intense concentration of thought on his part lasted for a few seconds only, for the matter was urgent. Wishing to have his hands free for this great venture, Pamphile got rid of his bouquet and his hat, while at his beloved's back he made the wry face of a man about to leap into the water without being quite sure of his ability to swim. Then, half demented by his feelings, he sprang at Flavie Lacail and attacked her brutally, panting with long-suppressed desire.

Having been seized from behind, and feeling a rough hand on her breast and her hip assailed, Flavie uttered a cry of indignation and of fear. At the same time a moustache was roughly laid upon her neck, and the smell of a pipe, breathed over her hair, was extremely unpleasant. (It should be mentioned that on his way to Flavie's, Pamphile, to get a little courage, had indulged in two or three glasses of white wine at a public bar. These drinks, absorbed on an empty stomach, were not calculated to give him a perfect young lover's breath.)

Pressed between a window ledge which separated her from the empty space below and a raging individual with some horrid exhalations, the young woman became extremely frightened. The daily papers are full of shocking news items and the servant often forgot to shut the door which opened on to the landing. Fortunately Flavie was a rather compact and stocky little person, with firm strong legs. Summoning up all her strength, she managed by a desperate effort to shake herself free. But this sudden movement had disastrous results for the lovely vase. It received a push and was dashed outwards and downwards through the empty air—a disaster which drew a loud cry from the young woman.

But this was certainly not the moment to worry about the vase! She had to confront her attacker, and perhaps to shout for help. In the first moment of surprise this had not occurred to her. With great coolness, and very nimbly, she threw herself back a long way from the window, seized another large vase, and struck a blow at the man's face with it. Not until that moment did she recognize her adversary. Beside herself with anger, she followed up this first attack with a resounding box on the ears. Pamphile, now in very poor fettle, retreated, then went and sank onto the sofa, saying:

"But it's me, Flavie! Me, your old Pampan!"

"You stupid old fool!" Flavie said.

She was half naked, with her breast uncovered and shaking with anger, with what still remained of her terror and distress. Facing this indignant and lovely bosom, Pamphile sat pitifully dabbing his bleeding nose. Holding his handkerchief to his face, he went over and took up his bouquet, which he then held out to his angry inamorata, saying, in a hesitating murmur to which the linen over his mouth gave a strange sound:

"Many happy returns, Flavie! It's your birthday."

"Old imbecile, you!"

She seized the flowers from him and hurled them violently into the street. But this furious woman, feeling herself to be mistress of the situation, was in no special hurry to expel the pitiful Pamphile, who was now back once more in his usual state of cowardice induced by the pretty creature's gaze, which at that moment was filled with hatred. Enjoying her position of vantage, Flavie told her ridiculous admirer exactly what she thought of him and how she rejoiced at being rid forever of such a figure of fun as he.

"For you will never set foot here again—you'd better be quite clear about that!"

"Oh, Flavie dear, forgive me! Dear Flavie, I just lost my head for a second, the first time in six years—do forget it, please!" Pamphile said, sighing, his voice muffled by the handkerchief over his mouth.

"A thing like that, done at the home of a man who trusted you—it's unpardonable! And it's unpardonable for anybody with a face like yours!"

"And what about Félix?" Pamphile cried. "What will he be thinking if he doesn't see any more of me?"

"He won't be surprised when he hears what has happened. I shall tell him everything."

"Flavie," Pamphile groaned, "you surely won't do that! You can't. Félix and I did our service together. You know, Flavie, don't you?—we were in the grand manœuvres together. You can't break up a friendship like ours."

"And who was it betrayed that old friendship?"

"Ah, Flavie, it's all your fault! That wrap of yours got into my head . . ."

"You idiot!"

"Flavie, why are you so beautiful! I've loved you ever since I first knew you. And why do I come here every day? It's for you, Flavie, because I love you to dis——"

"You're dotty, that's obvious!"

"Very well, then, Flavie dear, I am! And can one be in love without being dotty—and hopelessly clumsy too? Ah, if only I didn't love you so much .."

At that moment an urgent peal at the bell effectively drowned the gloomy utterances, the regrets and solemn oaths which were filtering through the cotton handkerchief of Pamphile Garambois. Voices were heard in the waiting room, and the housemaid came in:

"The porter is asking for you, ma'am. You must come at once," he said.

Flavie Lacail found the porter on the landing. and the stairway, which was filled with people the whole way down, was humming with a strange, abnormal murmur of voices, in which there was a dolorous and plaintive note.

"You haven't dropped anything out of the window?" the porter asked.

"Yes, that's just what I have done," Flavie said. "My lovely vase full of flowers. It's broken, isn't it?"

"Well, I never," said the porter, "that's a nice thing to have done! Yes, a nice thing, I must say. . . . And it'll cost you a pretty penny, I shouldn't wonder. . . ."

Flavie lived in Grenoble, on the fourth floor of a house in the Rue Turenne. The reader is already aware that the wife of Félix Lacail, a little enervated by the warmth of early spring, was alone at her window, day-dreaming, at a little before ten o'clock in the morning.

It so happened that at this very same hour M. Constant Euffe was arriving in these parts, having made a slight deviation by way of the Rue Charles-Testoud. Fate was in a deadly mood as she guided his footsteps thither. It must be added that Fate on this occasion was disguising herself with most charming features, those of Mlle. Riri Jumier, an attractive person of twenty-two, and equipped in every respect to enliven, strictly in private, a generous old man's leisure hours. M. Euffe was the old man whose declining years were being brightened by the pretty Riri. It is true that she did not do this for nothing, seeing that the value of the time set aside by a beautiful girl for the benefit of a man of sixty-seven can hardly be estimated. Riri was, in fact, a very great expense to M. Euffe, who had earmarked for this pretty person a capital sum of considerable dimensions, and moreover continually increasing, to such an extent as to be a source of worry to a respectable middle-class family, who were in despair at seeing the results of vast commercial undertakings which had been brilliantly successful for forty years past materializing in jewellery and furs for the adornment of a saucy baggage; while M. Euffe, at the period when his behaviour had been quite correct (i.e., when he was amassing his fortune), had shown a sordid stinginess over giving such presents to Mme. Euffe, pretending that a man's own wife is always beautiful in her husband's eyes without his having to bolster her up with an expensive and vulgar display fit only for a jade. When in her young days Mme. Euffe had been dying for some piece of jewellery, M. Euffe gave her another child instead. This new child kept Mme. Euffe away from all empty ostentation and idle caprice.

Born into the retail grocery trade, M. Euffe had soon given proof of a spirit of enterprise and a tenacity of purpose which in due course were to be crowned with such success that by the time he had reached the age of fifty he held the proud position of being one of the richest men in Grenoble: this was on account of the Silken Net, a catering business with large numbers of branch establishments, which spread the network of its agencies throughout the Department of the Isère and the two Savoys. In these regions the Silken Net had created a system of bounties or free gifts (in exchange for coupons), and the prizes themselves, chosen with a display of bad taste that amounted almost to genius, were the joy of every housewife's heart. Whole districts ate from table services of the same pattern, drank from the same glasses and the same cups. There was a certain kind of bulging soup tureen which was all the rage in the valley of the Grésivaudan and the Tarentaise; a certain pattern of doily held a place of honour on the tables of Voiron, St.-Marcellin, Annecy, and Chambéry. M. Euffe's sets of carvers (2,500 coupons) were used for the Sunday joints of the small shopkeepers and wage earners. With an eye to everything, the Silken Net offered also umbrella stands, perambulators, hygienic feeding bottles, flowerpot cases, coat-and-hat racks for waiting rooms, console tables, sets of shelves, et cetera. For a three years' contract for an over-all supply of goods, including wine, margarine, lard, furniture polish, iron shavings for scrubbing floors, et cetera, with a fixed minimum of monthly expenditure, one could choose between a Louis XV bedroom or a Henry II dining room, "inspired reproductions of furniture in our national museums," according to the prospectus.

M. Euffe, whose brain was seething with new ideas and who had an itch for writing which must be a rarity among grocers, was continually drawing up new circulars and compiling illustrated catalogues of his prizes adorned with emblems, allegories, and maxims. His style, being remarkably well adapted to the taste and understanding of his customers, was in itself a special adornment to the business; and his effusions found their way into the kitchens and the farms, where they were scrupulously preserved with the copies of *The Perfect Cook* and *Father Benedict's Almanack*. M. Euffe must also be given the credit for having invented, long before the great latter-day publicity campaigns, new formulæ, easy to remember and repeat, by which feminine minds were greatly impressed. Let us quote at random:

Presents for your marketing basket—Miracles at the Silken Net— Food which is an adornment to the home.

These phrases fixed themselves in the good women's brains. The splendid catalogues, which appealed to their imagination, did the rest. M. Euffe had also instituted an "Order book competition" for the best-kept and cleanest books, and in which the coupons were the most artistically disposed inside. A double page in the middle of the book was reserved for an attempt at a new way of displaying these. Fifty of them set out on this double page had to make up some decorative design or arabesque, and the books retained by the adjudicators had their value doubled. This artistic research was an excellent occupation for the long winter evenings, everyone in the house taking part in it; while from the commercial point of view it had this advantage, that so soon as people had finished looking at the pictures in the *Vermot Almanack* they could then think of nothing but the Silken Net.

Having risen to a position in which he enjoyed the highest authority and respect, M. Euffe wished that there should be no greater popular idol in three Departments than the Silken Net, and that all their inhabitants should swear by that organization and by that alone. He was planning to have his own almanack too, and that this should be a compendium of all the good recipes for cooking, advice on housekeeping, rearing of children, elementary medicine, care of animals and of plants, a handy reference for the formalities required in connection with births, deaths, and inheritances, and all the solemn occasions of life, down to specimens of the standing forms of words used in letter writing, including those suitable for young people of an age to venture along the path of tender avowals: "Speak to my parents, dear Alfred . . ."

All this, as will be seen, constituted a grand, imposing scheme, which demanded an enormous accumulation of material drawn from every branch of human knowledge. M. Euffe had had in mind the names of a few distinguished professors who are always quite glad to see their academic distinctions in print in popular treatises; and he had paid visits to bonesetters, fortunetellers, and astrologers, feeling as he did that, with his class of customer, stock prescriptions, old wives' remedies, warnings and interpretations of dreams, and the movements of the stars were not to be despised. He even became immersed himself in encyclopædias of many pounds' weight, a study which left him astounded at the vast extent of the learning from which the grocery trade had cut him off. Too absorbed in catering, he had quite forgotten the nourishment of the mind. He had glimpses of a mission of high moral import, which should add another bright distinction—philanthropic achievement—to all those of which the Silken Net could already boast.

Unfortunately, while reading his encyclopædias with bursting head, M. Euffe lighted on the word amour (love), which, through the exigencies of the alphabet, comes at the very beginning of these bulky works. M. Euffe realized that there also—in love—lay a territory in which his assiduous and in some ways missionary practice of the art of grocery had prevented him from making any great advance. At about his sixtieth year he discovered an unknown world with its own mysteries, its thrills, its heroes, and its glory—themes in constant use by poets. From that time onwards the life of M. Euffe was changed, and he went somewhat to pieces. He began seriously to doubt that grocery was everything in life, that a Silken Net prospectus included the very essence of earthly activities and happiness. These doubts came as such a shock to him that he made some blunders. He paid three farthings a pound too much for a consignment of thirty tons of sugar, and had a stock of chocolate palmed off on him which was beginning to turn white from age. There were whispers of this being the first sign that he no longer had all his wits about him. What people meant by this was that he was losing that admirable power of concentration which, whether as buyer or seller, gave him equal skill.

This was the first sign; the second was that M. Euffe was observed to be paying unwonted attention to a typist in his offices, a young hoyden as provocative as a piece of unripe fruit, whose instinct as a good native of Dauphiné whispered to her that attention from her employer was giving her an excellent start in life. As things turned out, the harvest to be obtained from these attentions was not reaped by her but by her parents, no less typical of Dauphiné than their daughter. These good people came solemnly and asked M. Euffe, with loud lamentations, whether it would be to his taste that a certain scandal should be made public, as a case of a girl underage, and with no means of protecting herself, being exposed to the tender mercies of an immoral set of employers. It fell to M. Euffe to calm this virtuous indignation and repair the damage done to the susceptibilities of these respectable parents by offering them compensations to be chosen from the complete catalogue of his prizes. By the time he had extricated himself he was the poorer by furniture for two rooms, a porcelain dinner service, a large copper vase, and two or three terra-cotta statuettes. His sole consolation was that he had bought the lot at wholesale price, much below the value which he had temptingly assigned to them.

This incident made some stir in Grenoble, where nothing that happens to its citizens remains long unknown anywhere between the Place Victor-Hugo and the Place Grenette. The comments which were made greatly extended the area of the scandal, and Mme. Euffe received some anonymous letters, the work of worthy souls who wished to put her on her guard against the dangers which were threatening her home.

Firmly pursuing his downward and fatal path, M. Euffe turned his back on the old principles which had established his respectability and made his fortune, and hurled himself blindly into a maelstrom of loose living and wild excess. His enjoyment of these pleasures was extreme to the point of being diabolical, and as things always balance each other, a life of economy and hard work had left him with fine vigour for a man of his age. Matters had gone so far that his elder daughter, Lucie, was desperately afraid lest part of her dowry should find its way into the hands of "Daddy's horrid women."

As for Mme. Euffe, the thought of all the rings and the furs of which she had been deprived during the years when she looked her best, and which now were going to shameless hussies, filled her with bitter regret.

"I was a nice fresh young woman and no one could say a word against me; I've been a good mother, too, and he was closefisted and stingy with me. And now, today, he is smothering those wretched creatures with finery and jewels."

"Why," asked Lucie, "has Father, who is getting so free with his money outside, always been so miserly at home?"

"Your father used always to declare that he couldn't take any money out of the business, that he must continually be adding to his trading capital, that his real fortune was in his stocks and the different shops. When you were born, do you know what his present to me was? The purchase of his big branch at Chambéry. And shall I tell you what he kept on saying to me for thirty years? 'We'll have a good time when we're old.' "

But alas! reparation for the offence of many years of cheeseparing and meanness was no longer possible. Anything like a display of sparkling jewellery would now have drawn too much attention to the respectable but superannuated appearance of Mme. Euffe. It was far better that the only impression she should give should be that of a blameless and irreproachable lady; that she should receive the honour due to her good name. On this good reputation she did in fact take her stand for the purpose of indulging in severe criticism of the young women of the new generation, whose behaviour was quite different from that of their predecessors in former days and who were slack in their methods of bringing up children and no longer giving all their attention to their homes, were dispensing with corsets and often with hats, and so flimsily clad and, generally speaking, relapsing into bad form. . . . Offended by all this, Mme. Euffe turned to a zealous display of good works, with manifestations of piety which no one could fail to observe. She brought God into her picture, but she did it in such a narrow-minded way that it could only make Him appear hateful; this may have been because for the past twenty years she had had blotchy cheeks and a red nose. In the name of the limited and bad-tempered deity to whom all her prayers were addressed, she inflicted penalties on the members of her family which were quite undeserved, cutting down their food and depriving them of home comforts and jolly parties, with a secret habit of searching her children's pockets and of reading their letters. That Mme. Euffe had been born in a shop was a fact which was still evident.

"There's no reason why," Edmond Euffe, the elder son, would say, "because Father has a high old time, we should all worry ourselves about it. After all, whatever you may say, Mother has had advantages; she has a very good position in Grenoble, she's a sort of lady of the manor at Montbonnot. and Grandfather kept a cutlery shop at the corner of the Rue Notre Dame. If we don't see those millions very often, still they do exist, we've got them, and they'll come out of their hiding place some-day."

"If there is anything left!" Lucie said bitterly. She was the ugly duckling of the family, had nearly reached the age of twenty-eight without finding a husband, and her nose, like her mother's, was also beginning to grow red.

"Yes, yes, but all the same, this Riri person isn't going to gobble up everything!" Edmond Euffe replied. "And Father has learnt to count."

The effect of the expiatory privations imposed by Mme. Euffe was to send M. Euffe hastening more often than ever in the direction of Riri Jumier—whom he had now set up with a flat of her own—where everything was warm and smiling and cosy and soft. Austere maxims, sighs, and the clicking of beads were sounds hardly calculated to retain in the family circle an abandoned old man with a pretty young woman in his pay who was anything but a reciter of long prayers, but was pink and white and never lectured him, and called him, in a roguish, chaffing sort of way extremely flattering to a man of his age, "you young rascal."

When he was with Riri, M. Euffe would often regret that his career as a pioneer of catering had swallowed up so many years of his life. He would say to her, lisping, and with much chaff and banter:

"What do you think I found right at the bottom of the Silken Net? A Riri!"

"And what is he hiding at the bottom of the net, for his Riri?"

"Ah, the little minx! That, my pet," M. Euffe would reply, taking some precious little package from his pocket.

From that time onwards M. Euffe preferred this youthful frolic to any study of the fluctuations and progress of food products. In the Place Marval, where Riri Jumier lived, he found a fresh flowering of his youth, which was all the richer, more urgent a growth for having come to him late in life, when the prospect of its approaching and inevitable loss had been weighing heavily upon him. Nevertheless, his arteries and blood pressure were remaining normal, his complexion clear. He walked well, his sight was good, all his bodily faculties were in good working order. He had taken up physical culture under the direction of a professor, while his doctor was giving careful attention to his heart. Two ladies of the Euffe family were saying to each other in despair that Constant Euffe seemed disposed neither to stop those pranks of his nor yet to die, and that the family millions had started a dance which had every appearance of being well-nigh endless.

But Edmond Euffe, who could not help feeling a certain admiration for his father, would sometimes exclaim:

"Father is an astonishing man. It's marvellous the way he keeps his end up, and he seems to me to be less nervy, to have more go in him and be in far better spirits than he used to. If you come to think of it, this house has always been a bit gloomy. He used to get bored to death at home."

"Now about this young woman of his," Lucie Euffe said to her brother, speaking of Riri Jumier; "you're a man, couldn't you go and see her? Perhaps if she were given money she would drop him."

"But it's he who won't drop her! As for money, Father can give her more than we could, and the lady would certainly know which side her bread was buttered! Now just remember, there's a man who has worked like a slave, who brought us up and made us rich, and will leave us a business that's going at full blast. He's enjoying himself a bit late in life, perhaps. All right, then, let's jolly well leave him to it!"

"You're approving of Father now, then, are you?"

"It's not only he who is to blame. After all, if it had been made more pleasant for him at home . . ."

14

"You're forgetting all Mother's troubles when you talk like that!"

"Oh, Mother! . . . Mother, she has her church, she's got God to complain to!"

"Edmond, how can you . . ."

"But look here, she said herself that she'd chosen the better part! It seems a pity that though she's so well provided for herself, she makes such a nuisance of herself to other people and is so hopelessly dull and boring at home!"

On that May morning when Flavie Lacail was dreaming at her window, M. Euffe, no less bewitched than she by the stimulating warmth of spring, was hastening with sturdy footsteps and in splendid trim—though this was not his usual hour for dalliance—to his pretty Riri's flat at the corner of the Place Marval, close to the Rue Turenne. As a man of good feeling, always anxious to arrive at his fair charmer's in perfect physical condition, he made a brief preparatory halt. He had a little perspiration on his face and neck. M. Euffe took out his handkerchief and, removing his hat, exposed to the air his bald and shiny head which on this warm and happy spring morning was taking on the rosy hue of a burnt-almond sweet. He was smiling, and thinking of the pleasures that were now so very, very near. Alas and alack! . . .

This was the moment at which, high up above him, the all-too-fervent Pamphile Garambois was springing wildly at the alluring Flavie Lacail. This was the moment, the exact moment, at which Flavie's fine vase was departing into empty space at terrible speed, which increased in accordance with the weight and square of the distance. . . . This big bulky object came crashing down, bottom foremost, flat onto the bald and unprotected cranium of M. Euffe, and split it open as though it had been a nutshell. Knocked senseless, M. Euffe collapsed onto the pavement, and the vase, by some inexplicable vagary of ballistics, came to rest intact at the side of his head, with its sheaf of lilac still in place. Just a little water had trickled out from it, and this was bathing the temples of M. Euffe, whose blood was flowing from his mouth, his nostrils, and his ears. But this kindly attention on the part of inanimate objects was powerless to revive him from a deathly swoon, and already the soul was preparing to quit this worthy body, which was being shaken by the convulsive movements of approaching death and an obscure revolt of the subconscious, which was probably thinking, in a last glimmer of lucidity, that it was absurd to be dying because somebody else had been clumsy, and when one had at one's entire disposal an adorable and more than friendly Riri. It was doubtless the profound stupidity of

15

human arrangements that was dealing with M. Euffe, as he lay stretched out on the pavement, a fatal blow, for his wide-open eyes expressed immense astonishment, and the little muttered, grunting sounds which came forth from his slack and dribbling lips had a reproachful intonation. A rich man, M. Euffe was not accustomed to have Fate treating him with a lack of respect and dealing him heavy blows on the head. He was dying in a state of extreme indignation, seeing that Providence was henceforth allowing Destiny's wayward tricks to include the taking, for targets, of hoary heads which were the pride of the Chamber of Commerce and the local Association of Provision Merchants.

This terrible crashing of the vase on a man's head and the dull, muffled sound of a body collapsing onto the pavement had drawn the attention of some passers-by. They came up and, seeing how M. Euffe was dressed, his short beard so carefully tended, his massive gold watch chain, his pearl tiepin, and the expensive quality of his linen and his shoes, realized at once that the victim of this stupid accident was by no means one of the ordinary herd. The incident made all the more commotion on this account, and the news spread round the shops in the neighbourhood with astonishing rapidity. Some of the local gossips, wearing their morning petticoats, hastened with groaning and lamentations to the scene. These ladies, admirably posted in the comings and goings of people in the district, came and bent over M. Euffe.

"Looks to me like Riri's boy friend, doesn't he?"

"Monsieur Euffe?"

"Yes, of course it's him, I'm certain of it, that blood don't make no difference. Why, I used to see him go by every day, I did, on the stroke of five, and always carryin' some little parcels—for his ladylove, of course."

"Oh, so it's Monsieur Euffe of the Silken Net?"

"Well, I don't think it is, Madame Poitte! I know Monsieur Euffe just as well as you do, and I don't think he's as tall as that. I should take him to be a squat, dumpy little man, Monsieur Euffe, I should."

"Oh, don't say that, Madame Couffon! Don't say things you're not certain about, when there's such tragic things happening to a man like him, a man who's a big bug in Grenoble! That's Monsieur Euffe all right, lying stretched out down there, and it makes one feel kind of awe-struck, seeing him on the ground like that. But just you stand him upright and you'll see it's Monsieur Euffe himself."

"So that really is Monsieur Euffe of the Silken Net and those coupon prizes?"

"Yes, and you can't think how rich he is! A millionaire he is—as rich as Crœsus! Everyone's got to eat, they're bound to, and there isn't a soul who doesn't deal at the Silken Net or the branches they've got all over the place. Just think of the money those people must pile up, with all the food that's sold!"

"And that's him there, all the same."

"And it's got to happen to all of us!"

"P'r'aps he's not going to die after all."

"That depends on what storey the thing was that fell on him—how high up it was. Anyway, he's lookin' pretty bad, I must say! This reminds me of when Granddad fell off the roof of the barn a year or two ago. He came head downwards smack onto the . . ."

"They do say that fortunes don't stop accidents happenin'!"

"You're right, they don't! Well, we've all got to go through it, haven't we? Someday or other."

"Yes, as you say, Madame Poitte, we shall all have to push off to a better world someday."

"And that poor Monsieur Euffe—it do seem as though his time had come to do it!"

"This'll mean a posh funeral here in Grenoble with all the nobs followin' along behind!"

"He'd got a finger in every pie, Monsieur Euffe had! A rich man like that, they couldn't do without him on committees and suchlike . . ."

"And now . . ."

"Yes, now! . . . As young Raimuzat used to say—he's the son of the dyer and cleaner in the Rue Condorcet, and been in the army and done some fightin'—you must know him . . ."

"Tony Raimuzat's son, you mean."

"Yes, that's him. Well, he used to say, 'Once he's dead, the colonel stinks as much as the tommy.' That's the sort of way the soldiers used to talk."

"That's the kind of saying that really teaches people—makes 'em understand things!"

These exchanges of conversation were continuing outside the chemist's shop into which the dying M. Euffe had just been carried. That it was indeed M. Euffe, the papers taken from his pockets amply confirmed.

It was at this same chemist's shop that Flavie Lacail and Pamphile Garambois arrived a little later, conducted by the porter from the Rue Turenne and followed by various people from the flats there. Some obliging person went off to look for a policeman, while others debated the question of the best method of breaking the news to the family, of sparing their feelings and softening the blow.

Some of the witnesses of the accident then drew attention to the fact that, looped round his finger with a pale blue string, M. Euffe was still holding a little package bearing the gilt label of the confectioner. Some persons well aware of the circumstances then suggested that the presence of this package might be very distasteful to the family if the victim—as was indeed to be inferred—had intended it for some unacknowledged lady of his acquaintance—of whose identity they had little or no doubt. With the consent of everyone present, the chemist then untied the string and removed the paper. It contained a small bag of stuffed and candied nuts, a Grenoble delicacy in great favour. The name of Riri Jumier was pronounced with discretion, for this was no time for criticism or heaping coals of fire. There were many things which the chemist himself knew. . . . He handed round a few nuts, then put the little bag just as it was into the hands of the woman whom he found the most pleasing of the assembled company. This was Flavie herself.

"Look, madame," he said to her politely, "if you take them, they will have lovely teeth to crunch them."

Flavie shrank back.

"Oh, but I couldn't dream of it! That vase belonged to me."

"Forgive me," the chemist said. "I understand, I understand . . . But I am sorry, I am very sorry," he murmured, casting at Flavie a glance from which it was evident that his thoughts were leagues away from chemistry.

Taking advantage of the crowd of people present and the diversion caused by the sorry state of M. Euffe, he added, very softly:

"Do you usually come here for what you want? I don't think I have seen you before."

"I am so very seldom ill!" Flavie said.

"Well, that's a pity, a real pity!" the chemist said, sighing. "But you must surely need some small articles, like toilet soap, tooth paste, eau-de-cologne, or beauty preparations? I should be delighted, I can assure you, to supply you . . . at special prices, very special prices."

"I think I need something at this very moment," Flavie said. "I'm not feeling at all well. This business has upset me."

"Just a moment, madame. I'll give you a pick-me-up."

"Look after that poor man first," Flavie Lacail said, pointing, without daring to look at him, at M. Euffe as he lay on a stretcher.

"We have already done what is required. My assistant won't leave him. And as for the rest . . ."

The chemist raised his eyes to heaven and pointed upwards, through the ceiling, at the higher regions of the universe.

"*Ad patres!*" he said simply. "There goes another man who's finished with pills!"

"Oh dear! Oh dear!" Flavie cried out. She had suddenly turned as white as a sheet.

There was only just time to hold her up and bring her a chair: she was fainting. Pamphile Garambois dashed forward, but the chemist pushed him aside.

"Now then, out you go, out you go!" he said roughly. "There are too many people in here. The wounded man must have more air. Keep that door locked, Eusebius," he said to his assistant.

He wished to be quite undisturbed while he was restoring a pretty woman to consciousness, and making sure, by way of taking every precaution, that a brassière she was wearing was not dangerously tight. These fine, well-developed bosoms are apt to be a sensitive spot and very liable to congestion, and some prompt action may be necessary. . . .

For thirty years past, ever since the brilliant success of the Silken Net had made it inevitable, the name of M. Euffe had been a household word in Grenoble, and was probably uttered thousands of times every day. And now M. Euffe had become the victim of a stupid accident and was dying an obscure death in a small chemist's shop, far from the Avenue d'Alsace-Lorraine where his offices were situated, far from his château of Montbonnot and his villa at Bouquéron, far from his La Monta and Vif properties, and far from his own family and household staff—and Grenoble, in all its morning splendour, beneath a sky of cloudless blue, knew nothing of this grave and solemn event.

The town was looking delightful, with a delicious, carefree charm and grace. A light, transparent mist which lay over the Rabot redoubt and the Bastille had now almost dispersed. In the far distance, on the rocks of the Moucherotte and St.-Eynard, some silvery tints were beginning to appear, while over their summits the last remaining little white clouds of mist were breaking up into clear bright strips, which were gently driven by the wind in the direction of the Lautaret. In the Avenue Jean-Jaurès the market was in full swing, and tramcars were coming in from all directions in the vicinity of the Place Victor-Hugo and the Place Grenette. In the quiet Place Verdun, the administrative, intellectual, and military centre of the town, some bemedalled army pensioners were seated on benches, reading their newspapers. Beyond the level crossing the Berriat parade was discharging its stream of vehicles in the direction of the Drac, whose tumultuous waters have a bluey-green and leaden tint. The white church tower of Seyssinet, rising above the chestnut trees of its little square, was gleaming on the mountainside. The plain of Echirolles was swept by little currents of air which stirred its tangle of young verdure, still looking immature with its tints of pale and yellowish green. In the bright sunlight the valley of the Grésivaudan was displaying the splendour of its old country houses, its ancient trees, its parks, its scattered formless villages with their swarms of little shanties put up on the mountain spurs, below the great ridges of precipitous rock.

Built on a level and with macadamized roads, Grenoble is essentially a town of the bicycle or, as it is commonly called, *vélo*. No sight could be more pleasing than that of the young Grenoble girls, supple and fearless riders, with their backs hollowed and bending forward over their narrow handle bars and gliding rapidly along on their gaily coloured machines, with an occasional flash of a white leg seen high up despite the modest little gesture by which the flying skirt is pulled down to its proper place. That morning the young female centaurs with streaming hair were enjoying themselves to their hearts' content as they scoured the avenues, taking the longest route for the sheer joy of pedalling, and sweeping round sharp corners and turns. Smiles were opening out in blossom on their lips, worthy rivals of the mountain flowers. The beginnings of perspiration from their armpits were lightly moistening their bodices beneath the armholes, and their young breasts were tossed and shaken with each slight jolt. Grenoble was sending forth its gaily coloured troops of pretty cyclists, eager entrants for the great competition of the season of light and brilliance and the race for happiness. The clearness of the azure sky was beyond description.

And M. Constant Euffe was dying! His shattered cranium was losing its colour of a pink burnt-almond sweet and gradually acquiring the yellow tint of a Chinese porcelain figure. . . .

Outside, Pamphile Garambois was hastening to a bar in the Rue Condorcet. He too, like Flavie, was feeling ill, sick at heart with this tragic turn of events after his high hopes on this lovely morning only an hour ago. For all he knew, he had lost everything; in any case, troubles loomed inevitably ahead. He had reached a point at which he almost envied the fate of M. Euffe whom, as he was hastening to the welcome of a youthful embrace, Destiny had just laid low.

Pamphile had hardly sat down when, absent-mindedly, he drank a small decanter of white wine. His thoughts then turned to a duty which friendship was requiring of him. This duty was to inform the faithful Lacail that his wife had fainted in a chemist's shop and that there were certain worries of a dismal nature awaiting him at home. He rose to go and telephone to Flavie's husband and, on reaching the counter, ordered a drink and swallowed it at a gulp. He was tempted to ask for a second glass, for he felt insufficient courage for what he had to do. He decided, however, that it would be better to have that second glass later, as soon as he had finished telephoning.

"You've had a nice jab on your nose!" the waiter remarked as he handed him his change. "An accident, I take it?"

"Yes," said Pamphile, "an accident."

"Lucky you didn't break anything! And in some ways it's better to cop it on the nose. It bleeds and swells, but it isn't dangerous. Think of boxers. You don't know Tom Krim, the featherweight?"

"No," Pamphile replied, in no hurry whatever to go and hear Félix Lacail's voice at the other end of the wire. "Give me another glass."

"Same as before?"

"Yes," Pamphile said.

"To go back to Tom Krim, I saw him coming along one morning, just here where you are, with his nose all purple, almost like yours is now. 'Well,' I said to him, 'you've had a nasty knock training!' And what d'you think he told me! It was his best girl, that big fat Fernande, that had given him a swing right across his dial!"

"Here now," Pamphile said abruptly, "here's what I owe. And tell me where the telephone is."

"Along there, to the right, then to the right again, past the w.c.s. And watch out—it's dark. Don't go and bang your nose against that door. It's bad enough already!"

2. SEQUELS

With the help of the blue sky, of a framework of mountains lightly shrouded in mist, fresh foliage, lawns of brilliant green, and the rosy tint of the courts—on which young people clad in white were expending their energies in graceful movements—springtime was painting a picture, at the Lesdiguières tennis club, in which the harmony of colour was a joy to see. For the first time that year an enjoyable warmth prevailed. of the kind that does not overwhelm but gladdens the heart, and on the threshold of unclouded, happy days is, as it were, a herald of the bright summer months to come. The breeze, blowing in the direction of the tree-lined walks of Pont-de-Claix, fell with a light gentle touch upon foreheads slightly damp with perspiration. The garden chairs, the parasols in gaudy colours had all been brought out, and from the tables where they were enjoying miscellaneous drinks a few spectators were calling out encouraging comments to the players:

"Oh, pretty, Bob!"

"Good shot! Bravo, Alberte!"

On court number one Alberte Euffe was playing a single with Bob de Bazair. It seemed almost as though the white ball was their own heart which they were sending back and forth to each other with joyous exclamations and some affectionate chaff, in reality more concerned to give pleasure, to harmonize with their surroundings, than to score points. To miss the ball mattered nothing if only it were gracefully done. Alberte was in well-fitting shorts and a light woollen jersey which charmingly displayed, from the waist upwards, the outlines of her figure. This getup suited her. She had well-rounded calves, and no muscles could be seen. Above her smooth, polished knees and the small cavities behind them, the widening out of the thighs indicated a fine development, with firm flesh still white at this beginning of the season, the skin having had no time as yet in which to become bronzed. The girl's game was not strong, but it was free from clumsiness, and the onlookers would have found greater satisfaction in a pretty posture than in a fine stroke. They were not demanding first-rate play from a pretty person with supple hips and wearing shorts which clearly displayed a modelling that was a pleasure to the eye and a source of reverie and dreams.

Opposite to her, Bob de Bazair, who had a knack for finding unimpeachable trousers and sensational sweaters, for keeping rather pale while taking violent exercise, was playing below his usual game, keeping an eye on his positions for each stroke, his changes of foot, and the angles of his body. In each light spring he made there was exceptional rhythm together with intentional slowness, and these were not unmixed with affectation. He played for his own self-satisfaction, to make of himself a harmonious spectacle. It is not improbable that he was committing some slight errors of taste in failing to bear sufficiently in mind that moderation and restraint are the crowning point of perfection, as they are of efficiency in games. In Bob de Bazair's game there were rather too many flourishes, though that did not lessen his own attractiveness. After a winning stroke, up would go his hand to his head of fine brown hair to make sure that the waves were still in place and their arrangement as it should be. A young ladies' champion, he played his strokes as though they were the verbal give-and-take of a flirtation in which the direction and control of its speed and rhythm, its half-confessions, its audacities were entirely his. Nevertheless Alberte Euffe was beginning to miss the ball more often and late in starting for her stroke.

"Tired, Albe?" Bob asked her.

"Yes," Alberte said. "I think I've had enough of it. I did too much running at the start."

The heat was by no means sufficient to make them perspire very freely. Bob de Bazair placed a sweater over Alberte's shoulders and put one on himself, and they sat down side by side and watched a professional on a court near by who was coaching a player for the coming tournaments. The player was dashing about in every direction with a tremendous expenditure of energy and putting an unnecessary amount of strength into his strokes. But the professional, whose name was Cols, was playing with the utmost economy in the matter of movement, of stroke gesture, and of muscular outlay. The ball would shoot from his racquet in a swift, unswerving flight along one of the lines, impossible to return. To each one of his pupil's attacks he had an answer and seemed to know in advance what he intended to attempt.

"Cols is terrific," Alberte said. "It's magnificent, that precision of his."

"It's simply professional play," Bob replied, "which has become purely automatic. When it gets to that stage, it's just work."

"Work which is done with great ease."

"Certainly, I agree with you! But it *is* work, all the same. We come here for pleasure, and that young fellow to make money. For all we know, he may be more bored than anything else, and be wishing he was up in the mountains, or fishing."

"But his being here, in a place like this, is really a necessity, isn't it?"

"Yes, Albe, it *is*. But you've got to put him where he belongs, and not get hypnotized about him. What looks like talent has often meant a lot of sweating and swatting. For real superiority you have to look elsewhere."

"Where do you place it, then, Bob?"

"It means putting yourself above talent, and making use of it for your own pleasure."

"And what about merit, Bob?"

"Merit, Albe, is sometimes a great bore. It stinks of the schoolmaster and the specialist, merit does! The man who is really superior should take his right place everywhere, that is, one of equality with the most important person—and he should do so without effort."

"Then do riches come highest of all?" Alberte Euffe asked.

"Wait a moment!" said Bob. "Wealth ought not to be in the hands of just anybody, indiscriminately. The management of wealth may need more talent than anything else."

They were now moving towards the cloakroom.

"By the way, Albe," Bob asked, laughing, "how is the old rascal?"

He was speaking of M. Constant Euffe and his notorious way of living, which was common property in Grenoble. The young people had adopted this manner of speech for referring to the follies and absurdities of their elders.

"Father is still being a great worry to us," Alberte said. "And how is the noble count?"

"The count has been in excellent form for some weeks past. Present-day society disgusts him more than ever. He feels extremely sorry for me and my own future in that same noisome society."

"Do you think you are so much to be pitied, Bob?"

"That depends . . . There's that great big question, you know—happiness."

"Happiness," Alberte said. "Why, that ought to be such a simple matter!"

"For you!" said Bob as with gentle fingers he put back in place a wisp of dark hair which had fallen over the girl's forehead.

As he did this he looked at her, with a rather enigmatic smile. There was a whole host of questions which they were on the point of asking each other, and might well be serious questions, perhaps decisive. But that morning Bob wished to avoid any sort of anxiety, even though it related to an affair of the heart the happy issue of which was, he felt, hardly in doubt. So he merely asked her:

"Shower bath?"

"Yes," Alberte said. "And you?"

"Yes, I'll have one too. Shall we meet here at ten to?" he asked, looking at his wrist watch.

"Right you are, ten to. Whoever's first waits for the other."

"Are you meaning to be late?"

"No, but women take longer to get ready, just a little longer."

"Because of their tender beauty?"

"That beauty that's always having to be patched up! Well, perhaps."

"While men, with their well-known ugliness . . ."

"Their ugliness!"

In this exclamation there had been a touch of sincere indignation, which made her blush, thus betraying the fact that she thought Bob de Bazair very handsome; of this, he himself had been in no doubt for a long time past. Alberte retreated hastily to the ladies' cloakroom to hide her embarrassment. Bob de Bazair, pleased with the little incident, made his way quite calmly to the men's dressing room, which was deserted. He undressed rapidly, and as soon as he was under the shower, murmured to himself:

"Alberte is at the top of her form just now! And her figure has come on splendidly since last year . . . and very pretty skin. . . The Silken Net really has produced something lovely!"

He dried himself and lighted a cigarette. Then, as he was putting on his silk shirt and knotting his tie with care, his thoughts turned once more to the march of events as it affected himself, and the favourable turn it had taken. But he was in no hurry to bring matters to a head. He still had pleasures to enjoy before finally making his future secure. In the meantime he need do nothing but retain firm possession of those affections which were to give his own life a safe and solid foundation.

Bob de Bazair had had some dogged fights with the examiners for his bachelor's degree, and these had lasted for several years. By clever cribbing he had twice been successful in the written examination in the first part, but had always been hopelessly ploughed in the viva voce, where little notes are no help. These experiences made him declare that the examination for this degree, a test which gave an unfair advantage to chatterboxes, was an institution which would prove fatal to the future of France. Since he thus criticized this institution, he had no choice but to give it a wide berth and despise the diploma which it confers. After his failure for the fifth time Bob adopted this uncompromising attitude for good and all. He must finish his education by other methods.

This young man, however, was by no means a fool. But he had a horror of effort, and of everything which gives a man an appearance of working hard or of being subject to authority. He took little trouble over anything except the pursuit of pleasure, and not much over that, for he did not like pleasure to result in fatigue. His real talent lay in his membership of a noble family and bearing its name, even though name and family were threatened with beggary at no distant date, thanks to the de Bazairs of bygone days, all of whom had squandered money right and left with the splendid jauntiness and unconcern of their class, treating wealth as a jade who would always yield complacently to any advances they might make. These gentlemen wrought havoc one and all in feminine hearts; they were dauntless lovers, disastrous husbands— and they were worshipped.

Bob's father, the Count de Bazair, had been a cavalry officer, first, because he had a liking for uniforms and horses, and secondly with a view to seduction of the indispensable heiress; but his whims and fancies, his vagaries as a noble lord had not allowed him to reach a higher rank than that of captain. The battle of Morhange put an end to all his military duties. In that battle he was so badly wounded in the hip that he could never ride again. This once shining light at horse shows went in the worst possible temper to live in retirement at his estate at Champagnier, where he owned an old family country seat. Unfortunately, the expenses attendant on a few hundred square yards of roofs ate up the proceeds of many acres of land, while there were certain unprincipled individuals who were merely reinforcements of the bad process initiated by the roofs. Of his wife's badly mishandled fortune there was barely enough left even to enable him to end his days in plain living. Nevertheless he completely refused to abandon any of that haughty demeanour which enabled him to flaunt his contempt of the millionaires of Grenoble, whose only armorial bearings were the trademarks of their firms. So far as he was concerned, anyone who sold anything was a clodhopper. His contempt was equally divided between the glove trade, chocolates, cement, biscuits, Italian pastry, and the manufacturing industries in general—for everything that contributed to the fortunes of Grenoble. He was a royalist and a Catholic on principle, a subscriber to the *Action Française* also on principle, without, however, reading that publication, for he read nothing at all, leaving all such pedantry to "those little pettifogging priests." Such was his designation for learned young men. Neither did his religion include observance of the church's rites. So far as he was concerned, one either had or had not been born in the gutter, and nothing else really counted. The count was accustomed to come to Grenoble in a tilbury drawn by a splendid grey horse which he drove himself, wearing a monocle, gloves, light-coloured gaiters, and various soft felt hats of inimitable design. To the whole town he was known as "the Count," the most representative sample of a society which is now no more, and against which the Vizille assembly and a certain Grenoble newspaper dealt the first decisive blows.

With such a father as this, the future of Bob de Bazair was as little assured as it could possibly be. But tradition required the de Bazairs to marry. For the past two or three hundred years the men of this family had not lived otherwise. Bob could try his luck in this direction, for he possessed those things which had always got the men of his family out of their difficulties—an attractive appearance, the bearing of a young prince whom it is an honour to know, a rather engaging indifference of manner, the ethical code of a knight-errant, and a smiling egoism.

And thus it was that at the age of twenty-five it was Bob de Bazair's turn to be giving his mind to the career of marriage. The important thing was that the young lady should be well off, and in a position to make an immediate financial contribution to a marriage which would give her access to an illustrious nuptial couch and thus bring her great glory and a felicity that might well be envied. The girl's descent did not enter into the matter. The de Bazairs were so enamoured of their own lineage, so certain of its ascendancy over any other with which it might become united, that misalliances held no fears for them. They adopted the lady as well as her money, and then, if the worst came to the worst, cold-shouldered the family. Moreover, these mixed marriages are often a source of strength to an ancient breed.

But alas, since 1918 social evolution has been advancing in a most unfortunate direction, and it is now becoming a very difficult matter to live without doing any work at all! Fortunes are melting away in taxes, deductions of various kinds, bad investments, decreases in value, and swindles of every sort, including those by the state. No one will work for you now, and the farmers put the finishing touch to your ruin. It was seeming impossible to Bob de Bazair that he should be able to live comfortably, even with a rich wife, unless he did a little work. Fortunately, a relation of his, a M. de Saint-Romain, was the principal representative at Grenoble of an insurance company, the Rainbow. As he was getting on in years, this gentleman had an idea of taking his de Bazair great-nephew into the business, preparatory to relinquishing the entire control to him. This taking over of the business would be a matter of some hundreds of thousands of francs. It might be the first use—and what a sound, what a worthy one—to which a dowry could be put. . . .

Bob de Bazair's conception of insurance was that of a decorative profession, based entirely on one's circle of acquaintance. He happened to be a perfect dancer, a good swimmer; he went in for winter sports, was regularly to be seen on the Riviera; his clothes were all that a man's should be, and he was greatly sought after on account of his family name. Furthermore, he had just spent several years of frequenting bars, casinos, and other places where ladies of easy virtue abound. By medium of these latter a man may very quickly be on terms of "my dear fellow" with people of considerable importance, with means that enable them to finance feminine beauty; and it becomes difficult, where an insurance policy is in question, not to give preference to a young man who knows all about your little secret escapades in the establishments of the district, at Pont-de-Claix, Sassenage, Rives, Villars-de-Lans, et cetera. As between men who have knowledge of each other's lapses and departures from principles outwardly professed, business transactions are notably expedited. As for liaisons which have to be carefully concealed, it is well known that they are a source of thousands of previously unpremeditated life insurances. . . .

Bob de Bazair was by no means indisposed to keep pace with the times in which he lived, and he felt the count to be rather an old fossil. He had a certain admiration for M. Euffe's achievements in the wording of advertisements, for the vulgar talent he had for continually arousing covetous desires in housewives' breasts. He reasoned thus: "As the Silken Net supplies everything, why should it not do the same for insurance policies? There is still a lot to be done with the proletariat. It is a stratum of society that has not been sufficiently prospected; and it needs to be given an instinct for small savings." Bob himself tried his hand at the persuasive style and drew up alluring circulars the general theme of which was: "The Silken Net will take care of your old age. The Rainbow will illumine your declining years," et cetera. It must be added that this was the only kind of work to which he tied himself down, and in which moreover he was often halted by difficulties of syntax unsuspected by him when beginning his task. But he was the son of a horseman, a horseman himself; he cleared the obstacle boldly. It is true that the French language has become an easygoing young woman ever since she took up the streetwalker's profession in the daily press. And Bob knew an easy way of overcoming the little worries of editorship: he would engage a man with a university degree at fifteen hundred francs a month. Society, thank heaven, was not yet in such a disordered state that one could not get cheap the services of some young prig, a passer of examinations and drunk with knowledge!

The central point and pivot of this fine programme was the heart of Alberte Euffe, the trend of its emotions, its ardent love. So far as that was concerned Bob felt happy and at ease: for that heart, which had been his chattel already for a long time past, desired nothing so much as binding avowals and the mutual plighting of a troth. The young de Bazair knew that he was completely free to choose the hour for this, and it was of set purpose that he had postponed it, though Alberte's gentle eyes besought him often to keep her languishing no longer. But the de Bazairs, past masters of diplomacy in affairs of the heart, had a flair for the right moment in these matters and knew exactly how to heighten feminine uneasiness till it reached a point where it became unreasoning, touching, intense. No, there was no immediate hurry. . . .

There were some nasty rumours afloat in Grenoble, probably exaggerated like all the others about his neighbour which man likes to spread abroad. People were saying that M. Euffe was behaving outrageously and spending large sums of money on Riri Jumier, and that if this sort of thing were to continue much longer there might be some bitter surprises in store for his heirs. The fact that his fair hopes for the future were apparently well founded had at first restrained Bob from hastening to enfold his tender Alberte in a loving embrace. Then, later, he discovered excellent reasons for not alarming himself over the rumours which malicious tongues were spreading everywhere. The fact of his having been to a certain source to get his information somewhat complicated the situation for him. But this hardly worried him at all, and he relied on his usual good luck to bring about the happiest possible solution. A man who is genuinely loved has enormous forces of persuasion at his disposal, and the gods are his friends.

It was Alberte Euffe who was ready first and knocked at the door of the men's locker room.

"Hullo, Bob! Have you gone to sleep?"

Charming Alberte! There she was, waiting for him, fresh and smiling, in a light-coloured frock which showed off her graceful figure. She had an air of confidence and of happiness, of submissiveness and tender love. The weather was so lovely, the sky so blue, that Bob de Bazair decided to make a slight departure from his present plan of campaign.

"Albe," he said, "I'll take you on my motor bike. Let us go and have a cocktail at Pont-de-Claix, by the river. The mountains are lovely there."

"What about my bicycle?"

"You can pick it up again here when I drop you, later on."

"I must be home by half-past twelve at the latest."

"Oh, but you will be, Albe! Unless it bores you, what I'm suggesting?"

"Frightfully!" she said, with a slight blush which, beginning at her eyes, made her temples pink.

Bob de Bazair liked calling forth that little blush, a token of his ascendancy over a rich and pretty heiress. He seized Alberte's hand, a little hand still damp from its grasp of the racquet, and which submissively pressed his own.

"Come on," he said, "we'll just slip away without saying anything to the others."

He took her off along a bypath. But the noise of the motor gave them away.

"An abduction!" was heard in the acid tones of Maud Crémieux, the daughter of the Crémieux Stores in the Boulevard Gambetta, a plain girl with red hair, and a treacherous creature, who at that moment was lying stretched out and displaying the very white skin of her legs to a point which bordered on extreme indecency.

"Who is it?"

"Bob and Alberte on the same machine."

"Well, I never! It really looks as though something might come of this!"

"She's crazy about him!"

"I pity her."

"But look here—there's a pretty fair number of girls as keen as anything on Bob. I don't see that Alberte is so much to be pitied."

"I just wonder how far they go, those two," Maud Crémieux said. "Do you think that Alberte has given way altogether? The little ninny would be quite capable of it. When girls start staring at boys with that sort of damp look in their eyes . . ."

"Never mind, my dear, it'll be a wedding in the best Grenoble style. Nice loud peals of bells."

"Do you think that Bob will swallow that grocery business?"

"Why shouldn't he? He'll have to make up his mind to take up something or other in order to live, and the de Bazairs have always been fortune hunters, for all those grand airs they put on. And if he wants comfort and an assured future—well, the Silken Net can give him all that. The father has guaranteed it to his customers, and the daughter will see that Bob gets it."

"What will Alberte's dowry be, do you think?"

"There's talk of a million, at the very least."

"That is certainly enough to get going with. But you don't go very far with a million nowadays!"

"Later on there will be the profits from all those endless branches! And for Alberte, who started life as a grocer's daughter, the prospect of being a countess someday is a distinctly pleasant one. I shouldn't wonder if she thinks of that sometimes."

"She? No, my idea is that she's hopelessly gone on him, and that that's all there is to it."

"If that's so, all I can say is, 'Lucky Bob!' The dowry is one worth having, and Alberte is a pretty girl, with a charming character."

"You think so? Well, there may be men who like that type, after all. But she's a flabby, soft creature!"

"Don't you be too sure about that! I believe myself that she's a most enterprising, resourceful sort of girl."

"A silly little goose—but your willing slave. Exactly as you like them to be, gentlemen!"

"Yes, but when they're too clever, you know . . ."

"I don't think Bob will be in any danger on that score. But difficulties might crop up elsewhere."

30

"What do you mean, my dear?"

"Don't play the village idiot. You understand perfectly. Do you suppose we know nothing of your goings on? You're only too glad to boast about them, you boys, the whole lot of you!"

At about midday Bob de Bazair dropped Alberte at the entrance gate of the Lesdiguières tennis club, where she recovered her bicycle and returned to town. He himself started off again on his machine, which took him in a few minutes to the bar of the Majestic. There he found some young men of his own age, perched up on the high stools. While joking with them he scanned every nook and corner of the room. There was a young woman sitting alone at one of the tables, and she made a discreet sign to him before rising from her seat. She was smart, with a good figure, and there was a graceful swaying of the hips as she walked. Bob in his turn made for the cloakrooms, where the young woman was waiting for him. It was Riri Jumier. She seemed greatly disturbed, and without preamble she said to him:

"The old man's dead!"

"The old man's dead?" Bob repeated after her, not understanding. "What old man?"

"Old Euffe!" she exclaimed. "I haven't got a regiment of them!"

"But I've only just left . . ." said Bob. "That is to say . . . I thought I saw him. Where did he die? At your place?"

"No, thank goodness. But not far away. I want to talk to you seriously."

An unfortunate point about Grenoble is that it has a very crowded centre, where nothing that happens escapes the notice of the inhabitants, whose tongues are even more intensively employed than their eyes. To preserve an incognito there would be an impossibility, and no confidential talk could ever fail to arouse curiosity.

"Shall we meet again at the Beauty Spot?" Riri said.

It was a good restaurant, in the avenues of Pont-de-Claix. But it had the disadvantage of being in the direction of the Lesdiguières tennis club, and the proximity of that place made Bob feel uncomfortable.

"No," he said, "cut along straight to Sassenage."

"To Parendel's?"

"Too many people one knows! There's a danger of being spotted there."

"Oh," said Riri, "now that *he's* dead, there's not a thing I'm afraid of."

But this did not suit Bob at all.

"Yes, but that doesn't prevent its being quite the wrong moment for you to be seen about," Bob said. "Take a tram. I shall go along independently, and we'll meet at the Hotel Faure, on the right as you arrive. We can lunch in the little courtyard, if there aren't many people about."

"Do you like me?" Riri asked suddenly.

"Don't ask me such improper questions, now please!" Bob replied. "You're a widow of a few hours' standing, just remember that!"

"Do you want me to cry?"

"A widow—and out of a job!" Bob said severely. "Hardly an occasion for rejoicing."

"I have had time to cash my cheque," Riri Jumier said.

"How much?"

"Fifty thousand."

"That's the last thing you'll get from the Silken Net. So—be careful!"

"There's the insurance policy besides."

"You are certain there is one?"

"Absolutely."

"Very well, then, keep quiet about it. And look out for the heirs."

"I'd like to see them trying to lay a finger on me! There'd be the devil to pay, I can tell you!"

Within the restricted area, like that of a crucible hemmed in by mountains, in which the skein of life at Grenoble is continuously unwound, it would have been difficult for the most prominent young woman of the gayer circles of the town and the young man the most attractive to women of them all not to have come into contact with each other. The bestowal on Bob of feminine favours came to him by a natural and inevitable process compounded of these ladies' vanity, jealousy, and desire. He took these favours and resigned them, doing both with a carefree if kindly indifference, varying his pleasures and studiously avoiding any shackles of a love affair that would become embarrassing some day in the future. His feminine admirers knew of this dangerous quality of his. But his approval of the girls and young women of Grenoble—its degree and the extent to which it was seen in public —was the final touchstone of their attractiveness and good looks. The caresses of the young de Bazair gave them more confidence in their own charms. And he was commonly supposed to have so many love affairs that he was thereby enabled to escape the anxieties and the loss of freedom which every liaison involves. This happy state of affairs gave him indulgent little harems, which provided him with convenient opportunities, and suitable to his mood at the moment, all over the town.

From the day when, thanks to M. Euffe, Riri Jumier had begun to occupy the position of a star in the gay life of Grenoble, it became in a way indispensable that this distinction should be confirmed by Bob. On this occasion, however, that young gentleman required much persuasion and many advances before he would consent to bestow the last and only jewel still lacking in the triumphant Riri's crown. This was just the way to drive her half mad with resentment and at the same time make her as mild and gentle as a lamb. Bob de Bazair, while continuing to smile and be charming, was a past master at putting the bit on young women too sure about their "sex appeal." He was more of a star himself than these ladies, with the advantage—which they had not—of good birth, and he wished them to make no mistake about it. When Riri had reached a proper state of humility, he was then quite prepared to make himself responsible for completing an education which was threatening to come to a dead stop if it were to be left solely in the hands of M. Constant Euffe, who had none whatever of the qualities of Lauzun or of Casanova.

Besides her physical charms Riri had plenty of intelligence, and she realized how immensely useful a young man like Bob could be to her. He could raise her from her status of an ordinary "tart" to that of a demimondaine of a superior class.

"It will be from the age of thirty onwards," Bob said to her, "that you will get your chance. As for real talent, either you've got it or you haven't. The profession has to be learnt, and it takes a long time. The 'houses' are full of very pretty girls who have been too stupid to learn their job of being courtesans, and who will never be any more than cattle."

"There is such a thing as luck, Bob?"

"The only people luck does anything for are those who deserve it. In every success it's the personal element that counts. That element is sometimes quite hidden away, and other people don't see it at all. It is quite possible that someday you may be held in great esteem. It's up to you to make that your object. And whatever else you do—don't go and fall in love!"

"You're the only boy I love, or ever have loved."

"Well, that's quite safe. I shall cure you when the right time comes."

"You'll leave me in the lurch?"

"Of course I shall! We could only be an embarrassment to each other in life. You would be a constant failure if I were still in the offing, and I couldn't give you any compensation for it. And you'd be the same drawback for me. So don't let there be any ordinary, stuffy sentiment between you and me. And nothing gets commonplace more quickly than love does."

Bob de Bazair did not regard his relations with Riri Jumier, which he took care should not be too sustained and should take their turn with other affairs, as amounting to a liaison. It was no more than a caprice, a whim, a convenient arrangement, a close friendship carried to rather unusual lengths.

When Bob realized the lively interest taken in himself by Alberte Euffe, he wondered whether he should give up Riri altogether or merely see her less often. He chose the second alternative, saying to himself: "I am watching over this family. If Papa Euffe were tempted to play the fool too hopelessly, I should be able to make Riri less greedy over what she gets out of him." He set himself up as an unseen protector of the Euffe younger generation. In any case, he knew, through the young woman herself, that M. Euffe's generosity was kept within reasonable bounds and by no means on a scale likely to disturb a well-established fortune. For Riri sometimes complained of his being rather stingy.

"What do you get a year?" Bob asked.

"Oh, I don't know!—thirty-five, forty thousand . . ."

"Plus presents?"

"Of course."

"And there's that car of yours. Believe me, for Grenoble that's good. Indeed, more than good."

"You think so?"

"Yes, I do. There is only one town, and that's Paris, where to drag every penny you can out of the man who's keeping you is an excellent advertisement. But here, at Grenoble, it would make a very bad impression. Dauphiné people don't like greedy women. And if one day you have to get a successor to Papa Euffe . . . Just you wait, your time will come."

"But I shall be getting old!"

"In Paris the women most in the public eye are all about forty. Don't be in a hurry; it's sticking to it that's most difficult. Learn first of all what good manners really mean, get more self-confidence. If you want to play the vamp's game it will be a pretty uphill one!"

It was in these ways that Bob de Bazair had made a harmonious combination of his pleasures, his comforts, and his ambitions, with an elasticity of conscience natural to a young man who had had ancestors at the court of Versailles.

"The old man is dead—just think of it! . . . Well, that alters everything—everything—completely."

This was the subject of Bob de Bazair's thoughts as he travelled along the Sassenage road at the foot of the mountains. His motor bicycle was leaving behind him a slip stream, not of air but of lively sound, which seemed to be giving the machine its abounding vitality and strength, which responded so readily to the lever that projected slightly from the handle bar. It was a perfect time for speeding along in the sunshine through this valley with its lovely tints. Bob, though his thoughts were of death, found keen enjoyment in doing so.

Only yesterday M. Euffe had been breathing, talking; only yesterday he had been an active man, and with familiar ease and unconstraint, a little paternally too, had been telling Riri Jumier his little worries, with numerous details of his family life, his wife and children. Only yesterday M. Euffe represented a solid base, both social and financial, on which rested the lives and futures of certain people, which in turn influenced those of others. It was in this way that the old gentleman's presence supplied a landmark of safety for a certain frontier of Bob's own life, gave a more favourable light to some dealings of his. And now all that was falling to pieces. . . .

"You'll have to start thinking all over again, my dear boy."

Bob began imagining Alberte among members of his own family—Alberte whom he had left only a little earlier, showing such promise, looking so lovely . . . Thanks to some copious outpourings—things told in confidence by M. Euffe to Riri, and by Riri to Bob—the young de Bazair had come to know the Euffe family very well indeed.

"Of his children," Riri reported, "his daughter Alberte is the one he prefers. He says she's pretty and kindhearted. He would very much like to see her happy. She hasn't got Clémentine's awful character."

"Who is Clémentine?"

"Mama Euffe! 'Oh,' says old Euffe, 'she is a high-principled woman, an irreproachable woman. She is ruled by her own virtue. But her virtue is ruled by her liver, and her liver has never worked properly. The workings of livers play parts of outstanding importance in family life.' "

Thumbnail sketches of this kind had often enlivened the conversations of Bob and Riri; and indeed it was through the mistress of M. Euffe that Bob's attention was first of all drawn to Alberte and a good impression of her obtained. Then, later, he saw the young girl, and found that she had in full measure the gentleness, straightforwardness, and charm of which her father had spoken so highly, with a fresh, radiant beauty and a clear complexion which could only banish any lingering suspicion that she might have a defective liver!

Through Riri Jumier, Bob further obtained some precise information on the real state of M. Euffe's fortune. This was not because M. Euffe ever expressed himself freely on that subject; on the contrary, he was extremely reserved in those matters. But he would sometimes allow certain things to escape him in conversation which, when pieced together afterwards, furnished very useful clues.

"Life's an amazing thing!" Bob de Bazair said to himself, gaily accelerating at the same time.

Thanks to Riri, he had come to know the Euffe family intimately; and it was also thanks to her that the idea of associating himself more closely with them had occurred to him. It was through her, also, that he was now feeling a genuine friendship for M. Euffe, a friendship which had a touch of filial affection in it and was marked with gratitude to a man who had become the father of a tenderhearted, exquisite child who would have a dowry of a million francs and fine prospects.

If the bonds between these people should seem to be rather too closely knit, the fault must be ascribed to the smallness of Grenoble and its feeble contingent of families of any real importance. But it must be set down to the credit of Bob de Bazair that of all the people affected by the fate which had overtaken M. Constant Euffe, he, with the exception of the gentle, truehearted Alberte, was the one whose grief was the most sincere.

"Poor old chap!" Bob murmured as the first houses of Sassenage came in sight. "Poor old Daddy Euffe! It was idiotic to die like that! And he just didn't deserve it! There was a man who'd begun the last few years to get a little pleasure out of life."

He said to himself that Alberte would be genuinely distressed. He made up his mind to be as gentle and kind to her as possible, to kiss her and tell her there and then that he loved her, so that the poor girl might have this consolation in her sorrow.

We have seen that even in the matter of riotous living M. Euffe was accustomed to walk warily. He was at that first stage in the accumulation of a fortune at which the pleasure it procures is primarily to watch the volume of capital steadily increasing, and is so great that any withdrawal of that capital becomes a matter for regret, of something very like pain. It is true that M. Euffe, at the age of more than sixty, had very greatly increased his private expenditure, but this was from motives of a very intimate nature which, if any longer set aside, would mean a renunciation for good and all of certain joys from which he had long abstained.

Conscious of having done much for his own family and amassed large sums of money for them, M. Euffe was henceforth assured of being able to "have his fling" on a generous scale. He intended in any case that certain extraneous expenditure should become the reward and privilege of a ripe age and many years of hard work. Youth, he thought, has not yet earned the right to indulge in certain whims and fancies which also are more keenly enjoyed late in life. As regards his sons, M. Euffe considered that they should have a solid education together with certain restrictions in the matter of money, in order that the boys should not lose sight of the necessity of personal effort. So far, therefore, as they were concerned, he kept his liberality within bounds, as he did in the case of Mme. Euffe. He was not opposed to a certain amount of display in the family, which he considered necessary for the sake of his firm's reputation; but he kept a careful eye on the details of this display, as befitted a man experienced in overhead expenses, accountancy, and the handling of advertisement. In his opinion, a fortune still in its period of growth should be safe-guarded in every possible way and protected against the abuses and squandering which ruined the aristocrats in former days.

It may be said that in every respect M. Euffe gave evidence of fore-sight, that quality so indispensable to organizers and those at the head of affairs. If he was accustomed to make presents of sums which allowed only for careful and well-regulated expenditure, he nevertheless kept con-stantly in view the possibility of some unforeseen circumstance which would keep him far from his family and his usual activities. In the case, therefore, of people closely dependent on him, he supplied them with the means of providing against his absence. It was thus that he had en-trusted Mme. Euffe, on the one hand, and Riri Jumier, on the other, with a cheque already filled in and signed, to which in case of need they would only have to add the date. It was a deposit on trust, and in hand-ing it to them he had made the same precautionary remark to each: "People can diddle me once. But never twice!" For safety's sake M. Euffe, not wishing to burden these two consciences with temptations too painful to bear, asked from time to time to see these cheques before giving out the money required for ordinary current expenditure.

The two cheques, each slightly antedated, were paid in on the very day of M. Euffe's death. They were handed in over the counters of a bank in the Place Victor-Hugo, the first one at about eleven-thirty in the morn-ing and the second shortly after two o'clock, by two ladies, one of whom was young, smart, and scented, and the other elderly and dour; both of them appearing somewhat nervous and anxious while the cheques were going the rounds of the different departments for verification. In these two people so well known in Grenoble some of the bank's employees had no difficulty in recognizing the mistress and the wife of M. Euffe. This immediately did away with any difficulty or suspicion. A sum of fifty thousand francs was accordingly paid out to Riri Jumier, and a similar sum to Mme. Euffe shortly afterwards. At the times at which these payments were being effected, M. Euffe's death was known only to a very small number of people in Grenoble.

When this death was made known to the public in the newspapers of the following day, an employee of the bank, thinking of the transactions of the day before, sought out the manager and drew his attention to the fact that M. Euffe's account had been depleted to the extent of a hundred thousand francs on the very day on which the holder had died. It seemed a strange coincidence. The cheques were examined once more, but there was no doubt that the signatures were genuine. Furthermore, these payments could well be in accordance with former intentions on the part of the deceased. And the fact that the widow herself had cashed the cheque in was sufficient guarantee that these transactions had been regular and aboveboard.

"It's a strange thing, all the same," the clerk observed, with a touch of shyness and cunning in his tone.

"You never know what may happen," the manager answered evasively. "It may be just a matter of arrangements, of family arrangements."

"It goes a long way beyond the family."

"Well, then, of arrangements made on the family's behalf! And it's not our business, anyway." Thus the manager cut the discussion short.

He was anxious, in front of an employee, not to show the slightest disloyalty to the memory of a man who had had very large deposits at his bank and paid in big sums every month. The handling of other people's money necessitates discretion and a wide understanding of private needs.

But this bank manager himself spoke the same evening of these two cheques at a certain restaurant where, together with a few men of importance in the town to whom he acted as financial adviser, he was having a cocktail and playing a game. This indiscretion of his was repeated at some of the nearest tables and quickly spread throughout Grenoble.

Far from doing Riri harm, the story of the cheque added to her reputation and brought her a fresh crop of good opinions and some real esteem. People wondered at such a pretty person having shown herself, at a difficult juncture, to be a woman no less capable than Mme. Euffe herself, with her reputation for austerity and constant attendance at church. The men sang her praises loudly to each other. And these encomiums were reflected on the dead man.

"That old rascal Euffe made a good shot when he chose her for his little lady!"

"He had an astonishing gift for spotting things—everything!"

"He had a first-rate brain! Very little education, but a first-rate brain. He trained himself, really."

"And it was sporting of him to have left the girl enough to keep her going."

"Yes, it was!" so all these gentlemen agreed.

"And she must have deserved it for him to have done it."

"Yes, she must have, that's almost certain. Pretty girl!"

"Very pretty girl!"

It is difficult for a citizen who is growing in importance not to be assigned to some category or other by his contemporaries. M. Constant Euffe had occupied at Grenoble a position so prominent that he could hardly hope to be immune from public opinion, and he was bound to take this into account. During his lifetime it had been M. Euffe's constant endeavour to give satisfaction to two interests frequently hostile to each other. The director of the Silken Net was glad enough to come into line with the families of high social standing, to whose level the constantly increasing total of his assets was bringing him near, and he greatly hoped to become united with them through his descendants in course of time. But he had no wish to sacrifice the popularity he enjoyed in working-class districts and in the country. His intention was to remain the benefactor of the cottages and the humbler homes. For this reason he had abstained from political activity of every kind and from any open adherence to, or strong expression of, social or religious convictions. In these ways he had made friends for himself everywhere. This line of conduct resulted in his receiving some very warm posthumous eulogies.

On the day after the accident, the *Dauphiné Gazette* published an important obituary notice of M. Constant Euffe, the founder of the Silken Net, a judge in the Commercial Court, president of the Association of Provision Merchants and of the Consumers' Friendly Society, vice-president of the Dauphiné Automobile Club and of the Departmental Federation of the Sporting Association of the Isère, an honorary member of the Society of Friends of the Arts at Grenoble, of the Dauphiné Alpine Club, of the Grenoble Football Club, of the Dauphiné Cycling and Touring Association, et cetera.

The readers of the notice were reminded of the fine career of this upright and enterprising man, of this great and indefatigable worker, upon whom the smiles of Fortune had been so justifiably bestowed. High praise was given to the novelty of his conceptions, his feeling for social evolution, and his constant solicitude for the welfare of those in humble circumstances, all of which was seen in his supply of the poorer class of housewife not only with exceptional facilities in the purchase of provisions, but with nutritious articles of food hitherto unknown in Dauphiné. "In speaking of M. Euffe," this journal wrote, "we wish to pay our tribute to the lustre of a prosperity which had its origin in the service of the people by a man who himself came from the people and derived all his own vigour from that source; who used all the strength he possessed for the attainment of a single object—to secure for working people comfort and dignity of a nature calculated to raise their standard of life. M. Constant Euffe never deserted the liberal convictions of his younger days. He bears away with him the gratitude of those who worked under him and of the multitude of his customers, whose guide and friend he was, within the framework of a democracy which has brought the blessings of civilization.even to the tiniest hamlets in our lovely valleys."

The other Grenoble newspapers published articles couched in similar terms, except that they laid special emphasis on this or that merit of M. Euffe, which varied with the shade of their own political opinions. Thus *The Republic* wrote in the following terms: "As he rose higher and higher in public esteem, as the reputation of his firm spread far and wide and his influence was felt over an area that was continually increasing, M. Euffe found himself better and better able to define his attitude in face of those conflicts of opinion, of ideas, and of beliefs by which society of the present day is so dangerously shaken. It was due to this that his children were brought up in the great non-state educational establishments in this part of the country, and that Mme. Euffe, to whom we now offer our respectful sympathy, has for long years past taken her place among those people of consequence in our town who have won appreciation by their steadfast adherence to Christian principles and their devotion to good works. M. Euffe had won the friendship and esteem of the great families of Grenoble and identified his interests with theirs, keeping steadily aloof from all pernicious tendencies to mob rule. He had a strongly developed sense of orderliness and discipline, of the place that each person should occupy in the social scheme; and with his departure we bid farewell to a man who, among the body of employers in this district, was a striking figure."

Lastly, the secretary of the Dauphiné Academy, who was a close friend of the family, had contributed to the *Despatch* an article which attracted much attention, and from which the following is an extract. "M. Constant Euffe would have been entirely worthy of a place among us. Doubtless his intellectual faculties were absorbed in the management of a vast and fruitful undertaking. But each time he took up his pen it was to write down some picturesque and vivid sentences in which he made clear, in a manner sometimes audacious, always striking, the close connection which exists between a sound and well-balanced family expenditure and the moral well-being of the members. He never grew weary of trying to educate, and was continually showing how anxious he was to improve his own knowledge in order to communicate it to others. In this way his influence over large bodies of people was profound. In this way M. Euffe was both sociologist and thinker, and I have no fear of saying that there was a touch of Montesquieu in this Félix Potin* of Grenoble!"

The effect of these printed encomiums, spread abroad in thousands of copies, was to surround the death of M. Euffe with an appropriate atmosphere of grief and to bring to those nearest to the deceased a consciousness of his merits which familiarity with these, together with little family wrangles and friction, had made them forget. Taking note of the universal esteem to which public condolences bore witness, they began a private summing-up of all they owed him: their fine apartment in the Place Victor-Hugo, their magnificent properties of Bouquéron and Montbonnot, their houses and estates, their entire freedom from financial worries which was helping them in their bereavement and leaving each one of them with a fair prospect of a comfortable future.

Reading all those notices, even Riri Jumier became conscious of having played a part, thanks to M. Euffe's patronage, in Grenoble society, a by no means insignificant part even though she had to remain in the background so far as ordinary family life was concerned.

"He really was somebody!" she said to herself.

She cut out the newspaper articles and put them away together with some small objects which had belonged to the dead man. She did not yet know—it would depend on circumstances—whether she would have to expunge M. Euffe from her past, or continue to associate him with it, as a display of affection that might show her previous history in a favourable light.

Pondering on the uncertainty of her future, Riri went out to do her marketing, a task which she often undertook because of its association with respectable and homely virtues. She entered the grocer's shop in the Place Condorcet with which she was accustomed to deal, when the owner, a woman who was always particularly gushing, greeted her coldly and said to her in a supercilious manner:

"I have a small bill for you, mademoiselle!"

There was nothing in the amount of the bill to worry Riri, but the tone of voice offended her. Having finished her purchases and left the

*The largest chain grocer in France.

shop, it seemed to her that there was a less kindly atmosphere than usual in the street outside, that she was receiving fewer glances and friendly smiles. All of a sudden she realized that she was no longer under the protection of the Silken Net, and that she would feel sadly the loss of consideration—and credit—to which the tradespeople had accustomed her.

"The dirty tricks are starting already!" she thought to herself.

She returned to the Place Marval. On the ground floor of the flats she found the concierge, who always spoke very pleasantly about M. Euffe. In a quite familiar tone of voice the latter said:

"Well, it's a loss for you, that it is, you poor young lady!"

"Yes," said Riri.

"It does alter things, a death like that! And what about your flat: you're not thinking of leaving, are you? I happen to know some people who've got their eye on it and who'd pay well if they took it over."

"I'm not thinking of it," Riri said, "not at the moment, anyhow."

"Oh, very well, then," the concierge said, "you think you'll be staying on at Grenoble even after what's happened, and carrying on as before? Well, they do say that everyone knows his own business best. But if you should change your mind you might remember those people who are wantin' your flat. Money's no object with them—that's the sort they are."

Having reached home, Riri had a feeling that her loneliness would be unbearable. This was just the moment when she must guard against allowing the whole of Grenoble to see her overwhelmed by the blow she had just received. She made her toilet with special care. Then she went out again, intending to make for the centre of the town by way of the Rue Thiers. It was nearly midday when she reached the Place Victor-Hugo. She then walked resolutely along the pavement in front of the cafés, where she was conscious of being the cynosure of all eyes and had little doubt that her name was on everyone's lips. She came through this ordeal, which lasted the whole length of the Rue Félix-Poulat, with success.

At the Dauphins restaurant, where her entrance made a sensation, she chose a small table not far from the orchestra and began to turn over the pages of a magazine with which she had provided herself. She was waiting.

A little later Bob de Bazair came in, and a rapid glance round the room was sufficient to enable him to see who was there and to take in the situation. Acting in the most natural way, he went up to the lonely young woman's table and, after a correct and formal salutation, said to her, speaking in rather loud, clear tones:

42

"Dear lady, you mustn't stay and sit there all alone. Come over and join us, do."

He led her to a table at which a number of young men were sitting, all of them regular visitors to the restaurant and none of them over thirty. There was young Barge, Italian pastry business; young Piganon, son of the biscuit manufacturer; the Lideux brothers, in the cement business; Roger Mivois and Charles Morton, glove trade; Simon Crémieux, of the Crémieux Stores; Luc Noguier, of the big jeweller's establishment in the Place Grenette; and Jacques Courtil, hydraulic engineering. That is to say, a collection of young men who represented a large proportion of the wealth of Grenoble. Their hair was oiled and brushed with care, their clothes were of the smartest. Each face bore an expression which was evidence of an unshakable conviction on the part of its owner that he was an important young man with all his wits about him. Their respective motorcars were standing outside.

The effect of Bob de Bazair's manœuvre was to determine Riri Jumier's new status. For all that her protector had vanished from the scene, she had not fallen from her high estate; and jealousy must bide its time before attempting revenge. Now that these smart youths had welcomed her at their table, she ventured to scrutinize the other people present. A few martini cocktails completed the process of restoring her self-confidence. Furthermore, she had quite sufficient means to keep her going. People are never really defeated except by hunger.

Bob de Bazair's behaviour, on the occasion of M. Euffe's death, was perfect, and in his case this was specially praiseworthy. For this young man had such a horror of sadness and worry and trouble that he strenuously avoided the spectacle of illness and death, of sorrow and mourning, in the same way as he kept sternly aloof from solemn ceremonies, ugly people, lachrymose old ladies, sententious men, and starchy conventions. To him grief seemed always belittling and often absurd. He felt his good health to be sufficient protection against physical blemish of any kind. He believed in his own good luck and felt that to go always whither his pleasure and inclinations led him was the wisest and safest rule to follow.

One of the earliest to hasten to the Place Victor-Hugo, Bob de Bazair behaved with such confident self-possession, showed such delicacy and tact in his expressions of sympathy, that the family, and especially the widow, were greatly impressed. She asked who this young man was, so obviously a gentleman, whose manners were a pattern of refinement and good breeding: the grave, calm impassivity which seemed to radiate from him kept all manifestation of grief within limits consistent with faultless bearing and behaviour. They realized that such ease of manner was not simply the result of education: breeding alone could have produced it. Mme. Euffe was greatly touched at seeing under her own roof the son of a proud nobleman, who was generally thought to be unapproachable. She trembled with emotion and pride when Bob, from the foot of the bed, lightly sprinkled M. Euffe's remains with holy water and then came and bowed before her and said:

"I am a friend of your children. Believe me, madame, when I tell you that my family feels for you sincerely."

Bob then turned to Alberte, who was in tears, and the look which he gave her was so full of friendship, of intimate understanding, that the young girl's sobs broke out afresh. This excess of gentle kindness became suddenly mingled with her overwhelming grief, and at that moment the kindness proved more devastating than the sorrow. There in that room, in the presence of death and in revolt against it, an urgent, burning life force was surging up within and threatening to stifle her. To feel and know that she was beloved had become a necessity to her no less vital than food and drink. It was an irresistible physical reaction, as nearly allied to fainting as to sensual desire, and with it there came welling up a great flood of tenderness on whose surface, blurred and indistinct, there floated reflections of the prostrate body of M. Euffe, and in the foreground, clear and well defined, the pale face of Bob de Bazair with fond and loving eyes.

"You ought to take a little rest," Bob told her in a gentle voice.

"Yes," said Mme. Euffe, "go and rest, my child. I myself must stay here. But you—you must go off . . ."

Then, filled with gratitude for a young man who knew exactly the right thing to do and what to avoid at a tragic moment like the present, she added these words:

"My children won't listen to what I say. Take her away, monsieur, please!"

The two young people stole out of the room and entered the rather dark antechamber through which visitors passed in and out. Bob was holding Alberte's elbow as she moved along with her head bent forward and her handkerchief covering her eyes. She turned aside in a corridor, opened a door, and Bob de Bazair entered the room with her.

"Is this your room?" he asked.

She nodded.

"Now you are going to be a very good girl, my little Albe. You're just going to lie down and think of nothing at all. Come along, now."

As he was speaking he had taken hold of one of her shoulders and was softly stroking her cheek and her neck. His gentle voice and the touch of his hand were the climax of the turmoil into which Alberte's feelings had been thrown. Her legs began to give way beneath her, her thoughts were in complete disarray, and her body, relaxed and flagging, was being attracted, though she knew it not, to the kindly strength which was giving it support. Silent tears were flowing down her cheeks, while her whole frame was shaken by deep-seated quivering and thrills and little faint, barely audible sobs.

"Oh, Bob, it's frightful! He died while we were playing tennis."

"Sh!" Bob said. "You mustn't think of that."

And there is a certain category of events in which words are of no avail, he sought out the spot where lay a heart too filled with emotion, to soothe its rapid beating.

And then it was that Alberte Euffe was stirred and shaken and her whole body thrilled, and slowly, involuntarily, her fevered lips united with those of Bob de Bazair, while a veil of oblivion came down and blotted out the world, leaving them alone with their wonder and delight that the curve of Alberte's breast was charming, and that by its means the girl was feeling a stir and flow within her that was an abounding promise of happy days to come.

3. FILIAL UNDERSTANDING At her husband's funeral Mme. Clémentine Euffe attracted less attention by an appearance of grief, which everyone expected, than by a superb astrakhan mantle which came as a surprise to those in the know, who were perfectly aware of M. Euffe's intense dislike of making expensive presents.

During the night before the funeral there had been a sudden change of temperature. In the morning there was a chilly, cutting wind, as often happens at Grenoble. This inclemency on the part of the weather was some justification for the wearing of the mantle but did not explain where the latter came from. Edmond Euffe, M. Euffe's obvious successor in the management of the Silken Net, and who had adopted certain of his father's principles in the administration of a joint estate, said to his mother, with a note of suspicion in his voice:

"I didn't know you had that cloak!"

"It was your poor father's last present to me," Mme. Euffe replied, between a couple of sighs appropriate to her widowhood. "He had promised it to me for the thirty-fifth anniversary of our wedding."

But Mme. Euffe omitted to mention that it was a posthumous present, which the shop had delivered the day before.

The reader is already aware of the way in which Mme. Euffe had been stinted of everything beautiful and costly in the days when she was at her best, and the humiliation which she had felt ever since all those desirable things which her own blameless life had failed to win for her had been lavished on bold-faced trollops. No sooner had she obtained possession of the fifty thousand francs from the bank than she had gone off in hot haste to the furrier's and bought, with no haggling over the price, the most expensive mantle that the shop could produce. It had certainly needed a few minor alterations, but these could wait.

After this purchase Mme. Euffe returned home quickly, that she might give herself up entirely to her grief. Thanks to the mantle, mingled with this grief there were also feelings of forbearance, of forgiveness, and of gratitude—feelings for her husband which had died in her for many years past. Taking advantage of a few moments when she was alone in the room with the dead man, she lightly touched M. Euffe's cold cheek and murmured:

"Thank you, Constant. Don't be afraid, I have forgotten everything."

With these words she expressed his worthiness of eternal bliss despite his escapades. But it then occurred to her that her husband, suddenly and brutally stricken down, had perhaps died without having time for repentance of his sins—had indeed met his death at a moment when he might have been on his way to the commission of sin, in the Rue Turenne. . . . "I shall have many masses said for the repose of his soul," Mme. Euffe thought to herself. She began to pray fervently, with a feeling of regret that perhaps she had made the poor man's life too hard for him. "When one sees of what little account we are, how everything falls to decay . . ."

And thus it was that by means of a final cheque M. Euffe, in departing from this world, left his widow with a calm and peaceful mind despite the small diversions of his latter years.

All the notabilities and people of consequence in the town were crowding into the church of St. Louis, which was draped in black and whose space was not enough to contain the multitude; while the coffin of M. Euffe was buried beneath enormous sheaves of flowers and huge wreaths, on which could be read expressions of sympathy from the employees of the Silken Net, the Consumers' Friendly Society, and numerous other societies of Grenoble. In the Rue Félix-Poulat and others adjacent to it double rows of vehicles stood waiting. Numerous sight-seers, braving the chilly blast, were occupying the pavements in front of the cafés. A funeral on such a scale of importance as this had not been seen in Grenoble for a long time past. There was, moreover, a certain element of romance attaching to the ceremony: and this was in the minds of each and all as they sprinkled holy water on the earthly remains of a man for whom there had been no lack of the pleasures and contentments of this world here below. M. Constant Euffe had been struck down while on his way to some pleasant trifling, at the age of sixty-seven, on a lovely morning which smelt of flowers. . . .

"A fine end for the old rip!" said M. Gaffon, a town councillor standing in the middle of a small knot of men who were being faithful to an oath they had made not to set foot inside the church and were now shivering a little out in the square.

"That ceremony of theirs will go on forever! The curé's got hold of him and won't let him go, poor old Euffe! Well, we had better go and keep warm somewhere, while we're waiting."

"Yes, that's the thing to do. . . ."

They went off in the direction of the Three Dauphins restaurant.

Riri Jumier, knowing that the whole of Grenoble would be watching how she behaved, had debated long and earnestly whether it would be fitting that she should be there. She did not wish that her presence should appear in any way either a sacrilege or an act of defiance, but she was no less anxious that her absence should not be imputed to vulgar ingratitude. She decided to leave the last part of the service, that at the graveside, entirely to the family, just as she herself would abstain from deep mourning, but that she would appear at the church of St. Louis; for churches open wide their doors to the Magdalens of this world. She chose some half-mourning apparel, sober and discreet. And on the day of the funeral, a little before the appointed hour, she stole into the church, which was still deserted. She went and knelt in the darkest corner of one of the aisles and buried her face in her hands.

Though her presence was hardly noticed, it was nevertheless known. As happens in the case of most of our actions, this presence received widely different interpretations. The women were extremely harsh.

"Really, that creature might have stayed away!"

"It's just bravado on her part. And when all's said and done, that death was a bit her fault. It was her he was going to see when he got that vase on his head."

"Fancy her coming and sitting with us respectable women at a moment like this, when the family are in such grief It's positively indecent. . . ."

But once again, at the Meuse restaurant and the cafés in the Place Grenette, at the tables occupied by men, the criticisms that evening were of a different nature altogether and showed that leniency which beauty never fails to obtain.

"It was pretty plucky of her!"

"And that faithfulness to old Euffe—jolly fine, I call it! After he was dead and she'd got her money she might very well have thought no more about him."

"And after all, why shouldn't she be sad? Those girls have got feelings just the same as any others."

"And gratitude too, sometimes!" M. Bajassot added. He was the leading builder in Grenoble, and also kept a mistress. "Euffe had been her benefactor. Where did he find her, anyway?"

"She says she's an officer's daughter, so I've heard."

"There's a sight too many officers' daughters in that game! I know perfectly well that men in the army don't make their fortunes and that they've got their risks to face in wartime. But that's hardly a reason why their daughters should become kept women!"

"Well, there's one thing certain, and that is, that she's a very pretty girl!"

"And no fool, either!"

"Yes, she's played her cards well. . . ."

The days immediately following the tragedy were occupied in mourning and the preparations for an elaborate and imposing funeral. As soon as these were finished life resumed its ordinary course. M. Constant Euffe had represented for his family an unfailing source of kindness in the home, paternal vigilance, professional skill, civic authority, and, generally speaking, a high reputation in the town. Their consciousness of all these blessings had doubtless grown somewhat faint during his lifetime. But after his death it very definitely revived.

"Now is the time when we feel how much we have lost!" said Mme. Euffe on their return from the funeral, as she took off her mantle, which had been very useful to her; for there had been an icy wind blowing at the St.-Roch cemetery and the funeral orations had been prolonged.

"What a blank there is in the house!" Aunt Augustine said. "Poor Constant! When I think how we used to swing together once upon a time, at Grandfather Guigon's . . . And now he is dead!"

"And there was a man who never had a day's illness!"

"And what life and go for a man of his age! He astonished everybody."

48

"Your lot is a hard one, indeed it is, poor Clémentine!"

"Yes, you are right!" Mme. Euffe replied with a sigh. "It robs me of an old companion just when I want him most—when we had grown into two peaceful old friends who understood each other perfectly."

It was seeming intolerable that no search was being made for those responsible for the accident. That fatal "conglomeration of circumstances" had had human beings to help it on its way. That tragic happening had been their work, however little their intention.

This assembling of relations was utilized for arranging a family council, with the uncles presiding; and it was agreed that even if only as a matter of principle, the Lacails, the owners of the vase, should be asked for some pecuniary compensation.

"What sort of people are they?"

"He works in the prefect's office."

"Has he a lot of backing? Anyone pushing him?"

"We don't know yet."

"In any case," Edmond Euffe observed, "these Lacails won't be able to afford a sum anywhere near the damage done."

"That is highly probable," Uncle Victor said. "But even if it only covered the death duties it would be worth considering."

"Just to guide me, Uncle Théodore—how much do you think Father was worth? What I mean is—how can we fix . . ."

It was difficult to estimate.

"It is obvious that nothing we could hope to get will bear any relation to your father's value either from a moral or a material point of view, nor to your sorrow, dear Clémentine! That is not the point we are considering."

"Uncle," Alberte said, "all this won't give Daddy back to us. So what is the use of discussing this question of money?"

"It's a question of justice!" Uncle Victor said sternly. "And pious duty. It would make poor Constant himself turn in his grave if we failed to claim something for his loss."

"Really, I don't think it's at all right for Alberte to be here," Aunt Augustine said. "She doesn't understand these questions in the least. You had better leave us, child."

"I would rather do so," Alberte said, rising. "Thank you, Auntie."

"I believe the best plan," Uncle Victor continued, "would be to go and see these people in the Rue Turenne and get an idea of how much they could manage. What do you think, Clémentine?"

"The whole thing is very sad for me. But it seems to me that we ought not to ask for some absurdly small amount which could only be an insult to Constant's memory. Suppose the papers got hold of it . . ."

"Yes, true—that might happen," Uncle Théodore said. "Can you suggest anything, Clémentine?"

"It occurs to me," Mme. Euffe said, "that if we got St. Anthony interested . . . If we promised him something for his collecting box he would make us get more; I am convinced of it."

"Well, well," said Uncle Théodore. "I have the deepest respect for your convictions, Clémentine. But we can't commission St. Anthony to go to the Rue Turenne. Or if so, you can go with him yourself."

"I?" said Mme. Euffe.

"There is nobody, my dear Clémentine, who seems more suitable than yourself. Being the widow, you are the hardest hit of all. In any case, we shall not expect you to raise the question of money, but simply to give them the moving spectacle of your grief. The lawyers will follow later. But I should like them to see you in your full mourning first. It would have an excellent effect."

"I shall never be able to screw myself up to that," Mme. Euffe replied.

"But, Mother," Edmond Euffe exclaimed, "there's the question of duty! I will go with you if necessary."

"No, not you," said Uncle Victor. "but your brother Germain, who is younger."

"And shall I take my beautiful mantle?" Mme. Euffe asked.

"Good heavens, no!" Edmond cried, having a particular aversion for this garment. "You must go as plainly dressed as you can."

"You will have to think it out carefully," Uncle Théodore said. "Let them see your grief, Clémentine, but don't look undignified. People are always ready enough to say 'No' to the poor, but they feel awkward in the presence of the rich. That's a law of experience, as old as the hills."

"But after all," Edmond asked, "wouldn't it be simpler to leave the whole thing to the lawyers?"

"The less we need them, the less money will go into their pockets. Besides, you are forgetting that this visit will be in the nature of a pilgrimage. You will be seeing, Clémentine, the exact spot where your poor Constant was struck down. Remember that."

"Oh, I shall, Victor, I shall! But I can't go to these people looking as though I had come to make some sort of application."

"You will have nothing to fear on that score. The way will be prepared for the interview beforehand. I shall see to that. When you go to the Rue Turenne they will be expecting you. You will be in a very strong position. Everything will be cut and dried—you need have no fear about that."

50

A few days after the funeral Mme. Euffe, accompanied by her son Germain, made her way to the Rue Turenne, where Flavie Lacail was waiting for her—alone; this being in accordance with a joint decision by the husband and wife, who reckoned that Flavie, besides being thereby more easily able to sidetrack the question of money, would be in a better position for playing off her own distress against any display of grief on the part of Mme. Euffe. The latter might be sorrowing for her husband, but it was nevertheless a frightful misfortune for the young woman herself to have been the unwilling instrument of the death of such a man as he. A mishap so terrible as this could hardly deserve to be followed by her own ruin.

During the course of this interview there was a very singular manifestation of mutual attraction, intensely felt by both parties, and while it was quite unnoticed by Mme. Euffe, it left each of them woolgathering and apparently remote from the circumstances which had brought them together.

From the very beginning of a halting and painful conversation which each of the two women knew to contain innumerable traps, the rich maturity of Flavie Lacail had an overwhelming effect on Germain Euffe, who sat motionless on his chair without daring to open his mouth, while Mme. Euffe toiled painfully through the labyrinth of ticklish and insidious questions.

On the other hand, the freshness and youth of Germain Euffe, his shyness and faint blushes, his fair wavy hair, his smart, well-dressed appearance, an air of reserve which he owed to his education by the Fathers, threw Flavie Lacail into a state of perturbation as sudden and as profound as his. The Hollywood ideal of which she had often dreamed had become a living and visible reality, in that person of this young man in black clothes, with his entranced and tender gaze.

In these circumstances Germain Euffe became powerless to give his mother any conversational support. There was comparatively little reference to M. Euffe, while the verbal exchanges were keeping Fate, mistress of our fragile human destinies, well to the fore. Flavie cleverly sidetracked the question of her own responsibility. She did not dare to speak of the preposterous intrusion of Pamphile Garambois and the liberties which that coarse fellow had taken with her breast, for fear of shocking the youthful Germain Euffe and of his imagining that that lovely object was perhaps not inaccessible during the morning hours at a certain window in the Rue Turenne.

Flavie had much to say on the subject of her own sorrow and regret. She declared that if it was in her power, morally or even physically, to do anything to soften the effects of a cruel bereavement, she would certainly do so with all her heart. As she spoke these words she looked at Germain Euffe, who was looking at her at the same time, and a vivid blush spread over the cheeks of them both.

As the sources of conversation began to dry, they rose and went over to the fatal window and leaned out, that they might reconstruct in their minds' eye the fall of the vase on its way to shatter the skull of the jaunty and carefree M. Euffe. Over the soothing abyss of the street, with its rumble and hum of vehicles, of pedestrians, of joyous life, they pondered and dreamed. Scarcely could they believe that anything so grievous could have happened there through the fault of an amiable woman with an expressive, engaging face. . . .

As regards the possibility of an indemnity, nothing definite was said, Flavie taking great care not to understand the allusions of Mme. Euffe, though she piled them up to the best of her ability. Stimulated by the presence of Germain Euffe, and wishing the boy to take away a good impression of her, the young woman succeeded in expressing herself in terms and phrases of rare felicity. The interview came to an end with renewed condolences on the part of Flavie Lacail, while Mme. Euffe made this vague utterance: "We must think of the best thing to do next. . . ."

When they were once more in the street, Germain Euffe said to his mother:

"That person seemed very correct and well-behaved. What do you think of her?"

"I think we shall have a lot of trouble in getting anything out of those people. They are obviously not well off. Unless, of course, that woman is a wily creature, up to every trick."

"Oh, I don't think so. She had some style about her. And she dresses in good taste."

"Clothes don't tell you anything in these days. In the lower middle classes they put all their money on their backs, and among the poor it all goes on the table. It's only rich people who still know how to stint themselves—and to count. And indeed they have to, if they want to be rich!"

But Germain Euffe was bubbling over with the subject which occupied his mind, and within him were the beginnings of a feeling he wished to share.

"In any case," he said, "this young woman seemed to me to be very sincere. It's terrible, what happened to her! Put yourself in her place . . ."

"I know where I belong and how to stay there, thank God!" Mme.

Euffe replied. "Will you ever learn not to be so hotheaded and excitable, Germain?"

This first interview had left Germain Euffe with a keen desire to see Flavie Lacail again. Having reached the age of nineteen, this youth was anxious to enlarge the circle of his acquaintance—ladyloves included. He had always hoped to become on intimate terms with a woman older than himself, having heard that women of thirty are delightfully experienced, in a way which may be of great educational value to very young men.

Now Flavie Lacail was in every respect the incarnation of his favourite feminine type. It was the first time that he had ever met anyone of this type in such complete perfection and also within reach, and in a setting which was far removed from the sordid transactions of harlotry: her hips were rounded and the reverse of bony, her thighs well covered and plump, her calves firm and strong; she had a full figure, very white arms, dark eyes, and an attractive languor. . . . He was at the age for preferring the rich abundance of Junoesque charms. And it would be flattering to him to have a liaison with an atmosphere of mystery surrounding it. "Perhaps she is thinking of rebuilding her life. . . . Perhaps she has had disappointments. . . ." He thought he had detected a kind of sadness in Flavie's look which was interesting, and certainly expressed some secret sorrow. These feminine troubles are very moving for young men with a leaning towards the romantic, who always want love to have a tinge of heroism about it. Such feelings are often found seething in the depths of shy and affectionate natures.

One morning, at about ten o'clock, after days of hesitation and nights of insufficient sleep, and having passed twenty times beneath the windows in the Rue Turenne, Germain Euffe mounted the stairs and rang Flavie Lacail's bell, having provided himself with a sufficient excuse for his appearance.

The door was opened by Flavie herself, in a morning wrap—the same semitransparent garment as had robbed Pamphile Garambois of all his self-possession. She gave a start on recognizing her visitor.

"Excuse me," she said, blushing, "for receiving you like this. My servant never turned up this morning. Will you come this way."

"Madame," Germain said, "please don't put yourself out for me, I beg you. I was passing by and I thought you would not mind my coming up to ask you something—coming up just as a friend . . . as a friend, please believe me!"

"I certainly did not think of you as an enemy! But if you say 'friend,'

53

then I am only too glad, indeed I am grateful! I have never needed friendship more than I do just now, since I have been feeling so upset by all that has happened. . . . Will you wait two minutes for me?"

She disappeared for a longer time than she had mentioned. But the result of her absence was a marked revival of the brightness of her complexion, her lips, and her hair.

"Madame," Germain said, "so as not to have to hark back to it and add to your worries—are you insured against civil liability? That is a point we forgot to ask you about the other day."

"Goodness me!" Flavie said. "I really couldn't tell you. Those questions of insurance aren't in my line at all. If it wouldn't bother you to come again one day . . . But do sit down, monsieur! Is your mother well? I was so distressed to be making her acquaintance on the occasion of . . . Oh, it's frightful!"

"Madame," Germain said, greatly moved, "madame . . . Ah, I shall be sorry I came!"

"Forgive me," said Flavie. "It really does me a lot of good, you being here. . . . Have you many brothers and sisters?"

"One brother and two sisters," Germain told her.

"Are they like you?"

And so the conversation went on its way while they gazed continuously at each other. This private talk of theirs only served to confirm their first impression; each was enchanted with the other. There came a moment when Germain Euffe remarked, as he looked over at the window:

"You have a delightful view from here!"

"Yes," Flavie said, "it's very pleasant. That is the advantage of living rather high up. We get plenty of light and air, and the view of the mountains. Would you like to see?"

They went over to the window. The weather was magnificent. This time it was no longer a heedless onslaught of an impatient season, but a perfect collaboration, on a grand and imposing scale, of all the elements; a ripe plenitude, permanently installed in the sky, over the fields, the plains, and the banks of the rivers and streams, with its gorgeous blossomings, its hum of insects, its garlands of flowers and fruit. An invisible orchestra was playing muted themes of love and caresses and bliss. All that Nature had lost as an effect of surprise was amply replaced by full and radiant accomplishment. Spring was no longer an impudent schoolboy who has played truant and escaped to freedom, but a very young man with budding moustache and the ardours of that youthful period, a boy whose eyes are glistening with a winning and persuasive arrogance, so confident is he of his power to produce on women an effect of rapturous delight.

Flavie was now surrounded by a halo of the sun's warm rays. Against this background of golden light her splendid form, a trifle heavy perhaps, stood out clearly with every allurement it had, but with just sufficient chiaroscuro to lend a disturbing air of mystery to outlines abundant and rich. That lasted for a moment only, but long enough to carry the feelings of Germain Euffe to an extreme of rapturous emotion. He had been quickly roused, for amorous adventures had hitherto been few and far between and sometimes dull, with real preference not always a deciding factor therein.

Flavie was now leaning out of the window, with the young man beside her. In the narrow embrasure they were standing close together, a little closer than was altogether necessary, for their hair came in contact in brotherly and sisterly fashion each time they leaned over either to right or left in order to look at some detail of the panorama which lay spread out before them. Flavie's black, scented hair was tickling the face of Germain Euffe, fair-haired and blushing a little, and looking like a young lord or Oxford undergraduate who has hardly yet learned the ways of the world. But doubtless neither the one nor the other was thinking of convention, which enabled them to defy it in all innocence. Flavie seemed entirely occupied in pointing out different objects and explaining them, Germain in listening and admiration. Away in the distance, over the roofs of the houses, they were discovering chains of mountains, which in their imagination were overlaid with flowers, shady trees, mountain rills, and fairylike paths, all lightly touched by the winds of the heights above.

Nature's unfolding, her revelation of herself, had reached the moment of its greatest beauty, beneath the flood of light from the sky above and the gentle, bluish tint in which the whole extent of the horizon was bathed. Some slight movement on the part of either was the last and fragile barrier that still lay between these two young beings and the realization of a happiness of whose coming they were deeply, physically convinced. But the clearing of this obstacle was no simple matter. Everything hung upon a mere gesture, and was as liable to failure as all things are that depend on a gesture, on its perfect execution, on the choice of the exact moment for making it. . . .

Though it was indeed by mere chance, it so happened that Flavie's fine firm hip had come in friendly contact with the leg of Germain Euffe. By this means their bodies were receiving certain mutual impressions which, unhappily, were failing to give their minds sufficient courage to stir them to some kind of action. And as her hip relaxed and softened, so did Flavie's eyes avoid the young man's, while she turned her face away from his, and a look of coldness and detachment appeared in every feature. Germain was confused and baffled by this.

And now they had become quite unequal to any further exchange of comments on the scenery, while each was feeling that time was slipping by in an absurd and pointless fashion. There was a movement by which Flavie's wrap was partly opened, without her appearing to notice it. Germain Euffe's gaze could do no less than plunge into an abyss of fascinating whiteness, the sight of which brought him near to fainting. At that crucial moment, when the most alluring prospects were unfolding themselves before his eyes, the son of Clémentine Euffe, trampling upon the education received from the Fathers and the rigid principles of his family, besought Heaven to grant him the ease and skill of the born seducer. He made vast effort to think of some witty remark well adapted to the situation; but not an idea would come to him, shyness bereft him of speech, and he was in torture.

At last, when the silence seemed eternal, and trembling lest his companion should notice and suddenly deprive him of his exciting vision, he gave utterance to the most stupid remark that he could possibly make:

"It was there, madame—wasn't it?—that you had put your vase?"

"Yes," Flavie said mechanically.

At the same moment she turned round and looked at him. There were tears glistening in her eyes, tears of exasperation, for her stock of patience, modesty, and restraint was exhausted. Having now lost control of her nerves, and hardly knowing what she said:

"Your poor father!" she murmured.

And her tears, which had broken out afresh, became as it were pearls in a precious funeral wreath dedicated to the memory of M. Euffe. Germain Euffe, himself also in a state of turmoil, realized that it had become absolutely necessary to take some steps to assuage this poignant grief. He felt it his duty, without saying another word, to take the tenderhearted woman in his arms. He clasped Flavie tightly round the waist; her lovely bosom was crushed against him and he became dizzy with intoxicating delight. This splendid frame he held was indeed in urgent need of support, for it was losing all its strength. With eager enthusiasm, Germain Euffe laid kisses in plenty over Flavie's neck and shoulders, accompanying them with confused and muttered consolations. In spite of all this, there was one brief moment at which the young woman showed presence of mind. She drew Germain far away from the window, breathing out, as though she were in a dream:

"Mind the neighbours!"

Then, once more oblivious to everything, she guided the young man to a corner of the room at which there was a divan. Onto this she gently subsided, taking Germain with her—with charitable and kindly intent, for the poor boy must be tired too. But, anxious not to overlook a single prescription of the most delicate of feminine codes, with eyes closed she breathed out these words: "What are you doing, my dear, you must be mad . . ." thereby safeguarding her own honour, as though she in her poor frailty were succumbing to the superior strength and artful knavery of an astute and crafty Don Juan. . . .

A little later Germain Euffe found himself out once more in the Rue Turenne, which was bathed in dazzling sunshine, and blithely went on his way. In less than an hour he had become a vastly more knowing and wide-awake youth of nineteen than he had been before, and he would have liked to cry aloud and proclaim his joy to every passer-by. Still under the spell of the amazement and wonder of his first wild moment, still astonished at the ease and simplicity of an ending which he had thought impossible, he was filled with gratitude and pride in equal measure. Flavie, when they were saying good-bye, had held his face between her fervent hands and murmured:

"Why, you are like Freddy Glowes! Has no one ever told you that?"

Freddy Glowes, the champion of masculine beauty on the screen, was the idol of every woman devotee of the films. And thus it was that Flavie Lacail had reached the height of her ambition. She was now beloved by a boy who resembled a famous young leading actor, and this boy, through his family, was himself a guarantee for all the recommendations she could wish for. . . . She had come and leaned her elbows on the window sill in order to watch the retreating figure of him who so filled her thoughts. When the fair-haired Germain had vanished, she looked back unconsciously along the street and then at the pavement beneath her window. At that moment she saw once more in her mind's eye, and with horror, a picture of M. Euffe lying on his stretcher in the chemist's shop, and it was not until then that she remembered the relationship of her victim to the fond and loving young man with the "film face." It was at that moment that she had a full vision of the power of the god of Chance, of its terrible irony. . . . It was at that moment that her thoughts were turned to the decisive part which that window had played in her own life, within a few weeks. . . . Happiness, unhappiness—everything had had its origin there. . . . She had exercised no better control over her own feelings than that mad fool Pamphile over his. Are we really free agents in this life of ours?

But Flavie Lacail was a woman, and having to shake a fist at Fate in her strangest mood, and to give a satisfactory explanation of her own doings, daunted her not in the least. She had no idea what the future would bring forth, what would be the result of the morning's events. In the meantime, as she thought of the younger son of the Silken Net, she said to herself with a sigh:

"Poor darling, it was the least I could do for him. . . ."

At the corner of the Rue Lesdiguières and the Boulevard Gambetta, Germain Euffe felt that he wanted to walk a little before going home. Turning to the right, he passed between the barracks Hoche and de Bonne before coming out into the Place Gustave-Privet, from which there is a view that extends beyond the heights of Champagnier and d'Eybins, which themselves have still higher peaks rising above them, the Taillefer and the Pelvoux mountain group. This is the most airy spot in Grenoble, the only place where, thanks to the Echirolles plain, one does not get the oppressive feeling of the mountains at too close quarters. Germain was thinking of the delightful woman whose bounty would henceforth be giving him an enviable importance among the youths of his own age. He admired and wondered at the tact with which Flavie had managed this affair, leaving all the credit to him. . . .

Occupied with this subject, his thoughts turned naturally to M. Euffe, whose shattered skull had been the starting point of the journey to this mutual passion. A sad and painful coincidence indeed it was, but the accident had taken place entirely apart from the will of anyone whomsoever. Germain included in one greathearted feeling of warm affection memories both of his father and of the dear young woman who had shown such distress at his death.

"Poor Daddy!" he said, with a sincere and genuine outburst of sorrowful feeling, keener than any he had experienced until this moment.

He kept repeating to himself, with an undercurrent of optimism and happiness, the sad words "poor Daddy," giving a little spring each time he mounted a pavement, while a strong feeling of filial piety filled his heart, already touched and softened by Flavie's gracious deeds. . . .

"Poor Daddy, how much better I understand him now!"

He was feeling how truly he was his father's son, the son nearest to him and the most deeply affected. And in his heart he gave absolution to M. Euffe, accidentally killed while bearing a present of sweets to an abandoned young woman. To excuse it in others one must know the power of passion one's self. All afire with its incipient stages, Germain Euffe was feeling himself nearer to his father than he had ever been— so near, indeed, that he would fain have had him at his side that he might tell him in confidence in his boyish, ingenuous way that, like him, he had a mistress for whose sake he was already feeling inclined to spend money—to wild extravagance, perhaps. . . . Thanks to his new-found love, sentiments of a delightful kind were entering his heart. He determined to go to the cemetery in the afternoon and take a bunch of flowers, the cost of which he would defray from money set aside for his pleasures.

"Dear old Daddy!" he said in an affectionate tone of voice.

The weather was beautiful, his lady loved him, he was feeling in a generous mood, he was hungry. He hastened towards the Place Victor-Hugo. As he was crossing Post Office Square one last thought came vividly into his mind:

"One does owe a lot to parents! Yes, one does. . . ."

4. SORROW AND JOY With all the appanage of her mourning and her grief, Mme. Clémentine Euffe had found in widowhood a condition of life so satisfying that she might well have wondered (had the thought not been distinctly unchristian) why she had not become a widow at some earlier date. For long years past, her wifely status had been reduced to the playing of a very unobtrusive part in which she had been exposed to criticism and grumbling in the family circle, hard though she strove to retain some measure of authority over her children by the use of precepts and maxims of the superannuated nature of which she alone was unaware. If Alberte, with her natural sweetness, was to some extent amenable, Lucie on the other hand would not listen to her, while the boys completely disregarded her, refusing to admit that she had any right whatever to supervise their doings, either the hours (very late) at which they returned home or their Sunday excursions. As for M. Euffe, he had long ceased to pay any but the very slightest attention to family conversation, while he might often be seen smiling at unspoken thoughts whose source and inspiration were certainly not his wife and children. As soon as he had finished a meal he hastened to leave his house, humming the while some tune or other which was manifestly derived from the repertory of the younger generation. He would tell them that he was going to a company meeting.

Mme. Euffe's widowhood released her from her position of effacement, made her the most prominent lady for the time being among the women of her own age and circle, and brought the grandmothers of the leading families in Grenoble hastening to see her. Delighted at the unexpected occurrence of an event of interest to the people of their own generation, the dowagers came crowding to Mme. Euffe's where, as they sat devouring dainty cakes, they spent long hours in getting her to recount the most trifling details of a tragic death, a death which had made so vivid an impression on public opinion that the municipal authorities had just issued a new order relating to windows and balconies with flowers. A question was frequently raised as to what M. Euffe was doing in the Rue Turenne.

"It was just Fate, indeed it must have been! A man who hadn't a thought outside his business and his family, to be struck down like that, right out in the street, just at the very moment . . ."

Mme. Euffe agreed that it was indeed to Fate that this tragedy must be imputed, adding that a man like M. Euffe, who was still very active despite his years, would be prepared to expose himself to the blows of Fate with all the ardour and rashness of a young man.

"What a loss for you, my dear!" the old ladies wailed as they furtively helped themselves to another glass of black-currant liqueur.

"Yes," Mme. Euffe would reply, "it is a sore trial. If there were not prayer . . ."

"How do unbelievers get on without it, I wonder? Fortunately you've always got your hope of seeing your dear Constant again."

"It is that thought which keeps me going," Mme. Euffe would say as she drank more tea than usual, with a good deal of rum in it, so heavily did her sorrow weigh her down.

More than a hundred times did she repeat the story of the accident in the fullest detail, with constant improvement in the method of its recounting, as also in the intonations of her voice. It was many years since Grenoble society had shown such interest in her, and she was so touched by this that tears flowed without any effort on her part. Thus she made some effects which were highly appropriate to her sad situation, and this won her fresh sympathy. The widows' contingent was rejoiced at gaining a recruit of such excellence, and one who had reached an age at which there was no further danger of her escaping them. Mme. Euffe was admitted straightway into the sisterhood of long veils and mourning in perpetuity.

The first wave of curiosity was specially directed towards discovering in what manner Mme. Euffe, who had long been relegated to a shadowy background, would mourn the loss of a husband whose levity of conduct was known to the whole town. Clémentine was approved for having kept a decent silence regarding depravities of a kind by which the unions of human beings are often spoilt. Furthermore, her physical deterioration, which had long since begun, was no longer a fitting complement to the vitality and vigour of M. Euffe's declining years. These ladies were in any case well aware that such a condition is an incitement, with men, to certain behaviour which for themselves, with the age of fifty behind them, is no longer seasonable. Many of the widows, in this matter, had no regrets of any kind: it was enough (good heavens, indeed it was) to have been acquiescent for twenty or thirty years in complying with certain requests, when only one of the parties stood to profit thereby.

The other widespread manifestation of curiosity was aimed at finding out whether M. Euffe's squandering of his fortune, which was reputed to be on a large scale, had not dealt a fatal blow at his family. The financial ascent of the Euffes had been so rapid and overwhelming that one section of the best society, that which led the fashion and considered itself specially privileged, could not fail to take it to heart. The representatives of the old families in the district would not have been sorry to see some diminution of the Euffes' growing importance.

Now it is when inheritances are taking place that family setbacks are revealed. People get wind of them through the appearance and bearing of the heirs and any changes there may be in their style of living. This was the reason why the women visitors continued to pour in: they were waiting to be told what the lawyers had said. The bombardment of questions aimed at Mme. Euffe came chiefly from the contingent of the acrimonious dowagers whose widowhood had deprived them of their prerogatives, of dividends and other advantages, and who could not forgive the younger generation for having ousted them. Having once been in positions of authority, and able to save money, with an easygoing husband in the background, they were now ageing with bitterness in their hearts. With ruthless insistence they asked her:

"You had no disappointments, my dear?"

"Oh no," Mme. Euffe would reply. "No, none." But she vouchsafed no further information.

Thus the last will and testament of M. Euffe was shrouded in a veil of irritating silence. It was generally considered that Mme. Euffe was carrying discretion too far and that she was selfishly avoiding her duty to supply what was clearly some rich material for the conversations of others in the same plight as herself. The strange death of M. Euffe was of that rare type of event regarding which it was only reasonable to expect some inside information. Unless each of the widows made some contribution of her own, how would they end their days and what would they find to talk about? How would they disperse that fog of boredom which is so trying, and which drives people to resort to each other in order to fight against their inability to live in silence with nobody's thoughts but their own?

Now there was nothing that happened among the old ladies in the smarter circles that escaped criticism and judgment at La Tronche, the home of Mme. de Sainte-Foy, widow of the general of that name, and the most remarkable and strongest feminine personality in the whole of Dauphiné, with a formidable reputation that extended as far as Chambéry and Valence.

The general's widow, now aged sixty-two, had the fleshy countenance of a proconsul of the Byzantine Empire, with a voice which would have worked wonders at the head of a regiment of cavalry. This massive face was accompanied by a bulky frame encased in a whalebone corset and weighing some two hundred pounds. The general's widow was reputed to be an unusually capable woman with an exceptionally good head on her shoulders, though it was not with her head only that she had fought the battles of life, in which by means of four consecutive husbands she had achieved no little success: these were the late M. Prunavent, chemist; the late M. Mathias, barrister; the late M. Larbois, manufacturer; and lastly, the general himself.

Forty years earlier the intrepid Nathalie had plunged into marriage in the spirit of a suffragette; and her numerous unions had left her with such a terrible hatred of men that it seemed that the only object of her multiplicity of marriages could have been to take reprisals. It was at the age of forty-seven, when she was already well provided for, that she marked down the general, a feeble man outside his military duties and a perfect coward in face of love. It was, however, regarded as a rash undertaking on the part of this slayer of husbands, for it is well known that generals, hardened by a healthy open-air life, live to a great age, apart from accidents, which are rare and unlikely to occur. But this opinion showed ignorance of the true worth of Nathalie de Sainte-Foy. After continually storming at him as though he were a second lieutenant, to such an extent that the wretched man had often hoped for a European conflagration in order to get a little enjoyment and peace, she killed off her general as she had the others.

On the death of her soldier, Nathalie, who was then fifty-seven, remained "the general's wife," an entirely suitable designation, and strongly upheld her position. She had still some good fighting years before her in which to carry on the feminine crusade and devote herself entirely thereto. Her four marriages had given her only one son, a timid simpleton who lived a long way from Grenoble in terror of his mother. He was a student at the Military Academy, and his head was so befogged with figures that he was always getting into strange predicaments. He had ended his academy career at the bottom of the list for promotion, with his brain power spent beyond repair.

There was some talk of Mme. Euffe in the presence of the general's wife. This lady expressed her opinion in no measured terms, and with a sonority of voice that recalled the notes of a bugle: "Poor Clémentine, she's a silly little fool! She has never asserted her authority in the slightest degree at home. But I shall go and see her. I've got some things to say to her!"

It was the month of August. For spending the hot summer months, the Euffes had the choice between their residence at Montbonnot and their Bouquéron property. During the lifetime of M. Euffe, who liked to entertain and to play at being a lord of the manor, Montbonnot was usually chosen. But Mme. Euffe, as a place of shelter for herself at this time of mourning, chose the Bouquéron property as being easier to run and in a more airy position and with a better view. It was there that the general's wife came to visit her. What she had to say was certainly important. And she went straight to the point.

"It would be better, Clémentine, if instead of sighing and groaning, you would pay some attention to things that are happening! A woman in your position has duties to fulfil, active duties, because people are watching you closely. Are you one of those women who let everything in a social way go to the deuce?"

"In a social way?" Mme. Euffe asked. "What can I do about that?"

"Tell me, Clémentine, do you think society is in a good sort of state? Let me tell you, my dear, society will soon cease to exist! The highest in the land are on visiting terms with the lowest. Pork butchers are buying country houses and pub keepers are made Ministers. It's up to us to put up a few barriers and take a stand against the stupid things men do in politics."

"Constant," Mme. Euffe said, "had very little to do with politics."

"He was wrong. With all those means at his disposal, he ought to have gone in for politics. Have you any idea at all how badly things are going? And why are they? Because we leave all the power to men. Men

—I ask you! Well, you've seen them at close quarters! Less than I have, no doubt. But yours must have been enough to give you an opinion. Do you know what they think about—men? Well, it doesn't leave them enough time to undertake anything big. But tell me, my dear, have you been to the museum lately?"

"No," said Mme. Euffe, "I never go there."

"You are wrong, Clémentine. Not that it's interesting, but you ought to know something about it. You see what manners and customs and different ways of thinking are like, in museums. Go to the one here in Grenoble, and you'll be astonished at it. Go right to the very end, to the chamber of horrors."

"What, is there a chamber of horrors?"

"I can't think of any other description. They have hung up some things which are neither finished nor ever will be, by Pica—what was the name?—and some others by Utri—oh, I can't remember now. Just daubs, jumbles—you can't make head or tail of them. They're just making fun of people, with the Government in the know. Do you know anything about painting, Clémentine?"

"Very little," Mme. Euffe replied.

"Just like me. Still, all the same . . . Now when the general was alive . . . oh, the poor man didn't know much outside his reviews and parade grounds . . . but he was interested in military painting on account of the uniforms. In my drawing room we had two Detailles, battle scenes or something like that: you knew what it was meant to be. And in my dining room at the present moment I've got a trout on a plate, and some asparagus and peaches. It actually makes you feel hungry! Clémentine, what I have really come to say is, that you must do your duty."

"But what is it that makes you say that to me?" Mme. Euffe asked.

"Everything. Grenoble is getting into a bad frame of mind; people stare at one in the street in a most impertinent way. There is slovenliness everywhere. And about your own affairs in particular. Everyone is talking about them. Now listen. Clémentine, we are both women of experience. And we can't alter the past. Do you know that Jumier girl whom your husband was interested in?"

"Oh," Mme. Euffe said, "I didn't exactly know her . . ."

"No," said Nathalie de Sainte-Foy, "she was hardly on your visiting list! But you knew that she existed?"

"At my age," said Mme. Euffe, "and with all my complaints, Constant was quite free . . ."

"That was no one's business but yours. But it ought not to have prevented you from keeping an eye on him and taking certain precautions.

With men, you must never give them their head. . . . Do you know what is happening now? You don't? Well, that girl is on the point of getting two hundred thousand francs insurance money."

"Two hundred thousand francs!" said Mme. Euffe.

"And did you know that she has already drawn fifty thousand francs —the very day of his death?"

"The day of his death! Did people know what was cashed that day?"

"My dear, there's nothing kept secret in Grenoble! You know what gossips Dauphiné people are! So I ask you—what good do these posthumous gifts do? What sort of people do they encourage? Are you going to put up a fight—for morality's sake? It's your own children's money that is to be stolen by the concubine! . . . And yes—your children—you would be wise to give an eye to them. They are beginning to follow in their father's footsteps, in the way of loose living."

"But how?" Mme. Euffe asked.

"Ah, my dear, people are beginning to murmur certain things . . . I haven't got all the details yet, but I soon shall. You can rely on me to keep you informed. If you want to fight, I shall be with you."

"Fight," Mme. Euffe said with a sigh, "fight . . ."

"Why, yes, fight!" said Nathalie de Sainte-Foy. "Do you imagine that I didn't have to fight with my four husbands? And I kept them in good order, I can assure you. I should just have liked to see them leaving money to Jumier girls! Those young women would have made my acquaintance pretty quickly! There would have been something like a shindy. . . . And because we happen to have taken up the career of marriage, should that make us less competent than those hussies?"

"Oh, I . . ." Mme. Euffe said plaintively.

"Yes," said Nathalie de Sainte-Foy, "a woman who is only married once gets bogged. Women grow too accustomed to a man and think that unless they've got him it's all up with them. Fortunately I myself have had four. I never had time to get slack. And if I were a few years younger I would still be prepared to be putting some fine gentleman in his place! There aren't enough women, Clémentine; that's the root of all our social troubles."

"But there are supposed to be more women than men . . ."

"What—flabby, spineless softies—slaves! I don't call them women at all. Pull yourself together, Clémentine! Hear fewer masses and get a move on."

"But what can I do? People have their own reasons . . ."

"If you listen to people's reasons! That is how all disturbances begin, Clémentine! As the general used to say .. oh, he didn't do much thinking, poor man, but he reduced everything to a simple system 'I start by telling 'em to go to blazes. Then one can think it over afterwards,' he used to say. And afterwards the thing was settled. My word!—if I'd listened to the reasons of my four rascals . . ."

This period of mourning was for Alberte a time of complete, ideal happiness. She went nearly every morning to lay flowers on her father's grave, either on foot from the Place Victor-Hugo or on her bicycle from Bouquéron. Knowing that she undertook it gladly, the whole family relied upon her for the carrying out of this pious task—including Mme. Euffe, who preferred the church to the cemetery and, as she suffered from varicose veins, had difficulty in getting about.

As she engaged in all these activities there was genuine sincerity in Alberte's heart. She had no wish to discover whether her father had in fact behaved badly, as the sour-tempered Lucie declared and her mother's sighs seemed to indicate. All she did was to remember that her father had been kind, that he had always smiled tenderly at her, in a way which gently hinted at a preference for her which was hardly expressed at all, but of which she was very conscious. She was remaining faithful to the memory of this tenderness, to the intonation of M. Euffe's voice as he uttered certain commonplace words when speaking to her, giving those words a deeper meaning than they really bore. She was sure that, as a father, he had been a good, worthy man, more scrupulous and more affectionate than many people might suppose.

She was feeling in her heart a special debt of gratitude because, on the day of the terrible accident, in the shock of grief, a confession of her own love had escaped her. This confession had left her with neither embarrassment nor remorse, nor did she feel that it showed any lack of reverence for the dead man. It had been made to some extent under his protection, at a moment when her eyes were filled with tears which flowed for him alone. Her love, of which at that moment she had felt the full power, was helping her the better to cherish and preserve a fond memory.

And in the morning, before the full heat of the summer day, the cemetery was charming in the sunshine, with not another soul in sight, enlivened by the songs of birds and bright with flowers, in an amphitheatre of mountains showing pink and with outlines faint and blurred, and in slanting rays the church tower of Corenc a brilliant object on the mountainside. In no way was this picture spoiled by the dead, lying there so unobtrusively, in such tranquillity and peace. You felt that as they were human and now at last held the key to all mysteries, they had the power of hearing and of understanding all things and were capable of great indulgence to those still left behind. It was there that the earthly future of each one of us would end someday. . . .

But for Alberte the future still suggested an infinity of time. Neither her enthusiasm nor her courage had been even lightly touched by any thought of earthly evanescence. And apart from M. Euffe, the dead were not associated in her mind with any people in the town with whom she might have come in contact. They came within a category of life stories in which her own youth found no place. These made up for her a little mythological kingdom into which, in the morning's gentle charm, in the silence and the light summer breeze, she had brought a daughter's grief now much allayed, her unreasoning, instinctive joy, her heart's high hopes. She had her favourites among these dead, her friends and confidants. This had depended on the design of the tombstones, the species of the flowers, and the poetry of certain names engraved upon the marble or the stone. Those she cherished most among them all were Blandine Saint-Azur, Jean-Louis Coucou (who had died at the age of twelve), and Bertrand de Quisendor d'Oisans.

It was on her way to the cemetery that Alberte's faithfulness to her father's memory found its reward. She met Bob de Bazair. And soon she met him on that road every day. He would wait for her two hundred yards from the iron gate, at the beginning of a little path in Green Island park, quite close to the town but far from its inhabitants with their suspicions, their scoffing, and their intrigues. They had before them a lovely hour of morning, an hour filled full with sunshine tempered by the coolness of the trees, with a wide vista of the green valley of the Isère and noble mountains at the horizon beyond. And above them a cloudless sky, a sky of liquid blue.

"Good morning, Albe!" Bob said to her, smiling.

These little trifling words became for Alberte so charged with meaning that she had no wish for more to follow, and would have been content that Bob should always speak the same, while looking at her with his masterful air in which she could see nothing but delightful kindness.

For she thought herself silly, so moved was she, and was filled with wonder at the interest which Bob was taking in her. There were a thousand things that she would have liked to say to him, but they were too secret, too hard to put into words, and it would only have broken the spell of that gentleness, that pact of silence which was bringing them together. Her only wish was to walk forever in this park of dreams, with her hand in his and the murmur of a tender voice at her side, and that sometimes another hand might be laid upon her heart and feel its grateful beating. . . . Her love was there, her great, unspeakable love. She dared not look at it, nor let her thoughts dwell upon it when its object was so near.

Bob understood her so well that he spoke very little of love. He talked to her of people whom they both knew and she was no longer seeing, and of the tennis club where she had ceased to go and play. He brought to their conversation a tone of easy friendship, which went further than friendship in certain intonations of the voice and an occasional light caress. He confirmed her in the habit of spending together a full hour of their mornings, with some lovely scenery to gaze at, and thus made her join in sharing their youth and the heedless, carefree joy of holidays. Life with its many problems lay far ahead of them, like the return home in October and the indistinct and hazy summits of the mountain group of the Grande Chartreuse. For Bob it was pleasant and restful, with a freshness about it that was quite new to him. Alberte, with all her good health and her openhearted sincerity, gave him something that he had never yet experienced—the pleasure of a love affair entirely unspoilt by any haste, impatience for a climax, or questionable arrangement. For Alberte, who put her whole being into these meetings, it was the very essence of happiness. She knew that these would be the starting point of her life, and that her life would then go forward in a direction from which it would never, never swerve.

In returning to Bouquéron, Alberte often went by way of the Citadel bridge and the Allobroges pier. On those occasions she sometimes made a brief halt at the St.-Laurent church. Not knowing to whom to tell the secret of her happiness, she went to speak of it to God, not to the bad-tempered God of Mme. Euffe and the elderly ladies who came to see her, but the kind and tenderhearted God who was hers, a God capable of understanding our little affairs of the heart and of forgiving, say, M. Euffe for his Riri Jumier, simply because M. Euffe had had a good kind fatherly smile for his children, and because the tiniest fragment of kindness atones a hundredfold for faults on which the world lays such spiteful stress.

There exists with regard to God a great fundamental misunderstanding which assumes a thousand different forms, each man trying to bring God over to his own side and make sly use of Him for his own ends. And so men have invented a God of armies, a God of the rich, a God of the poor, and others, occult and all-powerful, who are not named. Thus there could be no doubt that Mme. Euffe's was the God of liver complaints, and that of Mme. de Sainte-Foy, the general's wife, with her incipient beard and masculine appearance, the God of physiological anomalies. And for the curé of the parish of St. Louis, it was the comfortable God of the Grenoble millionaires, people whose actions are considered and judged in the light of the priority due to wealth, because every grade of human society is classified according to its income and every hierarchy based on the possession of material means.

As for Alberte, whose faith was independent of theological creeds, she believed in the God of the human heart; and this was because she was accustomed to act in obedience to the promptings of her own heart and that that heart was a tender one. With guileless simplicity she prayed to a God of kindness and of friendship, a God with whom her own sweet nature could associate no trace of vindictiveness or cruelty. She thanked God that Bob existed, that those charming eyes of his had looked into her own. In the young girl's mind God and Bob were becoming a little indistinguishable, no longer existed apart, ever since the day of M. Euffe's death, when Alberte had known heavenly rapture in the arms of Bob. She did not say ritual prayers. She stayed a few moments in the cool church, with its clear echoes, smiling gently at the saints, at the Virgin in rapturous admiration of her Child, and the meaning of her fervent thoughts was something like this: "Everything that may come to me from Bob and through Bob will be Thy will, and I accept it, and I rejoice at it, and I thank Thee for it, dear kind Father." She would try to think if that was all she had to say; then, as there seemed to be nothing else, she would end with a broad, tender smile wherewith she placed herself with faith and confidence in the hands of Him who is the arbiter of our fate.

Then she would make her genuflection, her sign of the cross, with all a little girl's thoroughness, and go outside and take her bicycle. And soon, having changed gear, she would be enjoying the climb of the hill which brought her back to Bouquéron. She had her rhythm, her muscular effort, under perfect control, while she relished the pleasure of continuous motion with each pressure of a pedal and of feeling her store of youthful strength in reserve. She was at peace with the world, that is, at peace with herself, with the fair prospect of the valley and the wooded slopes of the Belledonne mountain group which were expanding before her eyes as she mounted ever higher and the cool air of the heights touched her forehead with a light caress. Hundreds of times since her childhood had she come this way, and always with a feeling of pleasure. But now she was far more deeply touched by the beauty of nature than she had been in former days. These rides gave her consciousness of a life of intensity and depth. In solitude she found rich treasure of which she had never known; and it enchanted her. And on her tongue came often the sweet savour of one small word—Bob.

Alberte was happy.

5. EXPLANATIONS When Riri Jumier found herself with two hundred and fifty thousand francs at her disposal, and also in possession of a well-furnished wardrobe, a pleasant flat, and a small car at the garage, she said to herself that as compared with the past, the problem of life had now assumed for her a very different shape. It might well be said that there was but a slight difference, of a quite conventional nature, between herself and an ordinary young widow. She had a solid background, and could claim to be treated with consideration and respect: she had certainly earned it!

She knew also that a woman can only be at peace in society if she has a man's protection. She spent much time in thought before giving a definite direction to her plans, and eventually arranged a meeting with Bob de Bazair at Rives, at the Hotel Durand, famous for its cooking and far enough away from Grenoble to ensure being undisturbed. She wanted to have a conversation with the young man which would affect her future. She dressed with special care that day, and wore flowers. She started at a rather early hour, while the depths of the valleys were still hidden beneath bluish vapour, and drove slowly, looking at the scenery.

Arriving first, she garaged her small car and secured a table at the edge of the terrace which overlooks the great bend in the Lyon road. Bob, who had come on his motor bicycle, joined her at about midday. The weather was altogether delightful, very hot but with a tang in the air. Their cocktails were served very fresh, and the hors d'œuvre, equally fresh, were appetizing and varied. Bob appeared to be in high feather. He paid her a compliment on her dress.

Towards the end of the meal, which had been copious and the cooking first-rate, they began to discuss serious matters, and the young woman asked:

"What am I going to do now?"

"That depends on your own plans," Bob replied. "You expect to be staying on at Grenoble?"

"Yes, I rather think so. I am quite settled there, and I know people."

"Do you want to take another protector?"

"Another old man?" Riri said. "Thank you, no, indeed I do not! I can do without them. Don't you agree?"

"Yes, of course, of course," said Bob. "If you prefer to be independent. . . . In that case, why not take a little business, some nice little place— a teashop, a bookshop, or woollen materials—really, I don't know what to suggest, but there is certainly money to be made at Grenoble, with all the tourists. People are travelling about more and more."

"I don't know anything about business . . ."

"All right then, you must start on it. You're no fool, you've got taste, and you're a good-looking girl. Look here, why not take a business that concerns men? You see what I mean? Cuff links, ties, high-class morocco-leather goods, scarves, dressing gowns, eau-de-cologne. Nothing but smart things. Quite a tiny shop, but in a central position and up-to-date, with a pretty assistant. It would be called The Little Shop or The Man's Shop. Well, it's certainly an idea. Would you like me to make inquiries for you? I know Madinier very well, and Garnier, the architect, would fix you up with a smart little place. What about it?"

"No," Riri said, "too many worries. Or anyhow, not alone."

"Oh, some woman to go in with you? Well, that would be worth considering. You'd be able to take on something bigger. But you must be careful about any partnership. Those things often turn out badly. People quarrel and fall out with each other."

"Oh, I'd never have a woman partner!"

"A man, then? Then there would be other difficulties which you know as well as I do. There's a danger of that turning out badly too. Unless, of course, you married."

"Why shouldn't I?"

"It's a solution. And not such a bad one, either. Have you got someone handy?"

"Possibly," said Riri pensively.

"Well, well," Bob said laughingly, "you're feeling a sudden vocation to become a respectable middle-class housewife?"

Riri Jumier winced, and a trace of bad temper appeared on her face.

"Shouldn't I make as good a lady as anybody else? It's not so hard as all that, you know! When you see the clumsy way they move, lots of them! You're not going to tell me that all the high-and-mighty swells among the Grenoble ladies are models of good manners and smartness! If it wasn't for their money nobody would look twice at them, you can take my word for it. And what sort of amusement there can be in those stupid, stuck-up creatures I can't imagine! Men do have a funny sort of time, it seems to me!"

"Now, don't be antisocial!" Bob said. "You're not going to queer your own pitch, are you? You'll never make a lady if you take that sort of tone! People in good society ought to have a high opinion of themselves, even those with ugly mugs and fortunes that don't smell too good. Come now, you *must* understand that."

"No, not at all!" Riri said obstinately. "When I see old Mother Simione in her sables and her twenty-horse car . . . dowdy old fright!"

"Exactly what I was saying—you're antisocial! But, my good child, Mother Simione before her marriage was valued at twenty million!"

"Yes, well? And you don't think she's a fright?"

"That's not the point. You don't want twenty millions left lying idle when there are so many needs to satisfy! In any case, you are not in a position to understand. The aims and objects of the governing classes —that's not your pigeon at all. What a pity it seems! Now at this moment you've got a good standing in Grenoble, with a sort of left-handed connection with the richest middle-class families. And you're going to spoil the whole thing by violence. Be very, very careful!"

"I'm only speaking the truth!"

"But I don't care a rap, Riri! It's only fit for children or half-wits, all that twaddle you're talking! Come along now, don't be an idiot! Finish your sherry and let us go and stretch our legs a bit. It'll do you good to walk a little."

On leaving the hotel, they climbed several hundred feet of the hill on the Lyon road. Then they made their way into a field and took shelter from the sun beneath a shady tree. Away below them lay the valley of the Fure, and beyond the hillside opposite, which screened off the Moirans district from their line of vision, they could see the mountain peaks which tower above Grenoble. They had lighted cigarettes and were daydreaming, in the scorching heat of a lovely afternoon. Suddenly Riri uttered these words:

"Bob, marry me!"

Bob de Bazair started.

"You said?"

"I say—marry me."

"So you've gone completely off your chump, have you? These little country excursions seem to have a funny effect on you!"

"What is there so extraordinary in what I am saying?" Riri replied, with some indignation. "I have 250,000 francs, a flat, a car, a diamond solitaire, and I'm not repulsive to look at. And now his high and mightiness stands on his dignity! And what sort of position have you got, I should like to know? Are you any use at anything? I mean what I say. I've only got to open my mouth and I could be a rich wife—yes, 'wife' I said!—and because I offer this gentleman all I have he makes fun of me. . . . You son of a count! A count yourself!"

"That's the sort of proposal I prefer!" Bob said, joking.

"Swank! But that doesn't stop you being stony broke! And your family's stony broke too!"

"Quite true. Not much to hope for from me."

"You'll be looking elsewhere, I suppose? Got anything better than me?"

"Different class . . ."

"You skunk! What have you got against me?"

"A slight error of judgment."

"I'm offering you all I've got, Bob, all I've got."

"With the partnership thrown in! We might take a little dairy together, perhaps. It would be a delicious little place. And we should be a huge success in Grenoble. Specially me!"

"You wouldn't have to bother about the shop."

"Better still! Daddy Euffe's pennies have turned your head, I can see that. But for heaven's sake be a bit more reasonable about your ambitions. A little while ago you were talking in a way that would have done credit to a socialist tub thumper. And now here you are setting up to be like some old woman on the Riviera as rich as Crœsus and dancing about after some fancy man! I should like to know . . ."

"And this gentleman is a fancy man for young ladies in good society, is he? So it's true, then, what people are saying?"

"And what is that?"

"You and little Euffe. It seems that people are meeting you . . ."

Bob de Bazair's face became expressionless, wooden.

"Drop that, Riri," he said curtly. "You had much better drop it. I don't interfere with your life unless you ask me to. So don't do so with mine until I invite you."

Riri Jumier gave a little shrill laugh, in very bad taste.

"That kid Alberte, oh dear, oh dear! Little ninny, and butter wouldn't melt in her mouth! So that's the sort you like now?"

"Drop it, I tell you," Bob said again, gently.

This gentleness was more dangerous than violence. There was the suggestion of a smile on his lips, and he lighted a cigarette with his gold lighter. Then he gazed for some time at Riri, who had looked away from him: he remembered her vulgarity, and it would be sure to

73

come back to his mind at brief moments. He compared her secretly with the dark-haired girl at the Green Island, so confiding and trustful . . . Then, as though no serious words had passed between them, he tickled Riri Jumier's neck.

"You're a bit dotty, you know, my good girl!"

But the young woman burst out into convulsive sobbing.

"And supposing I love you? Perhaps I've no right."

Bob de Bazair thought that this day of lovely sunshine and brilliant light was about to be spoilt for good and all. He answered in a bored tone of voice:

"Of course you have—but it's idiotic! And I *had* warned you . . ."

"Yes, but you did sleep . . ."

Bob, irritated by this piece of ill breeding, cut her short:

"Don't be sugary! Did you love old Euffe? If we had to love everybody to whom we showed certain kindnesses . . ."

"Say straight off that it was out of pity, with me."

"No," Bob said, "it was for pleasure. There was a time when you were charming. But it's coming to an end. It did come to an end, just now."

He looked at his watch and rose.

"We had better go back. There are some people expecting me at Grenoble."

"What have you got to do, I should like to know! Are you really in such a hurry?"

"Yes," said Bob. "Idle people have a very heavy programme, having no excuse for escaping their social duties!"

Riri Jumier stood up, and patted her dress to relieve it of some blades of grass, while Bob helped her absent-mindedly. Then she looked at herself in her hand mirror, put on her hat, powdered her face, and used her lipstick. Side by side they started off once more along the Rives road, in silence.

Within a short time they caught sight of the beginning of the big bend in the road, and the hotel buildings.

"When do we meet again?" Riri asked.

"Oh, when it so happens," Bob replied, with a vague gesture.

"Bob, you're not meaning that between us . . ."

"Yes, I am," said Bob. "I think we've got to put a full stop now. But we can stay good pals."

"Good pals?" Riri murmured.

"If you like. . . . But on condition that you don't behave like a lunatic, as you did today!"

74

"And there was I wanting to turn over a new leaf," the young woman said.

"But I'm not stopping you!" Bob said. "On the contrary . . . It's with me that you would go to the bad."

The young woman tried another argument.

"It *is* sad, Bob!" she said humbly. "Now that I was free . ."

"Yes, it is sad. So don't let us talk any more about it. Talking of sad things doesn't get you anywhere, and it spoils the scenery. We'll meet again when you are more cheerful."

Riri Jumier had a return of her aggressive mood.

"You know jolly well how to be selfish!"

"It's the only capital I've got," Bob said calmly. "I have to manage it properly. And as for you, you had better go and have a little bust at Rector's this evening. What you need at the moment is to be taken out of yourself."

"Will you come there? And dance with me?"

"I might," said Bob. "If you don't get sentimental."

He was astride his motor bicycle and his right hand was playing with the throttle. He gave a kick at the starter, and the engine turned over slowly. Then he put it in gear.

"Well, good-bye!" he said.

He gave his hand to the young woman, gradually released the clutch, and accelerated. . . . A little farther on he changed into second gear and drew back the lever to the full, so as to have the joy of a sudden spurt, a flight. He had turned in the direction of Lyon, wanting, as he said, to have a good gallop. Soon he was charging along the La Frette road, with six miles in a straight line ahead of him. He had a good firm seat in his saddle, his elbows and supple knees acting as shock absorbers for him. Beyond the level crossing he sat more tightly on his machine and accelerated. The needle of the speed indicator rose rapidly till it reached seventy-three miles an hour on the dial. He maintained this speed for about two miles as a soothing measure and to feel himself in good form. Then he brought the burst of speed to a close and slowed down. He gave a sigh of relief as he thought how he had left all that recrimination and stupidity behind him, adding:

"What bores women can be, with that sentiment of theirs! And their mania for thrusting it at other people, all over the place . . ."

He smiled. The needle had gone back to forty. With one hand he searched for a cigarette in his pocket and put it between his lips. Then, letting go the handle bar for a few seconds, he quickly lighted it. It was a small feat which he could perform very successfully. A sense of comfort and well-being pervaded him.

"We certainly had a first-rate lunch," he said to himself. "An excellent place, that Hotel Durand. One ought to go there more often."

As he was wondering whom he should take with him next time to Rives, Alberte's name flashed across his mind, and he was seized with a desire to see her again, as a lovely climax to a day which had not been without its uses: so far as Riri Jumier was concerned the situation had been cleared up, and in the case of Alberte also there were no obstacles to contend with. As he thought of the latter:

"She's a topping girl!" he said to himself, with satisfaction and with tenderness.

A "topping" girl indeed she was from every point of view, in the beauty of her eyes, the quality of her smile, and the proportions of her figure, her candour and sincerity, her dowry . . . A few months hence the son of Count de Bazair might very well be marrying the younger Mlle. Euffe. A splendid marriage—and a delightful one too.

"And it will be a change from all those tarts, who will never be anything but what they are!"

Alberte was of the race of the tenderhearted, the admiring, and the faithful. She was fond of children, and at her coming of age would have a good fortune. And lastly, she adored Bob so wholeheartedly that not even opposition on the part of her family would be the slightest deterrent.

The young man calculated that he would have time to put in an appearance at Bouquéron without missing cocktails at seven o'clock with his friends. At La Frette crossroads he took the road to Voiron and Grenoble. He accelerated, in happy mood. Life for him was tinted with the colours of this radiant summer day.

Weeks and months passed. Family life had resumed its normal round, which had been subject to the altered arrangements occasioned by the subtraction of one of its members, long considered to be the most important, but already being proved to be by no means indispensable. But the death of M. Euffe had revived some very serious questions which had never been settled, and with regard to which there had always been hesitation in coming to any definite decisions. On these subjects Mme. Euffe, having been plagued and pestered by General de Sainte-Foy's widow, had a long conversation with her son Edmond, aged thirty-two. Edmond Euffe was saying to her impatiently:

"Now listen, Mother, do be quiet! You have never had the management of anything at home, thank goodness, and you are not going to begin now. Running a family necessitates a line of conduct which is based on a comprehensive view. Leave it to me to judge what is best, will you?"

"My dear child, I am only repeating what the general's wife said to me. You will hardly accuse her of any lack of either discernment or energy."

"Yes, I agree, the general's wife has always shown energy. She has had enough to bring four unfortunate men to the grave. Still, that was their business, poor devils. But our own affairs have nothing whatever to do with her."

Mme. Euffe had had such an inveterate habit of sighing all her life that the members of her family had become exasperated by it. But since her mourning they had grown more tolerant of this mania. Before replying, therefore, she sighed.

"Anyhow, she says that the whole of Grenoble has its eyes fixed on us."

"Oh, does she, does she! And what does she mean by the whole of Grenoble, I should like to know? Twenty or thirty families she has picked out, and hardly more than half are on our visiting list."

"Exactly, Edmond. And the fewer well-known families there are, the more they should set a good example of justice and dignified behaviour."

Edmond Euffe threw up his arms.

"As far as justice goes . . . granted! But when you come and talk to me about dignity and good behaviour . . . well, all I can say is that we should cut a fine figure if we brought a lawsuit against this young Jumier woman and tried to get back two hundred and fifty thousand francs, which, if you come to think of it, she has earned. In a certain way . . ."

"Oh, Edmond, how can you dare . . ."

"Well, what I mean is that Father left her this money of his own free will, in recognition of a certain self-sacrifice . . ."

"But your poor father never expected to die so soon! If he had known, he wouldn't have given her so much."

"Perhaps so. But remember this—if he hadn't died he would have given this person far more in the long run. And I don't know if it occurs to you what kind of questions might be asked in court? Why, Mother, we should be a laughingstock!"

Defeated on this subject, Mme. Euffe returned to the charge on another, so strongly was she under the influence of General de Sainte-Foy's widow and so greatly did she fear the sarcasms of that terrible woman.

"And about the Lacails, Edmond. What have you decided? Have you settled the amount of the damages?"

"No, nothing definite," said Edmond Euffe. "And there again, I'm wondering . . . These Lacails are not insured."

"How do you know?"

"Germain told me. He is keeping in touch with them, so he says. You know that Félix Lacail is employed at the Prefecture. He is suspected of being a freemason. For the Silken Net's sake we have every interest in not getting these freemasons against us; they are a strong influence in Grenoble. And we need to be on good terms with the Prefecture on account of our branches. It would be very easy to make trouble for ourselves."

"But, Edmond, our business dealings are all honest!"

"They are, of course they are! Still, even in honest business you need a margin of toleration, if you want to do really good business!"

"Edmond, I wonder what the uncles will say?"

"Oh, never mind them, Mother. The uncles are old asses."

"Oh, my boy, how can you talk like that about the family?"

"Between ourselves, why not? Needless to say, we shouldn't go and shout it from the housetops. But after all, Uncle Victor runs a rotten hotel at St. Marcellin. . . . Uncle Théodore is a sort of carrier, with his transport business at Chambéry. They get a bit of reflected glory from Father's success. But you're not going to tell me that they are remarkable men or a great credit to us."

"All the same, Edmond, they are your uncles!"

"Yes, well, they're my uncles! I didn't choose them, did I? Is this all you had to say to me?"

"I should have liked to talk to you about Alberte too. Don't you think she is changing?"

"Yes, I do. But I think she is changing for the better. She is getting very pretty."

"I am speaking of her character. Do you expect she will marry?"

"She will certainly marry."

"You have no idea who it will be?"

"Her only difficulty will be to choose."

"Let us hope and pray that her choice will be a good one!"

"But it may! One would think, to hear you, that nothing but catastrophes ever happen. You didn't do so badly yourself. You've gone a long way since the days of Grandfather's little shop!"

"Yes, yes," Mme. Euffe said with a sigh. "But one sees so many bad marriages nowadays. . . . And how about Germain? He goes out a great deal, his thoughts seem always to be elsewhere, like your father's in latter days. . . . He hasn't got a liaison, by any chance?"

"He's no longer a lad, you know!"

"Oh, children are a worry!"

"We all start by being children. Your own parents in their day said exactly the same thing. I am beginning to say it about my children. The world is made up of a few old threadbare stories."

"Yes," said Mme. Euffe with another sigh. "But life has changed a great deal. Manners and customs are not like they used to be. You need only see the way women dress nowadays . . . I used to wear corsets and long skirts. . . . Well, anyhow, take good care of the family. And I will send the general's wife along to you if necessary."

Edmond Euffe had inherited from his father, that self-taught, full-blooded, and audacious man, a love of authority, direction, and control, with something else added which was an appropriate distinguishing mark of the younger generation, the one which, finding its fortune already made, puts the finishing touches, by its general attitude and by the marriages it makes, to the family's possession of wealth. Unlike M. Euffe, who had started from zero, Edmond Euffe was born a director, which greatly facilitates assumptions of authority and contacts with other men. Beginning life on a high rung of the social and commercial ladder, he had had sufficient leisure for some good study, which, after his bachelor's degree, was successful in obtaining him a diploma of the Commercial Institute of Grenoble University. And thus it was that through him the transition from primary to secondary education was accomplished for the first time—a thing which raises a family from insignificance, alters the character of its future, and gives it a new part to play in society; and it is the most critical stage in the evolution of a line of descendants. Edmond Euffe was secretly no less proud of his patrician knowledge than M. Euffe had been ingenuously proud of his millions.

M. Constant Euffe had been a self-made man who had shed but little of the evidence of his humble extraction; this left him with simplicity and simple goodheartedness, which redeemed his vulgarity. He doubted that his success in life could be a substitute for all other deficiencies. When he had become a rich man he recognized that there were other standards of value besides money, and he was always inclined to be humble in spheres other than his own. Though incapable of any sound criticism where they were concerned, he admired orators, lecturers, journalists, and writers for their faculty of expressing themselves in a medium of which they were masters. In the presence of a great doctor or statesman or scholar it was quite natural to him to exclaim, "There's a fine brain!" He recognized that there are more exalted ways of utilizing intelligence than those in which he had applied his own. He would bow before a contractor for plasterwork who had become a member of Parliament; that man had done something difficult—something of which he himself might not have been capable. He respectfully admired the holders of exalted official posts which his triumphs in the catering world could never permit him to occupy. In the matter of decorations he had wished for nothing more than the academic palms, which seemed to him to be a very suitable recognition of a certain devotion to social and philanthropic causes—and he obtained this award at the age of fifty-five. (Knowing that he was extremely anxious to get it, the authorities had by no means hurried themselves; for it is a fundamental doctrine that a petitioner must not be gratified too quickly.)

M. Euffe was a firm believer in men being in their right places and working hard at their respective jobs; he also liked to see some gratuitous rivalries, and was in favour of certain spheres of activity being reserved for people of outstanding ability. His own rise had been so swift and so remarkable that he still found pleasure in looking down from above at the friends of his youth and some vague cousins. He had certainly discharged some ballast, that is to say, he rarely paid them a visit, but he was not afraid to see them from time to time in order to realize, by comparison, how far he had outdistanced them. For this reason he was not jealous and was always ready to applaud other people's successes. He was content with what he had done, at being able to feel that it was something considerable, and satisfied with the results obtained. At the same time he did not imagine that the sale of sardines and margarine, of dried plums and bacon, of cod and olives, of oil and wine, even though it were in hogsheads and tons, had carried him to the topmost rung of the social ladder. He did not deny that others had accomplished better and more difficult tasks, in spheres in which he could never have shone. By these means, beneath a rough exterior, he retained until his death a freshness of outlook and a fund of common sense.

Edmond's case was different. What his father had had to secure by the strength of his right arm and a gift of the gab, he, Edmond, possessed at birth. The rise in the fortunes of the Euffe family, which he found at a certain level, it was his task to carry to a higher one, at which there would be more variety and greater refinement. He had a smaller capacity for work than his father and doubtless less flair (that characteristic of pioneers); but much better manners, together with a more elastic conception of honesty and a conviction—shared by all the other young men of his generation—that success is chiefly a matter of shrewdness, adaptability, and good connections. The questions he had to consider were no longer that of making a fortune—such being already definitely acquired—but those of social status and flattering marriages.

M. Euffe himself had in actual fact been simply an uneducated millionaire, at the earliest period of the acquisition of wealth, and a man who in taking too much on his own shoulders and continually touting for orders still had commercial broker written all over him. He represented the springboard from which Edmond Euffe would leap in order to leave far behind him the memory of the shopkeeper grandparents and the small farmer cousins and certain laughable characteristics of the founder of the Silken Net. The family had emerged from the destitution and poverty of its earlier history and the narrow winding streets of the old portion of the town. And now it must win the armorial bearings of the rich, and the grocery business be rather less to the fore though not renounced, seeing how rich its yield. It was Edmond's dream to place the Euffes on a level with the paper manufacturers of Voiron and the glovers of Grenoble, those rivals of the aristocratic glass blowers of former days. He was sometimes irritated to observe the ways in which glory is bestowed. Grenoble honours, amongst others. military men, Bayard, Lesdiguières, Randon, Vinoy; and politicians, jurists, men of letters, engineers, artists—Barnave, Casimir Perier, Cujas, de Boissieu, Condorcet, Condillac, Vaucanson, Berlioz, Sappey, and that unreadable, pretentious, irritating, and scandalous Stendhal, who was more or less a failure and who spoke ill of his own town. . . . But no one puts up statues of Félix Potin. Duval of the restaurants, Olida, Amieux, et cetera, whose products are famous and activities nutritive. Catering, on which all else rests, is indeed unjustly treated!

Edmond Euffe, as soon as he became a university student, had realized that he would have to make a clear and definite choice of the mental attitude he would adopt in certain matters. The different schools at the university were attended by some badly dressed but remarkable young men who could have thrown all their fellow students into the shade, if only by their powers of assimilation, their ready intelligence, and their intellectual subtlety. These young frequenters of cheap boardinghouses placed intelligence above everything and took on airs of superiority; in other words, they constituted a threat to established positions. The respect shown to them and their learning took the form of indulgence in expensive rounds of drinks, excursions into the mountains, week ends on the Riviera, expensive young women, and light sports cars. When lectures and examinations were not in question these young men, unable to keep pace with the rest, had to relapse into their normal function of constituting the less important framework of the social structure. They would be the workers of tomorrow: luxury needs them for its own safety and support.

Edmond was accustomed to meet, at the Lesdiguières tennis club, the Dauphiné restaurant, the swimming pool, and elsewhere, some lusty young fellows, idiotic for the most part and not particularly well-bred, and sometimes even caddish and vulgar boors. But several of these uncouth individuals belonged by virtue of their birth to the club frequented by the wealthy men of the district and were capable of raking in large sums at poker. Apart, however, from their mediocrity, no one was afraid of being let down by them. Edmond throughout his life would be meeting youths like these at every gathering or centre where consideration of profits, influence, or business connections would be in question. It is true that certain rich young men were far from being stupid. But they too preferred the brainless individuals in their own set to brilliant fellows who paid for things by monthly instalments, feeling safer thus from the point of view of money, and because that is the only sort of policy to pursue if one does not wish wealth to give openings to the attacks which are directed against it on every side. Only lately enriched by his father, Edmond might have chosen to consort with the young fellows who were trying to make a start in life with nothing but their own abilities to help them. Apart from the fact that one should not place too much faith in a mere promise of talent, the future director of the Silken Net would have fallen into discredit with the young men like himself, who were well supplied with pocket money and allowed very considerable latitude in the matter of their debts. He decided in favour of the monied set and threw overboard those students whose fathers were the reverse of millionaires. He knew what he was doing and the road he wished to take.

He had the satisfaction of seeing his choice universally approved. He was given to understand that if he persevered in this line of action he would very soon be on a level with the people descended from a long line of bourgeois ancestors. The stage of the journey associated with his father was now a thing of the past. The members of his set would be prepared to forget it if he, the son, would give them certain pledges. They would not demand austerity in his way of life, nor that he should forgo any pleasure, nor that he should restrict his profits from conscientious doubt or scruple. They would not ask him how he got his money, only that he should have a great deal. All they required from him was orthodoxy as understood by that section of the community into which he was making entry, that is to say, whole-hearted and drastic opposition to the rapid attainment of wealth by other people. The path of merit, that ambitious little creature that gives itself the airs of a moralist, must also be obstructed to the utmost possible degree. The thing that spoils wealth nowadays and robs it of its just prerogative is this, that it is becoming so disconcertingly easy to acquire that rich men no longer feel completely at home among themselves. Edmond Euffe adopted unreservedly these points of view.

So thoroughly did he adopt them that he made a marriage of a kind calculated to strengthen his position greatly. At the age of twenty-seven he married a Mlle. Bargès—of the firm of Bargès and Chouin—daughter of a large manufacturer in the Bourgoin district. The young woman was not very pretty. She had a hard, aggressive tone in her voice, and a disagreeable mouth; but she was an only daughter and would be heiress of an old and important firm. The newly made fortune of the Euffes was thus conjoined with another already old and a family with a great reputation in the district, strengthened by their possession of a historic country house. By this marriage Edmond was ranging himself among the most staunch and reliable members of a section of society in which henceforth he would occupy a prominent position. He took a fine apartment in the Boulevard Edouard-Rey, and with his wife's dowry he too bought a country house of baronial aspect on the wooded heights overlooking the Sassenage. Having attained his ambition, he would have nothing further to do but keep an eye on the members of his family to prevent their making social blunders which might prejudice his own efforts, remembering that the founder of their fortunes had begun, fifty years before, as a tout in grocery and had had his glass at every bar in the district.

M. Euffe had evidently lacked discretion in the manner of his death. For the man in the street it became slightly comic and it drew too much attention to the amatory escapades of a Dauphiné self-made man. It was for these reasons that Edmond did his utmost to diminish the conse-quences and repercussions of the tragedy, which had already made too much stir; and it was on this account also that he shrank from the idea of any dispute either with the Lacails or Riri Jumier. Haggling and strife could only end in a court of law, for Grenoble has produced numerous jurists in the past and still continues to produce redoubtable quibblers, all smiles and treachery. Edmond knew to what lengths an advocate may go, and what gems of insincerity they produce on their clients' behalf, especially when respectability offers a fine target in which their shots go well home. He knew what he would say himself if he had to plead in cases like those. Riri Jumier, thanks to her attractive appearance, would have all the masculine sympathies on her side, for the Bench would not be indifferent to the charms of a pretty litigant who had succeeded in squeezing an important sum of money out of a flighty old man who was clever at business. As for those Lacails, they would set themselves up as victims of a greedy plutocrat who was trying to make money out of his own father's corpse. That was the argument which would be used on their behalf, and they would have the Prefecture and probably freemasonry behind them. If the latter, with its many and far-reaching ramifications, were really available for backing up their cause, there would be every likelihood of the Euffes losing face over this action. There would be innumerable troubles and worries, and then the whole thing would end in ridicule. In a case like this one must start with a certainty of success or give it up altogether. We are living in a period notable for the humouring of appetites and passions, for the encouragement of jealousies and sharp practice, and for promises to the undeserving. It would be much better to give one's self the advantage of taking a generous attitude and, by sacrificing a few hundred thousand francs, get the whole thing hushed up. This was definitely Edmond's intention, acting on the advice of his wife, who as a member of the Bargès family was finding this Euffe family always in the way, hopelessly lacking in polish, and altogether a nuisance.

But the bustling widow of General de Sainte-Foy, always up-to-date with the latest Grenoble scandals as a person who kept tireless and energetic watch over the morality of her contemporaries, came to badger Edmond at his office in the Avenue d'Alsace-Lorraine, where he sat surrounded by his statistics, his samples of mustard, products of Italian paste, jams, and catalogues of free gifts. She burst into the room and sounded the bugle of her overpowering and masterful voice.

"My dear young man," she said, "your mother is a sniveller and only half awake. She won't stir a handsbreadth to do anything. I take it that you know that?"

"My mother," Edmond cautiously replied, "has always taken rather a back seat in our family life. It was the best thing she could do, at home."

"What you mean is that she is not intelligent? Well, anyhow, you have noticed it! Poor fellow—it's a great misfortune for you. It's a great misfortune for a family when the wife lets the husband lead her by the nose. The children suffer for it. You can never rely on men for moulding children's character. Men have other ideas in their heads—no need to tell you what. Think of your poor father! . . . Do you know what brings me here?"

84

"No," said Edmond. "But if it is confidential, dare I ask you to speak not quite so loud? I've got people working in the next room."

"Very well," said the general's wife, "I will remember, indignant though I am. The first thing I want to say is this. Your weakness is deplorable. Everyone is astonished at it. What about all those lawsuits, prosecutions?"

"Our counsel have got that in hand."

"They've gone to sleep, you mean?"

"Oh no, by no means. I am in constant communication with them. Have you anything else to say to me?"

"Yes," said the general's wife. "I have things to tell you which would send your mother into floods of tears. That is why I have come straight to you rather than to her. Your brother Germain has a mistress."

"That is his business."

"That is his business—exactly! Oh, I know that men all agree on that point! But it may be your business too. Do you know who this mistress is that I am speaking of?"

"No," Edmond replied. "Is it really necessary that I should be told?"

"You will see. Well, she is neither more nor less than the person who killed your father by hurling a vase onto his head—that Lacail woman. So far as I am concerned, I am rather wondering whether she didn't do it on purpose, if it wasn't a case of revenge. She may be an old flame of your father's, that gay old spark! It's just an idea of mine which you might consider. . . . Now, to go back to your brother—what have you got to say about it?"

"You are quite certain of what you are telling me?"

"Make your own inquiries, my boy, that's all you need do! But when I sound the alarm, you know, I am quite sure of my facts! Now, the second point. How old is your sister Lucie?"

"Oh, twenty-eight, twenty-nine . . ."

"Very well. Now, do you realize that that girl is going mad?"

"What do you mean?"

"She has sex on the brain. Her imagination is working on things she knows nothing about and which she feels she is threatened with never knowing. That happens sometimes to plain girls and it sends them clean off their head. . . . You may call it stupid, because if they only knew, the poor wretches . . . But still, there's the fact! Your sister will go mad one of these fine days if you don't get her married."

"Get her married, get her married," Edmond Euffe murmured.

"Oh yes, I know. It needs two, as they say, and the poor girl gets no admirers. You ought to pick her out some good honest young fellow from your staff. You would see that he gets promotion, and that would give him a position, and frankly, he would be earning it. . . . By the way, what is this new chauffeur of your mother's, that little dark-skinned fellow with the glowing eyes?"

"Bruno? He comes from Nice—a very sharp fellow and most obliging."

"Very well then, just you take care! Your sister looks at him in a funny sort of way. I know what it is to make eyes at men, as you may perhaps imagine! If this young man has a grain of common sense and determination, it's easy to see what may happen. You're not specially keen on having him for a brother-in-law?"

"All the same, you are not going to tell me that Lucie . . ."

"I tell you once more that she's mad! She's in that sort of condition that old maids and very often nuns get into when they are about forty. I advise you to get her married off quickly, or there'll be a frightful to-do very soon. And bundle that chauffeur out of the house, that Bruno, whom Lucie is so fascinated by. . . . Ah, you think it's an easy matter to keep up a position! You think it's easy to run a family! Don't you believe it, my boy!"

"You scare me!" Edmond said.

"Half a moment," said the general's wife, "that's not all! Have you been told that your sister Alberte is compromising herself with that young scamp de Bazair?"

"The count's son?"

"Yes, a count without a penny to bless himself with! And you know as well as I do that all the de Bazairs have been utterly cruel to women and fatal to their own families. If Alberte loses her head over this young rascal she's done for."

"Alberte is about the last girl I should expect it of."

"Oh, really? Well, you don't look to me as though you knew much about women! Just you go and take a turn round Green Island one morning and you'll know all about it. My goodness, how the Euffe children take after their father!—except you, Edmond. And they catch it young!"

"In any case, Alberte is under age."

"Not for much longer. She will have her legacy when she is twenty-one?"

"Oh yes."

"Then it's easy to see the game her fancy man is playing! . . . That will do for today, my boy. I shall leave you, now that I have given you these proofs of my friendship. For you won't imagine that I would do as much for everybody."

"I'm sure of that, my dear friend. And might I ask you—I hope it isn't indiscreet?—why we are the object of your vigilant and helpful attention?"

"Oh," said the general's wife, "I can certainly tell you, now that it is too late. If your father had been free during one of my periods of widowhood, I should have liked to marry him. I felt quite drawn to all you children, and I saw quite well that you needed a firm hand. I thought that your fretful, whining mother wouldn't make old bones. But she is one of those people who are always ill and never die. . . . Your poor father—well, there was nothing distinguished about him, but he was a man—a real man. That would have been a change for me, for once. . . . In four marriages I've had nothing but softies hanging round me!"

"What!" Edmond said. "There was the general."

"Oh, my poor friend. That thunderbolt of war was a man who at home loved his fireside and slippers and couldn't say boo to a goose. He was afraid of another general who had a tiny bit more on his sleeve. Oh, I've had more than enough of the Army! I am very sorry indeed that the flying men arrived too late for the women of my generation. I should have liked to sample . . ."

6. OPINIONS DIFFER There is a short work of comparatively recent date (it was published in 1937), which happens to be banned from the public libraries, entitled *Secrets of Grenoble*. It is from the pen of a man named Edgar Lapérine, an enigmatical person who has now entirely vanished and who has produced a certain number of very strange documents, such as *Rural Musings Outside Grenoble*, and *Lives of My Dauphiné Contemporaries: Their Seamy Side*, copies of which it is all but impossible to obtain.

This Lapérine was reputed to be a harebrained, eccentric individual, a hack writer, an odd kind of hermit who had adopted an indefensible attitude which was most damaging to his own interests in a post in which his promotion might be dependent on his general outlook and opinions. Being too much of a freethinker, he would never pledge himself to any political party, and this deprived him of any useful backing and only made him suspected by everybody. This self-sufficient personage enjoyed but little or no respect; he was indeed practically a failure, seeing that as he was devoid of ambition and sought nothing for himself, he gave offence to every party or clique. His career at Grenoble was an official one of an average sort, and on his retirement he disappeared from the town. Of the people who knew him, some describe him as a shy individual and a dreamer, others as a misanthropist who was also rather a rogue; some say that he was too sensitive and too easily roused to indignation, others that he had a hidden urge to cruelty. On the one side he is given credit for culture and a first-class brain; on the other, he is declared to have been a mediocre and embittered man. One may assume that any comments on this strange individual are coloured by some personal bias. It is certain that his detractors outnumber those who admire and read him. But that is what usually happens in provincial society, where everyone is suspicious and so ready to fight tooth and nail for his own interests that he cannot bear the idea of anyone else being superior to himself. And still less can he bear it when the other man is disregarding the rules of the game which he himself is observing. So there is still in existence a mystery about this man Lapérine which time will gradually unveil. He is said to have preserved among his papers some racy pieces of writing which he had deferred taking steps to publish. Any sound estimate of him will have to wait. The following is from his pen: "The town of Grenoble might well be thought worthy of two distinct reputations. For it has two eddying, whirling periods every year, summer and winter; it is the seat of two distinct societies, autochthonous and transitory, the first permanently installed, with its own customs, ambitions, and work; the second nomad and shifting, idle, and subject to change. For a real native the town doubtless evokes nothing more than a collection of habits, certain faces, business and other connections, and local rivalries, with a flow of life which must retain its provincial character, that is to say, completely at the mercy of a universal inquisitiveness and curiosity, simply because the town does not harbour an accumulation of human beings large enough for anyone to become isolated or hidden within it, and thus escape the constraint of petty jealousies, envy openly expressed, passions with nothing to divert their course, and deliberate hatreds.

"Strictly speaking, the town sees no horizon, but a corset of mountains both adjacent and high, which after a certain time give people the feeling of a corset of steel. There is the story of Corot being lured to Grenoble by admirers who had told him: 'You will find there scenery worthy of your talent.' But the great painter of the French landscape, ever in quest of the light airs of morning that ruffle the surface of a lake, and reflections in water over which some mist still lingers, when he found himself a prisoner within these walls of rock, and stifled by them, refused so much as to put up his easel and made all haste to return to a more even, measured countryside. The townsmen of Grenoble live in a deep hole which is bitter in winter and scorching in summer, and there they seethe, in sight of a row of mountain peaks which remain indifferent and aloof. From the summits of the Moucherotte and of the St.-Eynard, Grenoble looks like a mere ant heap. It is in the hope of becoming a slightly bigger ant than the rest that the inhabitants plot and plan.

"There is besides this a second Grenoble of which tourists have much to say in praise: it is a great centre of excursions and holiday delights, and there are relay stations for vehicles dashing to the south by way of the Lautaret or the High Alps route, or through Monestier-de-Clermont and over the Croix-Haute Pass, et cetera. Throughout July and August the great dusty cars unload their cargoes of visitors and mountain climbers at Grenoble. This motley crowd, part of which is in quest of outdoor sports and pastimes, gives the town an appearance of youthful hardihood, the same as is given to it in winter by the ski runners. It is possible that these sights have some effect on morals, the effect which may be observed wherever luxury and high living flaunt themselves. The presence of students must also be reckoned with, for with the prestige attaching to their learning and their free-and-easy ways of youth, they turn many feminine heads. Where there are students, women's dreams and aspirations take a tenderer and more fanciful form.

"But underlying this brilliant and seasonal aspect of the town there still remains the Grenoble of bygone days, in which people live, as they did in times past, an uneventful life wherein duties and habits make up between them a monotonous round. Despite crammed hotels and streets crowded with cars, these people, living in the hollow basin formed by the valleys, make up the old nucleus of the locality. Remaining patiently where they are, they continue to secure for themselves everything that is obtainable by a mixture of the doggedness, caution, and guile characteristic of their province. Beneath an exterior of a cosmopolitan city, Grenoble retains some of the forms and ritual observed in the typical country town. These go hand in hand with subterranean currents of jealousy and treachery of a ruthless nature, all of which is coldly planned and deliberately carried out. . . ."

Lapérine often takes up these themes in different forms. It seems that this man, who is still only half explained, became bogged, at Grenoble, in provincial mire, and that at the same time he managed to find pleasure in a moral climate which he found difficult to breathe, because it favoured his meditations. He seems to have understood his own case, for he himself has written: "It is possible that great thinkers, like great observers, need shackles at which they violently protest, but which supply them with material. The acute discernment displayed in the writings of La Rochefoucauld and Saint-Simon was born of frustration and constraint. If Cardinal de Condi had supplanted Mazarin, if the other two had been more successful at court, would they have found time to write memoirs and maxims? Concentration is impossible without isolation. But nothing is less public-spirited, nothing less social, than isolation. And nothing arouses more suspicion."

In other passages of his works Lapérine alludes to persecutions to which he had been exposed. He speaks of a live viper slipped into his letter box by unknown enemies. He attributes to the citizens of Grenoble a taste for denunciation and anonymous letters, for secret societies and feuds, and declares that he himself was a victim of these things. He alleges that to show independence arouses more suspicion there, and is more unpopular, than elsewhere. We should, of course, make some allowance for the exaggerations of a solitary individual who dug too deeply into the same questions, while keeping aloof from all collective movements and activities. It seems probable that Lapérine's reserved and standoffish attitude, which smacked of contempt, irritated his contemporaries and turned them against him. However, it is not these questions of a personal nature that are important, but rather to discover in Lapérine's writings any statements from which some fairly wide psychological generalizations can be made. There are taciturn people who have an exceptional gift for observation, feeling, and analysis. The history of the Euffe family seems a thorough vindication of a certain number of remarks which are to be found in Secrets of Grenoble and Lives of My Dauphiné Contemporaries: Their Seamy Side. Later portions of this narrative will enable the reader to judge.

Claire Bargès, when she had become Mme. Edmond, was nicknamed "the Princess" by the Euffe family. This was on account of her pretensions to being a woman of fashion, her opinions on literature, art, and society, and her family connections either factual or merely alleged, which, if she were to be believed, included everything of note in French society of the day.

She was a fair-haired woman of the unpleasing type, with poor hair that was naturally inclined to be yellow (without any of those glints of sunshine or mirabelle plums which brighten the complexion of blondes at their best), with sea-green eyes which fell upon you with a stony gaze, and flesh that showed no tender, generous curves but was furrowed with visible sinews and hard veins. In a word, a frigid statue, but also a speechifying statue, mincing, affected, platinized, anointed with beauty preparations and adorned with everything costly. All this, which entirely failed to improve her looks, made her imposing in the eyes of shallow-minded people, of whom there are so many, and who are themselves but lay figures in appearance. This person was moreover obsessed by her own personal appearance, as she was also by her birth, her education, her intelligence—by everything that either closely or remotely concerned herself. She would take on an intensely witty air for making the most trite remarks, never imagining for a moment that anything commonplace could ever fall from those thin lips of hers. To kill time when she was a girl, she had managed to get a university degree. On the possession of this diploma she based an estimate of herself that assigned her—in her own mind—a place somewhere between Georges Sand and Mme. Curie, with a more aristocratic touch—reminiscent of the Duchesse d'Uzès, perhaps—thrown in.

This angular and bony lady of the manor, who gave herself the airs of an experienced Parisienne, held sway over a little court of people like herself, all of whom, both men and women, were thoroughly pleased with themselves. These people, all of them mutually convinced that they were the cream of Grenoble society and a shining light in the province, took their pleasure in an atmosphere of autoadmiration (not wholly free from backbiting and slander) from which they drew their pride of life. This competition in vainglory, this vanity fair, which was maintained at a high pitch, actually went far enough to invade and spoil the peace of a certain lovely site, when the mountains of Sassenage, blue tinted in the fading evening light, spread their vast shadows far and wide amidst an impressive and majestic silence. For the most select and crowded gatherings were held, in summer, at the château of White Terraces, which stood out, a conspicuous object, on the nearest of the wooded heights of the Vercors. Five hundred citizens of Grenoble had done various contemptible things to gain admission to this circle of pinchbeck and boredom. It was Claire Euffe's great feat to have brought into being this provincial movement in which the participants fondly imagined that, in gatherings of the newly enriched in the great manufacturing industries and trade in excelsis, they were reviving a little of the refinement and charm of Versailles. . . .

Edmond was a mere plaything in the hands of these jarring people, believing as he did that he would have to go through with it all in order to climb that new rung of the social ladder which would bring him to the level of the genuine old families of his time. Eager to banish all memories of the Euffes, of their relations, and all else that lent itself to ridicule, he had meekly performed all the smirks and smiles and came entirely under his wife's spell. He applied himself to the task of thinking her a superior woman—since he could not think her pleasant to caress—perhaps because some hidden prompter whispered in his ear that that chilly creature, were she once deprived of this social influence of hers, would be the emptiest, most useless, and least desirable of companions.

Edmond had been enraptured by his discovery of the art of being "in the swim," which he regarded as a quintessential one, with very few initiates. Detesting games, at which he was a clumsy performer, he had forced himself to go to Uriage and play golf, as that would place him. In the same way he would drink cocktails and whisky, because white wine and vermouth-cassis, which he really preferred, are too undistinguished as drinks. He played bridge, which bored him to death, thinking that it was the card game of the *élite*. He had even tried to read certain writers of lofty thought—who from his wife drew screams of delight—but that was just more than he could manage. He could not cope both with the literature of the sublime and the market prices of foodstuffs; for the Silken Net sold hundreds of different kinds of articles or products, from flypapers to cheese graters, with everything that gives nourishment included. Edmond could not divide his brain into compartments in such a way as to reserve on one side a place for the strophes of *La Jeune Parque* and on the other for the prices of tunny fish in oil and mackerel with white wine. In painting he contrived to appreciate the Abbé Calès, but that was certainly the furthest he could go. If the truth were told, he would have been glad enough to dispense with painting and even with books, thinking as he did that one should stick once for all to the classics —and those of not less than a hundred years old—which one is quite safe in admiring, in those portions which one learns from one's schoolbooks. For it is unreasonable to suppose that a man who is running a hundred different branch establishments will ever have the head to read *Phèdre* or *Les Fleurs du Mal* more than once, when it is such a simple matter to listen to the wireless, which tells you practically all you need know and is an ample substitute for the lack of conversation which prevails today.

While driving back to Sassenage after his interview with the general's wife, Edmond was pondering anxiously over the disturbing items of news which he was bringing back to his wife. He was feeling that a time was at hand when the characters of his family would be laid bare, in conflict with himself, each member of it revealing, under the spur of passion or self-interest, some Euffe hereditary trait. For all he knew, there might have been among their Euffe forebears some clodhoppers of a scandalous and disgraceful type and some reckless, devil-may-care trollops, hot as hell, whose exploits would still be remembered by the older inhabitants of Domène, La Galochère, St.-Martin-d'Hères, Jarrie, and Bresson. If such instincts still lingered in these people's descendants, there was every prospect of strife and scandal—terrible scandal—which would completely demolish the results of years of social effort and ambition.

"Oh, the family," Edmond sighed, "what a curse it is! And how will Claire take it all?"

He knew well enough how biased she was against the Euffe contingent and foresaw a truly delightful discussion on the well-known theme of "your family" and "that crew." He was genuinely afraid of those airs of a goddess out of her element which his wife was accustomed to put on in such circumstances. He decided that he would start his revelations with the most harmless of them, Alberte's and Bob's flirtation, for he did not wish to believe it to be anything but a mere flirtation, a young girl's imprudence, which they all commit when they first begin flirtations. In any case, he refrained from considering the question of how far this particular imprudence had gone. After all, Bob had a handle to his name, and later on would have a title. Claire might fall for this: it would be for her to declare her opinion.

And that was what happened. Claire asked at once:

"This young man will really be a count one day?"

"Certainly," Edmond replied, "as his father is now. The de Bazairs are the oldest noble family in the district. There were already some of that family in Dauphiné at the time of Louis XI. I can get you the full particulars."

"And your sister might be a countess?"

"Yes indeed. It may be worth thinking over."

Claire was divided between two feelings, each very strong; longing to see a count in the family, and indignation at the idea of this honour coming to her through little Alberte whom she considered completely insignificant. (The lady of Sassenage belonged to that category of women who cannot admit the existence of beauty or charm in any other woman, still less so when those qualities include an element of gentle sweetness that is itself physically attractive and wins men's devotion.) It was the second feeling that prevailed when she reflected that some day or other Alberte with a title would be more important than herself and perhaps by no means anxious to entertain her. She proffered some advice with considerable emphasis:

"Your sister is too young to know what she wants. I think I have summed her up pretty well. She's a nice little thing, but she has no conversation and is rather limited. She is certainly lacking in a will of her own."

"Everything will depend on whether young de Bazair gets a hold on her," Edmond said. "These de Bazairs are said to be very dangerous."

"This young man," said Claire, "may be losing his head over her. Alberte is very fresh and attractive now. But she is not the sort of girl to keep her prettiness long. She'll lose her figure after her first baby. Do you know this young fellow?"

"A little. Everyone knows everyone else at Grenoble, more or less."

"Well, if I were you I'd have a talk with him, if Alberte won't listen to you. I should tell him that Alberte has much less money than he might suppose and that we have got other plans for your sister."

"What plans?"

"We must wait and see. Alberte needs safety rather than brilliance in her surroundings. We must try and find her a young man who could manage her fortune well. I'll stir up my friends about it."

"You think, then, that it would not be desirable for her to marry young de Bazair?"

"No," Claire said with emphasis, "in Alberte's own interest, I don't think it would. In some society Alberte would be quite out of place—she would feel constrained, awkward. She takes a good deal after your mother, you know."

"Very well, then," Edmond said, "if you think . . ."

Proceeding with caution, he spoke next of his sister Lucie's case, following the description of it given to him by General de Sainte-Foy's widow.

"Poor Lucie is certainly very plain," Claire said. "I am afraid she won't find a husband at all easily."

"But we have got to get her married," Edmond said, "and quickly too, if the general's wife is right in what she says. Can you think of any way to do so?"

"I am trying . . . She can, of course, be married for her money. Some young man who is very hard up—he shouldn't be difficult to find."

"Yes, but what sort of fellow shall we unearth? You can imagine the kind of brother-in-law?"

"Wait, I've got an idea. Grenoble is a town of soldiers. Your sister could marry a young officer. Officers don't make their fortunes, as we know."

"I should think not!" Edmond said. "There are no risks in their job!"

"Except in war, all the same . . ."

"Excuse me," said Edmond, "war means similar risks for every Frenchman liable for service. In wartime I shall be doing an officer's job under circumstances as dangerous as they can be. Do those gentlemen come and do mine, just when payments are falling due?"

"Oh, I agree with you!" said Claire. "All I meant was that from the social point of view marrying an officer wouldn't bring her down in the world."

"No, that is true," Edmond said. "But there is less to it than there used to be. If you come to think of it, war ruins armies, because it lowers the level of recruiting. The perfect soldiers are those who never have to go to war and serve as an adornment of peace, by cultivating a tradition of good manners, a fine bearing, and honour. I shouldn't be surprised if those qualities were seen at their very best among the pontifical zouaves and the bodyguard of the Prince of Monaco. The Swiss Army, which hasn't had a fight for years, is said to be magnificent. War kills off the finest military specimens and they are hard to replace."

"I think," Claire broke in, "that an infantry officer would be too showy for Lucie. It's not at all to her interest to draw attention to herself. But I often see officers passing who look like quiet, unassuming civil servants. They carry a leather portfolio which appears to be stuffed with papers."

"Oh," said Edmond, "those are administrators, or engineer officers in charge of military buildings."

"That would be exactly right for Lucie. It's not for her to be too particular. And officers are moved to different garrisons?"

"Usually."

"In that way we should lose sight of her after she was married, and then see her again later on if her husband got good promotion. Something of this kind will have to be arranged. Speak to the general's wife about it. She is sure to have kept up some connection with her military circles. She will be very useful to us."

Edmond finally plucked up sufficient courage to speak of his brother Germain and Flavie Lacail.

As he expected, his wife burst into loud cries.

"You must get that stopped immediately. You quite understand?"

She then gave utterance to a maxim which from her lips sounded astonishing; but she had a plentiful store of such sayings that were completely inconsistent with her actual behaviour: "One should think of others before one's self."

"What can I do?" Edmond asked.

"Come, come, your brother must know that there are things which in certain circles simply aren't done! Tell him so, firmly."

95

"Yes, I'll tell him, I most certainly intend to do so. And supposing he won't listen to me?"

"See this woman. Frighten her. See the husband too."

"Not quite the best way to avoid a scandal! We have given up the idea of taking proceedings, so as to avoid a lot of fuss and bother. We can't go now and tell this man that my brother has stolen his wife."

"That is true. In any case, he will hear of it without your telling him."

"I am afraid so."

"Oh, it's the limit, really it is!" Claire exclaimed. "A charming family you are indeed! And you make life so much easier! How she'll laugh, old Mother Simione, that old creature who was kept and then married after she'd inherited an industry on her lover's death. And how about your mother? Has she been doing anything stupid or extravagant?"

"Not that I know of. The general's wife would have told me."

"Oh, that will come! And all these troubles are her fault. If the poor woman was less of a nonentity you would have had a better education. It's true that you can't expect an uneducated woman to have any feelings about her children's education. What was he—your mother's father?"

"He sold cutlery, Claire, you know perfectly well!" Edmond replied in a vexed tone of voice.

The conversation was taking a trend which he greatly feared. There was now every prospect of his life being often embittered by allusions to the instincts and past history of the Euffes. He had a presentiment that his relations with the members of his family were about to enter a difficult phase full of wrangling and friction and bitterness, with the revival of old scandals as part of the programme for the day. On all this there would be daily comments from Claire of the usual scathing kind.

All things considered, Edmond knew his brother and his sisters very little indeed. He had known them as one knows children, with their characters still unformed, and had maintained an elder brother's rather lofty detachment; while since that time, though he was constantly rubbing shoulders with them, he had not kept in touch with their development as adults, which had but little interest for him. And now he was suddenly discovering that he knew nothing of their deeper feelings, their ambitions, or their passions. Was it possible that they really had passions of their own, and that these might become a millstone round his neck which would hinder his ascent to the highest social circles in Grenoble?

More than ever he was being haunted by the question of predominance. The incessant upward thrust of the proletariat into the ranks of

96

the middle classes, the rapid multiplication of those classes, and their enormous facilities for enriching themselves were becoming a menace to the pick of society (to which he considered that he belonged) before it had time to dig itself in. There was a forward march towards a con-fusion and disorder of ideas and appetites in which people would cease to recognize themselves. The Euffes had now acquired a position in society which they were in danger of losing unless they fought with might and main against these new manifestations of ambition and greed. This was Edmond's reason for believing in the urgency of reconstitut-ing certain coalitions of employers, of a hereditary nature, which would give society some new foundations. He contemplated laying himself the first stone of one of these foundations, to be cemented with the blood of his own family. Was it possible that Lucie, Germain, and Alberte were now about to hamper him in this task instead of helping him by a scheme of marriages arranged with a view to the founding of what was known in days gone by as "great families"? Those dangerous modern theories of the superiority of the individual, of "a place in the sun" and "the right to happiness," were leading to a fragmentary conception of the social structure, which itself is continually raising new problems, owing to the mixture of its elements which is perpetually taking place.

The foregoing will provide the explanation why Edmond, when choosing his friends from the age of twenty onwards, had elected to join forces with mediocre young men who were already in a safe finan-cial position rather than with gifted but poor young fellows who did in reality constitute the new waves of assault whose objective was the con-quest of power and wealth, of which latter he himself, with the Silken Net and the Euffe millions, possessed no mean share and which it was his duty to defend. (Moreover, these rich if mediocre young men had actually some idea of the meaning of elegance, luxury, and good breed-ing, which made them easy enough to get on with, and after one genera-tion had entirely died out, they might very well become fathers of in-telligent children. No dynasty can be entirely free from defective and unsatisfactory members, but that which has been already won, all solid worth, remains in being and reappears in more efficient representatives of the line. This in any case is better than no dynasty at all. M. Con-stant Euffe had grown up as a man playing a lone hand in a game of chance. But his rise to fortune would have neither sense nor meaning unless it served as a point of departure for a line of descendants inured to the employer's problems as to those of catering, and experienced also in the management of wealth, an art for which apprenticeship is re-quired. This line, enriched by choice graftings, would form a chain of beings whose links would be the Euffe traditions, which would tend towards increased refinement and a distinguished bearing.)

M. Constant Euffe, rich in money and experience, used sometimes to say at informal gatherings towards the end of his life, in his bluff, good-natured, rather vulgar way: "A rich man can think as he likes." There was a good deal of truth in this, lacking though it was in that restraint in the manner of expressing one's self that is essential to courtesy; and people of the upper middle class would never be guilty of such crudity of language, which would only give a handle to their enemies. For the chaos of the present day is fostered by traitors and embittered people (owing, perhaps, to the misuse of education, given to all and sundry). . . . It is thus that one constantly sees sons of lower-middle-class families refusing to submit to the forms of discipline which are necessary at the earlier stages of life and throwing themselves into the arms of the proletariat, taking control of the masses and organizing them and guiding them along the paths of insurrection. As to the myth of a world in which there will be no more downtrodden people, a world where everyone will be rewarded as he deserves, that is simply a piece of electioneering claptrap. Individual merit is now once for all measured by the extent of the man's possessions—whether he acquired them by merit (which may assume a thousand different forms) or whether his possessions *ipso facto* confer merit upon him.

These were the conclusions to which Edmond, a man of property, had come while banishing from his mind the confused mass of ideas in which quibblers and thinkers alike take pleasure. He needed to maintain an unswerving adherence to a way of life which would leave his mind free for the management of his business and the maintenance of a superior social position on the lines of the great manufacturers of that part of the country whose equal he considered himself to be, since, like them, he possessed a large country house, servants, and several cars. Any examination of the prejudiced quibbling of sociologists will enable one to perceive that our forebears acted soundly in recognizing the rights of birth and in basing them upon divine right. It is here that the Church gives a necessary support to institutions, granting them recognition by a superior will of hers which can neither be explained nor can it be disputed, and which is responsible to nobody. A great employer, Edmond Euffe thought as did Napoleon that the people need a religion, for it is good and right that the people should find in religious faith a safety valve for their agitations and their claims. It was when the strong and mighty had forsworn their alliance with the gods that they were swept away by plebeian revolts; witness the end of Athens, the end of Rome, the end of the French aristocracy given over to the atheism of the eighteenth century. It is accordingly wholesome and right that the *bourgeoisie* should be in unison with the Church and give a good example of submission to the Divine will which governs the universe. Edmond was not evading this duty: he was going to Mass. His father, still too much a member of the lower middle class and entirely absorbed in his constantly growing business concern, and also rather cold-shouldered by the whole body of people whose social standing had long been assured, had hesitated in the matter of adherence to any political party. Edmond, however, had put his tiller hard over to the right, and both by his outward behaviour and his own mental outlook had identified himself with the Conservative party, considering as he did that the time had come for putting the brake on what was too rapid a social evolution, and that it was best to do so while the fortunes of the Euffe family were winging their way aloft to heights of dominion, authority, and power.

"One must be logical about one's self and one's position. And besides, managers and people in authority, and, generally speaking, people of a superior type, are a necessity and always will be."

Edmond thought that wealth was the crucible in which all these were forged, and as he himself possessed it he took his stand among the leaders of his time. This meant that a certain mental attitude in different matters became a duty for him. For so far as duties of the active kind were concerned, he thought that, apart from his management of the Silken Net, these were sufficiently covered by his parochial offerings, his financial support of certain groups of people engaged in political activities, his subscriptions to journals with orthodox views, his adherence to certain Grenoble societies in which he had succeeded his father, and his presence at certain public ceremonies at which he sat somewhere near the prefect, the general, or the mayor.

In the army he was a lieutenant on the reserve of officers, with the probability of promotion. He had lately got himself transferred to the quartermaster general's department, thanks to certain influential friends. In the event of war he would be employed in revictualling, either at Grenoble itself or in the neighbourhood. In view of his knowledge of catering in general, this was reasonable and just.

Lastly, his wife, whose special task it was to see that the intellectual supremacy of her home was properly maintained, bought rare books, pictures, furniture, carpets; read reviews, attended lectures, and went every winter to Paris for several weeks, thus enabling her to get in full touch with what was fashionable at the time, by visiting exhibitions, seeing a few successful plays, watching the general trend of fashion and taking note of those things that had then become "all the rage." It was due to all this that her receptions were the most brilliant, the most "up-to-date," of any in Grenoble.

The extent to which members of the same family can remain unknown to each other was revealed to Edmond when he had Alberte before him fighting for her love.

Edmond's conception of his sister was that of an amiable young girl who had hardly outgrown the ways and thoughts of childhood, had barely said good-bye to her dolls, and who had come suddenly to maturity and blossomed into beauty, without losing any of her artless simplicity, her quiet sense of fun, her natural sweetness, or her tender grace. Everyone who came near her with an unprejudiced mind declared how nice a girl she was, and praised her happy disposition, so entirely free from ill temper and jealousy. At a social gathering she would never express any preference of her own, but fell in with any suggestion made by others and seemed to be using all her wits in order to give pleasure. Of all the Euffe children she was the easiest to control; so much was this the case that she was never consulted about anything, so ready was she to agree wholeheartedly to whatever was proposed and to find pleasure therein. She was constantly smiling.

And now within a short time she had gained remarkable beauty, a serene, a luminous beauty, which recently—since the death of M. Euffe —had acquired an extraordinary brilliance. It was this that surprised Edmond as he looked at his young sister more closely than usual because he was preparing to say some very serious things to her. Alberte had in truth become one of the prettiest girls in Grenoble, perhaps the prettiest of them all. So evidently now was she at the crowning point of her grace and charm that even her brother was struck by it. That little girl whom no one took seriously only a few years ago, that quiet submissive little Alberte stood there now before his eyes as though she were haloed with some secret happiness, and adorned with a self-confidence whose source was derived from some mysterious quality of her girlhood. The young girl's warm gaze had the same open candour as before, the same clear, honest way of resting upon the people she met and the sights she saw. But now there burned within it a steady gleam of bright and shining intensity, which drew its light from some secret fire within her, whose presence was reflected in Alberte's cheeks, and her forehead lightly gilded by the sun, in tints of rosy pink. She was as pure and flawless as honey, warm bread, or fresh milk. But the outline of her lips had grown firmer, and their rich rounded form had acquired the tint of certain crimson roses which shine and glisten in the morning dews. She had lost all the hard, ungracious lines of adolescence and the awkwardness and lack of grace of that period. Every curve and line of her modelling had improved, had acquired a plenitude which gave her a sudden flowering of all a woman's loveliness. While losing nothing of her adolescent charm, she was now aglow and shining in the knowledge of her beauty newly found, as though that knowledge had come to her through an unshakable conviction that in her own heart she had discovered the shape and outline of her future and her fate.

Alberte had come to her brother without suspicion, but no sooner had he uttered the name of Bob de Bazair than something shrank within her, her face clouded and assumed an expression whose meaning it was impossible to read; her features hardened and her clear, bright gaze became tarnished and dull. The thing she had wished to keep apart, beyond the reach of anyone whomsoever, was now no longer intact. It was all very well for Edmond to speak of objections, of rashness and imprudence on her part—to argue the case and to promise his help to an Alberte who would be amenable to guidance; she did not listen to him, nay more, refused to do so, to give a single minute's attention to that which assailed her inmost beliefs and was an insult and desecration. In a flash Edmond had become her enemy. She kept silence before him, with her face turned away, leaving him to flounder in embarrassment in a maze of clumsy and sordid arguments, in which money was involved. He had no right, she thought, to lay a coarse and clumsy hand on that part of her life that was now sheer bliss. She who had always said Yes because nothing hitherto had really counted, felt surging up within her the strength to say No, the strength to resist and fight until the very end. During a momentary silence she rapped out these words at her brother:

"Be quiet, will you? I shall marry Bob, or no one. I have promised."

"But," said Edmond, misunderstanding her, "that was not an absolutely binding promise."

"I made it of my own free will," Alberte said.

There was nothing inhuman about Edmond. Seeing that his sister's mind was entirely made up, had he had only himself to consider, he would not have sought to put pressure on her. But there was Claire in the background, Claire with all her influence and advice. Never would she agree to Alberte's having her own way.

"Oh, no doubt, no doubt," said Edmond. "But there may be more to it than that. There are certain things which you may know nothing about . . ."

He hesitated. . . . But he heard Claire's affected voice saying to him, with an unpleasant sneer, "That family of yours!"—and thought of the reproaches awaiting him at home if he should fail. He played his last card.

"Now listen," he said, "do you know that Bob de Bazair has been Riri Jumier's lover? It may be going on still. People know about it in Grenoble."

In an instant he wished he had not spoken these words, when he saw Alberte turn pale and her pure lovely face transformed by an expression of the utmost pain and grief, while her eyes became suffused with tears. He wondered whether he had not hurt her too deeply, and if it would now fall to him to sustain and comfort her. But the blood flowed back in a burning stream to the young girl's cheeks. For the second time Edmond became aware that it was a stranger that he had before him, and that her reactions were astonishing and showed no trace of the adolescent of recent years.

"You were a cad to say a thing like that to me!" Alberte said.

Edmond tried to explain himself; but his sister would give him no time to do so. In a calm, steady voice, in which she made no effort to conceal her indignation and contempt, and with her tears forced back and not allowed to flow, she added, with a power of divination that laid her brother's motives bare:

"It was your wife who suggested that piece of filth? That *lady* . . ."

Edmond blushed, and as he made the gesture which implies that one is prepared to let everything go hang, he felt a strange need of self-justification.

"Forgive me," he said. "And please believe that I didn't want to hurt you."

As he spoke these words he had realized that Claire herself, with all her knowledge of the world, would be unable to get the better of the new Alberte, whose gentleness in the past had contained no hint of her present transformation. The girl whom he was now discovering, who cared nothing whatever for the views and motives of his wife, would fight to the death to save her lover; for she was one of those for whom their love is all there is, and who live for it alone. Deep down within him he felt a whiff of Euffe family feeling, which was not far removed from pride. "She takes after Father," he said to himself, "and Granny Guigon, who kicked over all the traces for a man." But this proud feeling left him when he reflected that his sister's insubordination would have a most unfortunate effect on his own home life, and perhaps his social position too, since this had been Claire's opinion. But Alberte's case was not, after all, the most serious of them. He asked her:

"You wouldn't care to come and spend the day at Sassenage, tomorrow or the day after? We should be so pleased if you would."

"No," Alberte said listlessly, "not just now."

He felt that he had lost her confidence and her esteem. He went with her to the door and kissed her on the forehead, then let her go without trying further to persuade her, while he said to her: "Well, well, things will work out all right!" Then he went and sat down again in his office, as he murmured to himself:

"There seems no end to one's worries!"

He had to deal with two transactions, one relating to kegs of anchovy and another to soda. He opened his files and compared the latest prices he had received with those of previous orders. He was feeling the need of some sort of action, of taking revenge. He rang for a typist and began to dictate at great length. "Yours of the 10th inst. to hand. We are surprised by your latest schedules of charges. We think we should warn you that other firms are making us decidedly more advantageous offers. We shall be compelled to give them preference if, failing to bear in mind the extent of our facilities for sale, which are unique in this part of the country (please, mademoiselle, underline 'our facilities for sale,' and 'unique in this part of the country'), you persist in maintaining the prices which we have before us. Therefore . . ."

The girl was bending so far forward over her paper that through the opening at the neck of her dress Edmond Euffe's eyes were roaming at will between two white and somewhat heavy breasts, which were moving gently with the girl's breathing and an occasional small jolt involved in stenography. Edmond Euffe, tired of the unjustified pretensions of Claire's meagre form, was suddenly attacked by a wave of coarse desire, which called for quick satisfaction and total submission to his superior position of authority. Indulgence in this sudden fancy was becoming necessary to his comfort and well-being. He asked her brusquely:

"What is your name?"

"Josiane Bigeois," the typist replied.

She was looking at him, waiting, her pencil in the air, and a little surprised. He for his part was thinking: "These affairs must be brought off immediately, without discussion, otherwise the whole staff gets wind of them, and your subordinates get a poor opinion of you. There's a right way of doing these things."

"Are you a virgin?" he asked her bluntly.

"What, monsieur?"

"Virgin, I said!" he exclaimed, his nerves rather on edge. "I am asking you if you are a virgin. You know what that means, I suppose? Well, then?"

"Oh yes, monsieur," the girl stammered out, blushing.

He thought her a ninny, despite her fine bosom and her ample form. However, this would be no hindrance, rather the reverse. But he feared that she was a little fool, likely to make a fuss and quite capable of crying out for help. . . .

"All right, then, out you go!" he said. "Clear out, and quick about it!"

She rose, her pad and pencil in her hand. She was completely mystified. She asked him:

"Will you want me to come back—the letter's not finished?"

"When you're not a virgin," he said with a growl. "Now get along with you."

As soon as the girl had gone out he fell into a state of profound depression as he realized that he himself had just been a victim of a remnant of the old Euffe instincts and that he had had a narrow escape from giving way. "If that little imbecile . . ." Then he said to himself:

"All these family bothers about love don't seem to have done me the slightest good!"

He rang for his commercial director and addressed him harshly:

"I say, Michard, what's the meaning of this? Desmarais is asking us for some packing cases and cans. Haven't they been sent back?"

"I should be surprised . . ."

"I'm asking you, have they or have they not? You don't know? Well, who does? If I have to verify everything myself, what's the use of my having people to help me? Let me know in five minutes."

"It's quite true," he said to himself, "if you give them their head, those people, they're as difficult to keep in hand as a family!" Alberte had shaken his faith in his own authority. The little Bigeois with that bosom of hers had given him doubts about his self-control. He must pull himself together. He asked himself: "Am I becoming like Father?" He happened to know that M. Euffe's belated outbreaks had begun with a typist. . . . When a man starts that sort of game . . . He was becoming conscious of a desire deep within him of some fresh and different feminine curves, rich and ample—vast if necessary—skin of some new texture, and sighs (Claire uttered no sighs, remaining too lucid always).

"What a bore it is, what a bore it is!"

He had organized his life on methodical, prudent lines, and he was wondering whether he would always find that life enough. . . . In any case, after such a lapse he hardly felt prepared to remonstrate with Germain on the subject of Flavie Lacail. He decided to postpone this.

"Got some big worry, Albe?"

Seated on a bench on Green Island, in a secluded corner of the gardens, Bob de Bazair was pressing Alberte with questions.

"Something gone a bit wrong? Have they been blowing you up at home?"

There was such sympathy, such kindness in the tone of his voice, he was so clever in anticipating her trouble before she had confided in him at all, that Alberte was quite overcome by it. No one read her thoughts so well as he, nor spoke so readily the words she longed to hear. Why must this boy be false to her? But was he false? She asked no more than to be undeceived and delivered from her suspense.

In the meantime Bob was making a mental review of certain possibilities. Circumstances in which he himself might be a cause of Alberte's present sadness seemed unlikely and remote. In a still more tender voice he asked her:

"Have they been saying something spiteful or unkind, Albe?" and his tenderness was quite unfeigned, for he found her very touching and he truly longed to scatter the dark cloud which overspread her face. It must surely, he thought, be some childish sorrow now grown beyond all proportions—and it had come to spoil their lovely morning. As he for his part was feeling only comfort and well-being and a sure hold on happiness, he wished to see an end of that intruding pain.

The young girl dared neither raise her eyes nor make a reply. The intimate nature of the cause of her unhappiness made it too hard to explain, while contact with Bob, who was just his usual self, carefree and full of charm, seemed to deprive it of all reality. That doubt which had been torturing her for the past twenty-four hours—suppose he were to find it insulting? And what right had she to doubt him already? After all, her suspicions were based on a few words of Edmond's only. And her ideas regarding the outward manifestations of love were very vague. All she really knew of Bob was his irresistible smile and that look in his eyes that was in itself a caress. Was it possible that he could bestow that same smile, those same fond looks, on some other woman? It would be not only heart-rending, but a monstrous, dreadful thing.

"Come, Albe, look at me!" Bob said, and moved her head gently so that she turned her face towards him.

But the girl's eyes evaded his. And at the same time, blushing and weighed down by her feelings, she seemed to be appealing for help, as though Bob could have given her the comfort of which she stood in need.

Bob de Bazair guessed that this enigmatical behaviour was merely the outcome of natural modesty of feeling. He pursued his investigations without dropping his voice, thus ruling out any idea that there might be serious reasons for Alberte's sorrow, or that life was anything but a simple, pleasant business, which held every promise of smiles and happiness and bliss to come.

"Have they been running me down, Albe?"

She did not answer, but from a slight start she gave, he knew that he had hit the mark.

"They told you that I was a rake?"

She picked up courage to cast a furtive glance at him, in which there was more of fear than anger, and in which he read an appeal for help. There was a little quiet smile on his face for the rather childish sort of remark that he was expecting to hear. He seized both Alberte's slightly feverish hands in his own.

"But it's true, Albe! Or rather, it was true. What reason could I have for not being fast, before I knew you? If I hadn't been, I should have a liaison now, or be already married. I shouldn't be free today. And I should be sorry. Wouldn't you?"

"Are you entirely free?" she murmured.

"Entirely," Bob said, with sincerity in his voice. "Do you doubt it? Come, come, dear one, you're not going to make yourself unhappy for no reason at all? We have never yet spoken about my past. Very well, then, let us do so now once for all and then never again. Did they mention anybody?"

Alberte bent her head forward and gazed steadily at the shoe on her right foot, this leg being crossed over the other.

"Who was it?"

"Riri Jumier," she said in a whisper, still not looking at him.

"Good Lord! Was that all? Nothing more?"

"No," said Alberte.

"Well," said Bob, "it simply isn't worth while your worrying yourself over such a trifle as that. It isn't really! Now, listen, Albe, I could lie to you and assure you that there has never been anything between Riri and me, and no one would have any proof to the contrary. Perhaps, Albe, you would prefer me to lie? But I don't want there to be anything of that kind between us—not even if I do give you a tiny trouble to bear. I want you to be able to trust me absolutely. I did have a flirtation with little

Jumier—a rather violent one, and I didn't even start it myself. And at that time I had not met you. But that's a thing in my life that is over and done with. Or rather . . . See now, Albe. I'm going to tell you everything. It was through little Jumier that I heard about your father and felt that he and I had become friends. And if that happened, it was because he said so many nice things about you. Your father was very fond of you, Albe! Oh, very!"

The effect of these last words was to turn the flow of Alberte's sorrow in another direction. At last she could weep, and relieve herself through tears of the burden of her grief, within the shelter of her father's memory, that father who was still hovering as a guardian angel over her love at the most touching and most decisive moments of its course.

And Bob de Bazair, as with tender caresses he brought her comfort in her sorrow, continued thus:

"It was through this little Jumier, Albe, that I heard of you, before I actually saw you. Perhaps if it had not been for her I shouldn't have had the curiosity to get to know you. Are you so very vexed with her for that?"

"How long ago was that?" Alberte asked.

"Those talks we had about you?"

"No. I mean since you noticed me?"

"The first time," Bob said, "was at the very beginning of spring. One afternoon you were with some lady on the terrace of the tea place opposite the Dauphins. You were wearing a red frock with twisted white and jade trimmings. I was looking at you and saying to myself: 'She is charming!' We caught each other's eyes several times. I smiled at you."

"I remember the dress," Alberte said.

"And I saw you again really properly at Lesdiguières, thanks to the tennis. Do you remember the day when I asked you for a game?"

"You must have thought I played very badly. I was a bit nervous . . ."

"You played rather cleverly. But your style wasn't quite right."

"Still, I had had some lessons from Cols."

"Lessons are not everything. You have to work them out in practice. As Professor Grémillet says: 'The way you shape for each stroke must become completely mechanical if your reaction to the flight of the ball is to be infallibly right.' And Lacoste himself says that his tennis improved when he practised against a cement wall. I bet you don't try shots against a wall?"

"No," Alberte said, "it's so monotonous."

"You're wrong, though. A wall is the most patient and most accurate opponent you could find and it adopts and keeps up the rhythm of your own strokes better than any other. And gives you a chance to correct your own mistakes."

This conversation on the subject of tennis, a game to which she owed her meetings with Bob de Bazair, banished from Alberte's mind the picture of that odious creature, Riri Jumier, a young woman who distributed her favours with cynical impartiality among old men and young. All her trust and confidence returned to her, and with it all her adoration. September was already bringing to foliage the first russet tints of autumn, though barely discernible as yet, for the slopes of the Grésivaudan still kept their greenness as a whole and the sky its blue, while there seemed every promise of a late season of warmth and sumptuous colour. But in the evenings at Bouquéron, as she watched the stars shimmering in the pale sky and the white mist gathering in the valley below, the young girl was feeling, now that autumn was already on its way and a tinge of melancholy was mingled with the shortening daylight hours, that the weeks and months had flown away and left her poorer because those days of precious happiness could never be recalled.

Since the springtime she had known love only by the joy and gladness which it brought her, by a layer of bright colours with which, for her, it adorned the commonplace and the ugly, by the humming of what seemed a song in her honour by the trees, the insects, and the winds—a song of which her heart could never tire of taking up the refrain. And now for the first time she had come to know, through the agency of grief, the depth and the intensity of the feeling which bound her to Bob de Bazair for all time. She was thrilled, almost shattered by it, and filled now with gratitude for the enchanter who was giving her faith, hope, and the light of life, with the warm blood beating in her temples and the joyous flow of life deep within her and clear as a crystal stream, while as she breathed, her nostrils, accepting none save the sweetest scents, were bringing back to her that rapture in which, since the death of M. Euffe, she had walked as though she trod on air.

"Little Albe, little Albe," said Bob as he fondled the back of her neck, "did you really doubt?"

Tears came to Alberte's eyes, tears of repentance for having sinned against her dear, her all-absorbing, her indispensable love. . . .

As she returned to Bouquéron that morning she was happier than she had ever been. She paid a visit to the humble Virgin of the church of St.-Laurent, the confidante of simple minds and guileless hearts. She thanked her for the great happiness that had been given to her, and wishing to give pleasure, added, on an impulse essentially feminine, as she looked at the Child Jesus in the arms of His mother:

"He's nice, your little one! He's nice, he's a darling. . . ."

7. AN AMAZON ON THE WARPATH At the instance
of her son Edmond, who had himself been hard pressed by the widow
of General de Sainte-Foy, this lady having returned to the charge,
Mme. Euffe dismissed her chauffeur, the young and attractive Bruno
Spaniente, whose dark velvety eyes exercised a powerful attraction for
Lucie Euffe, whose feelings were unrecognized and misunderstood. It
is true that this young woman's natural instincts were being heightened
and inflamed by a stifling celibacy from which, at the humiliating approach of her thirtieth year, not even her reputation as a rich unmarried
lady seemed likely to rescue her—so complete was the failure of her personal appearance to suggest any idea of the mutual enjoyment of amorous delight.

Pondering on her disastrous lack of physical charm, Lucie Euffe had
realized that she could never be the joy of any refined or fastidious
young man, and that she would always be handicapped, so far as the
sons of good families in the district were concerned, by the existence of
plump and dimpled little ninnies with their superior physical advantages, and themselves by no means lacking in this world's goods. For
pretty girls are not necessarily poor. They may, of course, be stupid—
and Lucie Euffe considered that, generally speaking, they were—but
men have never found any serious obstacle in this. It is indeed only
too evident that feminine intelligence is not a thing over which they
grow enthusiastic. One might even say that there are many men who deliberately shun it, fearing criticism from their better halves, over whom
they claim a right to exercise their masculine authority at the least possible cost to themselves. What they demand from the other sex is that
kind of attraction of which poor Lucie knew that she was dreadfully devoid. So conscious was she of this that she envied the coarse tributes
which the street provides in plenty for creatures the reverse of shy. She
would have given much, if a company of soldiers were passing, to hear
coming from their ranks those appreciative remarks which with their
forcible expression strike blows at a pretty passer-by at the most vulnerable points of her femininity. But at sight of her only a painful silence
reigned, while a few yards farther on a laundrymaid, a factory girl, or a
young woman of easy virtue would unleash a torrent of acclamation,
coarse and vulgar in its attempted lyrical flight, but able to turn your
cheeks scarlet and give you some distinctly pleasant thrills.

In her cruel isolation, Lucie Euffe was meditating on the laws which govern the pairing of the sexes, and constantly observing how this mutual attraction takes place. In actual fact her discoveries were not altogether discouraging, for it is not always the pairing of two handsome beings that is the occasion of passion and mutual good feeling. One day outside the Cathedral of Notre Dame she had seen an expression of utter and complete mutual adoration in the eyes of a pair of poor puny little lovers, absurdly ugly, who were going forward on life's journey with their fingers interlocked and their faces transfigured with happiness, between a double row of smiles and expressions of astonishment. This fervour gave them a sort of grace which was touching and disarmed criticism. From this incident Lucie had come to the conclusion that as the eligible young men in her own circles were turning up their noses at her, she would have to take time by the forelock and force her own destiny. After all, she had the money to get a husband, and there are plenty of instances in society of rich but ill-favoured girls counting on their money to achieve that end. If she secured herself a husband, why not choose a handsome one? She was haunted by the idea of beauty. Furthermore, whether it were from resentment or desire for revenge, she snapped her fingers at both education and birth. She wanted a man who had the beauty of a lovely object, of a fine animal, being herself exceedingly well able to dispense with the famous masculine intelligence. Nay, more, she wished to avoid it; for she feared that such intelligence would create a feeling of embarrassment between herself and the man of her choice.

When she saw Bruno Spaniente she was conquered. He was the type of male to whom she was peculiarly susceptible and who could stir her to her depths, the virile type at which, subconsciously, her virgin aspirations had aimed while she was suffering the torments of disdain. In her eyes he was so fine a man as to be a humiliation to all those idiots at Grenoble who had declined to notice her.

Bruno Spaniente was without doubt a good-looking young man with a natural grace about him. He had the strongly defined features so frequently found in the South of France and which resemble the Roman cast of countenance, with a clear-cut, sharply defined chin, rendered bluish by the very dark growth of his hair, an upper lip with a sinuous outline, and dark eyes with a fascinating fiery glint. Not very tall, but agile and wiry, he had a muscular torso with broad shoulders and narrow hips. A slight wave, which went in a slanting direction, in his black and very abundant hair gave it some rather odd reflections of light; this hair ended off on either side of his face in whiskers of the kind favoured by leading tenors. It must be admitted that he looked a rogue, but a good-natured one for all that, with the endearing shyness of a young wild animal which has been tamed.

Before getting his situation with his present employers he had been a door opener in the approaches to the casino at Nice, a ball boy at a Monte Carlo tennis club, and a taxi driver. He went through life in haphazard fashion, waiting for his rather rascally charm to get him his chance. He had only one passion, but it was an overmastering one—his Southern laziness. He knew nothing more agreeable or gratifying than whole days devoted to lounging in small bars, bareheaded and wearing a sweater and canvas shoes, with the blue serenity of the Mediterranean before his eyes. Now he had left the South, but he was hoping that Fate would direct him to the discovery of a definite and lasting opportunity for doing nothing, while in the brilliant light of the Riviera he enjoyed a life of leisure given up to friendships quickly made, and boasting and jests, to say nothing of dark-haired, chattering girls, whose love is redolent of mimosa, garlic, and the sea. . . .

Bruno Spaniente had come from a part of the country in which there were too many men living on women, or awaiting an opportunity to do so, for him not to take note of the effect he was producing on Lucie Euffe. But he was by nature too lazy and unconcerned, and also too wily and astute, to wish to precipitate matters in any way. It seemed better to allow this rich girl to fall in love without any encouragement on his part, and consequently to do no more than give her such smiles as a deferential servant might offer—smiles which incidentally displayed an even row of white and shining teeth—look at her from time to time in a tender, dreamy, rather shy sort of way, and be always well shaved and smartly dressed. For he was undoubtedly playing for big stakes in wishing to make this young woman so infatuated with himself as to forget her social position and her very ample means.

The strength of Bruno Spaniente's position lay in his playing of this game without feeling entirely convinced of winning it—playing it, therefore, with a serene detachment which suited his own indolent nature. He was still further helped in this undertaking by the young woman's utter lack of appeal to his senses, while there was a pretty servant in the Rue Félix-Vialle who was affording him every possible kind of satisfaction. He was afraid neither of losing his head nor of making any gesture to which the slightest objection could be taken. And every member of the Euffe household considered Bruno to be the perfect chauffeur—polite, obliging, tactful, and smart—in fact, a rara avis, with an equable nature and never robbing his employers. In this respect, also, Bruno showed his cleverness; with his eye on big profits, he cared nothing for small ones, and would never think of falsifying his accounts with the garage proprietor or the man who sold petrol.

It was indeed Lucie whose feelings were getting the better of her and becoming increasingly obvious, thanks to her inexperience as a virgin who is too mature and gets excited through being in a hurry. These feelings could not escape the eagle eye of the widow of General de Sainte-Foy, as determined as a ferret in poking her nose into other people's business, and whose interference came near to ruining the plans of the young man from Nice and breaking the heart of Lucie Euffe. But as often happens, the general's wife, wishing to convey a warning when no one had asked her to do so, merely brought matters to a head. Passion was already mistress of the situation.

The widow of General de Sainte-Foy prided herself on having a long arm, a determined and striking faculty for making decisions, and an aptitude for command; and certainly from her own point of view this was no exaggeration, for her boldness and impudence in matters of intrigue, of stirring people up, of prying into the heart of their affairs, of casting them into a state of perturbation and unrest, of laying traps which led them into rash and hasty unions, were nothing short of marvellous. This whirlwind driver of other women had a positive passion for matchmaking, and was ceaselessly launching attacks by members of her own sex on the positions of the male enemy. Her own numerous marriages had been more than enough to show her how to bring people into each other's presence and rapidly into the same bed. Her matrimonial experience had taught her that fifty per cent of humanity have only a vague idea what to do with their lives and with their bodies. When one sees the astonishing way in which those same human beings cling to one another, does there seem to be any reason for using tact or standing on ceremony in the matter of stowing them away in couples? The general's wife didn't think so. Men and women (and the men more so, in her opinion) are lacking in determination. And the more they lack it, the longer they dawdle and hesitate in shyness which they can't subdue. The general's wife regarded celibacy far less as a piece of selfishness than as an example of cowardice, of sheer funk, and above all as a shameful flight from virile duty, on the ground that a man's principal mission in life is to support a woman (whether he enjoys it or not—and could anybody imagine that women get any enjoyment living with those wretched creatures?) because it is a fundamental law of this world that women should live on men.

There was to be no question, in this marriage business, of happiness or sentiment, or any of the twaddle that is talked on this subject; all that mattered was that poor weak, gentle women should be protected. (It was indeed somewhat strange to hear this terrible dragon speak of the weakness and gentleness of a sex to which her own contribution was a combination of Mother Angot and a lady with a moustache and of powerful build.) Just as she had married and remarried in order to take reprisals on men, so did the general's wife arrange marriages right and left with the object of bringing men into ever greater subjection to the law of her own sex, being unable, with her tyrannical nature, ever to admit that a man under a woman's control should be anything but appropriately and suitably fettered, and reduced to the utterance of a docile Amen. And thus it was that the idea of chaining a man to Lucie Euffe, who she thought was frenzied and mad, and ugly to boot, gave her a glimpse of new expiations for the sex she abhorred. Filled with a spirit of enterprise and zeal, she started her campaign and quickly found the very thing she sought.

In Captain Eugène Bidon, of the Engineers, there was neither push nor glamour. He had never read either Jomini or Clausewitz, or Moltke, or Dragomirov, or Napoleon. He was ignorant of this teaching of Foch: "To be disciplined does not mean keeping silent, remaining aloof; it is not the art of avoiding responsibility, but it involves *acting* in the sense of orders received, which means discovering in one's own mind, by investigation and reflection, how far it is possible to carry those orders out." As an officer he was punctual in the execution of his duties, with no fancies or opinions of his own, and avoided initiative as though it were the plague. He might just as well have chosen a career in civil life, as a chartered accountant, a draughtsman, a cashier, or a commercial manager. But by going into the army he had eliminated the risks of a civil career: his employer would never go bankrupt, he himself would never be dismissed, he would get a pension on retirement. Furthermore, his promotion would take place in due course, without any excessive activity on his part.

Completely in his element with administrative duties on the staff of a district officer of Engineers, he found therein his heart's delight in dealing with matters of accountancy, reports, affidavits, returns, schedules, plans of landed property, etc.

Responsible for the upkeep of military buildings, he enjoyed prowling about in the Dode, Vinoy, Alma, Bizanet, Hoche, and de Bonne barracks, and at the Rabot fort, the Polygone, the forage park, and the military stores. He had all the regulations at his fingers' ends, and was well up in all the dodges of officialdom for getting a question pigeon-holed forever and saving a man from responsibility. The notion of time never entered into his rough estimates, for he was well aware that in any case the "usual channels" of official or army life constitute an automatic and powerful brake, a check on all rash impulse, just as he knew that one officer succeeds another, and that a man who completes a job is seldom the one who began it.

The captain had acquired in the lower ranks of the army a taste for war material somewhat out of date (for instance, he was delighted that a certain type of forage wagon had to all intents and purposes remained unchanged since the days of Napoleon, and that the same old sheet-iron boats were still in favour for throwing a bridge over a river). In the same way he preferred to stick to the theories which had stood the test of wars of long ago, thinking as he did that the army—one of the last remaining bulwarks of French tradition—had no need of novelties that endanger and undermine the good old army orders, which are never sufficiently pondered over, and which one gets well rammed into one's head after twenty years of barracks or office work. In this way he inspired confidence in his superior officers, who as men older than himself were hostile to innovations, and became more and more so as they approached the age limit. The senior officers had the same prejudice against modern methods as they had against the young women of the present generation, who in their opinion were put completely in the shade by the little lady friends of their youth, whose hips and bosoms were of ampler and more generous design.

"Bidon's as safe as a house," was said of him in the Engineers at Grenoble. "He never gives any trouble."

That was a good mark—the highest he could get, perhaps—and set the seal on the possibility of his attaining high rank in a learned branch of the army, even though he was known to have a certain reluctance to put pen to paper. But this difficulty—which was as though his pen were afflicted with a stammer—was counterbalanced by his never boring people to death with reports, and by the fact that, generally speaking, his activities involved a minimum of correspondence. His fellow workers were grateful to him for giving his superior officers confidence in his observance of all regulations, thus protecting everyone from criticism.

At every stage of his career, Captain Bidon had kept marvellously within the limits of the rank he held, without any vainglorious desire to distinguish himself therein or purpose to achieve too rapid promotion which might give offence to his brother officers. In the presence of an officer of higher rank he was inclined to keep in the background as though overcome by the other man's grandeur and power, and everything in his attitude expressed utter and complete approval. So truly was this the case that an inspecting general had actually made this remark about him to his colonel:

"A good fellow, that Lieutenant Bidon! Knows how to keep his mouth shut! Intelligent! Record good?"

"Very good indeed, sir," the colonel had answered with alacrity, never having noticed Lieutenant Bidon much.

"Recommend him," the general had said. "Useful fellow to have on the strength."

The outcome of this incident was Lieutenant Bidon's third piece of gold braid, the colonel having no wish to displease the general. The latter, however, who had large forces to attend to, had completely forgotten Lieutenant Bidon when he wrote "approved" on the colonel's recommendation.

And thus it was that Captain Bidon was the complete personification of a type of officer-official current in an army resting (or going to sleep) on its laurels and forgetting its ideal of military efficiency, so widespread was the opinion among all ranks that no enemy would dare to try conclusions with its very obvious strength. He spared his subordinates nothing in the way of work which contributed to their own safety, but expected nothing from them beyond a prudent conformity with the rules and regulations. For he applied those regulations in the letter, but fought shy of interpretations in the spirit, since these would rarely agree with other such interpretations emanating from higher ranks than his.

He considered himself a humble cog in a machine whose construction was unalterable, and of whose power he himself held a satisfactory fraction.

He thought it a specially fine thing that that powerful institution, the army, the bulwark of all other institutions, should rest on certain conspicuous signs leaving no room for mistakes, including one that was a stroke of genius, namely, that a man's professional intelligence should be inscribed on his sleeve and discernible at twenty paces; a sleeve is more easily read than a face. Civil life mixes people up in an anonymity which is dangerous and which favours imposture. There is nothing like this in military life, where a five-stripe intelligence cannot be confused with a four-, three-, or two-stripe one. It is one of the army's great outstanding qualities, this creation of simple classifications which remain conspicuous and clear even amid the disorder and confusion of battle and the rush and scrimmage of assaults.

Captain Bidon felt a calm satisfaction in the knowledge that henceforth he would be a three-stripe intelligence after having thought, acted, and obeyed for years past with only a single or a two-stripe one. He thought that his intelligence would increase still further with seniority; and this is another advantage of military as compared with civil life, where intelligence tends to diminish as a man grows old. He was not dissatisfied with his lot. He was waiting for his Legion of Honour, being quite high up on the list. His uniform gave him undeniable prestige despite his being rather bald, a little corpulent, and his beard carroty when he had neglected to shave. He was nearing forty and a widower. This condition had its advantages and its drawbacks. Whether it was the former or the latter that loomed the larger in the captain's mind depended on his prevailing mood.

Such was the military officer selected by the widow of General de Sainte-Foy as the tool for the fulfilment of the destiny of Lucie Euffe. Captain Bidon was free, as we have said, from devouring ambition; but the idea of becoming a millionaire officer, and in a position to anticipate his retirement at any time he chose, worked on him in such a way as to predispose him to face an amorous venture which was far from tempting. At sight of Lucie's photograph he had still stood firm, discipline having long accustomed him to uphill tasks. And the attack on this young woman was certainly a less dangerous task than throwing a bridge of boats across a river under artillery fire or blowing up a bastion defended by machine guns and flame-throwers.

Before starting his campaign, the captain went and ordered a new outfit at Moréteau's, and bought a few shirts and a pair of shoes with high insteps and pointed toes. Alas, despite his own efforts and the recommendations of the general's wife, he felt shy and awkward in the drawing room at the Place Victor-Hugo, rather as though he were a company sergeant major who had strolled into the officers' mess. His manners were defective, and his conversation, with far too many references to barrack buildings and quartering of troops, could make no effect whatever on a feminine mind in an emotional and excited state.

It sometimes happens that conspirators become entangled in the web of their own conspiracies. This was what happened to the widow of General de Sainte-Foy. Her own nature was too domineering to allow her to pay much attention to those of other people; and the result was that she made mistakes. She who had been a pretty woman unaffected by masculine contact could not understand a plain girl's being aroused and stirred thereby and having preferences of her own.

Captain Bidon, who a year earlier would have received an enthusiastic welcome, now filled Lucie with horror. She found him insipid and dull; for this virgin with a blotchy face and bony frame was now wallowing in romance.

Lucie was now subsisting on a love against which all the gold bands and all the generals' wives in the world would have been powerless. This strange girl had formed an ideal of a lover based entirely on physique, and could no longer conceive of a man otherwise than in the guise of a lover to be passionately cherished. Contrary to ordinary young women whose lives are settled at an early stage and rather at haphazard, she had had time in her solitude to give thought to the problems of love. She knew what stir within her love's approach would cause, and what kind of partner could bring her ecstasy and thrill. She did not ask to be passionately loved, but that she herself should be allowed to love; this plain-featured person was conscious of possessing a fund of devotion and of gratitude to an Adonis who was a bit of a rascal, with a glint in his eyes and a fine figure, who had not got that silly Christian name Eugène, but Bruno. Her passion was at its height when Captain Bidon made his appearance in Mme. Euffe's drawing room, with his solemn, embarrassed air. Lucie was having secret meetings away from home with the handsome chauffeur, to whom she paid the tribute of compromising herself and sacrificing the family good name. This was the delightful outcome of the activities of the general's wife. The reader must be taken back a month and shown how it had come about.

Against her will, and without Lucie's knowledge, Mme. Euffe gave Bruno Spaniente his dismissal, at the same time making him a handsome present of money so that he should leave the house without delay. This generosity on the part of a lady of her class, being distinctly unusual, made the chauffeur realize that there was something serious in the wind. He contrived to be in a corner of the park where Lucie—who was never far away from him—would be passing, and there, cap in hand, he spoke to her with an air of mingled shyness and sorrow.

"Well, miss," he said, "it seems I'm saying good-bye to you. It makes me very sad to be leaving you because you've always been kind to me."

"What," Lucie said, "are you going away?"

"Haven't you heard, miss? It's the mistress who's sending me away, on someone else's advice, so I understand. She wants me to leave in no end of a hurry, just as though I'd suddenly gone wrong. And yet I've always given good service here, and I'd got fond of the place—on account of you, miss," he added, with a special inflexion in his voice.

Lucie was too overcome to reply. Seeing that she had turned pale, Bruno burnt his boats behind him. But he had nothing more to lose.

"On account of you, miss," he went on, "not being treated as you deserve. Anyone can see that they think more of Miss Alberte and Mr. Germain than you!"

"You realized that, did you, Bruno?"

"It wasn't hard to spot that, and I've felt so sorry for you, miss. I said to myself, 'Miss Lucie,' I said, 'they simply don't understand her. She's got a kinder heart than the others, yet she's the one to suffer, not being loved!' And you deserve to be loved as much as any other lady, miss. And p'raps a bit more!"

"Do you think so, Bruno?"

"I should just say I did! And even . . . But I'm only a chauffeur . . . though I might be doing much better . . . it's all a matter of luck, as they say . . ."

Lucie Euffe's eyes shone bright with adoration.

"And suppose you were something else in life and not a chauffeur, Bruno? If you had occasion to love a girl who, shall we say, was above you in station? It might happen, you know."

"Oh, then . . ." said Bruno. "Ah, if I had just a bit of encouragement . . . There are things one doesn't dare to say. It's what one's feelings are . . ."

"But do speak out, Bruno! What is it you want to say?"

"Well, I'm leaving—going away for good and all. . . . It'd give me something to think about later on, it'd be a sweet memory . . . if I could speak . . ."

"Yes," Lucie said vehemently, "I understand you, Bruno. I understand what noble feelings you have."

"If I could see you somewhere else, miss . . . just talk to you for once not like a servant, before I go away forever . . ."

"Forever!" Lucie exclaimed, with the wild expression of a woman in love who is plunged into a situation tragic to the last degree.

"Bruno," she said, flurried and upset, "I am going into Grenoble presently. Do you know any place . . . any place where you would feel at your ease? . . . There are lots of things I can understand . . . I feel that you are a friend of mine, too, Bruno."

"Thank you, miss, and I shall never forget what you've just said."

"Do you know any place, Bruno, where we could talk in a friendly way?"

"Oh," Bruno replied, "there are plenty of them. If you liked, miss,

118

you might come, perhaps, to the Shady Nook. If you want to be quiet and not meet people, there's no better place."

"Look," Lucie said as she handed him a book which she was holding, "write this down, will you? 'I will be there at five o'clock.' Five o'clock, don't forget."

Thereupon she hastened to leave him and went a roundabout way along a small path in the park, in the opposite direction to that which he was taking. At first she made up her mind to speak to her mother about Bruno's departure, until something warned her that it would be better to say nothing and appear ignorant of the whole matter.

Situated at the top of Green Island, the Shady Nook was a sort of small suburban tavern, with a garden, frequented chiefly by workers of various kinds and soldiers, and there were games of ninepins and a snack bar where white wine was served. On Sundays the place resembled a tenth-rate dancing hall, that is to say, there was dancing to the accompaniment of a penny-in-the-slot machine which dispensed waltzes and tangos that sounded somewhat weary. There were arbours for the benefit of loving couples. Lucie Euffe liked the place enormously, tinted as it was with the hues of her own love. She was weary to the point of loathing of all that reminded her of the people of her own class, of their duplicities and their rules of life. Furthermore, at the Shady Nook one had fine glimpses of the Isère valley, with views of Bouquéron, Corenc, and the bluffs of the St. Eynard.

In this rustic and popular setting, amid the deep silence of the evening hours which at the foot of the mountains is so striking and impressive, Lucie literally threw herself on the neck of Bruno Spaniente, with a clumsiness born of inexperience and in mortal terror of losing the handsome young man who was at once her life's torment and its bliss. This tremendous gesture brought her a radiance that gave her a touch of real beauty and made her sincerity a moving thing. Bruno felt that this too trusting girl was not to be despised and that he must not treat her lightly. He was without doubt an unscrupulous man, but with a good reserve of decent feeling. All he cared about was that the pleasant things of life should come to him without effort or work on his part. In Lucie he saw a means of a brisk clearance of some social barriers, but he had no wish to mystify or cause suffering to the emotional and excited girl now his for the asking. He was doing the best for himself, that was all. And if it happened to suit Lucie too, that would be all to the good. He was now starting his programme of "respecting" her until further orders. He wished her to see how chivalrous he was.

Lucie paid further visits to the Shady Nook. She hastened there impatiently, in terror lest she should not see Bruno, who on one occasion gave her the painful experience of a fruitless wait. He had wished, by the amount of distress given to this girl of good family, to gauge the extent of the hold he had upon her. He had been enabled to judge that this hold was immense and that his affairs were taking a definite and durable shape.

Above all, he must not leave Grenoble—not at any price! This was Lucie's oft-repeated prayer as she feasted her eyes on the handsome face of the young man from Nice. In order that Bruno should have time to look round and find another situation she offered him money, since it was through her fault that he had lost everything. The offer did not come as a surprise to a young man who, living on the Mediterranean coast, had known many others like himself whose activities had no other object than to obtain a similar offer, and who regarded it as indispensable evidence of a woman's love.

Bruno accepted a few gifts of money in order that the principle might be well established from the outset; as between Lucie and himself there could be no question of necessary funds being supplied by him. But he was careful not to take unfair advantage of this. Expenditure on a large scale he was reserving for later, when his life should be properly organized.

As for Lucie, she was delighted at Bruno taking her money. This transaction freed her from a mass of stifling convention associated with the bleak and dismal years of her life and the sighs of Mme. Euffe, and she was enabled for the first time to feel that she was really useful to a fellow creature. She would even have liked Bruno to have more needs and fancies, to give her great opportunities for devotion, and to owe his entire happiness to her. It was she who implored him to accept a new suit, ties, and socks. Bruno consented. He had a partiality for smart clothes, and there was no harm in Lucie's seeing him to advantage, dressed like a gentleman. Unfortunately, Bruno's taste in ties and in the colours of shirts was somewhat disastrous. In addition to this he had a predilection for shoes with bright uppers and the leather too highly treated. . . . But Lucie's happiness was too complete to allow her to notice trifling details of this kind. She thought Bruno handsomer than ever, and Captain Bidon more absurd.

The latter was at grips with the widow of General de Sainte-Foy, enraged at her protégé cutting such a poor figure.

"Well, Captain," she said to him, "are you asleep? What are you waiting for if you want to get on in life? If the army had nobody except people like you to carry enemy positions, France's enemies would have a grand time! Attack, my friend! It's at the sword's point that you carry off a woman. You're not waiting for me to come behind you and sound the charge?"

"I have a feeling that she doesn't like me . . ." the captain said.

"Doesn't like you!" the general's wife exclaimed. "Good heavens, if you start off with ideas like that . . . When I married the General, do you suppose I asked myself whether he liked me or not? There was only one thing I really did know, and that was that I wanted the general. Oh, not for himself, the dear old mug!—but so as to be the general's wife. Very well then, I stormed the title as though it had been a fort! And now the general is dead. May he rest in peace in the warriors' paradise. Do you or do you not want your Lucie?"

"Certainly I do, madame."

"Well then, my boy, what on earth are you waiting for? Heavens alive, man, why don't you give her a child!"

"There would have to be an opportunity . . ."

"An opportunity! There's always an opportunity for giving a woman a child! And it's a woman who's telling you so! What idiots men are!"

"I still have a feeling that she has lost her heart to someone else," the captain said.

"Oh, very well then!" the general's wife cried out. "If you're one of those silly fools who believe in women's hearts! That famous heart of theirs—why, it's women themselves who've invented it! Do you think that I had a heart? No, thank goodness—or where should I be nowadays? No, it's only poor ninnies, girls of the poorer classes, young skivvies . . . But when you get higher up in the world, the heart becomes a mere pretence. . . . Ah, if only I could have been a man! A fat lot of attention I should have paid to women's hearts!"

"Then it must be her nature—she must be difficult to . . . er . . . rouse."

"My poor friend," said the general's wife, "if there were only temperamental women to go to bed with! What on earth did they teach you at St.-Cyr?"

"At Versailles!" the captain said by way of correction. "The school of Engineers is at Versailles. . . ."

The general's wife was forced to admit defeat. Despite her efforts with Mme. Euffe and with Lucie herself, the latter remained steadily indifferent to the prestige of the army and displayed a pigheadedness that was truly surprising.

Captain Bidon was extremely upset by his failure to win Lucie's heart. He had been chosen and sought out at a time when he had no particular ambition to satisfy, and new and brighter prospects were held out before him. He had yielded to the spell, and had done so the more readily in that Lucie Euffe, hopelessly in love with another man, was going through a period at which she was, comparatively speaking, radiant and aglow—radiant, that is to say, in the eyes of a man of forty who was afraid of too much beauty, feeling it to be dangerous.

When he saw that he had been ousted, Captain Bidon had a feeling of resentment which produced an effect quite foreign to his real nature: it filled him with a keen desire for revenge, and with unbounded ambition. The captain conceived a horror of Grenoble, where he thought that his misadventure had become a subject for mirth. Having developed a sudden craving for promotion, he applied for the Colonies, having just read, at the Military Club, that Marshal Joffre, an engineer officer like himself, had had a colonial career, most of which had been as an engineer, that had carried him to the highest rank of all. After the recent blow to his natural pride, the captain's dream was to return one day to Grenoble with stars on his sleeves and there appear with a halo of distinction before the woman who had scorned him, and fill her old age with bitter regret.

This plan, however, came to naught. Captain Bidon departed to Indo-China, and was there posted to a particularly unhealthy district on the frontier of Siam. There he was bitten by a poisonous snake and died in a far-distant land, a victim of the machinations of the widow of General de Sainte-Foy. As for Lucie Euffe, she was destined to remain forever in ignorance of the fact that she had been the faraway heroine of a colonial tragedy of ill-starred love.

But the news of his death reached the ears of the general's wife, who still kept up her connection with military circles.

"Bidon?" she said. "Yes, I remember now. A young man who was only half awake. Just think, I had given him an opportunity of making a splendid marriage—splendid for a little captain. You knew that crazy young woman, Lucie Euffe of the Silken Net? It was before she left Grenoble to do all the mad things I should expect of her. I wanted to get her married—and Heaven knows it seemed pretty necessary at the time! But I wanted her to make a more or less suitable marriage, seeing that there was enough scandal in her family already with the death of old Euffe under the very windows of that hussy of his . . . So, just imagine . . ."

This account of the abortive marriage of Lucie Euffe and Captain

Bidon became one of the most ruthless of the general's wife's stories. She continued to tell it until she was eighty-seven, an age at which, with her dictatorial energy deserting her as her strength ebbed, she gave up the ghost in true military fashion, convinced to the last of having wrought a useful work upon this earth of ours and set a fine example of force and vigour to the people of her time.

8. A TOUCH OF MELODRAMA Edmond Euffe had just brought off two big deals, one connected with sauerkraut and sausages, the other with preserves of tomato juice. He had bought these stocks at half their normal price because they were within a few months, only, of the time when they would no longer be fresh enough for consumption. These stores had become available as a result of the liquidation of a co-operative society, and Edmond Euffe was proposing to use them as items for a special sale which would act as an advertisement for the Silken Net. While selling these preserves at a lower price than rival firms, he would still stand to make a forty-five-per-cent profit on the sales. From the point of view of advertisement it was a first-rate transaction, but it rested on the possession of very wide facilities for sale. The *Dauphiné Gazette* would publish some enticing paragraphs, under the titles "A Week at the Silken Net," and "A Pleasant Surprise for Housewives."

Edmond Euffe was pondering on this transaction while eating, in his own home, some of the sauerkraut with sausages which his many shops were about to put on sale. In so doing he was remaining faithful to an Euffe custom derived from his father. M. Constant Euffe had made a rule of trying at his own table the items of food which he was offering to his customers. His intention was that everything he sold should invariably be of good sound quality, though he brought a special effort to bear upon certain foodstuffs which made an outstanding contribution to his firm's reputation for excellence. It was known, for example, that the Silken Net's Gruyère cheese was unrivalled, and that every confidence could be placed in its butter, eggs, vermicelli, and filleted herring. The Silken Net had likewise two or three specialties in the biscuit line, with design and taste which the manufacturers reserved exclusively for the firm.

"It makes very good eating!" Edmond said, after swallowing a few mouthfuls of his sauerkraut and sausage. "And there's a little smoked taste in it, too. . . . Won't you try it?" he asked his wife.

"No, thank you," Claire answered, rather curtly.

"But your opinion would be a help to me."

"I don't think so," said Claire. "My taste has got nothing whatever to do with those people's."

This was the expression she used to indicate her husband's customers, with a slight difference in the tone of her voice that raised an impassable barrier between her and them. Claire found fault with the tasting experiments in which Edmond indulged at home, and never took part in them herself. Whenever her husband fed on his own samples she was served with dishes prepared specially for her.

"Perhaps you are right," Edmond agreed. "One couldn't say it was up to much—no, not up to much."

"Then why do you eat it?"

"Duty," Edmond answered. "My poor father always used to lay this down as a principle, and he thought the firm's prosperity was due to it: 'One ought not to poison people.' And he used to fix his prices as he tasted. I think, as he did, that taste or high flavour can be a very useful guide for price. I was hesitating whether to sell these boxes of sauerkraut at nine francs or nine francs forty-five. I think decidedly that I ought not to go beyond nine francs. I don't mean that the stuff is in the very slightest degree doubtful. But it has to be used up quickly. A reduction of a few pence will get rid of a thousand boxes more within the first week."

"Well, if you think so. . . . All that is your business, my dear."

"Yes, certainly. . . . The bacon has held out well," he added as he bent over his sauerkraut. "It's the sausages that have taken on a slight metallic taste—oh, very slight. After all, an uneducated palate may find that this taste gives the food a certain originality. I have seen stock on the point of getting high—oh, but very slightly—which was specially favoured on that very account. Customers came back and asked for more. Oh yes, and there was something that happened once over a quantity of salt bacon . . ."

"Oh dear, oh dear!" Claire said, tapping her plate with the point of her knife.

"Yes, bacon. It was when my poor father was still alive, and I'm not sure if we were yet married . . ."

"Oh, what does it matter!" Claire said, tapping more loudly.

"Well, my father was wondering whether he ought not to throw the whole consignment away. Then he had an idea that was really a

124

stroke of genius. He put the price up fourpence a pound, and recommended the stuff as something special. And do you know what happened?"

"No, I don't!" Claire exclaimed, her patience now exhausted.

"That bacon sold like hot cakes! The customers were almost snatching it away from each other. What do you say to that?"

"Oh, most remarkable!"

"Yes, wasn't it! Yes, those strange sort of things do happen in our business. But it wouldn't do to make a rule of it. . . . Do they eat this sauerkraut in the kitchen?"

"I gave some out," Claire replied.

"And what do the servants think of it? Their taste would be a useful guide."

"Now listen," said Claire. "You can ask them afterwards. We are not here to discuss the tastes of servants!"

"Oh, all right, all right." Edmond said. "I will ask them. . . . The opinion of underlings is often most valuable, you know. There's an odd-job man I've got at the office—Lepitois, his name is—who has an amazing palate for the Roquefort we sell for snacks—they serve it in the cafés with white wine. I never buy any Roquefort without consulting him. And we have a girl, Adèle Glatard, in the forwarding branch who knows the tastes of our customers to a T. I always rely on her when we are stocking our branches in outlying districts."

With his mind wholly taken up with the cares of his profession, Edmond fell into a profound reverie. His methods of managing the Silken Net differed from those of his father. M. Constant Euffe had never wished to depart from the principle of selling only high-grade goods of the best quality. But he was a formidable buyer, a champion exponent, such as one never sees nowadays, of the dictum that "a penny is a penny," and well able to reduce commercial brokers and producers alike to a state of exhaustion. He showed himself to be ruthlessly exacting, with an incredible capacity for stubborn bargaining. In addition to this he was, until his later years, an indefatigable worker. He had indeed, as he himself was wont to say, carried the whole business on his own shoulders. And what efforts, what wholesale sacrifice this had cost him!

Edmond was already beginning to drop these compulsive and exacting methods. He was giving up much less time than his father to the Silken Net, did not himself receive all the brokers nor all those with goods to sell, and was ceasing to give the firm its customary smooth running by means of personal pressure and drive and constant and unremitting vigilance. He was throwing over old purveyors, giving up brands which had stood the test of time—a thing which his father would never have done—and had an increasing tendency to go in for speculation, saying to himself: "The business is in full swing." He thought of the Silken Net as an organization which most conveniently supplied him with his wealth, and he did not regard catering as a kind of priesthood.

"In any case, our generation is more emancipated," he said to himself. "And Father had a poor sort of life, a restricted life. What is the use of money if you don't take advantage of it?"

He allowed himself a certain amount of leisure. And so it was that, feeling rather overworked after his business with the sauerkraut and tomato juice, he had decided that day to take an afternoon's rest, although Saturday was an important day in the catering business.

"What are you going to do now?" his wife asked him.

"I thought of going to the club."

"Yes," said Claire, "it would be a good thing if you put in an appearance there more often. You keep too much in the background. And before that?"

"I don't know . . . I shall rest a little . . ."

"You wouldn't care to come with me to the private view of this art exhibition?"

"What exhibition?"

"Oh, come, I've talked to you about it!"

"Oh, so you did! So sorry . . ."

"There will be paintings by Grenoble artists. Flandin, Sahut, and water colours by Jean Hesse, and some pictures sent by the Lyon group, with Morillon, Didier, Laplace, Ponchon, Salendre, and that young Couty—you know who I'm talking about?"

"No, not exactly," Edmond said.

"Well, it doesn't matter. Are you coming?"

"Well, Claire, I don't think I am. I'm not feeling very well. A bit of a headache . . ."

"It's that sauerkraut of yours! You ought not to have eaten that beastly stuff. . . . Yes, I know your father used to do it. But you are not as strong as he was, and you haven't got his digestion—nor his manners, thank Heaven! Is it cold outside?"

"No," Edmond said, "not at all. But it will be chilly this evening."

"I'll take a fur. It looks smarter. The prefect will be there, and the general, and the curator. I simply love Andry Farcy's stories, when he's

126

in good form. And he's a man who has managed to bring our museum into great prominence."

Edmond Euffe, now alone, had coffee served to him in a small room which he kept for his own use. The radiator was on at full strength, giving out a suffocating heat, and his stomach was very uncomfortable.

"Claire was right," he thought. "It's that beastly sauerkraut."

But he corrected himself straightway, feeling that he could hardly apply this description to a commodity which he was about to put on sale and for which he had a bill outstanding for a sum of eighty thousand francs.

"After all, it's not the sauerkraut's fault if I don't digest it."

He was feeling slightly feverish, with little shivers which, however, were by no means disagreeable and inclined him to sleepiness. He let his thoughts wander at will and they went off at a somewhat erotic tangent, a thing which had been happening to him much more often lately, especially when his digestion was not working well. He called to mind a certain person who was applying for the management of his Voiron branch. He had received her in his office three days previously. She was a dark-haired woman, solidly built, with keen, bright eyes having considerable warmth in them. Her appearance suggested firm, white flesh, an ample posterior with tightly closed median parting, and armpits like a jungle. Doubtless this exciting person had but little distinction about her. But Edmond had had a surfeit of distinction in love. What he now preferred was rich physical abundance and an appearance of eager consent. He turned up his applicant's name in his small notebook: it was Irma Moufeton. She was a young widow, and Voiron is not far from Grenoble. Arrangements could easily be made, with visits two or three times a week. This would be in no way to the detriment of Claire, who never responded willingly to effusions nor without endless preliminary fuss and preparation at her dressing table. What Edmond Euffe desired was something more primitive and brutal, with more savour of the wild beast about it.

He drank a glass of liqueur brandy and diverted himself with some imaginary liberties taken with the sturdy frame of Irma Moufeton. But this must have fatigued him, for he closed his eyes and went to sleep in his armchair.

He was awakened later by the sound of his own voice, and heard himself declaring:

"Nine francs a box, that's surely a good price to get!"

He realized that his subconscious was still struggling with the sauerkraut and sausage. The clammy state of his mouth warned him that his digestive processes were not yet entirely completed. He poured himself out another glass of brandy; and as he was raising it to his lips, a servant came in and announced Bob de Bazair.

"How are you, old chap?" said Bob, with the offhand, free-and-easy manner of the young lordling. "I'm not disturbing you?"

"No, no, not at all," said Edmond grudgingly.

He was not prepared for this interview, and was afraid of being caught unawares. A poor improviser, he was one of those men who, whatever the business may be, prefer to be armed with relevant documents which they have studied in advance.

"Look here, old man," said Bob, "perhaps you can guess why I am here?"

"No, I'm afraid not," Edmond said in a feeble tone of voice, suspecting that there was trouble ahead.

"In actual fact," Bob said, "it is the count, my noble father, who should be paying this visit, and paying it moreover to Mme. Euffe, your worthy mother. The object of this meeting of ours today is therefore only to pave the way, to tell you of the count's proposed visit and to judge of its timeliness."

"The count wishes to see my mother?"

"Yes," said Bob, "and the sooner the better."

"What about?—if it is not indiscreet to ask you . . ."

"Not the very slightest, my dear chap. . . . You have a taste for old brandy, it seems?"

"From time to time," Edmond said. "Will you have some?"

"What year is it?"

"Eighteen ninety."

"Then I should like some. As my kinsman de Romain says, 'Liqueur brandy must be perfect, otherwise I've no use for it.' Yours is excellent. Now to put it shortly, this is what I've come about. Your sister Alberte and I have quite made up our minds. We think, therefore, that the time has arrived for informing the two families and proceeding in the usual way. The count will pay his formal visit when I ask him to do so. Do you know him?"

"Very little," said Edmond.

"Quite so!" Bob said. "Very few people can flatter themselves that they really know him. And I myself, his son, hardly know him better than you do, though I go and see him regularly. He's a queer stick, but a gentleman to his fingertips."

"Of course," Edmond said.

128

"Yes, and a gentleman who never puts himself out in any way except for great occasions. For though he may not show it, he looks down on everyone born later than 1900. But I introduced Alberte to him, and he was kind enough to think her charming. I think we should now take advantage of his being in such a good frame of mind. Don't you agree?"

"Look here," Edmond said, "I don't quite follow you. What has my sister Alberte got to do with all this?"

"You really are an amusing fellow," Bob said, smiling, "you don't listen to what I'm telling you! Well, I must start all over again. I intend to marry your sister Alberte, and she intends to marry me. Oh, I can see a possible objection of yours. . . . But when the count raised this question of birth—to which, my dear chap, I myself attach little importance—I told him very definitely that I intended to disregard it. He had the good sense not to insist. And Alberte's charm did the rest. You can see now that everything has been smoothed out. The count will be courtesy itself, you need have no fear about that."

"But this is the first I have heard of the proposal," Edmond said. "And Alberte is under age."

"A few months only. We could have waited for her coming of age. But this would have been a shoddy thing to do, it seemed to me. It would be better that your sister should become a de Bazair with the full consent of her own family. You would not see any objection in her becoming a countess someday?"

"None at all, doubtless," said Edmond. "But in the meantime . . . Forgive my asking you this question. What sort of job have you got at the present time?"

"My dear Edmond," Bob replied, "I have been devoting this early portion of my life to my own culture."

"To your culture?" Edmond exclaimed in astonishment.

"That is what I said—to my culture. I know that this word is usually given a narrow and stupidly pedantic meaning, with which I do not agree. What I am speaking of is the culture of a nobleman of the twentieth century, corresponding to that of my ancestors, who were instructed at an early age in the use of arms and the arts of riding, hunting, love, and insolence. Now listen, my dear chap. I am regarded as a good tennis player; I have driven Bugatti cars in races; I hold the Laffrey amateur hill-climbing record for motor bicycles; I can do the crawl stroke in swimming and I do the 120-yard sprint; I fence; I am a very cool poker player; I dance, and I go in for yachting and skiing; I play golf; I am a trout fisher and I shoot; I have had a few very eligible mistresses; I have some experience of fast living, cocktails and cigars. I know people of every class and in every walk of life, from waiters to dukes. I think I have made good use of my time and acquired enough experience to give me a successful and happy future."

"Oh, I think you have. . . . But I must go back to the question I asked you: what means have you for keeping up a certain style of living?"

"That, my dear fellow, is one of those questions that one doesn't put to a de Bazair! However, I will tell you that I am in no difficulty. I have several plans which I shall choose from when the time comes. In any case, with the name I bear I shall be on all the administrative councils in the district within the next few years. The count has kept steadily aloof from business, but my own ideas on that point are more up-to-date. And by the way, only to mention the Silken Net, I shall be having suggestions to make to you. A business that is not going forward is doomed."

"You need have no anxiety so far as the Silken Net is concerned. It is doing very well indeed," Edmond said stiffly.

"I'm quite sure it is," said Bob. "But businesses get ill sometimes just as people do. You have to have remedies in store for them. . . . But I don't want to intrude any longer. May I rely on you to let me have your family's reply as regards the count's—my father's—visit? You will understand that I cannot expect the old gentleman to make the journey here unless he is assured of a good welcome! And Alberte, who is a sensitive girl, would be distressed if in a few months' time she had herself to get you to do certain things. I am counting on you, my dear Edmond. And thanks for the brandy, which is really excellent."

"Well, of course, it was bound to happen!" Edmond Euffe said to himself after Bob's departure. Thinking of the latter's easy, assured manner and his sister's air of determination, it seemed probable to him that in spite of Claire and the general's wife the marriage would take place, and he felt no inclination whatever to put up a fight.

"After all, why not? . . . Alberte will bear a fine old name, and this boy seems quite equal to shifting for himself in life. 'The nobly born must nobly do,' as the saying goes."

He wondered whether he should go out. But it was to be a day of mishaps. Edmond poured himself out a third glass of liqueur brandy, when a servant appeared and told him that a lady was asking to speak to him.

"What lady? Did she give her name?"

"She said that it was personal and confidential."

"Show her in," Edmond said, after a hesitation.

He saw approaching him a pretty young woman, of generous build, with red eyes and apparently in terrible distress. She had hardly sat down when she burst into a flood of tears and seemed scarcely able to breathe. The air was no longer reaching her lungs, and her rather strongly developed bosom rose in quick spasms, which were moving to witness. After some time she succeeded in getting out the words "It's frightful!" and her paroxysm grew even worse than before.

Edmond Euffe was completely helpless in face of this despair whose origin he did not know. The lady was dressed with a certain elegance which, however, included some small details in poor taste. "She's not our class," he said to himself. Nevertheless, as her tears were not spoiling her dull complexion and were giving an interesting brilliance to her dark and sombre eyes, he began to feel that she held a certain fascination for him. He realized why this was so: she was like Irma Moufeton. She belonged to that type of woman of strong build whose bodies move and stir like the gentle eddies of a tranquil ocean, and who moan in the night, sirens with dishevelled hair. He poured out a little brandy and offered it to his visitor, who took the glass from him almost unconsciously. She swallowed the alcohol, and with it her tears. But this restorative failed to give her back her speech, nor did it still the surge and swell of her breast, whose rich abundance could be seen through the opening at the neck of her dress, still heaving with the violence of her grief.

"Well, madame, who are you?"

Amidst her sobs and fits of coughing she managed to utter these words:

"Madame Félix Lacail . . ."

"You don't mean to say . . . Madame Lacail of the Rue Turenne?"

A nod indicated that this was only too true. Then she said again:

"It's frightful!"

"Oh, no doubt, no doubt . . ." Edmond said, wishing to convey thereby that the past was the past and that nothing could be done to alter it.

He was greatly surprised by this belated display of hopelessness and grief. And he continued to be much affected by Flavie Lacail's opulent charms, and the vast movement as of a surging sea which was pervading this body of a Juno in despair. He would fain have lavished consolation on her—consolation of an affectionate, indeed of a physical nature—have sunk like a stone into some oblivion shared with her, so deep that embraces and caresses would become a primitive and simple need, her only means of rescue and salvation. There are moments when one could wish to see opening out before one's eyes a yawning chasm in some other sphere, wherein one would have but to open one's arms to find within their embrace some lovely, throbbing form, so wrapt and lost in sobbing and distress that every vestige of all that holds us back from yielding to age-old instinct would vanish and be destroyed. Impelled by such feelings of dizziness and bewilderment as these, Edmond had come and bent over Flavie's neck, whose scented emanations he inhaled; and he was beginning to take the young woman by the armpits with a feeling of pity that was unconsciously desperate and wild, and was about to say words to her with which some obscure impulse was prompting him: "Oh! my darling, my darling, what is the matter with you?" But Flavie herself intervened.

"Your brother!" she cried out. "Your poor brother!"

"What is that you're saying—my brother?" Edmond murmured.

"I am wondering whether we should warn the police . . . I wanted to ask your advice . . ."

At the word police Edmond had drawn back. He was gradually becoming able to take stock of the situation in which he was placed, and his own social importance.

"The police? Explain yourself, madame!"

"Monsieur, come with me. Come with me, I beg of you!"

"But where do you want me to go?"

"To my flat," Flavie said. "Your brother is there."

"My brother Germain?"

"Yes. He is wounded. Come, monsieur. Quickly."

"Yes, I will come. But will you explain?"

"Oh, it's frightful—frightful . . ." Flavie said.

The winter had seemed endless, and its dispersal long delayed. March and April, following in its train, were damp and rainy, buried in a thick mist by which, save for an occasional lift therein, the mountaintops were continuously concealed. These were capped with low clouds which filled the valleys with a damp, depressing white mist. A raw, bitter wind swept the avenues of Grenoble, bringing heavy showers of ice-cold rain that lashed the faces of the passers-by. In the flats and houses, where large fires were still burning, people were depressed and bored, ill-tempered and benumbed with cold, longing for their outdoor pleasures and excursions and a gay and cheerful countryside. The hotelkeepers were looking upwards each morning at the hostile skies, whose threatening aspect would not allow their establishments to fill with guests. The café proprietors had despaired of being able to set out the tables on the pavements. The snow was still up there, up on the heights, a dirty snow with bare patches in it, which was refusing to depart from the high grasslands and let their whole extent be seen. The Sapey and the de Porte passes remained hidden in the mist, and the motorcars were skidding on a thin coating of ice. There was already talk of the season becoming a failure for mountain climbing, touring, and cycling, a season interlarded with rumblings and roarings, mountain cataracts, and storms.

And then suddenly, on Friday the second of May, there was a little burst of spring. It was not an obvious, wholehearted spring, but nevertheless one could smell its breath of lilac, and the sky, above the mountain peaks which could now once more be seen, had hung out a fine new standard of heavenly blue. There are certain times of the year, at the passing of the seasons, when the women burst into blossom like flowers heavy with pollen. The women of Grenoble, walking briskly along with sprightly swaying of the hips, put themselves out to smile and look their best, and the men saw therein a good omen. But was all this a foretaste, a signal, or was it mere deception? Time would show. In Dauphiné spring may make false starts, may bring joys that have no real foundation.

The Saturday fulfilled the promise of the day before. The quality of the light which set the Moucherotte and the St.-Eynard sparkling could only be the herald of a perfect day. Thousands of hearts began to beat with a different rhythm, songs came welling up on many lips. The pretty cyclists of Grenoble brought life and movement to the avenues with their graceful riding and the spectacle of their agile legs. Plans put aside were taken up again. Happiness seemed a thing of marvellous simplicity, already in one's grasp.

That day at about one o'clock, in the Rue Turenne, a man was making his way downstairs in a block of flats, carrying on his shoulder a precious bicycle of aluminum tint, which he was taking great care not to knock against the walls. The man emerged from the exit passage, propped up his machine on the pavement, and set about completing the preparations with which a cycle-touring fanatic starts off on a long and methodically conducted trip.

This fervent cyclist had a carefully thought out rig for the practice of his favourite sport. He wore golfing plus fours which leave the knees plenty of freedom for pedalling, with the pockets buttoned up with safety tabs. He had woollen stockings which kept his feet warm in his low, light shoes, a woollen sweater over his jumper, and over the sweater a loose waterproof garment cut like those worn by skiiers, which was done up with a zipper.

133

The cyclist weighed his machine with satisfaction, happy in the knowledge that its weight barely reached twenty-four pounds, with its half-balloon tyres of pure Pará rubber, its two infallible brakes, its mudguards, its loud bell, its electric lights, and its speed indicator. It was the best machine of its class obtainable, with duralumin accessories throughout, and strong, handy, and light. With no less satisfaction he raised the wheels one after the other and set them revolving, and verified the perfect centering of the rims. He tested the chain on each of the eight gearings, which gave ratios varying from $2\frac{1}{3}$ to $8\frac{2}{3}$ yards, a scale devised to enable the rider to go everywhere, whatever the gradient, road quality, or wind resistance might be.

Having done all this, the cyclist then turned his attention to his equipment. He put away in his knapsack and secured on his luggage carrier a small camping outfit, provisions, a surgical dressing case, a repairing outfit, a flask of brandy, some easily accessible tools, et cetera. Every object had its right place, interior or exterior, which varied according to the likelihood of its being required. Everything was done up with straps or elastic bands. When this was finished the man stood back and gazed at his machine, wondering whether he had forgotten anything. And he had: upstairs in his flat, on a corner of the mantelpiece, he had left a little box containing a spare link of a chain, some valve caps, and some insulating tape. He went back into the house and once more climbed the stairs. As he opened the door a feminine voice called out to him:

"Have you forgotten something?"

"Yes," he said impatiently.

"You'll be late."

"I know, I know."

He found the box and took possession of it.

"Good-bye!" he called out.

"You'll be back tomorrow evening, then?"

"Yes, tomorrow evening."

"Don't go and overtire yourself."

"No fear of that!"

Félix Lacail left his home again in haste, leaving the tender Flavie alone, and without having observed that she was making elaborate use of beauty preparations in her room. He made his way down the stairs at great speed, and on arriving at the bottom in the passage, as he was still holding his bunch of keys he automatically opened the letter box, where he found a note addressed to himself and marked "Personal." The handwriting was unknown to him.

"Oh, bother it . . ." he said to himself.

He stuffed the letter into his pocket. Nothing seemed so urgent as to jump onto his machine and hasten to join his friends, fervent cyclists like himself, who were waiting for him near the level crossing, at the entrance to the tree-lined walks of Pont-de-Claix. There is an extraordinary feeling of pleasure as one starts pedalling with lively and supple movement that speeds you along a sunny road in a spirit of happy, carefree adventure that has its stiff, difficult moments of hard exertion. But these toilsome efforts bring a feeling of conquest as the cyclist takes their measure and rises superior to them . . .

Félix Lacail had not been out for a long excursion for a considerable time past. He was wondering whether his leg muscles and wind would be in sufficiently good trim to enable him to tackle the mountain slopes. But no sooner was he spinning along the macadam of the street than he had the pleasant sensation, so dear to the cyclist's heart, of "slipping along on butter." His pedal strokes carried him forward with no effort on his part, and he would then slide along listening to the click of his freewheel. He felt himself amply rewarded for the care he bestowed on his machine, constantly improving its mechanical adjustments, dismantling chain and bearings, cleaning and lubricating, and so forth. It was his chief diversion, his one great pleasure on the dark winter days. He would then install himself in his kitchen surrounded by a miscellaneous collection of tins and cans, solutions, lubricating grease, keys, pliers, rags; and there, softly whistling old tunes and messing about with dirty oil and grease, he made his different adjustments with finicky, meticulous care. When he had got through all this attention to his machine his thoughts still dwelt upon it, and he was never tired of looking through the most recent of the manufacturers' catalogues. He tested every one of those small inventions that make cycling an art of diminishing, of lightening points of friction and lessening this resistance to movement. He had needed two years and numerous timekeeping tests to reach a final state of perfection in his gear ratios and adjustments.

"Ah," Flavie said one day, in a state of exasperation, "you pay less attention to your own wife! If I got one quarter of the care you take of that filthy bike of yours that clutters up my kitchen . . ."

"A woman," Félix Lacail calmly replied, "doesn't carry you to the highest point of the Grande Chartreuse mountain group or help you to cover a hundred and twenty to two hundred miles every week end."

"You haven't always argued like that!" Flavie said. "I can remember a time when you used your bike to chase after me. I couldn't go out without running into you at every street corner."

"There's a time for everything," Félix replied. "Now the bike gives me some healthy pleasure. I strengthen my lungs and do no harm to anybody."

"But I am left alone!"

"It's a pity you don't care about riding! I know women who go with their husbands every excursion they take."

"Oh, thanks!" Flavie remarked, with the listless indifference of a voluptuous woman. "I prefer the movies."

"Everyone to his own taste! Now, if you liked a tandem . . "

"A ghastly thing!" Flavie exclaimed. "Spending hour after hour behind a sweating back that shuts out the view. And toil and moil into the bargain!"

"You're no sport. Still, I don't care a rap for the movies—nor Freddy Glowes. He gets on my nerves, that chap does, and I don't think he's as good-looking as all that!"

"You don't think Freddy Glowes good-looking?"

"No!"

"Well, you've got some nerve to talk like that! It's just jealousy makes you say it. Anyway, all the men are jealous of Freddy Glowes. That only shows how much he's liked."

"Pooh!" said Félix. "In any case, what do I care whether people like him or not? He doesn't come to Grenoble, your Freddy Glowes. And if he did, you can take my word for it there'd be plenty of his fans who'd get a look-in long before you would, my poor dear!"

"Before I should!" Flavie flashed back at him, nettled at this last remark. "What do you know about it? I'm every bit as good as lots of others!"

"You aren't smart enough and you haven't got the right manners. As far as women go, they get the pick of the basket, those young dogs do. Just give a wink, that's all they need to do. They might be princes."

"I'm only the wife of a humble official—that's what you mean, I suppose?"

"Humble—all right, if you like—but highly respectable, and I'll claim full credit for that!"

"A man who's got nothing to talk about, and all he does when he's not playing cards or careering about the roads is to polish up his bike!"

"Look here, Flavie, you weren't a duchess, you seem to have forgotten that!"

"Well, even if I wasn't I might have done better. When I think of Sylvaine Marchaillou . . ."

"That's quite different!" Félix said. "She was a tart."

"Oh, that . . ."

136

"And how did she make her bit of capital? Who was it paid for the shop that started her off? I know her myself, yes I do! She began in the glove business, as an assistant, in the Place Grenette."

"Anyway, she got out of the glove business all right!"

"Yes, and we know how she did it! A thankless sort of job that must be, don't you think? While you've got a name that's far from having anything shady attached to it. You can carry your head high in Grenoble."

"Yes—and without a sixpence to bless myself with."

"A safe future, and retirement to end up with."

"Retirement in poverty after a second-rate sort of life! We shan't even have a car."

"Shall I tell you something, Flavie? The reason you're discontented is that you don't ride a bike. If you had a good sweat on Sundays it'd do you far more good than all those boring things they dish you out at the movies. You wouldn't like me to buy you a jolly little eight-gear machine like mine?"

"I should want dresses and hats before I'd want that!"

"It's a pity," Félix Lacail said, "that you haven't got the same tastes as me! Yes, it's a great pity for you! People are right in saying that ambition wrecks the world, and not being contented with what you've got."

But Félix Lacail did not draw any alarming conclusions from these disputes. He regarded it as a universal rule that women are changeable and do not know exactly what they want. A proof of this was that for a year past Flavie had ceased reproaching him and allowed him to go out as much as he wished. "She's quieting down," he said. "With her, you've only got to stick to it." And that day, as he was on his way to join his companions for the trip, and smiling as he rode along at the thought of how shrewd a husband he was, Félix Lacail kept saying to himself: "I knew how to manage her. I knew exactly how to manage Flavie! Now I can do anything I like with her." He believed that a woman once conquered is conquered for good and all, and that you can then pass on to other occupations.

For this first day out it was always a question of a trial spin. The itinerary chosen would be Seyssinet, La Tour-Sans-Venin, Pariset, St.-Nizier, on the way to Villar-de-Lans—even though that meant climbing from seven hundred to three thousand eight hundred feet over a comparatively short distance. This was invariably one of the first of the long training runs. As soon as they had arrived up in the mountains they would make a final decision as to the route, whether it was to be by Chevranche or by the Grands-Goulets, descending to Pont-en-Royans and returning home along the Isère valley, on the left bank if one felt lazy, on the right —a longer way—if one were brave.

There were sure to be a few fainthearted people who would suggest sleeping at Villars-de-Lans. But Félix Lacail would resist such a proposal tooth and nail, on the ground that it was not worth while to have gone out with one's full equipment and then sleep at a place as near Grenoble as that. His sedentary profession allowed him to amass considerable reserves of strength which he wished to use up entirely between Saturday midday and Sunday evening. It was delightful to return home dead beat, in a bath of perspiration and overcome by all the keen open air, and then fall asleep immediately after one's last mouthful of supper.

(Flavie had been accustomed to grumble and growl at this, but now she put up with it as with everything else.)

And there was nothing unpleasant in feeling on Monday mornings a certain stiffness which gave some queer sort of pleasure to one's life at the office, which is so helpful to recuperation.

Among the friendly batch of cyclists there were some robust and sturdy fellows who were excellent riders on the flat. But none of them was a better climber than Félix Lacail, a small, sinewy man with a bit of the devil in him. He wanted a triumph every time he went out, with sufficient material to enliven the staff of the prefect's office with accounts of his exploits for a whole week. This man who spent his life in filling up printed forms, examining these, and drawing up lists and returns, thought that athletic feats accomplished on a pair of wheels in the mountains constituted life's finest achievement. It was when riding up gradients of 12 in 100 that he both took his revenges and created new standards of prowess. Lacail could be seen bending low over his handle bar, twisting about in his saddle, and crying out with sneering laughter at a hated rival: "I'd like to get him up here, that Freddy Glowes of theirs!" He was speaking of the foppish individual at Hollywood who wrought havoc in feminine hearts. He knew nothing of Freddy Glowes beyond the picture supplied by his own imagination, but there was hatred in his heart for this dandified person, for something seemed to warn him that this too handsome youth was an offence to every husband. This was the reason why Lacail, at moments of great exertion, would sometimes hurl defiance at Freddy Glowes and challenge him to a trial of strength up there on the Porte or the Lautaret passes. "He'd end up miles behind us and walking, that American would! Flavie would be looking pretty sick!" He believed that cycling exploits could have an overmastering effect on a woman's feelings. He had no doubt that Flavie was in reality flattered by his reputation as a famous hill climber.

For approaching the mountains Lacail was accustomed to adopt a gear of nearly five yards as far as the village of Seyssinet. He then changed to one of four and a half yards and maintained this as far as he possibly could, reserving developments of about four and three yards respectively for the last miles, and beginning at the same time to accelerate his pedal stroke. Once more he now repeated the same process. Making a slow start, he was at the tail of the party as far as Seyssinet, but when in sight of Pariset he began to make up ground. At the sharp turn in the road at Rochetière he went ahead of the rest. Two or three miles before reaching St.-Nizier he made his maximum effort, for it was a rule with him to arrive there first and count the number of minutes by which he had outdistanced the second man.

Everyone had worked hard. A halt was decided upon. The cyclists went to an inn to get refreshments. Lacail remained outside to tighten a strap, and it was in any case against his principles to drink during a run. As he drew out his pocket handkerchief to wipe his forehead, the letter marked "Personal" came with it and fell to the ground. As he was alone, he opened and read it, then read it again. It was a horrible message, with a coarseness and vulgarity that were certainly intentional; the handwriting was faked. and the spelling purposely incorrect. It read as follows: "Lacail, you wretched idiot. Your Flavie is giving you the go-by all the time you are playing the giddy goat on that bike of yours. She has a high old time with her young rascal Saturdays and Sundays when you think she's at the movies. Don't you notice *anything?*"

"Don't you notice *anything?*" That sentence drove suspicion home and anchored it firmly in Lacail's mind. Yes, by jove, indeed he *had* noticed that his wife had become nicer and kinder and easier to live with, and likewise more detached, more indifferent, as though there were some *other source* from which all her needs were being satisfied. A thousand small details of their life together recurring to his mind, and among them Flavie's abstention from unreasonable demands, which only two hours earlier he had attributed to his own cleverness, suddenly became alarming signs. That absent-minded look of hers, that careful attention to dress, that kind of radiance that came from her on certain days . . .

No thought could ever have been farther from the mind of Félix Lacail than that of his wife being unfaithful to him. He could never have believed that a disgrace of that nature would befall an official of the Prefecture, particularly himself. He lived in an armour of self-satisfaction which effectively shielded him from possibilities of such a kind as that, which were reserved for ridiculous and laughable people devoid alike of intelligence and charm. And then, suddenly, up there at an altitude of three thousand five hundred feet, with the world away below him in all its littleness, and Grenoble a mere ant heap at the bottom, his self-confidence began to waver. In the depths of that blue and green abyss where watercourses were sparkling and tiny roofs glittering in the sunshine, a treacherous woman and a young scoundrel were holding him up to ridi-cule. He had a sort of fainting fit, an agonizing sensation which he had already experienced on one occasion two years previously, after climbing the Galibier with an exaggerated expenditure of energy.

He had an impression of an immense void and a deep silence. Red lights danced before his eyes. Nevertheless he found strength enough to go to the inn and join his companions, all of whom noticed how pale he was.

"Listen now," he said. "I'm not feeling well. Carry on without me. I'm going back to Grenoble."

"Oh, it'll go off, Félix. You're feeling a bit faint because you went up too fast."

"I've been up faster than that before now," Lacail said, rather an-noyed. "And I'll do it again. But I'm off colour just now. Something I must have eaten."

"Sort of poisoning, perhaps? It tires you, that kind of thing does."

"Yes," said Lacail, "a sort of poisoning."

"You feel a bit tottery on your legs, and sort of queer all over?"

"Yes," Lacail said.

"And very weak all of a sudden?"

"Yes," he said.

"And a kind of cold shivers?"

"Yes," he said again.

"Then you'd better stop and go somewhere where it's warm. Wait till the weakness goes off."

"I'm going home," Lacail said.

"You wouldn't like someone to go with you?"

The question was put without emphasis. No one was pleased at the prospect of returning to Grenoble and spoiling a week end.

"No, no," Lacail said. "Don't you bother about it. I shall go off, quite slowly. If I should find I couldn't manage it at all, I'd hail a car."

"It's true there are cars passing all the time. Ah, it's a pity you have to leave us, Félix. Very well, then, till Monday. We'll come and inquire."

Félix Lacail got on his machine once more and almost unconsciously started to glide down the great slope, in the reverse direction from that already traversed. It was true that he did not feel well; he was feverish and shivering, and he looked haggard and drawn. Thus he covered a few miles.

He remembered that he had some brandy in his knapsack. He dismounted and drank half the contents of his flask. Then he sat down at the roadside, in a dazed condition. Far away below him he could see the waters of the Drac seething in their stony bed, the church towers of Seyssins and Seyssinet and the roofs of the châteaux of Jarrie, de Bresson, and d'Eybins conspicuous in the sunlight. It was a very lovely day, warm and mild, and gay with flowers and fresh green trees and grass. He thought: "It's some blasted idiot who's trying to make fun of me." He regretted having left his pals: what could he do with himself all alone in Grenoble? But it was too late now to go back. And his doubt and fear broke out afresh. He took another drink from his flask, and the sudden and violent absorption of the alcohol affected him. "The hussy!" he said to himself. "The damned hussy!" He jumped on to his machine, took the firmest possible seat, with his feet pushed tightly into the toe clips and the handle bar closely gripped, and began riding down the slope in a rash and foolish manner, taking wild and senseless risks at the bends and corners. This savage outburst of riding—for such it was—left him no time to think. A certain instinct of self-preservation was working in him; nothing else.

On reaching the level road he began pedalling with all his might. And soon, in a bath of perspiration, he saw Grenoble just ahead of him, with himself on the point of entering it before his brain had come to any decision at all. He drank all that was left in his flask. Then he crept into the town, trying to think out the best way of reaching the Rue Turenne at the point nearest to his house, in order to escape notice by his neighbours. He arrived just opposite the passageway and there he nimbly stowed away his machine. Then he crept stealthily upstairs until he reached his own door. It was bolted and locked. He dealt with this, and opened the door, and closed it again noiselessly. He was now in the passage of his own flat, like a thief in someone else's abode, and bewildered at finding himself surrounded by a silence of empty houses which is only found on days of rest and holiday, and in the midst of which a distant wireless was actually giving out the result of a cycle race—and Lacail wanted to listen . . .

But he must get quit of the business—somehow or other. Still without making any noise, he half opened a door. And there before his eyes, on the sofa, was his wife, a Flavie who was quite unknown to him, with her eyes closed and a transfigured expression on her face, which was resting in surrender on a man's shoulder. He was bending over Flavie and whispering some words with his lips close to her hair—quietly, calmly, with depraved and vicious skill. *And this man was Freddy Glowes*—yes, the man himself—that filthy, conceited young puppy from Hollywood, who had taken up his abode in Félix Lacail's flat as though it were his own—Félix Lacail, a member of the staff of a French prefect's office!

"Grinchard is leading, fifteen seconds ahead of Speicher," was heard on the distant wireless.

The shot rang out without Lacail—who nevertheless had taken aim—having any real consciousness of what he was doing. The report was followed by cries. He saw Flavie, her face distorted with terror—and blood, a thin trickle of blood . . . Then he threw his weapon away. It was his "dog pistol," a small pistol with leaden bullets which he used on his bicycle for firing at certain large dogs which jumped at his calves. He opened the door and dashed down the stairs four at a time. On reaching the bottom he took his machine out from the passage, leapt on to it and made off, pursued by the nasal tones of the wireless:

"Grinchard is increasing his lead. Speicher is dropping back among the other competitors. The race will soon be over . . ."

Lacail did not see a man with a sardonic smile who was prowling about in the vicinity and had remained for a long while in a small café in the Rue Lesdiguières, as though he were expecting someone. It was Pamphile Garambois, old Pampan of earlier days. . . .

The Prefecture employee, trying to find a way out of the situation in which he found himself, dashed off in the direction of Vizille without knowing whither he went. He was in such a state of mental disturbance and excitement that over the whole of the five miles which separate Grenoble from Pont-de-Claix the needle of his speed indicator was oscillating around the twenty-two-miles-per-hour mark. Never before had he made such splendid time over that section of road. He went into a wine shop and ordered some white wine, of which he drank two small carafes with a doltish look on his face. Oh, what a to-do there would be at the Prefecture when the story became known! He would lose his job. . . . Wouldn't it be best to go and throw one's self in the Drac, off the old bridge with the Gothic arches? But what the devil was that American doing at his place? In a thick, heavy voice he sought enlightenment from a man who was drinking at the counter and appeared to be a person of vast experience, for words were pouring from him in a ceaseless flow.

"I go home and I find an American kissing my wife. What do I do?"

"You heave him out of the window," the man said.

"Ah," said Lacail, surprised that this had not occurred to him at the time. "And supposing I kill him some other way?"

"Doesn't matter. You'll have done a good bit of work anyway. What about drinks?"

"Yes," said Lacail, delighted to have found so comforting a friend.

142

Nevertheless his uneasy feeling had not entirely left him.

"Don't you think life's a stupid business?" he asked his new companion.

But the other man was unaccustomed to such profound thinking. Especially at a bar where white wine was flowing.

"Well," he said at last, "did you kill the American or didn't you?"

"I did," Lacail answered.

"Then what are you worrying about? You're lying doggo now!"

"Yes, but——"

"Did you kill your wife too?"

"No," Lacail said, "not her. I didn't think of that."

"Perhaps you were wrong," his friend said. "As you were there . . . Once you've got your teeth into a job, better to polish it off at one go."

But Lacail made no reply. Overcome by alcohol, fatigue, and emotion, he had sunk into a chair, and with his head between his arms, which were resting on a marble-topped table, he was already snoring, his wife, the American, and his leap into the Drac now completely forgotten.

. . .

These leaden bullets have very little penetration. They flatten themselves on a hard frame and plough up the flesh, making impressive wounds. Lacail's bullet had struck Germain Euffe in a slanting direction, above the ridge of his brow, and glancing over the bone, had made a diagonal cut in his forehead. There was a deep furrow from which the blood flowed freely, blinding the victim and staining Flavie's dress. She would have fainted had she not been sustained by her very genuine love. Germain, moreover, was speaking, and assuring her that he was not in much pain. She put a first-aid dressing on the beloved forehead while waiting for the water to boil and enable her to cleanse the wound. Then she wrapped up Germain's head in a gauze turban, through which the blood continued to ooze slowly.

The pretty woman was possessed of presence of mind at moments of crisis. It did not appear to her that her lover's life was in any danger, and she took stock of the situation. It would be better that Germain should not be in a doctor's hands until after he had returned home. The Euffes' chief concern would certainly be the avoidance of scandal. He must therefore get away from the Rue Turenne as unobtrusively as possible and return to the Place Victor-Hugo without being observed.

"You must see my brother Edmond," Germain said. "I know it's a nuisance. But one can't rely either on my mother or my sisters. And I can't go home until everyone has agreed on the explanation to be given."

It was settled that Germain should remain shut up in Flavie's flat and not open the door until there was a prearranged signal from her. So Flavie departed to look for Edmond Euffe. Not finding him at his office in Alsace-Lorraine Avenue, she took a taxi and drove to Sassenage, to White Terraces, his country house. It was on the way there that, yielding at last to her emotion, this capable woman burst into sobs and arrived at the home of the director of the Silken Net in a state of the utmost distress.

"Well, madame, I congratulate you! First the father, then the son. You have sworn to destroy our family. Oh, don't cry. Tears have never brought anyone back to life. Otherwise there would be less crying at funerals!"

In his own car, which took them back to Grenoble at great speed, Edmond spoke harshly to Flavie, impelled by the irritation which he was feeling at the prospect of a fresh family complication. His bad temper was also partly due to a secret grudge because the young woman sitting by him had a pleasant scent, a scent which he would have enjoyed if his brother Germain . . .

"Do you think the newspapers will mention anything?" Flavie asked.

"One can always come to some arrangement with the newspapers. The *Dauphiné Gazette* is perfectly safe. I am one of its big advertisers, and they will do anything for me. The *Dispatch* and the *Republic* have other reasons for dealing gently with us. But we shall have to act quickly."

What in the meantime had happened to the murderer, the stupid Lacail? It was to be hoped that that imbecile, seized with a sudden desire to speed the course of justice, had not gone and got himself imprisoned by blurting out the whole story to the first man he met! There were people who would be only too glad to give information. The Euffes had had political enemies ever since Edmond had been more openly siding with the great Conservative upper middle class. In any event rich people, exposed as they are to feelings of envy, always have enemies who may be known to them or not.

"Tell me, now," Edmond asked, "what sort of a man is your husband?"

Flavie made a gesture of contempt.

"Yes, one thinks that sort of thing, and then see what happens! And moreover, it isn't the fools who give one the least trouble—quite the contrary. Ah, you may congratulate yourself on having put us all in a nice hole!"

"And what about me," Flavie said, "am I not the person who is most compromised?"

"You were a perfectly free agent in the matter," Edmond said. "Why on earth couldn't you have chosen a lover somewhere else? What made you set your cap at a member of my family?"

"My heart!" Flavie said.

"Yes, yes. I understand," Edmond murmured, in a way which seemed to attribute to Flavie Lacail's heart a warmth of feeling capable of very interesting manifestations. "But at least you might have refrained from enticing my brother to your own house."

"It was Germain's fault. He wanted to see what my surroundings were like. Sometimes he came here to fetch me. It was just our luck, his staying on here today."

Edmond harked back to his previous question.

"You have no idea what can have happened to your husband? But surely you would know what places he goes to. You ought to start looking for him. He must be feeling fed up and worried just now, and he will be glad to see you again even after what has happened, if you tell him that this business won't have any further consequences. It certainly is deplorable that it won't, if you look at it from the moral point of view. But I don't see anything else to be done about it."

"Oh," said Flavie, "I have no intention of seeing Lacail again. I would rather go away. I shall go back to my mother."

"Where does your mother live?"

"At Domène."

"Domène—well, that's not exactly a lively spot all the year round! If I were you, I shouldn't be in too great a hurry to decide on anything so drastic as that. Were things going very badly at home?"

"Very badly? . . . Well, no."

"There you are, then! And I hope you will leave my brother alone now!"

"You mean that I mustn't see him again?"

"Oh come, come, what do you think I mean?"

"I think," said Flavie, "that I would rather die!"

"Now listen," Edmond said, "you had better postpone your death for a bit longer. I can assure you that we have had quite enough trouble for today!"

At that moment they were turning off into the Rue Turenne. Flavie pointed out the house.

"It is here," she said. "And what are you going to do with Germain?"

"I think I shall take him with me to Sassenage. I shall warn our mother of his absence. That will give us a little time to look around."

They got out of the car and were about to enter the building when Edmond suddenly stopped and gazed at the pavement.

145

"By the way," he said, "it was here that my father got the vase?"

"Yes," Flavie said, turning her head away.

"On the fifth of May last year."

"It will be a year ago in two days," Flavie said sadly.

Then she added, with a sigh:

"When Fate is dead set against you . . ."

They went upstairs to Germain, who was waiting for them in a state of mind divided between pride at being a central figure in a catastrophic love affair, terror lest he were permanently disfigured, and fear that he might have brought the family good name into disrepute.

In the course of the following night a cyclist was picked up, on the Pont-de-Claix road, who had run into a motorcar. No responsibility was incurred by the driver, owing to the fact that the cyclist was zigzagging dangerously on the roadway, appearing in and vanishing from the beam of the headlights in a reckless and disordered fashion. It was a miracle that there had not been a head-on collision with the bonnet of the car.

The victim was very badly bruised, and his knee could be seen bleeding through a large slit in his breeches. But the only information that could be dragged from him was contained in these strange words:

"I killed the American with my dog pistol!"

"The poor fellow is suffering from shock," a bystander said. "We mustn't hurry him. It seems to have been the end of the American!" he added gently. "Let us forget about that."

"I tell you I killed Freddy Glowes. I killed him a little while ago, while he was kissing Flavie."

"He must have seen that in the film that's on now at the Palace."

Other cars had stopped and were drawn up at the side of the road. Their occupants had assembled in a small group beneath a dark canopy of trees.

"What does he say?"

"He says he killed Freddy Glowes this afternoon," was the answer as people touched their foreheads with their forefingers.

By a piece of good fortune there was a doctor who left his car and approached the scene of the accident. He was a man accustomed to dealing with wounded people. He opened his medical pouch and bent over the ill-fated cyclist.

"There, there, it's nothing, my friend . . . I will put on a field dressing. . . . And now tell me who you are."

"Never!" the victim replied with energy.

"Have you no family at Grenoble?"

146

"My wife is dead. Dead as far as I'm concerned—the whore."

"That is a misfortune," the doctor said patiently.

"No!" the victim cried out.

"Or a blessing," said the doctor in a conciliatory way. "Where would you like me to drive you?"

"Give me an injection and throw me in the Drac. And say nothing to the prefect. He thought a lot of me, the prefect did."

The doctor got up slowly, with a grave expression on his face. In a low voice he gave his opinion.

"It is a case of cerebral derangement resulting from shock."

"Poor man! Will he stay mad?"

"One can't say for certain," the doctor replied. "They're such strange things, these disturbances of the brain. Just imagine, a clot of blood or a bone splinter is quite enough to put one of our faculties out of action or to affect a whole region of our vasomotor system."

However, there was a less learned gentleman who also bent over the victim and was anxious to make to the diagnosis a contribution of his own.

"Tell me, Doctor, don't you think he's just merely drunk?"

But the doctor, who had just given his verdict, rejected point-blank this ignorant suggestion.

"My dear sir," he said curtly, "while I admit that he may have been in that condition, you should know that a traumatism nullifies instantly the effects of ethylism. That is a theory on which I have had the honour of lecturing at the Academy of Medicine. Are you acquainted with the part played by the humoral glands in cases of wounds?"

"No," said the gentleman, who was a manufacturer of footwear in the Romans district.

"Indeed I thought not!" the doctor said.

He called the bystanders to witness, and added:

"It's extraordinary the mania people have in France for poking their noses into everything and talking at random!" Then he finally settled the matter by saying:

"I am going to drive this man to the hospital, and he will be put under observation there."

While the gentleman from Romans, much vexed, kept on saying, "Well, I don't care, I say he's drunk!" the doctor went off to his car. The injured man was placed on the back seat. He appeared to be in a bad way, with his head rolling from side to side. Nevertheless he had a lucid moment, when he cried out at the top of his voice:

"For God's sake, where's my bike?"

He refused to be parted from it. The lovely bicycle was in a lamentable state: the rims were broken, the fork twisted, and the frame buckled. They succeeded in strapping it onto the bumper at the back of the car.

And Lacail set out for the hospital under the shadow of an indictment, not for murder, but for insanity, the charge having been preferred by a doctor who was consigning a man to a padded cell at two o'clock in the morning at the side of a steep road and by the light of an electric torch.

There was another doctor about to step in, a Dr. Lavigerie, a rather intimate friend of the Euffes of Sassenage, having been taken up by Claire, a woman prone to violent fancies. In actual fact her favour was bestowed on him more on account of his social qualities than of his medical skill. Dr. Lavigerie, a handsome, buoyant, even-tempered man, a good talker, an athlete who carried all before him, was a doctor whose patients were healthy and high-spirited people, to whom he expounded his theories on the beneficial effects of swimming ("crawl" stroke), skiing, tennis, bicycling, et cetera. His medicine took no account of illness, but was specially concerned with the harmonious development and general well-being of the human frame. In all places, therefore, where human bodies disport themselves in the open air, you would meet the doctor, in shorts or jersey, or flannel trousers, but usually naked from the waist upwards, for he was a fervent devotee of sun-bathing. He was a sort of doctor for Olympic games or life at a country house, in splendid form at cocktail time and at meals alike, being a fine judge of cooking, wines, old brandy, and cigars. He was amiable, easy to get on with, and a man of considerable culture, the very man, in fact, for doctoring the Venus de Milo, Aphrodite, Apollo, and the Discobolus, that is to say, for moulding perfect muscles and harmonious frames. He was well off, and found difficulty in keeping regular hours for seeing patients. The best of his practice was made up of people who came to him for moral consolation, and drank port or liqueur brandy. And charming women came to tell him all about little physical troubles whose origin was predominantly sentimental.

With an attractive personality, a good talker on many subjects with a plentiful store of anecdotes and of social gossip from Paris, the doctor had the run of the Prefecture and the town hall and was received at the bishop's palace. He was pre-eminently a man in whom one could confide in an embarrassing situation. He could understand everything—and forget it, for his feelings of kindness and indulgence towards humanity were unlimited, as was his aversion from pain, and he had a deep horror of sadness. Edmond sent for him to attend Germain, and without speci-fying any details gave him to understand what had taken place.

"Oh, so he's been playing pranks!" the doctor said. "Well, we all took those risks when we were twenty. Any of us might have been up against a spiteful husband."

He examined the wound and gave his verdict:

"The wound is not at all a serious one. But it must be sewn up at once. That is the first thing to be done to reduce the scar to a minimum. The boy needs that jolly little phiz to be taken care of."

"Where will you do the sewing?" Edmond asked.

"At the Deschailles clinic. I know him very well. I shall ask him to let me use a room there for an hour. It's not the first time he has done this for me. Your brother's name will not be mentioned. And we will bring him straight back here. We can have a rubber of bridge after din-ner, and that will enable me to keep an eye on him for part of the night."

"Will you stay the night here, Doctor?"

"I could manage it, if it will make your mind easier."

At about midnight Flavie telephoned to say that she had seen nothing of her husband. Lacail's disappearance continued to be Edmond's chief anxiety. So long as he remained undiscovered no one could say how things would turn out.

Edmond then decided to tell Dr. Lavigerie the whole story, in strict confidence. It would be easier for the doctor to discover the missing man than it would be for himself, since he would find it difficult to explain why he was taking such keen interest in a man employed by the Prefec-ture.

The doctor then made these comments on the situation as it appeared to him:

"The reactions of a man whose wife has been unfaithful to him are sometimes surprising. But in any case running away doesn't do him any good, for he's got to stop somewhere. This chap may have got himself run in by the police. But he might have had an accident. Before we warn the police it would be as well to try the hospitals. I'll see to that first thing tomorrow. Let us have another whisky and then go and sleep."

With the assistance of friends in his own profession, Dr. Lavigerie had no difficulty in tracking down a strange monomaniac describing himself as "the man who murdered the American." The description of the mad-man supplied by them was similar in every detail to that of her own hus-band given to him by Flavie. whom he had been careful to go and see

149

at the outset. He found her physically interesting, but morally in a state of great indecision and doubt after a lonely and sleepless night during the whole of which she had been pondering on the dismal prospect of a return to her mother's home. At Grenoble, Flavie Lacail was included in the category of "ladies." What would she be at Domène, with a scandal behind her, without much money, and alone with a miserly old woman in her dotage? She had a certain fondness for her mother, but could not bear her company for more than twenty-four hours on end. In the same way the widow Pansaque was fond of Flavie and complained at not seeing her more often, but her daughter's presence failed to bring about the slightest interruption in the dreary round of her fads and fancies and her endless tales of woe. She was becoming like an old witch, with her attentions divided between a patch of garden which she scratched up with her fingers, a mangy dog, and a few wizened old gossips who were forever harking back to the same old stories of a bleak and lowly past.

The situation in which the Lacail husband and wife now found themselves was one of those which Dr. Lavigerie was accustomed to go ahead and unravel with gay and hearty courage. Above all, life must not become a thing that irritates and annoys! Such was his leading principle. He tried hard to persuade Flavie that a resumption of her life with her husband would be by far the least disaster that could occur.

"If I were to tell you the number of alarums and excursions of this kind that have been followed later on by real and deep affection! There are certain couples who need these shocks to enable them to appreciate each other as each deserves."

But Flavie, who was filled with a great love from which she could not tear herself away, felt horror and dismay at the mere possibility that such sentiments as these could be applied in Lacail's case. Thereupon Dr. Lavigerie summoned immorality to his aid, a course from which he did not shrink in case of need, knowing as he did that there are certain poisons that heal.

"And what of Germain Euffe?" he said. "Think of that boy with a bit of affection in your heart. What will become of him if he sees you no more?"

"Oh, Domène isn't far away . . . And I shall be free. But will he ever forgive me?"

"If he knows that you are here and thinking of him, I am sure he will," the doctor said. "Believe me, everything can still be arranged, arranged as it was before."

"As it was before? It would be too lovely!"

"Come, come now," the doctor said, "don't get disheartened! I shall bring your husband back to you soon. Be firm with him. And make him see where he was in the wrong. For in some ways he most certainly was."

"I should just say so!" Flavie exclaimed.

"I am going to convince him of that myself. And I assure you that I shall bring him back as humble as you please. And you can take my word for it that he will not be sorry to see his house and his pretty wife again, after thinking he was done for. And after that it'll be up to you to take him well in hand."

The doctor had not been telling the truth. It was no part of his plan that Flavie's and Germain's affair should be resumed. But he did not hesitate to employ any means whatsoever for bringing the husband and wife together again, which would debar Flavie from any further pursuit of Germain and from playing the martyr.

Dr. Lavigerie found Félix Lacail in a condition most favourable to his purpose, that is to say, ill from his excesses of the previous day and in a state of complete moral collapse. Obscure regions of his memory clutched at certain gestures of which his actual recollection was hazy and indistinct, but which he knew intuitively to have been disastrous. His mood was that of a man condemned to the gallows and awaiting the last fatal summons. The doctor read this state of mind at a glance and took full advantage of it.

"Well, young man, you killed the American, so I hear?"

At these words a ray of understanding, of sinister intent, made its way into the brain of Félix Lacail and gradually spread therein. He remembered certain allusions to the waters of the Drac. . . . Nevertheless he seemed doubtful that it was the waters of the Drac that had brought about his present disastrous physical condition, which was manifesting itself in a burning sensation in the stomach and an iron band encircling his temples, to say nothing of the contusions which seemed to have stiffened all his limbs. Then he had a glimpse of his wife in the embrace of a shameless and brazen young fop. And finally he had a connected picture in his mind of everything that had been destined to bring about the inevitable ruin of the career of a discreet and careful official, whose best energies were devoted to the all-absorbing ventures of cycle touring. But still he kept wondering about his peregrinations of the night, and how he had managed to become stranded in the cell in which he now found himself. Perhaps he had been shut up in an annex to the prison? . . . But what could Freddy Glowes be doing at Grenoble, and how did he come to be at the Rue Turenne? And what an utter idiot he, Lacail, had been to defy Flavie to attract the notice of the famous young star!

Nevertheless the doctor, speaking down to him from his imposing height, let fall these words, spoken in a calm and ironical tone of voice:

"A pretty piece of work, my boy! And it will make a fine impression at the Prefecture! And what will you be telling the judge at the Assizes, eh? Have you thought about that?"

"Is he dead?" Lacail asked.

The doctor made no reply.

"There is no doubt." he said, "that I can boast of having known some blundering idiots during my life! But an idiot of your calibre makes all the other imbeciles I know look clever by comparison."

Despite the severity of these comments, there could be detected in the doctor's voice some cheerful modulations that could not be associated with a ruthless administrator of justice. The unhappy Lacail, humbly resigning himself to being considered an outstanding and superlative ass, plucked up enough courage to ask timidly:

"Is it very serious?"

Dr. Lavigerie burst into a loud and ferocious laugh, in which, however, a touch of good nature could still be detected. But it was nevertheless disturbing.

"Very serious? What—the Assizes? But that's the road to the guillotine!"

Lacail had a sudden and extremely disagreeable sensation of cold in the nape of the neck, and at the same time was shaken by the nauseous hiccup familiar to executioners which has given rise to the delicate attention, on the part of a tenderhearted community, of the condemned man's nip of brandy. And in fact, in the state of collapse in which he felt himself to be, Félix would have given much for a glass of brandy or a bumper of rather strong white wine. But the doctor kept him fasting, and left him to face the prospect of a pale and ghastly dawn, the last he would ever see—for so long a time as he deemed necessary for the wretched man to wish once more to live.

Seeing him suitably reduced to an utterly limp and helpless condition, the doctor addressed him thus:

"You were a happy man! You had a pleasant, warm, comfortable home. a restful job, a lovely safe outlook, an assured future. Is that so?"

"Yes, it's true," Lacail replied dolefully, thinking of his past life in much the same way as he would of the guillotine set up at early dawn in some open space in Grenoble.

"And you prefer penal servitude or capital punishment to all that?"

152

"But," said Lacail, "my wife . . ."

"Don't speak of her!" the doctor said peremptorily. "You *had* a wife whom you didn't deserve, and who now, thanks to you, is plunged in grief. Now just confess straight out that you were drunk!"

In these last words Lacail saw a faint glimmer of hope that he might yet be saved.

"Yes," he said, "I was drunk."

"Is that any reason for murdering people?"

"But the American was in a nasty sort of attitude . . ." Lacail said.

"How could you tell, if you were drunk? Now, could you—possibly? And you have paid Mme. Lacail the greatest insult that a respectable woman can receive! And now . . ."

A convulsive shudder ran through the wretched Lacail's whole frame.

"Ah, the dirty dog!"

"Of whom are you speaking?"

"The filthy rotter who sent me the anonymous letter!"

"Ah, there we have it!" the doctor said. "There was the fatal anonymous letter! Lacail, you are even stupider than I thought! But look here, you wretched man, if we had to take into account all the anonymous letters that are written in this town, and if every one of them meant that a shot would be fired, how many people do you think would still be alive in Grenoble? You who sort out index cards, you ought to know better than most people that slander and false accusation are merely innocent jokes, and don't in the least prevent people from being friendly to you!"

The doctor had lighted a cigarette. Lacail looked at it with avidity.

"You mayn't smoke in prison," the doctor said. "You will have to get used to that."

Tears began to pour down Lacail's face, the tears of a man who thinks he is done for and has lost all hope. It seemed to the doctor that this was the moment at which to put his scheme into effect.

"Listen to me, Lacail: I am Dr. Lavigerie. You have heard of me?"

"Yes, Doctor."

"You would be very glad if everything became as it was before, and if nothing of what has actually happened had ever happened at all?"

"Oh yes, Doctor!"

"Very well, then, listen carefully to what I say. If you will obey me blindly—I say *blindly!*—perhaps I shall be able to get you out of this hole. . . . Do you promise?"

"Yes, Doctor."

"You have now a choice between going back to the Prefect's office and taking up your work again as though nothing had happened, or standing your trial at the Assizes and going to prison. You have chosen?"

"Oh yes, Doctor!"

"But I make one condition, which must be strictly observed. There is one day of your life which must be forgotten, completely forgotten, and to which you must never allude in the presence of anybody, especially your wife's. Do you swear?"

"I swear, Doctor. . . . But—the American?"

"There never was an American! Being drunk, you fired at a shadow, a hallucination, and risked killing someone who is dear to you. Loss of control, Lacail, is a very serious matter. Whatever you do, keep off drink! I am going to take you home, and you are going to ask your wife's forgiveness. And I will give you a doctor's certificate for the Prefecture. You need a good fortnight's rest. And most important of all—forget everything!" .

9. THE YOUNGER ONES RUN STRAIGHT

"These wounds in the head are either a very serious matter or else they amount to nothing," Dr. Lavigerie had said. "Your brother is young and in perfect health. With good antiseptic treatment the wound should heal in about ten days. Keep him in the country, it will do him good."

The trouble was that Germain, with the ardour of his nineteen years and his taste for chivalrous display, believed in undying passion and the matchless quality of a certain woman's heart. Nothing seemed to him more sublime than Flavie Lacail, nothing more indispensable to his happiness than the sighs and surrenders of this misunderstood and slighted woman, who was exposing herself to the worst dangers for his sake. This young man was now filled with the delirious enthusiasm of a first love, touching in its artless innocence, which nevertheless predisposed him to commission of the grossest follies, of the kind which bring irreparable ruin to a young man's prospects of a career and to his family much distress.

In Germain's eyes Flavie was an incarnation of all the glamour that attaches to the woman of full development and maturity, whose caresses are flattering to a youthful lover's self-esteem. There was some very powerful bond uniting them, some sort of cohesive force that was a mutual attraction of their two natures, each of which was the perfect complement of the other. There were hidden affinities between them, to which

154

Germain was more ready to yield than she, still ignorant as he was of the precautions we need to take on life's journey and what hidden dangers the realm of feeling contains. Of all these, Flavie's thirty years made her the better judge, and her outbreaks never robbed her entirely of lucid and balanced thought.

Germain and Flavie had given no really serious thought to the future, having seen no farther ahead than the wonder and amazement of their mutual pleasure one morning of springtime amid the universal joy of rising sap and seed. The success of their first embrace had been too complete for them not to be tempted to meet again. There was something fervent and tender in Germain—something very young if the truth were told; while in Flavie long-standing aspirations, which with Lacail had found no outlet at all, were now finding sudden and almost overwhelming realization in the arms of a young gentleman with fair skin and blushing cheeks (but eager to a degree) and soft and pleasant wavy hair.

The future . . . This was the problem set by Lacail's pistol shot, and it demanded an immediate answer and some big decisions. Strongly urged by Edmond and Dr. Lavigerie, Flavie was occupying, in her own home, a position of withdrawal, while awaiting the turn of events. She would have felt stronger had Germain been there to support her, and would have been quite capable of following him blindly if he had said to her: "Let us go." Deprived of the only masculine protection which had any importance for her, she was allowing her destiny to be shaped or decided by such events as might occur. She kept saying to herself that she could not live without Germain, but did not dare to make any decision with her lover away.

That young man straightway showed more spirit and determination, and perhaps also more ignorance, as his brother declared. The pistol shot, while it had in no way lessened his passion, had increased his pride. He thought Flavie wonderful—Flavie who had had no thought but for him, to care for him and to save his life. He spoke seriously of making her leave everything and taking charge of her himself. Edmond Euffe was enraged at this.

"But, you young idiot, what will you do with her when you've got her on your hands? You will marry her, perhaps?"

"Why not?" Germain replied, his head encased in bandages.

"And can you see yourself with a woman ten years older than you are?"

"Age doesn't matter."

"You don't think so? Wait till you are ten years older and then come and talk to me about it again. Or rather, about something quite different, because this business is finished and done with. Get that well into your head. Can you see yourself married to a woman of no birth whom no one will want to come and see and who won't be asked anywhere?"

"I don't care two hoots for people. I don't need them."

"Now, now!—if you think you can shut yourself up with a woman and do without seeing another soul! You'd soon be sick of it. It's pleasant enough to meet a mistress here, there and everywhere and spend a few hours with her. But don't you ever fall under the thumb of a jealous old woman to whom you will have given rights. And this Flavie of yours hasn't got a sixpence!"

"But I shall be rich!"

"Still more reason! Let beggars marry each other, that is as it should be. But wealth brings duties with it. And the first of these is to show a united front. We have to build a solid wall to keep out all covetous people. If the rich don't stand shoulder to shoulder it's all up with them. Surely you must see that! Just take my own case. Do you imagine that I enjoy everything in life? Don't you think there are times when I feel I should have preferred some nice, pretty, simple girl? Don't you think . . ."

"Are you not happy?" Germain asked, a little disturbed by his brother's questions.

"I'm not discussing happiness at all! Happiness isn't a matter of enthusiasm and excitement, but of an average, calmer sort of feeling that is made to last. That is what I mean! Good heavens, we all get fancies into our heads. . . There are women who flit across our path and seem to us . . . But that isn't life!"

"What is life, then?" Germain asked. "Boredom, perhaps."

"Yes," Edmond said solemnly. "Yes, my dear chap, you must learn to face boredom. You must learn renunciation."

"For what purpose? To go—where?"

"To go straight!" Edmond said. "You are an Euffe. One day you will feel you need a certain dignity to display to the world."

"You make me laugh!" said Germain. "Mother is half mad, Lucie entirely so. And Alberte is going to make a marriage that you are all opposed to. I don't see why I should be the only one to be sacrificed. Do you think that Father, at my age, would have given way in a case like mine?"

"Oh," said Edmond, "that is not the same thing at all! Father married Mother. He might just as well have married someone like Flavie Lacail. At the point he started from, it wouldn't have mattered in the least. He could do anything he liked. But Father worked the whole of his life in order that you should not marry a divorced Mme. Lacail. Do you understand?"

"No," Germain said obstinately.

"Look now, my boy, Father put us higher up than he was himself. Are you going to fall back again, straightway?"

"Your beastly vanity, your dirty pride!" Germain cried out.

"Yes, yes," said Edmond. "Call it what you like!"

"It's your 'princess' who puts those ideas into your head!"

"I know," Edmond said slowly, "I know what you all think of Claire. But Claire has meant for me a rung in the ladder—and I've climbed it, and I am climbing others every day. If Father were alive, I am sure he would say to us: 'Go on, children, you must go still higher.'"

"Oh, Father," Germain exclaimed, laughing derisively, "he climbed a long way up—with his Riri!"

"He had every right to her, after all he'd done for us—and it was no business of ours anyway."

Suddenly Germain burst out sobbing. He stammered out:

"I didn't want to say unkind things about him, you know I didn't! I was very fond of him."

"I know, Germain," Edmond said. "Each of us loved him in our own way, perhaps without knowing it. One day you will understand how much was accomplished by that simple, uneducated man. I often think of it—I who have control of the organization he left us."

Edmond truly meant what he said. He was speaking of his social mission with a seriousness which seemed to increase his moral stature, while it committed him to a strict loyalty to the interests of his class. At the same time he was discovering that he had a feeling of affection for his brother stronger than he would ever have suspected. Germain realized all this.

"Then what am I to do?" he asked.

"You are going to close this chapter of your youth, which is only an unimportant preface. And you are going to turn your real life in another direction."

"Then I shall never be happy again!" Germain exclaimed. "Never, never!"

"Child!" Edmond said, putting his arm round his younger brother's shoulder. "You don't know what you are talking about."

"Oh," said Germain, "you don't in the least mind condemning me to suffer!"

"I am not denying this suffering of yours. But do you think you are the only one? Don't you believe that others have suffered before you? That I myself have suffered in the past?"

At this point Edmond was exaggerating slightly. But as he watched his brother's grief, he felt that he himself had once endured some sorrow no less painful than his.

"You?" Germain asked.

"Well, yes," Edmond said, "why not? What has happened to you is nothing out of the way. When I was just about your age I broke off a liaison, because it was necessary that I should. It was *necessary*, you understand. You won't remember it, you were too young at the time. But I was like you, I thought there was nothing left worth living for. . . And now I never give it a thought. And fancy, it's you who are reminding me of it!"

"And there's nothing you regret?"

"Absolutely nothing, old boy, I swear!"

"That means you didn't really love her!"

"Anyhow, I certainly believed I did, and it came to the same thing. (Don't go and imagine that you have invented love!) I did violence to my own feelings and I knew later on that I had acted for the best. . . . But look here, I can tell you, without giving her name. It so happened that I met her again by chance a few years later. And I thanked Father for having advised me as I am advising you today. It is really as a memento of what he once said to me that I am talking to you in this way. I am paying off a debt that I owe to his memory. As he is not here, I am saying it myself: 'Drop all that, my boy. Be a man.'"

"And if I couldn't manage to?" Germain said. "If it were to kill me . . ."

"If it were as bad as all that, well . . . But that is an argument you've no right to use until you have tried all your power of resistance. Start with a really genuine effort—some months of it. If in a few months' time you come back to me and say, 'I would rather die,' I promise you, Germain, not to stand in your way any longer. So now I've given you my word. Will you give me yours?"

"But suppose I meet Flavie?" Germain said. "Grenoble isn't such a big place."

"You won't have any opportunity. You are going away."

"Going away—where?" Germain asked.

"I'll leave that to you. Which would you prefer to improve, your English or your German? Choose between Heidelberg or England. You will have plenty of money, I will give you letters of introduction to people with whom I correspond, and you will have a fine trip. There are people worse off than you. Which country is it to be?"

"The English make splendid motor bikes," Germain said. "Will you let me buy myself one?"

"As a matter of principle I regard the motor bicycle as a dangerous implement. But it is, on the whole, less dangerous than a Flavie. You shall have your motor bike."

"A 350 with overhead valves?"

"Very well, then. Are you pleased?"

"Yes," Germain said.

But he added:

"But that won't stop me from being very unhappy!"

"I don't expect you to do that in a moment. But I do ask you to be brave for a few months. This is a trial that you have got to face, and it may set the whole of your life straight. You can say to yourself that Grenoble will still be in the same place when you return, and that the people who are fond of you will be waiting for you there. I am not even asking you to make a clean break. Only an interruption."

"You don't think that I shall be behaving pretty shabbily to Flavie in going away?"

"Do you think she behaved very well to you?"

"But she gave herself to me," Germain said.

"Which is quite the worst thing that certain women, in certain circumstances, could possibly do!"

"I am certain," Germain cried out, "that she did it unselfishly!"

"That doesn't make it any better!"

"I forbid you to say anything against her!"

"Far be it from me to do so. Flavie Lacail is an amiable woman, and physically attractive . . ."

"And with a good, kind heart, Edmond!"

"You are in a better position to know that than I am. But being kindhearted doesn't give her any right to make a hash of your life. As long as she was circumspect in giving you pleasure and didn't overdo it, well and good. But now things have gone beyond that stage."

"I shall be longing to see her again," Germain said.

"Indeed I hope you will. It would not be nice of you if you didn't."

"And if I miss her too much . . ."

"You have my promise. But I also have yours, that you will stay patiently in England for a few months, haven't I?"

"Shall I order the motor bike as soon as I get there?"

"Whenever you like."

"Shall I see Flavie again before I go?"

"No. Write to her if you like. I promise you that the letter will be sent. But be careful what you say, and don't make any rash promises."

"Where is she now?"

"She has returned to her husband. Where else did you expect her to go? Passion is one thing and life another. She knows that better than you do."

"She'll be unhappy! Promise me you will keep an eye on her."

"I promise, Germain."

It was at that hour of evening when a faint, bluish tint still lingers in the sky, on a terrace of the château of Sassenage, whose noble architectural design stood out against a sombre background of forest. The mountain group of Vercors, a dark mass against the setting sun, spread its deep shadow over the valley, and with it a profound, majestic peace; while far above it all there lay the almost overwhelming silence of the mountain peaks. At a great height in the sky above were some rose-pink, billowy clouds which cast their reflection upon the shining surface of the Isère, with its leaden hue. A wave of damp and chilly air was rising from the river and spreading in tiny liquid pearls over the grassy fields. The two brothers stood gazing at the beauty of the scene. Then Germain drew nearer and spoke to his elder brother:

"Edmond," he said, with a touch of awkwardness that was charming, "there is something more that I would like to say to you. I am feeling that I didn't know you very well . . ."

"Why, neither did I know you well. One never knows people well. They are capable of more than one thinks—of good as well as evil."

"Do you think me absurd?"

"I think you are young, Germain. You have much freshness, many illusions still to lose."

They heard Claire's voice and saw the outline of her figure appearing on a flight of steps.

"All this is between ourselves!" Edmond said quickly.

He took his brother's arm before they made their way back to the building. They were conscious at that moment of being united by a deep clannish feeling, which might never have appeared had it not been for the intervention of Flavie Lacail in a young man's life.

Splendour of the early spring, of that still chilly time which casts off its heavy mantle of fog and mist and dons once more the light garment of the luminous season, on which flowers are pinned like a lover's nosegay resting on a young maiden's breast! Bursting forth of youthful ardour that surmounts each gloomy obstacle which prudish reason sets! Bright, shining paths of happiness along which amid the incandescence of the fragrance and sweet odours that have come from the mountains and the trees now green again, warm, eager hearts go forward in answer to the great summons and appeal! Laughter that is like a thrill: thrills that are like the sobs which some too poignant melody has drawn from you! Sky that recalls the blue seas on which one morning the navigators set sail, staking their all on fair winds, and steering for some realm of their imagination in whose far recesses the happy isles were gleaming, the continents of emerald and coral, with their strange, unheard-of fruits and their goddesses of mythology and legend! Force that no words can tell, quivering, throbbing force, which gives back to the universe once more its courage of those first mornings of the nebula, when it wandered, scarcely yet turned cold, among the vast and solitary spaces of the starry heavens. Fallen petals of hope destroyed! O my heart, my heart! And thou, my love, see, I am on my bended knees, dazzled at the realization that it is myself whom thou hast chosen from among all others—dazzled because this annunciation has entered the very depths of my being and of my enchanted life! I am hyacinth and mignonette, I am the young shoots, the tiny buds in that bed of earth on which thou treadest in stepping down from thy plinth, O thou giver of sweet pain! But 'tis my heart's delight, my inmost joy to be the carpet beneath thy feet, the cushion upon which thy head reposes when thou dost come to dream away the hours, and I am mute as I behold thy long lashes like blinds drawn down upon the dim half-light of thy musing and thy thought!

Things she knows not how to express, thoughts that make her heartbeats race and temples throb. Humming, buzzing murmurs of her joy, bird song within her heart, bud and blossom of the years, innumerable, that lie ahead—and radiant smiles, like lights on Christmas trees, at every anniversary of the future which has now begun. World, how lovely thou art, adorned with the countenance of him who is my choice, who is coming, coming to meet me on the road! Mountains, mountains, how brotherly your heights, how purifying your solitude! And thou, valley into which I descended to meet him, valley which has beheld his sleep, his awakening which I now share, and the care of himself which he takes because of me, how tender and how friendly is thy dress of green! Town where I have known him, town unique among all others, my only, my indispensable, my beloved town—Grenoble!

Alberte, on her bicycle, lets herself slide down the toboggan of the road, with the air whistling in her ears. There is a smile on her face, and such a radiant smile it is that people turn round to look at her, for she is a picture of perfection that causes astonishment and reminds them of ideals long since forgotten. She smiles and the world seems then a lovely place. She is on her way to meet Bob de Bazair. All difficulties have been smoothed away, the two families see eye to eye. She will marry him whom she loves, with all his radiant charm. Can she think any further than that? Does the rose think upon its stem, or the cloud that floats along an azure sky, or the water that dances in the sun, or the foliage in the sighing wind?

She is in advance of the appointed hour, and knows she is. At the bottom of the hill she puts on her brake and props up her bicycle at the edge of the pavement and fixes the padlock on the machine. Then she makes her way into the church of St. Laurent to dream awhile and thank that great beneficent power which is giving her a happiness almost too great to bear. She goes forward to the chapel of the Virgin, and like the Lady of Heaven herself, she bends her head a little over her shoulder, on the side on which it will be drawn down by the weight of the child which later on she will be clasping to her heart.

"I shall have a little one like yours!"

She does not add: "He will have Bob's face." But the Virgin has guessed that, for she smiles at her. Then Alberte grows bolder and offers up this prayer:

"Give me grace to please him always!"

She lays at the edge of the altar the flowers which she gathered a short while ago, slips a coin into the alms box, and then is out in the open air once more, the pure morning air of Grenoble, where Bob awaits her at the far end of a park bathed in sunshine, near the house of the grandfather of Stendhal. She loves Stendhal for the sake of Clélia Conti. She had read La Chartreuse de Parme. There is much in this novel that escapes her. But she knows the happiness of loving just as Clélia did, and Bob is for her a Fabrice for whom she knows there is nothing she would not do.

At this time of preparation Alberte has to give her mind to questions of her trousseau, dresses, presents, journeys to be made, and miscellaneous plans, a quantity of things which are ordinarily regarded as being of consequence and which add a pleasurable feeling of self-importance to the event itself. Alberte cares but little for them, just as she feels nothing of the stings of jealousy which the announcement of her sensational forthcoming marriage has produced. It has been decided that the wedding shall be a great and impressive ceremony. Bob feels no objection to this; it amuses him. As for Alberte, she would have liked the quietest and simplest possible wedding, and would wish that no one that day should be able to read her feelings in the expression of her face. But Edmond has pointed out that the prestige of the Silken Net is at stake, and Mme. Euffe has urged that "your poor father" would certainly have wished that his daughter should have a brilliant wedding. It must be made clear to the whole of Grenoble that this marriage is no hurried, perfunctory affair in which there is some secret grudge involved; but on the contrary the alliance of the two families, the Euffes and de Bazairs, should appear as no small triumph. The "whole of Grenoble" here in question amounts to no more than four or five hundred people, including officials, the shining lights in the glove trade, cement, pastry, biscuit manufacture, et cetera, in addition to a few members of noble families and the pick of the basket in the liberal professions. But the limited number of these people is in proportion to their distinction, and it is with an eye to their presence that everything is planned. In the meantime there are whispers—people are always so kind!—that this marriage is an urgent necessity. None of this gossip reaches Alberte's ears. Nothing in any case has power to hurt her. One being and one alone has disposal of her suffering and her joy.

Bob! Always there is a feeling of wonder as she sees him, though from sheer modesty she dare not look into his eyes, so evident, when he is near her, is the rapture in her own. She prefers to have him at her side, for then she can study him in profile at her ease, study him and listen to him, and see him smile. His smile, tender and with a touch of mockery in it, is of a kind of which she could never weary, and it makes her feel so little, and with no will but his. Bob's voice, with its melodious tremors, acts upon her heart as a bow upon the string.

This morning they have to go to the jeweller's, where Bob has had some rings put aside for Alberte to see and make her choice. As they are coming out of the alley which connects the Municipal Garden with the Place Grenette, they come suddenly face to face with the bulky form of the widow of General de Sainte-Foy, who is brandishing a lorgnette as though it were a field marshal's baton and looks as if she were holding a review of all the riffraff of the capital of Dauphiné. It is customary with her to be furious at the behaviour of people who do not instinctively show her deference when they see her (she used to value the apprehensive immobility into which large crowds of people were plunged on the appearance of her late husband the general. She used to enjoy it in the old days when, wearing a hat with an ostrich feather and seated in the front row of official rostrums, with her notable stature and powerful bosom, she was a conspicuous feature of the ceremony). It always seems to her that something is owing from the community to the woman in whose presence the general himself might have had to stand to attention.

Alberte's nature surprises and scandalizes her. She thinks the girl is a little fool, and more deplorably so in that she is pretty. (The general's wife has never understood that feminine beauty can be anything but an instrument for the persecution and subjection of men.) As for Bob de Bazair, she has a violent hatred of him, for she feels instinctively that he has a gift of effortless sway over women's hearts.

"Well, my dear," she says to Alberte, "so we are gadding about with our young man, are we! You know that as one makes one's bed so one must lie on it, don't you? You will have time to think that over. Pray Heaven it's not too late!"

"Have no fear, madame," Bob de Bazair said in a pleasant tone of voice, "Alberte will be very happy. I am making myself responsible for that."

"Oh, to be sure you are!" the general's wife exclaimed. "There's a conceited young man for you! I'm not sure whether you look as if you could make a woman happy. And I know something about men, my boy!"

"Oh," said Bob, "you knew several specimens of the same type. Not the same thing at all."

"Come, come, I like that!" said the general's wife. "With me, you would have had to mind your step just like the others did."

"Nay! Not I!" Bob replied. "For I should have fled from the barracks of your charms. I myself have never cared for company sergeants major, even in private."

"Alberte," the general's wife cried out, "you won't see me at your wedding! And the whole of Grenoble shall know the reason why. And I shall tell Clémentine exactly what I think of the young scamp who is to be her son-in-law. I shall see that various people decline to know you, Mr. Impertinent!"

"The people I choose to know will always be delighted to see me," said Bob. "My respects, General!"

They left the general's wife standing on the edge of the pavement, where the spectacle of her wrath and her crimson face caused astonishment to passers-by.

"Oh, Bob," Alberte said, "why did you treat her like that?"

"To shut her up, Albe. The less we see of her the better. It will be advisable to start now getting rid of the people we shan't be visiting—people whose only object in knowing you would be to do you harm."

"Do you think she is really ill-natured?"

164

"I think she is a mischievous woman. And you hardly want this Scottish drum major planting herself on us!"

"She is a friend of Mummy's," Alberte said.

"Your mother is more to be pitied than blamed."

"What does that mean?"

"Oh, she has plenty of excuse—and it's you being here with all your loveliness that makes me say it! Have you noticed something, Albe?"

"What, Bob?"

"That these fine mornings in Grenoble are divine and make everything look lovely. They've got blue eyes and sweet breath. Are you happy, Albe?"

"Yes," Alberte replied in a serious tone of voice. "You think it will last?"

"I am certain it will," Bob said.

"Tell me why?"

"Because I could never bear to have an unhappy person near me. And if that person is pretty and trusting, it would shock me in the same way as seeing a beautiful flower in an ugly vase. You will be calling that selfish . . ."

"Oh no!" Alberte said.

"Well, you might call it that. The general's wife certainly would. But one has to put a little bit of selfishness into love, like one puts pepper into sauces."

"Oh, do you think so?" said Alberte.

"But not you!" Bob said gently. "You, my little Albe, have no need whatever to be selfish in order to be happy!"

He seized her hand and laid a kiss on her fingertips.

They arrived at the jeweller's, and Alberte chose her ring, that is to say, she asked Bob for his opinion and her choice was his. Next they went to the florist's, where Bob pinned some flowers on her dress, and then did a little shopping together. There they were in Grenoble, like a couple of carefree tourists, in summer clothes, breathing the pure fresh air, smiling at the mountains as they appeared over the rooftops, and sauntering at the shopwindows. People looked at them with warm and kindly feelings, because they were young, well matched, and each had beauty. Bob noticed this. He felt that there was a bright and happy future in store for him, thanks to this tender Alberte now receiving these glances of admiration, and whose trust in him was so complete. Her charm was a compound of simplicity, ingenuousness, and faith; her attractiveness was due to her extreme naturalness. Some people might have said that she was lacking in "style." But her style was this

—that she was completely devoid of affectation, of selfishness, and of guile. She was resplendent with happiness, and made no attempt to conceal its origin. It was flattering for Bob de Bazair.

This unqualified success of hers was irritating for others. . . . They met Maud Crémieux, the treacherous and jealous girl with red hair who allowed boys to take extreme liberties with her (they could give precise details of her physical make-up), without securing a single one of them. She paid them little compliments which were a mixture of ferocity and derision. She had once displayed all her charms for Bob, who had subsequently ignored her.

They also met Mme. Simione, who was known at Grenoble as the Merry Widow, though she was now married and had never been a widow in the legal sense of the term. The death of a man who had kept her had left her positively wallowing in wealth, at a time when the voluptuous charms of her maturer years were already on the wane. This, however, did not prevent a certain handsome adventurer, Simione by name, from conferring, by his marriage of the lady, a legal status upon these highly desirable millions; which secured him the acme of luxurious living, with all the privileges of a prince consort. And as nothing can resist money for long, the Simiones, complete with country houses, estates, and the very solid business of the manufacturer now deceased, played a part in Grenoble society. It was said of them that they knew how to spend money and that they were generous people.

Mme. Simione showed a certain tolerance where love affairs were concerned, remembering as she did that improper behaviour had contributed to her own success. (The story was that M. Miollet, her former protector, had fished her out of some very shady surroundings twenty-five years earlier.) Her elevation to the dignity of the life of a respectable citizen had been sufficiently long and difficult for Valérie Simione to regard legitimacy as an asset indispensable to the consummation of a career. This feeling was increased by the fact that she aged badly, growing to resemble a retired "Madame," as is often seen in the case of handsome women of maturer years whose carnal life has been a stormy one. Valérie Simione's past was in fact comfortably relapsing into oblivion, whilst her millions, which were a permanent and obvious reality, gave her a place among the important ladies of Grenoble. She was at the line of demarcation which ran between two differing shades of opinion in the town as to the part that should be played in the community by wealth. All those with tolerant views received her, because she was a good sort and because there was liberal and handsome entertainment provided in her house, and one was never bored

166

there. She was kind to young people. She complimented Bob on Alberte's prettiness and the happiness she so plainly showed; and to the girl herself she said that she would make a charming little countess and that she was very lucky in having such a fine start in life.

"Why does the general's wife—Madame de Sainte-Foy—say such unkind things about Mme. Simione?" Alberte asked later.

"I think," Bob answered, "that it is because Valérie never rams her virtue down people's throats. There's a little collection of old dowagers here who would always have had great difficulty in being anything but virtuous, and the capital they make out of it now is merely laughable. A little more generosity and tolerance would be more to the point. However, people usually pride themselves on the things that have given them the least trouble."

The weather was too lovely for them to leave each other at midday. The town, swarming with motorcars, trams, and lighthearted pedestrians, seemed to be in genuine holiday mood.

"Albe," Bob said suddenly, "you remember the cocktails we had at Pont-de-Claix a little more than a year ago? What about going there again? And this time we'll lunch there."

"Yes, but I haven't let them know at home . . ."

"Oh, that's nothing," Bob said. "We can ring them up. Come along with me."

They telephoned from a café, where Alberte left her bicycle. Then they took a tram, the shaky little vehicle which bumps along the avenues at Pont-de-Claix. They stood on the front platform, out in the open air. The avenues were shady throughout the whole of their length and the leaves on the trees still a fresh green. The journey seemed brief and delightful. After a short walk they sat down, ravenously hungry, on a terrace overlooking the Drac. They smiled at each other, and Bob asked for the menu.

"Get married, my boy!" Such were the words which had been spoken to his son by Gonzague-Stanislas-Gontran de Bazair, Count of Haute-Jarrie and lord of the manor of Champagnier, thus carrying on a tradition of the de Bazair family several centuries old, by which the prosperity of the men of that lineage had been dependent on women ("Love supports me" was their motto). In each generation these men had been ruined, but always their fortunes had been restored through their ascendancy over tender hearts. So far as riches were concerned, all the de Bazairs were born younger sons, but these younger sons of Dauphiné were in every respect the equal of those of Gascony in the

167

boldness and daring of their assaults upon the heart, in making their way in the world by battering down the defences of heiresses and rich maidens, in juggling with married women's wealth—all of which served to rebuild the tottering, crumbling manors of these lords, half warriors, half squireens, courtiers at times, but all of them drinkers and lovers of the chase, reckless spendthrifts, insolent men, given over to pleasures of every kind, to hunting and spicy wenches; and fathers of many a son who met his end in battle or affray, or went to distant parts to conquer colonies and Creoles. It is true that the rhythm of these ways of life had slowed down somewhat since the close of the First Empire, under which the last great de Bazair adventurers had distinguished themselves throughout the length and breadth of Europe. Their descendants, chafing at the bit, had had to make shift with a society which, with the middle classes continually enforcing more prudent, cautious ways of life, witnessed the growth of fortunes acquired in business, the founding of an aristocracy of manufacturers and the triumph of priggish little whippersnappers who, armed with a diploma, had the impertinence to face up to men with family escutcheons and to speak of merits of their own. This new form of society was exasperating to Bob's father, who had been one of the last cavalry officers to be a shining light at horse shows and in the hunting field, to become famous for his duels, his gaming debts, and his mistresses with nineteenth-century corsets.

This "Get married, my boy" was the only marriage gift which the grumpy old count could make to his son, for he was getting to the end of his financial tether. He had just enough money to enable him to keep one half-bred horse in his stables, and to buy some beige hats which came from London, check trousers, gloves, gaiters, a special kind of ties, cigars, and brandy. The last luxury in which he had indulged was to give flowers and a few presents to some young ladies. Both flowers and presents cost rather more than he could afford. But the family tradition required that anything that was left of a fortune which had come through a woman should be squandered on other women. In actual fact the old nobleman's outbreaks were becoming few and far between, and they were the last festivities in his disgruntled life. He spared nothing to make them a success, thus giving himself the illusion, for a few days or hours, that he was back once more amid the splendours of 1900. The de Bazairs had been neither lawyers nor ecclesiastics: their occupations had rather been fighting and love. In the whole of his career Gonzague-Stanislas-Gontran de Bazair had cared for nothing but the smell of horse dung, the alignment of squadrons on parade, and the scents of boudoirs, and mistresses who, while they brought financial ruin, had mouths as hard as that of a stubborn mare, with quivering flanks which, once they are brought into subjection, give you the finest, softest seat.

For the rest, he was brutally obstinate, uncompromising in contempt, and had never at any period of his life had the faintest understanding of money. During her lifetime the countess, a slave to her husband's pleasures, had done her best to supply this deficiency herself, by dealing and negotiation with purveyors and process servers. Since her death, which had taken place ten years earlier, the widower had let everything go hang, with his accounts getting into a hopeless tangle, and he was on the point of succumbing to the blows of the revenue authorities, who somewhat foolishly struck at him after merely taking note of exterior signs of wealth, that is to say, by basing their taxation on the superficial area of buildings which were not only old but in a tottering condition, and were of themselves a redoubtable instrument for bringing a man to ruin. But the count shrank from any failure to bear the hereditary burden of the great barracks of his ancestors, the home of owls and bats, and adorned with the dusty lace of cobwebs and with stalactites of plaster which had come unstuck from the ceilings of French pattern. Such was the château of Haute-Jarrie, an ancient haunt of forbidding aspect, in a commanding position above the slopes which lead down to Eichirolles and Eybins. And scarcely better was the château of Champagnier, lording it over a number of acres that was being continually diminished, where the farmers led a lazy life, cheating over their dues and cutting down the amount of their rents in kind. As for disputing with those people, or setting the lawyers after them, the count was incapable of either. Since the suppression of the gallows he could not conceive of justice being carried out in any shape or form. He had no belief in justice as administered by the sons of grocers, ironmongers, and scribblers, in a state governed by café owners, advocates, and professors. There is a certain way of wearing an opera hat and frock coat, seen at election times, which made him howl with fury. There were certainly old blockheads among the King's ministers in days gone by, but damn it all, those men did wear clothes that you could look at!

"Get married, my boy!" That meant "Don't count on me. I have given you what the de Bazairs have always received—a name, pleasant features, a good presence, breeding. Behave now in the same way as your ancestors did."

Those ancestors—one had only to look at their portraits in the semidarkness of the two castles—had been all of them hearty fellows, gay dogs who would stick at nothing. There is a certain element of scruple and conscientiousness which is suitable enough for ordinary clodhoppers, but with which noblemen are quite unconcerned. Humble people should be apprehensive and respectful. For the powerful, the elect, the anointed it is a different matter altogether. Bob de Bazair knew this well enough, and if there were some qualifications in his respect for his ancestors, he nevertheless regarded a right to a certain freedom and licence exclusive to his class as a sacred inheritance.

To enable him to marry he needed a sum of fifty thousand francs, this being indispensable for the purchase of presents, the renewal of his wardrobe and the expenses of setting up house. His only capital consisted of debts—which could wait; but his credit was momentarily at a low ebb. At poker he was having a run of bad luck, and the proverb "Happy in love . . ." was recurring to his mind. It was at this point that, like a worthy specimen of his ancient breed, he took bold action and never turned a hair.

At the bar of the Majestic he sought out Riri Jumier, whom he had forsaken for long months past, and sat down at her table.

"Riri," he said, "could you cough me up fifty notes—a thousand each?"

"What—just like that?" she said, dumbfounded.

"Just like that!" Bob replied calmly.

"Have you gone dotty! And you used to be so nice to me!"

"That's quite a different matter," Bob said. "If I'd been too nice I could quite well have pinched all you've got and then run out on you. That's not my way. I'm not one to grab savings. I am suggesting a perfectly correct bit of business, and I shall pay you back the money with interest."

"And what will you pay me back with?"

"The money of the dowry," Bob said, "as soon as I'm married. Look here, you're not a little tart who's afraid for her pennies!"

"Well, I like that! Let me tell you that that's not the way to talk to me! And as for you, Bob, you're a bit of a pimp anyway!"

Bob de Bazair smiled.

"There are some things, Riri, that you will never understand! The Court of Louis XIV was full of pimps and whores, and there was no mistaking them, either. But they were the bricks that built Versailles. It takes every sort to make a world."

"All the same," Riri said, "you can't mistake the Place Grenette for Versailles, nor the people who go to the Dauphins for dukes and marquesses!"

"I should just think not! But I am probably the only man here who can still show a little of the spirit of Versailles. Just think. There isn't a single boy in Grenoble in the position which I am in with regard to you and to—someone else, who could come along and say to you 'Lend me fifty thousand.' "

"Yes, that's true," Riri agreed.

"I should have no difficulty in getting those fifty notes," Bob said. "But I said to myself, 'It would be a sporting thing to go and ask Riri. That will show her that I still feel friendly towards her, and perhaps it will give her pleasure.' But now, if I was wrong . . ."

"Oh no," Riri said, "you were not wrong. One day I offered you all I had. . . . When will you be wanting the money?"

"As quickly as possible."

"The day after tomorrow, here, at the same time?"

"Right you are," said Bob. "I will make you out a receipt."

"So that I can show it to your wife later on? Is she nice, your Alberte?"

"Very nice," Bob said. "One day she saw you go by. She thought you were charming, and very well dressed. She is not at all jealous of women. And that is saying a lot."

"Well, she needn't be!"

"Oh!—that's nice of you, Riri!"

"It doesn't mean that I like her! I hate her, because of you."

"You shouldn't. If it were not her it would be somebody else. It's better that it should be her."

"You couldn't have done differently?"

"Out of the question, Riri. Come, think of Versailles!"

"And that fifty thousand—a receipt's all I shall get? I really don't care a hang for your beastly receipt!"

"Listen now," Bob said, "I'll take you on Friday to Lyon for the day. That suit you?"

"Yes," said Riri. "And a bit of love?"

"Take care now," Bob answered. "No sloppiness, please! If you swear you won't cry . . . Well, we'll see."

This conversation had taken place a few days before the choice of the engagement ring. Sufficiently provided with cash, Bob could face the future with confidence; and marvel at the fact that it was money which had belonged to "Daddy Euffe"—Bob's friendly way of referring to the latter—which, after a slight diversion, had reached him as a means of preparing Alberte's happiness.

Then again, the loan had given him proof that his ascendancy over women's hearts was still the same, and that Riri Jumier was a very excellent young woman. This, of course, made no difference whatever to the nature of his feelings for Alberte, who would make as pretty a lady of the manor as you could wish to see, and whose oval face would in due course be no mean adornment to the gallery in which the family portraits hung. For the de Bazairs, though they married money, were insistent always that it be brought to them by girls whose physical charms would alone have been sufficient to engender rivalry among other suitors. Plain Janes had no hope of entry into a family where they would have caused damage to the stock of males, whose constant task it was to regild a somewhat tarnished name.

Plans, happiness, success—all that became a matter of doubt, the whole structure of it came near to toppling stupidly to the ground. Travelling at upwards of fifty miles an hour on his motor bicycle, Bob de Bazair had a fall at the hairpin bends on the Uriage road due to the bursting of his front tyre. He was picked up seriously hurt and in a fainting condition. He had to be urgently conveyed to a nursing home in Grenoble, where for ten days he lay between life and death. Among other contusions, he had a fracture of the hip, with regard to which the doctors temporarily withheld diagnosis: he might be lame. And he had a deep gash in his face, traces of which would doubtless be permanent.

This event provided an opportunity for those who disapproved of the marriage to make an attempt to detach Alberte from Bob. Instructions to that end, issued from Sassenage, where Claire ruled the roost, were observed by all the members of the family—except by Lucie, who was upholding the rights of love, and Germain, who was adopting English manners somewhere near London. The widow of General de Sainte-Foy hastened to the rescue, with a truly military instinct for the counterattack. But all these efforts came to naught in face of the attitude of gentle firmness of Alberte, who would not agree even to the slightest discussion of the question as to what was proper and becoming and what was not. Disregarding all protests, she went off each morning to the nursing home and there shut herself up, a gentle, silent figure, in the room where Bob, unconscious, was fighting for his life. In face of her youth, her beauty, and her persistence, the attendants at the home had given up all attempts to induce her to leave the room, where she remained for hours on end, sitting alone in the dim light with a beloved face that was often twitching and distorted with pain.

The echoes of Bob's wandering in his mind resounded in her heart and drained the colour from her cheeks. But as she bent over him as she might so bend over a sick child, she dared at last to murmur things which until that time she had kept within her own heart. No longer was she the young girl in love half dazzled by her happiness, the girl who had walked smiling in the leafy shades of sun-kissed parks and likened the future to the magic enchantment of the Grésivaudan valley in the morning hours. Now she was a woman, a true woman, bending over this spectacle of suffering and bearing her own share of pain. It was this suffering of his, this weakness, and his deep unconscious need of her, that was making Bob her very own. She was feeling that she must be there, thinking of none but him in his loneliness, breathing in the rhythm of that erratic, struggling breath, stabbed to the heart by the groans and murmurs coming from that bed, in order that some hidden emanation, born of her own fervent love, might give this flickering life the strength it needed to find its way out of those dark labyrinths where evil spirits lay in wait for it.

"Courage, Bob!" she murmured softly as she wiped away the sweat of fever from the sufferer's brow. "Courage, I'm here!"

This was what she meant: "She whose life or death is in your hands, she whose mission it is to share all sorrow and pain that may come to you, and to leave you always the larger portion of the pleasures and the joys. For my pleasures and my joys will always be the reflection of your own." Vestal virgin with one sole task and one faith alone, she was fighting for Bob with the powers of darkness, with the evil spell of nightmares which kept him apart from her and drew from him some hoarse and fearful cries.

"Oh, my dearest dear!"

Words were coming to her lips which she had never uttered when Bob was himself and happiness was spontaneous and free. She was watching over him as over a young god laid low, on whom at last she dared to feast her eyes, fearful lest he should wake and catch her unawares in her mute ecstasy, should see her look of rapture and of pain. She knew that he would live, because the sun cannot cease to shine nor the earth to revolve, because for her the rhythm of the universe was bound up with this prostrate frame, with this half-conscious, torpid mind, and her own thoughts would be halted, dulled, extinguished should he come to die. Such a possibility as this she rejected with horror, calling to her aid her friend and ally, the Virgin of Saint-Laurent, who knew her dazzling secret. This Bob half shattered, wailing like a small child with hidden pain, was now dearer, more indispensable to her than ever. For the first time she felt that in his weakness he was hers; for the first time she felt that she was useful to him, raised to his own height by the boundless devotion which she held in store for him. There in that room, with its odours of fever and the chemist's shop, she had some moments of a great, solemn happiness, which went deeper into her soul than the bliss of spring and summer mornings.

Later, Bob was taken to the château of Champagnier, and there Alberte took up her abode as sick nurse and companion despite loud protests and prohibitions from the members of her family, who asseverated that "such things are not done." She set at defiance her own family and the scandalmongers of Grenoble, and cared naught for Claire's contempt or scornful treatment by the widow of General de Sainte-Foy; and this she did in fulfilment of a duty which she was the only one to feel as such, for it was the outcome of a complete surrender to Bob of her own destiny, and even her personality, motives, and will.

There was someone, however, who understood her and approved of her conduct. This was the old count. He treated her in the most courteous fashion, with a politeness that savoured of a period long past and raised her to the level of a great lady. She seemed to him to have the same gentle sweetness, the tranquil beauty, the faithful submissiveness of the traditional de Bazair wives. He even went so far as to say: "This girl is a true de Bazair," thus paying her the honours of his ancient name and his hereditary home. He saw in her an element of nobility with which, at Champagnier, Alberte also felt herself imbued. She went there as to an enchanted abode, with a touch of melancholy also within its walls: she was like a little girl who is confronted with the grandeur of certain places and is filled with awe. In the maze of the great state apartments, empty now, in the silent, tree-lined walks within the park which in places reverted to a tangle of vegetation run wild, in the corner turrets of the castle and the little private chapels built within the thickness of the walls, she could all but feel the presence of those princesses with their hearts enslaved, who in days of old had awaited the return of the de Bazair warriors, whose proud portraits gave an air of life to those murky drawing rooms that were always closed, wherein there floated the dust of legend and of passion long since extinct. She was linked to those princesses by the spell the de Bazairs had cast upon her, which was binding her to those surroundings wherein she lived as though she were in a dream.

Bob de Bazair was lying in a large, airy apartment on the ground floor, which was adorned with old furniture, ancient tapestries, full suits of armour, and trophies of the chase. The french windows, left wide open, led out to a terrace bathed in sunshine, and enclosed within a railing of very handsome design, through which could be seen the effects of light airs ruffling the blue-green surface of a sheet of water in which deep masses of foliage were reflected. The air entered freely, bringing with it perfumes of flowers, open country, and lovely summer days. In this room Bob and Alberte spent the daylight hours, rejoicing in the bright cheerfulness of the mornings, the lulling torpor of the afternoons and the wondrous beauty of the departing day. In vases there were roses blooming, birds' were singing in the trees, and the gentle stir of life outside could be seen in tarnished mirrors in which in days gone by arriving coaches had been reflected.

Bob loved Alberte to place herself so that her figure stood out against a scenic background of verdure and of mountain peaks. Within this setting of the ancient castle the young girl, whom Bob had judged too hastily to be easy to understand, took on an air of mystery which until that time she had not held for him. He smiled to see how pretty she was, to see her so silent and so grave, which was her outward sign of happiness. It was she who held him up when, leaning on a stick, he made his first hesitating, awkward footsteps. He struck his foot against a large paving stone which had come loose, and stumbled and nearly fell. So upset was Alberte that she cried out:

"Oh, Bob, my darling, you haven't hurt yourself?"

It was the first time that she had used this term of endearment aloud. (In thought she had long addressed him thus.) From that time onwards she acquired the habit of using it often, but for some long while when doing so she could not look at him. She could not say these words without blushing and confusion, so greatly had she longed for the happiness it gave her.

The month of August, magnificent that year, was a time of exquisite enjoyment for them. Then September brought the golden tints of the first approach of autumn, the first evenings in which there was damp-ness in the air, the first blazing log fires in a somewhat dark and gloomy room. For Alberte, time seemed to fly. She was near the end of the second year of her great love. It seemed to her that that love had begun only yesterday, that it was yesterday that Bob had clasped her in his arms, in the Place Victor-Hugo, while M. Constant Euffe, his head en-veloped in a bandage, was lying dead.

To Bob de Bazair, whose recovery was on the way, this time of trial had been of great use. It had allowed him to discover Alberte's great worth, and his own good fortune, which he had never sufficiently ap-preciated, in having won the love of this trusting, faithful heart. He had come within a hairsbreadth of disaster, either maiming or death.

Without Alberte's care perhaps he would not have escaped so lightly. There had been comparatively few visitors to Champagnier during his convalescence. Had he been disfigured or lame, the people in Grenoble would have been quite capable of leaving him in the lurch and ceasing to treat him as a privileged person, which they had done hitherto. He realized now that Alberte's smile was for him the smile of Fortune herself, that the goddess must be paid some tributes of respect, that Alberte was his best ally, the only one who would be left him if he came upon evil days.

It seemed to him that he would find his greatest safety in marriage, and that he must sell his motor bicycle. He had promised Alberte to do so. And in any case he wished to have a car.

He had had much time for reflection at Champagnier, more than at any other period of his life. And the result of all this thought had been a resolve to have greater consideration for Alberte, to show her more kindness. Sometimes he would call her, laughingly, "pretty countess." Alberte was then quite overcome by her happiness, not on account of the title itself, but because it meant that she was definitely and finally accepted by the de Bazairs and that Bob was saved.

Bob was beginning to walk normally once more. The scar on his face had almost vanished. The wedding date was fixed.

10. MISALLIANCE The summer had been no less a period of emotion for the elder of the Euffe young ladies than it had been for her sister. While Alberte was playing the part of a loving and devoted sick nurse at Champagnier, Lucie Euffe, at the Shady Nook, bright with flowers and fanned by breezes which brought to that place of refreshment all the sweet scents of the Grésivaudan, was tasting the cruel delights of meeting almost every day a handsome young waster of twenty-five who was saying to himself that love might be a decidedly profitable venture.

Bruno Spaniente, devoid of culture and with a commonplace mind but much physical beauty, was a prince after the fashion of a Donatello model, whose features, though somewhat plebeian. would have deserved the honour of reproduction in bronze. Artful in rather a feminine way, he had that kind of physical make-up which causes one to stare at certain Spanish gipsies in whose bright shining eyes there is a fiery glint which is supposed to give these people an air of mystery, but which is perhaps no more than the reflection of an animal nature. In the same way there are men in whom a suave and gentle exterior is but a covering that hides their perfidity and guile. In the warmth and ardour of their gaze there are glints of gold that bewitch and fascinate the objects of their scheming or desire. It is, of course, a fact that some of these men are comedians rather than professional adventurers. This was the case with Bruno Spaniente, the strength of whose appetites was lessened by his native indolence and unconcern.

Lucie was more madly in love with him than ever. But she was remaining steadily incapable of taking the step which would decide the remainder of her life, of committing herself to the physical consequences which her affections would involve. It must here be stated plainly that she had much of the bashful modesty of an old maid. She had done too much private thinking on the subject of love not to feel shy and undecided now that the moment for initiative had arrived. She was lacking in spontaneousness and self-confidence, and had already lost that youthful enthusiasm and glow which makes one yield to impulse without thought or hesitation.

Bruno for his part was afraid of making some untimely gesture. He wanted Lucie at his feet, to avow her love, and not just Lucie but Mlle. Euffe of the Silken Net, heiress in her own right and free to act as she might wish. It occurred to him that it would help his cause if he were to make himself scarce. He accordingly secured a job in the Ricou transport business as driver of a motor coach which did the trip between Grenoble and Nice once a week. Besides enabling him to throw Lucie into a panic by the threat of a total disappearance, there were other reasons why this occupation was to his taste. It meant that every week he would be seeing once more his beloved Mediterranean and his friends in the old quarters of his native town; he loved the picturesque and ever-changing life along the route, and to feel himself in control of a powerful machine in which some thirty passengers were at his mercy; at the big relay stations there were jollity and meetings with friends; and lastly, this free, expansive life brought him money with the tips he received. The effect on Lucie Euffe was exactly that which Bruno had anticipated.

"Why do you do this appalling job?" she asked him on his return after his third period of absence.

"Oh well," he said, "I've got to live somehow. What do people think of a man who does no work, eh?"

"But I can help you, Bruno!"

"Help me, help me . . . A little, that's true. . . . But what do I look like, taking your money when I can't do it openly and aboveboard?"

"But you've no need to make a secret of it, Bruno!"

"Oh, don't pretend you don't understand!" he said. "What am I to you, when I'm only a poor chauffeur? You're just a rich young lady who's got a fancy into her head. And when that's over you won't want to see any more of me, like your mother, who's turned me out. And then what's going to happen to me, with no job? Turn dishonest, I suppose! And end up in jail!"

"Bruno, be quiet!"

"Mind you, Miss Lucie, I'm very fond of you, and that's a fact. But I'm nowhere near your level. As far as you're concerned, I'm simply a man who's paid wages."

"Wages!" Lucie exclaimed. "Bruno, Bruno, you mustn't talk like that! I just can't bear it!"

"Well, I don't want to lose my self-respect," Bruno said.

"I know how proud you are, what a fine man you are, Bruno!"

"It was a bit of bad luck for me, meeting you, miss. I lost my situation. I know you've been kind, and that you wouldn't have let me go hungry. But all the same it won't do me any good to pay attention to what I'm feeling about you. I shall just be an outcast, same as I was before! You're a young lady of good family who's having a bit of fun outside her own circle!"

"Bruno, you are everything to me!"

"Just a passing fancy you've got—this lovely weather has to do with it, I shouldn't wonder! But you wouldn't say that in front of your mother, or Mr. Germain, or Miss Alberte. You wouldn't say it in front of Mr. Edmond and his lady, with the grand life they lead in that castle."

"I would say it before God and everybody on earth. I would even say it in front of Madame de Sainte-Foy!"

"And then," Bruno said, "there's the question of reputation and only doing what's correct. When there's money passing between husband and wife, that's quite all right, it all comes out of the same purse. But between you and me, miss—well, it isn't the same thing at all."

"Bruno," Lucie said in a tone of entreaty, "why must I always be miss? Doesn't some other name come into your mind when you think of me?"

"Sure it does," Bruno said, "if I was to let myself go . . . Then I should be done for! Could I dare speak to you like I do to the little creatures one meets and has a good time with? I have to treat you very seriously. And then at Grenoble I feel restless, out of place. It's too cold for me here, right under these mountains of yours. The people here seem to me to be always holding themselves back, not wanting to be happy or kind. See now, what about coming to Nice with me?"

"With you, Bruno?"

"In the coach, and not say a word about it. I'll keep you the seat next the chauffeur. We'll do the whole trip together, there and back. You'll be seeing the sea, the Promenade des Anglais, the St.-Roch and Riquier districts, Cimiez and Carabancel. You'll see lovely Nice and the Bay of Angels!"

"Bruno, Bruno . . ."

"The palm trees and the blue sky . . ."

"Bruno . ."

"Well, Lucie?"

"I shall never have done with this blasted family! Mother is a fool not to have kept a better eye on that young woman. She's barmy!"

Edmond Euffe had taken his personal correspondence away with him when leaving Sassenage. He was reading it in the car while being driven to his offices in the Avenue d'Alsace-Lorraine. One letter, with a Nice postmark, was from his sister Lucie. It read as follows: "I have found happiness and I intend to live my life as my heart and feelings and aspirations bid me do. If you are opposed to my happiness, to which nobody at home has ever paid the least attention, I shall quarrel with you and take my money away from the Silken Net. Tell Mother this, and also your wife—specially your wife. I am going to marry Bruno Spaniente, a straight, honest fellow, who is worth more than many of your Grenoble people with their airs and graces." "Well, that's the last straw!" Edmond said to himself. "The general's wife was most certainly right! That girl is raving mad. And I spend my time trying to straighten out their affairs—for the whole lot of them."

The car had slowed down as it was passing through the suburb of Fontaine and crossing the bridge over the Drac.

"On the other hand, if she takes out her money it might be awkward for us. . . . Oh, what an infernal nuisance everything is! And people will be saying nice things at Grenoble when they hear of her bolting like this! And there's Claire . . . And here am I, having taken every possible care to get my life settled on solid foundations, and now the members of my own family are doing all they can to put spokes in my wheel. It's just madness!"

As he was getting out of his car in the Avenue d'Alsace-Lorraine, Edmond met M. Philibert Mivois, of the glove trade, a man of great influence. He had a high opinion of Edmond Euffe and was grateful to him for his general policy and way of life, which was of a kind calculated to place leading businessmen on a high social level. M. Mivois backed up the Euffes in the more exalted circles of Grenoble society in which they were still liable to be given the cold shoulder. Edmond was to some extent his protégé.

"How is your mother?" M. Mivois asked, in the tone of condescension peculiar to him. "And your sisters? I heard that the younger one is to be married? And is your elder sister well? She is a most excellent and most worthy person. There was a rumour some time ago that she was to marry an army man. Is that so?"

"No, I don't think so," Edmond replied. "The officer in question seemed rather shy."

"A pity!" said M. Mivois. "Yes, really a pity! The army, don't you think?"

"Oh, of course!" Edmond said.

"Especially here, at Grenoble, the district where our Alpine light infantry comes from!"

"As a matter of fact," said Edmond, "the officer was not an infantry officer."

"Ah, that is a pity!" M. Mivois said. "Those Alpine fellows, you know . . . Ah, those Alpine fellows . . ."

"Yes, rather!" Edmond said.

"And then, too, those chaps do belong so much to these parts!"

"Yes, they do, don't they!" Edmond said, with a touch of awe in his voice.

"Anyhow, we've got some lovely weather," M. Mivois remarked. "Splendid for the tourists!"

"Splendid!" Edmond agreed very earnestly, glancing automatically at the sky.

"And for us here in Grenoble, tourists mean . . ."

"Yes, don't they," Edmond once more agreed, with a sly and knowing air.

"Ah," said M. Mivois with a sigh, "if only our municipal authorities weren't such party people . . ."

"Yes indeed," said Edmond, with a grave and anxious expression on his face.

"Well, never mind!" M. Mivois concluded, dismissing all such serious matters from his thoughts.

"No, quite so," said Edmond, politely following suit.

"And is your wife well? Please remember me to her, will you? She is a very remarkable person."

"You are too kind," Edmond said gratefully.

"Yes, yes, my dear fellow, very remarkable! She has the unmistakable manner of the great governing classes! And the great governing classes . . . Ah, the great governing classes . . ."

"Yes," said Edmond, "the great governing classes."

"Don't you agree!" M. Mivois exclaimed.

"Yes, yes," Edmond said, with two little nods which had a world of meaning in them.

"I am happy to find you in this frame of mind," M. Mivois said. "You are one of us now!"

"I do my very best to keep up my position in life," Edmond said modestly.

"Ah," M. Mivois cried out. "position in life! You have said the word: 'position in life.' And how essential that is, my dear fellow! Position in life . . . Bravo!"

"Oh . . ." Edmond said modestly.

"Yes, yes, bravo, I congratulate you. . . . Your father was a bit strange, a little out of place among us here. But with you it's quite a different story. You have come to realize that one has to make distinctions between different people, fundamental distinctions!"

"I understand that better and better," Edmond said fervently.

"Better and better! That is well spoken. Yes indeed, well spoken."

They were walking side by side along the avenue enlivened by some very lovely sunshine at the beginning of July, taking very short footsteps and wondering what they could still find to say to each other regarding the great problems of social and fashionable life in Grenoble. The initiative in referring to these matters and the manner in which they should be approached rested entirely with M. Mivois by reason of his recognized importance in the district. Edmond Euffe, not a little awed by this encounter, was awaiting some definite turn in the conversation, and watching carefully to see whether by chance some other inhabitant of social importance might be passing by and see him hobnobbing with M. Philibert Mivois. (The latter had just been gratified by an elaborate salute from the dean of the Faculty of Science, of which Edmond had taken his share. And the director of the *Dauphiné Gazette*, who was on his way to the Rue Denfert-Rochereau, had turned round in surprise at seeing the director of the Silken Net in such dazzling company.)

But M. Mivois became aware of having given to the son of M. Constant Euffe a quite exceptional proof of his esteem, and felt that he had done enough—to say the least—in that direction. This man had an unrivalled faculty for keeping people at a proper distance and cutting short all attempts to take too great advantage of any concessions that he might make. His expression became suddenly cold and indifferent as he proclaimed:

"Now then, that will do! Good day to you!"

He touched his hat with the tips of his fingers, gave a curt little nod and abruptly departed, in the manner of a person of distinction who has once more to give his mind to affairs the scope and importance of which would be almost beyond the comprehension of other people. In the meantime Edmond Euffe, who was well aware of the great value of this conversation in a public street, was bowing deeply and addressing these words to the retreating back of his important friend:

"Thank you, Monsieur Mivois. My respects to you, Monsieur Mivois."

But M. Mivois no more turned round to hear him than the person of charitable intent slows down his footsteps to listen to the beggar's thanks. . . .

Edmond had now to reach his offices, from which his walk had taken him some little distance away. What had surprised him most had been M. Mivois's leaving him without even shaking hands, thereby indicating that this conversation, flattering though it was, did not denote a new stage in their relations. Nevertheless there was no mistaking the fact that this interview in public was to some extent a mark of favour, and this rejoiced Edmond's heart, admiring the man as he did. "How subtle he is in drawing distinctions," he said to himself. "How clever at managing men and putting them in exactly their right place! That's what you need if you want to rule—a sense of proportion."

He was feeling in an excellent humour as he made his way into his office, where his chief clerk came every morning to hand him a report on the operations of the Silken Net. He was unusually amiable to his subordinate.

"Lovely weather, Monsieur Pimolot! Splendid tourist season."

"Yes, it is indeed, Monsieur Edmond," the old employee replied. He had seen the elder of the Euffes start work in these offices under his father's guidance.

"And as Monsieur Philibert Mivois was saying to me just now, the tourists, for us here in Grenoble . . ."

"Yes, yes, Monsieur Edmond," M. Pimolot answered, a little surprised.

"Do you know Monsieur Philibert Mivois, Monsieur Pimolot?"

"Dear me, Monsieur Edmond—well, I might say I know him and I don't know him. In the sort of way one knows Rothschild."

"He's a thorough gentleman, Monsieur Philibert Mivois is. Good luck does come to the right people sometimes, whatever you may say."

"Yes, anything may happen, Monsieur Edmond."

"And do you know, Monsieur Pimolot, what counts more than anything else in society? One's station there, one's position, one's rank. Do you take my meaning?"

"Well, Monsieur Edmond, I did my military service in 1887. That's a long time ago now."

"Your military service? Ah yes, the army . . ."

"I had a Corsican company sergeant major. A man called Santicchini. He was a frightful drunken brute. I heard that he'd ended up by getting drowned in the Rhone. He'd been chucked in, one foggy night, off La Guillotine bridge. It was at Lyon, Monsieur Edmond."

"That man's being drowned," Edmond said severely, "does nothing whatever to weaken the principle of authority and discipline. Discipline is a necessity, Monsieur Pimolot, it is needed everywhere."

"I haven't reached my present age without understanding that. Monsieur Edmond. Discipline's a good thing, it certainly is. But drunken brutes are never anything but drunken brutes. In the same way I knew a man called Machefouille who was a police constable in Paris, in the tenth ward. Now you might well say that a policeman, who at least should set a good example, ought to behave . . ."

"Quite so, quite so, Monsieur Pimolot," Edmond broke in. "And now tell me how the firm is getting on."

M. Pimolot returned to his normal functions, from which his employer's exceptional mood had for a brief space diverted him.

"Well, Monsieur Edmond," he said, "things are going well. Our figures last month were 48,432 francs better than for the same month last year. There's a falling off in the sale of bottled beer and preserved foods for picnics, due to the bad spring. But there is a rise on wines and drinks, olives, cod, and Camembert cheeses. Filleted herrings rose twenty per cent since we went in for the Floupet variety."

"Nothing else, Monsier Pimolot?"

"There's a rise of a penny a pound on margarine. And an advance in the prices of pepper and cloves is expected."

"Then we shall have to raise the sale prices. Good day, Monsieur Pimolot. We shall meet tomorrow."

"Yes, Monsieur Edmond, tomorrow."

Edmond Euffe once more started thinking complacently of M. Philibert Mivois, who was championing his career. Thanks to his protection, a subtle distinction was already being made in certain circles, and those the most distinguished and least accessible, of Grenoble society, between the Euffes of Sassenage and the rest of the family. Thanks also to the very considerable impression made by Claire, that member of the Bargès family, there was a growing tendency to cease to regard the Silken Net as a very ordinary grocery business and to think of it as an extensive and important catering concern. In this way Edmond was gradually taking his place among the pick of society, that is to say, about twenty families of the first flight, who were living entrenched within an enclosure compounded of their own conceit, self-satisfaction, and scorn.

This happy progress of Edmond's affairs was certainly rendered easier by the disappearance of the founder of the Silken Net, who had formerly been known as an ordinary commercial canvasser or tout at Grenoble. M. Mivois, with the candour which in his case was permissible, had summed him up perfectly when he said: "Your father was a bit strange, a little out of place among us here." It now rested with Edmond, supported by M. Mivois's kindness upon which it seemed that he could henceforth definitely rely, to wipe out in people's memories the vulgar and plebeian element which his father's nature had contained. It rested with him to raise the Euffes to those lofty heights from which one gazes down upon a world far away below, in which men toil and struggle in a daily round of trivial tasks and petty cares.

Then, suddenly, as he was revelling in the bliss of ambition on the way to fulfilment, he remembered the letter from his sister, that crazy sister, Lucie. He took it from his pocket and read it once again with care. Its terms were precise and clear, and the matter was certainly not one that could be settled by correspondence. In any case it must be stopped at once, before the story should be noised abroad and provide a subject of entertainment for Grenoble.

Edmond made a mental survey of those whom he could send to Nice to rescue his sister from the clutches of a schemer of low degree. There was no one in his own circle suitable for this delicate task; neither Mme. Euffe, who had never had any maternal authority; nor General de Sainte-Foy's widow, who was too blunt and outspoken; nor Claire, who would be offensive; nor Bob de Bazair, who was too high and mighty a person to be mixed up in such depravity as this. He was marrying a young lady of the Euffe family with an air of granting favour. Edmond feared to expose himself to the shafts of his irony and his superior upbringing.

There was no help for it; he must go off to Nice himself, and the sooner he started the better. Would he have any influence with Lucie?

When a girl of that age goes off her head, and especially when her madness takes that particular form . . . Oh, those Euffe children had been showing terrible tenacity in their love affairs! (Just like their father and Grandmother Guigon!)

But an idea occurred to him:

"Of course," he said to himself, "all I've got to do is to see the blighter myself! It's not the wretched Lucie herself that I must tackle, but that adventurer fellow who is playing ducks and drakes with her. How much will he want to let her go?"

Everything now seemed as clear as daylight. Bruno Spaniente wanted to blackmail the Euffes, to get a large sum of money out of them.

For this purpose, no less, he must go to Nice to negotiate. Fortunately Lucie had given the address of the hotel at which she was staying. Edmond consulted the timetables. Then he went to his bank where as a measure of precaution he obtained a letter of credit on a branch at Nice. He was feeling inclined to make a sacrifice of money in order to spare himself the shame of seeing his sister marry his mother's former chauffeur, an event which, with the help of the general's wife, would be the talk of the whole town: for that good lady would be only too happy to spread the news. (In any case the greater portion of the money would be obtained, without her knowing it, from Lucie herself, by deducting it from her share of the profits of the Silken Net. Alberte and Germain, whose interest in the matter was the same as Edmond's own, would pay their quota.)

After leaving the bank, Edmond took the road back to Sassenage in order to let Claire know about this preposterous business, and to make preparations for his departure.

"A jolly sort of summer, this!" he said to himself. "And I ought to be having my holiday now . . . And what will it be like telling Claire . . ."

Then he had a little vision of M. Mivois asking him in a friendly tone of voice, as he stood on the pavement in the Avenue d'Alsace-Lorraine: "There was a rumour that your elder sister was marrying an army officer. Is it so?" And he imagined himself replying:

"No, not an officer. A chauffeur. She is marrying a chauffeur in a middle-class household; a servant!"

He had a mental picture of an expression of extreme disgust on the face of M. Philibert Mivois, champion of the great governing classes! The mere thought of it sent an icy shiver running down his back, despite the warmth of that lovely morning and an atmosphere that was a joy to feel and breathe . . .

"Twenty thousand—that suit you? I'll give you twenty thousand francs cash down, here and now, and no receipt wanted, and no fuss or bother, and then you just clear out and leave my sister alone. An interesting offer, don't you think?"

"Oh, Mr. Edmond," Bruno Spaniente said, with quiet indignation, "what do you take me for?"

"Why, Bruno," Edmond replied, determined to be patient with him, "I think you're a very nice, decent sort of fellow, an excellent fellow. That is why I am interested in you. Look here, I'll run to twenty-five thousand, just to please you."

It was at Nice. Edmond Euffe and Bruno Spaniente were strolling along the Promenade des Anglais, where beautiful shining cars were gliding swiftly and noiselessly, driven, many of them by intrepid young women who made one think of female centaurs, with their hair streaming in the wind, fearless and bold. The sea was an exquisite pure cobalt blue, with an edging of white wavelets along the whole extent of the shore. The sky was blue like the sea, but of a less vivid tint owing to a thick dust haze in the atmosphere.

"Yes," Edmond Euffe continued. "I will give you a thousand francs at once, in cash. And the rest by a cheque which can be cashed at a bank in Paris. You can take a nice little trip to Paris, where you will arrive with your pockets full of money. A pleasant stay you should have there, I think you will agree! To say nothing of the fact that a young man like you, with twenty-five thousand francs in his pocketbook, may get some fine chances in Paris. Other people have pulled it off who had nothing like your capital to start with. Well, Bruno, what about it?"

"Mr. Edmond," Bruno said solemnly, "you distress me! It's true that I've been your mother's chauffeur. But that's no reason for treating me as though my honour meant nothing to me, Mr. Edmond!"

"Now listen, Bruno, I haven't the slightest intention—not the very slightest—of hurting your feelings. If I hadn't a good opinion of you I shouldn't be here. I could have gone and told the whole story to the police, for instance . . ."

In saying this, Edmond was putting out a feeler. There are some people on whom the word "police" has an immediate effect, and he wanted to see . . .

But Bruno did not flinch. On the contrary, he replied in an indignant tone of voice:

"And what is it that's making you talk to me about the police?" he said. "Have I stolen anything?"

186

Edmond beat a hasty retreat.

"I am not accusing you of anything whatsoever, Bruno. Of course one can always ask a man what means of livelihood he has. The police are authorized to do it. I meant no more than that. Look now, Bruno, would you like thirty thousand—thirty thousand, Bruno?"

As he spoke these words he looked thoughtfully at the young native of Nice, trying to guess how long he would continue this play-acting and these endeavours to strike a fine bargain.

Bruno Spaniente was wearing an immaculate vizored white cap and white-and-fawn-coloured shoes with the leather very highly finished. His shirt was of light grenadine tint, and his tie a graded mixture of some extremely bright colours ranging from canary yellow to turquoise blue. His jacket, which his tailor had cut on very generous lines, gave him horizontal and powerful shoulders, with an impression of highly developed pectoral muscle. Bruno had a rather swaying gait, with a peculiar way of shooting his legs forward that made his wide trousers twirl slightly round with each step he took and then fall back again over his shoes, which they covered almost entirely. Edmond found this brand of smartness a trifle loud. He would not have liked any of the people in Grenoble to meet him in the company of this gentleman of the South, with his chin of a bluish hue and a walk that suggested the rhythms of a slow-motion tango. But Bruno was feeling quite confident that his getup blended in unimpeachable fashion with the blue skies and lovely climate of his native town, and the stylish elegance that the Riviera displays. He doubted not that his own charm, combined with those invitations to happiness that the climate of the South extends to those in love, would bring a decisive influence to bear upon the destiny of a young woman whose cheeks were somewhat blotchy but who in certain other respects was decidedly interesting.

"I don't want any money, Mr. Edmond."

"You don't want any money?" Edmond exclaimed in amazement. At the same time he was saying to himself: "The blighter's coming it strong!" He thought that he had not offered enough. He was in a hurry to be done with it.

"Fifty thousand," he said curtly, and in such a violent hurry as to prove that he would never make a buyer of the stature of his father, the late M. Constant Euffe. "It seems to me that that is a pretty sum of money, and that we are doing our business on correct lines."

"Neither fifty nor a hundred," Bruno said calmly.

"Oh, really!" Edmond thought to himself. "Well, we shall soon get to the figure he has decided upon. The scoundrel seems a pretty grasping fellow." Bruno was looking at the sea in a listless sort of way, as though he were a young man particularly sensitive to beauty. The director of the Silken Net was gazing intently at the Sybilline profile of the young native of Nice and steeling himself against a coming shock which would be entailed by some doubtless enormous claim. At last, ready for anything, he stopped and planted himself solidly at Bruno's side.

"How much?" he asked. "How much do you want? What sum?"

"Nothing. Not a halfpenny, Mr. Edmond."

"Does that mean that you are giving up Lucie for nothing?"

"I would rather give up my life," Bruno exclaimed with pathos in his voice.

This solemn declaration was accompanied by a little wink and a mechanical gesture which carried his hand to his cap and slightly shifted the position of the latter upon his head, while he elegantly cocked his little finger in the manner of those gentlemen who take their drinks in a public bar.

"What a frightful little cad!" Edmond thought. But he restrained himself. He did not wish to have a scene.

"Bruno," he began again, "be reasonable. I will go to seventy-five thousand. You will never have such an opportunity again in your life. Well— is it yes or no?"

"No, Mr. Edmond," Bruno said, in the sad tone of voice of a man the fineness of whose feelings is unrecognized and misunderstood.

There was a brief moment of silence, which was filled with the calm and dazzling brilliance of the Mediterranean Sea.

"And supposing I love her—Lucie?"

The effect on Edmond of this familiar reference to his sister was that of an insult hurled at him by an ill-bred cad.

"I see!" he said. "You're a bad lot!"

"Oh," said Bruno, touchy where his honour was concerned, "gently now, Mr. Edmond! I'm a straightforward honest fellow. Your sister loves me and I love her. You've got no call to be insolent to me. And you might be sorry for it later on."

He spoke slowly, spacing out his words, with the singsong accent of the Riviera, and said:

"When we're brothers-in-law!"

"Brothers-in-law!" Edmond exclaimed, with a scornful laugh. "You're pretty certain of things aren't you!"

"Say now," Bruno replied, quite unmoved, "your dad, what was he before he made his fortune?"

"Leave my father alone," Edmond said harshly. "So you'd thought of that, had you! You're even more of a blackguard than I supposed! To play on the feelings of an old maid . . . with no charm."

"Oh, she's not so bad to look at, Lucie isn't! And she's a real good sort. Character's a thing that lasts a lifetime, while prettiness . . . goes phut. . . . It's the heart that I'm always after, in a woman!"

"With her money thrown in, perhaps?"

"Oh," said Bruno. "if the character's all right, a bit of money's always welcome enough. This is what I always say—you'll meet poor girls whose character's all wrong anyway. I know 'em, the little darlings! What I put higher than anything else, Mr. Edmond, is feeling. And Lucie, she's got feeling."

Edmond was pale with anger, and quite incapable of further argument with the villain who was about to bring ridicule and scorn upon the Euffes' good name which, through the behaviour of an infatuated and crazy woman, he had now the power to destroy. It would have given him the greatest pleasure to kill this handsome young man. Surely, he thought, there should be a law to authorize the destruction of low scoundrels when with brazen impudence they set you at defiance and leave you speechless.

Bruno then added these remarkable words:

"The trouble is that you have no family feeling, Mr. Edmond. As for me, I'd have made no difficulty about coming to see you sometime, and your lady too—I've driven her several times to Grenoble. Miss Alberte is very agreeable and pleasant, and Mr. Germain's very nice too. But it's just this—as Tonio Mascoulade at the Mascoulade bar down by the harbour always says—you very seldom see families that get on well together! All the same, Mr. Edmond, you mustn't come and put all the blame on me. In the whole of this business no one could have behaved more correctly than I have!"

Edmond saw Lucie, who also was dressed in bright colours to blend with the lovely blue of sky and sea. She looked like a bony English girl and was in a state of excitement and not entirely sober. Since her arrival at Nice a week earlier, Lucie had had certain revelations, and she was now under the sway of the ecstatic joy that they had brought her. This young woman, who had long ceased to receive anything in the nature of a compliment or to have even the slightest notice taken of her, was now enjoying the tribute of marked attention from a man. Her pride and joy were becoming frenzied, were breaking all bounds. At the first words her brother uttered she broke out into fearful cries, let fly a volley of insults and poured out violent criticism of her own family, who had always sacrificed her and kept her in the background. She had made an idol of

Bruno. There was danger of her causing a scandal either at the hotel or in the street. Henceforth she would care for nothing in the world except to gaze at a handsome head of dark hair outlined against a background of blue sea beneath the canopy of an enchanting sky. Never before had the blood of the Euffes been stirred to such a frenzy of passionate love. Edmond left her, in great distress.

Being at a loose end and alone at Nice, he went in the evening to the Casino, where he won fifteen thousand francs, joylessly, for he had only gambled as a means of drowning care. On the following day he took the train back to Grenoble. He spent the time occupied by the journey in evolving details of an explanation of Lucie's disappearance to be given to all the people of social importance in Grenoble. For this disappearance a motive had somehow to be assigned which would not be inconsistent with the maxim of M. Philibert Mivois: "One's position in life! Never to forget one's position in life—everything depends on that!"

11. UNFOLDMENT   Several times already, since the death of M. Constant Euffe, the mountain groups of the Moucherotte, the Grande Chartreuse, and Belledonne had changed their aspect. Several times had the waters of the Isère and of the Drac come down in seething spate with the melting of the snows. Several times had the lovely valley of the Grésivaudan come back to life with the bright glories of another spring and the warm breezes that flit and stir within it in the month of May, whilst in the hours of morning sunshine its country houses and its tiny hamlets perched high upon the hillside stand out clear and bright. Several times the village of Sappey had received its summer visitors and the mountain pass of Porte its skiing parties. Several times had the plain of Eichirolles seen its willows, birches, and young trees with tender leaves grow green again, while above the dense leafy masses of the trees that line the walks at Pont-de-Claix, the church towers of Seyssins and Seyssinet stood out in sharp relief against the mountainside. Several times had Green Island adorned itself with jade and emerald, with lilac and green grass, opposite La Tronche and Bouquéron, where the successive tiers of villas with their flowery terraces and paths were flooded with the rays of summer sunshine. Gay or sombre, the seasons had come in their due time and the inhabitants of Grenoble continued on their daily round, each one more or less preoccupied, as his station in life should happen to require, with the affairs of the University, the Prefecture, the Town Hall, the army, or the commercial, industrial, or social life of the town. The Euffes, and in particular the Euffes of Sassenage, stood alone in their conviction that the destinies of their own family had a representative character, worthy of a place in the thoughts of their fellow citizens for a long while to come.

There was certainly a distinction to be made between the local people, the genuine natives of Grenoble, and many others only temporarily resident in the town, who filled the hotels, cafés, and restaurants and overran the avenues, and the floating mass of whom finally settled down within an area between the Place Victor-Hugo and the Place Grenette, where everything with any pretensions to smartness, elegance, or entertainment is necessarily to be found to the greatest advantage.

During the months of the dead season, the genuine natives of the town, now left to themselves, had to fall back upon the local news. With the colourful and brilliant crowds of tourists now scattered to the four winds of heaven, the restricted outlook of their daily lives returned once more. If we cut out the suburban districts which lie beyond the level crossings, the zones adjoining the Rue Très-Cloître and the Rue Chanoise, the barracks quarter and the area situated on the right bank of the Isère; if La Capuche, La Bajatière, and the Croix-Rouge are also omitted, the remainder of Grenoble, those portions of the town where intellects and fashions are to be found, is seen to be of very small extent. It is for this reason that, with such a limited number of interesting or outstanding people from which to make their choice, all the inhabitants of note are much taken up with each other. It is for this reason also that the possession of a title, of wealth, or of beauty gives its owner a supremacy that lasts. The conditions of life for these few people are the same as in other provincial towns, and are the inevitable outcome of their restricted numbers. There is but little chance of some new passion wiping out the traces of an earlier one, of a fresh appointment being found if a previous one is lost, of a fortune that is all but lost being quickly regained.

During his lifetime there had been an unconscious tendency at Grenoble to revolve around the person of M. Constant Euffe. By his death, what was to some extent their prop and stay was removed from certain beings who were unconscious of their dependence on him and now saw opening out before them a grim prospect of the total loss of their joys and of their precious security.

It is certain that had it not been for the disappearance of M. Euffe,

Félix Lacail would not so have lost his temper as to come very near to committing murder; that Germain Euffe would not have come equally near to death in the arms of a woman much beloved; that Flavie Lacail would not have known happiness in a romantic guise; that Bob de Bazair would not have married so soon; that the heart of Alberte Euffe would not so soon have gained its dearest wish; that Lucie Euffe herself would have shown more restraint in her fiery outbursts of passion.

The death of M. Euffe had had its real victims, such as Riri Jumier and Pamphile Garambois, each of whose futures was pledged in secret to another, on whose responsive feelings each relied. Riri Jumier wished for nothing better than that M. Euffe's paternal generosity, together with the very close and intimate friendship of Bob de Bazair, should be of lasting duration. As for Pamphile Garambois, he lived on hope. If he had not been entirely happy, at least he had been spared the distress of refusal, up till the fatal morning of the vase's fall. This dogged person was counting on time to bring him what would be his finest hour. The state of mind which is the prelude to requited love is often the happiest of all, that which best favours sweet amorous flights of the imagination. Pamphile could go each day to the spot where love for him was at once a torment and a bliss. With this he stayed content—waiting. The disappointments which inevitably befell this shy and timid suitor became as it were a cherished habit. There was a melancholy charm about this time of waiting that gave his life a serious aim with poetry in it. Sometimes, on leaving Flavie, Pamphile would find that he was being touched and stirred by evening twilight, by a piece of music, by moonlight, by a thousand vague, intangible things which would have left him quite unmoved had not thwarted love made him unusually susceptible to their influence. There were doubtless moments when he believed himself to be unhappy, but a time was to come later when he realized that the years passed in contact with Flavie and her husband at their home had been for him a source of deep if tranquil happiness.

Flavie was no less to be pitied, after Germain Euffe's departure for England. Up till the time of M. Euffe's death she had been a woman accustomed to dream of some other destiny, dispassionately be it said, for her dreams were vague and hazy and she fed her heart on vain imaginings. Misunderstood she certainly was, but no more than many other women. So many were the years during which she had been looking out from her window in vain for the appearance of him who would be her Prince Charming that she was ceasing to believe that he would ever come. The safety she enjoyed as the undistinguished wife of an insignificant official was obtained at a cost, renewed each day, of bitterness and sighs. There were times when she felt seething within her aspirations that bordered on the sublime, with a wealth of wasted feelings debased and ruined by the mean and paltry nature of Félix Lacail. But there was nobody in sight to whom she could dedicate that ardent passion which was the constant theme of her lonely reveries . . . Then Germain Euffe came into her life, with his fair hair, his blushes, his awkward eagerness, his gentlemanly manners, and his "perfectly sweet" appearance, as she had said to herself. . . .

With her happy time of love now past and gone, Flavie spent days and weeks and months of heartbreak. Left entirely without news of Germain, she was now alone with a dazed and bewildered Félix who did not know whether he was a murderer, whether his wife had been unfaithful, and who moreover made no effort to discover these things, and in order to forget everything had ordered, from a maker in the Avenue Jean-Jaurès, a new light road-racing bicycle of the very latest pattern. Every evening as he left the office, Lacail went off to supervise the assembly and fitting out of this treasure. But he no longer took the same pleasure in this as he had taken in the past, for some thread in his life had snapped. This lack of balance had appeared immediately after Pamphile Garambois's departure, and had been increasing ever since. Nevertheless Lacail felt that he must still cling to this, his love of the bicycle and long tours thereon, for without it life would have no meaning. With regard to Flavie, now disdainful and aloof, he wondered whether he should play the part of a guilty man or outraged husband. But he remembered that he had come near to losing both Flavie and his job, and as he still had both he clung to them, in all humility. Furthermore he knew quite well that his wife, with eyes red from weeping and her nerves on edge, would endure neither insinuations nor reproach.

Lacail remembered his ride down from St.-Nizier and its dizzy speed, and the horrible sound of the pistol shot which he had fired still rang in his ears. Of all that followed he had but the vaguest memory. He had tried to get some enlightenment, but Flavie had answered harshly:

"Never speak to me of that again! And consider yourself extremely lucky that I didn't leave you after what you did to me!"

"Very well," Lacail said. "Suppose I was in the wrong . . ."

"Oh," she cried, "there's no 'suppose' about it. You were most certainly in the wrong."

"All right, then, I did wrong. But tell me, why aren't you like you used to be?"

"There are things a woman can't forget."

"But what things?"

"Oh, things!" said Flavie. "And anyhow you bore me! If you aren't satisfied . . ."

It was in this sort of way that their lives dragged on, spoilt by dissension whose roots went deep, as Flavie's coldness showed. At first Lacail had been thankful that he was enabled to resume his calm and peaceful life. Then, when he had once more taken his full place as husband and official, he was overcome by sudden fits of jealousy. He had periods during which he was dejected and easily upset; his suppleness in pedalling was deserting him and he had to toil and labour, and was outdistanced by others, when riding uphill. He began thinking again of "the individual," the man whom he had held covered by the barrel of his pistol.

One evening he met him. He had left the Prefecture at about six o'clock. In no hurry to return home, he decided to go for a walk in the town, setting out by way of the Place Vaucanson and the Rue Saint-Jacques. As he was on the point of entering the tobacconist's in the Rue Félix-Poulat, the door opened and a tall young man with fair hair, of athletic appearance and with Anglo-Saxon stylishness, brushed past him.

"Good heavens!" Lacail said to himself. "Freddy Glowes! Still here, that fellow!"

He should have enjoyed the satisfaction of being able to say to himself that his victim was not dead. But this satisfaction was accompanied by a fear lest once again he should find his wife leaning shamelessly upon the shoulder of this young popinjay, the sight of whom evoked a clear and definite picture in his mind; and he could not doubt that this was the young man associated with a cruel happening in the past. . . . He brooded over this calamity, wondering what its real extent might be, and lingering for long periods in cheap wineshops, where he drank to excess. It was late when he mounted the stairs in the Rue Turenne. Flavie gave him a bad reception, telling him that she refused to put up with such behaviour.

He sat down, and at first remained silent. But the alcohol he had absorbed got the better of him.

"Now then," he said, "I've had enough of it!"

"What?" Flavie said, astonished. "I don't understand."

With an unpleasant, sneering laugh, he replied:

"I've met your American!"

"What American?"

"Why, Freddy Glowes, of course!"

Flavie should have said nothing. But her curiosity was too strong for her.

"You met him in Grenoble? Today?"

194

"Ah," Lacail said, "so you're interested, are you? You've never said much about him!"

Flavie had turned pale, with a hard, determined expression on her face. Lacail felt so strongly that there was a danger of the plain, unvarnished truth being hurled at him and thus wrecking the whole situation, that he became alarmed.

"All right," he said, "we'll talk about it some other time. Give me my soup."

He ate rapidly, without speaking, and rose from the table.

"Anyhow," he said, "I can see quite well that he's a fellow who won't want you to share his life. He knows better!"

And off he went to bed, leaving Flavie in the kitchen, where she wept, wondering what was to become of her. Germain was at Grenoble, and she could not go on leading this life of humiliation. . . .

She heard Félix snoring heavily. She felt that she wanted to go out; she would have given all she possessed to see Germain, merely to see him, even from a distance. She crept out of the flat, noiselessly, went downstairs and out into the street. The night, which was warm and mild with a clear, starry sky, reminded her of past nights of happiness. Had she but known where Germain was to be found, she would have gone there without further ado. But all she knew—and that through a stranger —was that he had returned ("stranger" was the term applied to Félix in her thoughts). She wandered aimlessly along the Rue Lesdiguières, from one end to the other. She then turned off into the Rue Casimir-Périer, went back in the direction of the Place Vaucanson and thence down the Rue Condillac and Lafontaine Row. At the corner of Lafontaine Row and Gambetta Parade she entered a café, ordered a chartreuse, and stayed there buried in thought. She felt heavy and dull with unhappiness, with an unhappiness which had lain dormant for months and was now coming back to her with the same searing pain as before.

Snatches of loud conversation reached her from a corner of the room, where a small group of men appeared to be engaged in a lively discussion. One of them was bawling more loudly than the rest, and Flavie guessed that it was the "Dictator," of whom she had heard. He was a little man of the name of Maliboin, with irregular teeth set in a most unpleasant mouth, and green and prominent eyes which he turned incessantly this way and that. He had had an undistinguished career in the army and retired with the rank of captain. Since his retirement he had been rescuing France daily, at cocktail time, with energetic and vociferous methods which otherwise he would be having no occasion to use, with the asperities of the military officer's job now left behind.

He belonged to that breed of petty tyrants who would be quite capable of stirring up a revolution in order to make a name for themselves in their own district. This would-be reformer lived on dreams of the Bastille, the guillotine, the firing squad, penal servitude, and the gallows. It was denunciation that gave him his most unalloyed delight. He had been given a job with agents of the C.I.D., whom he supplied with secret reports on a number of people in Grenoble whose opinions did not coincide with his own. Needless to say the police, having had a good laugh over them, consigned these notes to the wastepaper basket. The same thing was done at the military headquarters, whither this madman resorted to expose anti-military intrigues of a mysterious and sinister nature. But he was solemnly thanked for his shrewd insight and his zeal. All this provided further occasion for laughter.

It was because he was feeling a need of diversion that Pamphile Garambois had sought out the Dictator's company. For it was Pamphile who was there and answering him back with sufficient success to arouse Maliboin's fury. Suddenly he caught sight of and recognized Flavie. He rose, went to her table, and sat down facing her.

"Good evening, Flavie," he said to her. "But you don't look well. You are not ill, I hope?"

"I don't know," she replied.

"I am pleased to see you, Flavie. I'm very pleased. You know that I think about you as much as ever?"

"Ah," Flavie said wearily, "still got the same complaint?"

"Yes—loving somebody. Does one ever get rid of it? Do you really believe one does?"

"No, no, I don't!" Flavie said.

She was almost weeping. Pamphile noticed this.

"I'm certain you have a sorrow! You're wrong, Flavie! You will suffer at first, and then it'll be all over."

He looked at her, shrugged his shoulders, and said gently:

"That young Euffe—he's not right for you. He will marry in his own set. You'll disappear from his life."

He was guessing her secret. What he was saying was horrible, but it enabled Flavie to hear Germain spoken of. She let him go on talking. In him fidelity and devotion were plainly to be seen, and even his voice brought comfort with it. Pamphile took her hand.

"Flavie," he said, "do you remember what I said to you one day? I shall always be at your service at any time you want me. Just a hint is all you'll need to give me."

"My poor Pamphile—what's the use of it? If I loved you, well . . ."

"Oh," Pamphile said, "your loving me—that's another matter altogether, and I am not asking for so much as all that. But I myself still love you, Flavie. Isn't that enough?"

"Why don't you marry somebody?"

"Why should I? Does it make one so happy, then?"

"That depends," Flavie said. "It ought to be possible, I suppose."

"Yes," Pamphile said. "I think it ought. So I am waiting. When a man hasn't any charm and hasn't any luck either, he needs a lot of patience. And I spend my whole life thinking about you, Flavie!"

"By the way," Flavie said, changing the subject, "is your business doing well? Are you satisfied?"

"Very well," Pamphile replied. "But I am no longer doing agency work. I've bought a little cinema which pays well, without taking up much of my time. I could quite well afford to buy a car. Would you like to do some motoring, Flavie? Come now, at your age anything may happen!"

She made no reply. He handed her a small printed card.

"Look," he said, "here is a free pass for my establishment. I am showing a very good Freddy Glowes film there just now. You should go and see it."

"Freddy Glowes?" Flavie said with a start. "Perhaps I shall go. . . . Now then," she added, "I must go back."

"I will come with you," said Pamphile.

He took her back to her own door, and they were on the point of bidding each other farewell when Flavie said to him:

"You wouldn't have known this—but you should come here again— come just like you used to do. Félix would be pleased to see you again. He misses you."

"I will come," Pamphile said. "I shall come because you are there, Flavie."

"What—me? Oh, I've nothing more to hope for. I've nothing to hope for in life . . ."

"Oh, I shouldn't say that," Pamphile said, "there's always something good to be expected from life. Always! I shall come tomorrow. Let Félix know."

For those people who have not been favoured from the outset by the circumstances of their birth, a certain hardness is necessary for the conduct of their lives. It may happen that this hardness is not natural to them, but life itself contrives to instil them with the mistrust and suspicion they need, with the faculty of standing always in the breach, of being always on the defensive, which keeps their wills taut and ready for action.

A girl whose instincts were fundamentally good rather than bad, Riri Jumier was now undergoing an apprenticeship of this kind. It is most difficult in the provinces to turn over a new leaf and throw overboard a past of which everyone is well aware. Riri was assigned at Grenoble to a certain class—that of kept women; and the label remained securely tied to her charming person. The constant tendency of the offers which she received from men was to prevent her from emerging from this social category. And it is not every day that chance procures you a well-preserved elderly man with the kindly disposition and the generosity of a Constant Euffe. Many men, even when advanced in years, are skinflints in love; many men of a ripe age are uninvited and unwelcome guests therein . . . As for young men, they are generally short of money: while those who plunge into reckless expenditure and consequent debt do so for women much older than themselves, because that gives them prominence. It was on these lines, at any rate, that Riri was arguing to herself now that she was in search of a situation, and prepared to run straight or otherwise, as circumstances should dictate. But whether she continued her career of unofficial love or steered for a legitimate union, it was at something serious and lasting that she was directing her aim.

As regards starting a business, she was not prepared for this. "In any case," Bob de Bazair had said to her, "if you are quite set on making this experiment, you must assure yourself that the man who is backing you will make good any losses there may be. But don't run any risks with your own bit of savings. And you have every chance of getting done in by moneylenders. They're a dangerous crew." This was assuredly good advice, and it was prompted by a sincere friendship.

In reality Riri had quiet, homely tastes. She attached the greatest possible value to her charming flat in the Place Marval, which gave her the status of a lady, a little on the border line perhaps, but still a lady. At one period of her life she had known what slums were like, and promiscuous living. At all costs she would avoid any relapse to such depths as those.

It is curious to reflect that while Flavie Lacail was feeling sick and tired of her condition in life, it was exactly that regular, well-ordered existence that aroused the envy of Riri Jumier. Bob had sensed her real nature when he said to her, on one of the last occasions when they had met: "You should settle down. You haven't got the temperament of the out-and-out adventuress, you are much too sentimental for that. What you would like best would be doing your own marketing, polishing your furniture and washing your kids." This was true. Even during the time of M. Euffe, Riri had been accustomed to do her own shopping and keep her furniture bright. She was descended from women of the La Tour-du-Pin family, who had been great polishers, great scourers of pots and pans, and prolific mothers of children (which had obliged Riri, one of a numerous family, to shift for herself at an early age). These family traits were at work within her.

She had good reason for setting great store by her flat, for it became the means by which she got her life into working order. One day when she was looking through the advertisements in the *Dauphiné Gazette* (which was itself an indication that her mind was unsettled and that she was in search of some improvement in her circumstances), her eyes fell upon these lines, in the "Apartments to let" column.

"Engineer, 27, desires furnished room in light clean building. Careful and tidy. Good rent offered. Write Box 3905."

It occurred to Riri that to let one of her rooms would be a very material assistance in the payment of her rent; and further—and this was a still stronger inducement to do so—it would be a means of getting in touch with a decorous and well-behaved gentleman. An engineer . . . This word set her musing, as did the age—twenty-seven years. She wrote to Box 3905 and went out and took her letter to the offices of the *Dauphiné Gazette*.

On the following day a young man of pleasing appearance, tall, dark-haired, and well dressed, came and introduced himself. He explained that having been an engineer at Grenoble for some little time past, he now expected to remain in the town. He was therefore wishing to leave his hotel and find a more comfortable lodging. He inspected the flat and declared that he was delighted with it. He looked at Riri with an interest that was plainly to be seen.

"Are you the proprietress?" he asked.

"Oh yes," she said. "Does that surprise you?"

"Well, the fact is that I took you for the daughter of the house. Do you live alone in this apartment?"

"Certainly," Riri replied. "Do you find that an objection?"

"I should just say not!" the young man exclaimed. "What I meant was that I could never have dreamt that I should strike so lucky! But it won't be you that does my room? With such pretty hands . . ."

"Oh, you need not worry," Riri said. "I shall get a charwoman to come in the mornings."

Riri observed that he had a pleasant smile, fine teeth, and a nice, open manner. He gave her his name—Roger Lagarde. The matter appeared to be settled.

"Now there's just one thing more," Riri said. "You are young . . . And I don't want any women in my house. Just remember that."

"Madame," Roger Lagarde exclaimed, "I should be ashamed to bring a woman of any kind to the house of a proprietress so young and so charming. And if there is one thing I could hope for . . ."

But he blushed a little and did not say what it was that he dared to hope for. He offered to leave a deposit. Riri tried to refuse, but he insisted.

"Take it, take it," he said, "then I shall be quite sure that the room is mine. Shall I be able to come tomorrow?"

"Tomorrow if you like. Anyhow, I can only give you the room for a month. I have never let a furnished apartment before. It's an experiment I'm making."

"And it will succeed, you'll see!" Roger Lagarde exclaimed enthusiastically.

So far as Riri Jumier was concerned, a young man who had come from a distance started with less in his favour than a firmly established resident in Grenoble would have had. On the other hand, it was particularly rash to shut up beneath the same roof two young, ardent, unmarried people who slept badly, he in his place and she in hers, that is to say a few yards away from each other, and conscious of having within their reach everything they lacked and needed, and in the most agreeable, not to say entrancing, form. The tenant and his proprietress could hear each other move and sigh. It was inevitable that each should be thinking of the other, in a most tender, caressing way. . .

Roger Lagarde, so soon as he had finished his evening meal at a restaurant, had never a thought but to return to the Place Marval in the hope that Riri would be still stirring. He always had some requests to make, which served as an excuse for starting a conversation. This conversation would be continued at considerable length in a pleasant setting, in the gentle glimmer of a subdued and softened light, in an atmosphere of intimacy and of home. Riri wore indoor frocks of an extremely suggestive kind and the whole apartment was filled with her scent. She would offer him tea or a glass of liqueur brandy or chartreuse. He gave her Turkish cigarettes, bought specially for her. There was laughter; they were learning to know each other better.

"You go out very little for a young man?" Riri said to him.

"Grenoble bores me," Roger Lagarde replied.

"Still, visitors always say that it's a town to enjoy one's self in."

"But I'm not out to enjoy myself," he declared.

"Oh well, then . . ."

She did not ask him why. But he continued on the same theme:

"In any case, you don't go out any more than I do!"

"Oh," she replied, "that's a different matter. A woman who goes out alone in the evening gets a bad reputation in no time."

He suggested taking her to the cinema, and she accepted. They went every week; and they soon became what was to all appearances a couple leading a highly respectable and very united life. But this appearance ceased at the doors of their rooms, where they parted. Roger Lagarde had fallen in love with Riri Jumier within a few days. After two months of smiles, occasional light contacts, and pretty ways, he was becoming altogether crazy. Riri's charm made any compensations that he might have found elsewhere seem merely hateful.

In days past Riri Jumier had made but little difficulty about yielding to certain requests, and there had been a difficult period of her life at which these concessions had been pretty numerous. Her intention now was to make some atonement for these past errors by a mild display of prudishness. But her nights were as restless as Roger Lagarde's; and the task of confining herself strictly to the parts of landlady and friend, which she had hitherto been playing, called for a species of heroism for its accomplishment. She was now nearly twenty-five. She had no wish to serve as plaything for a second Bob de Bazair, who would be deserting her one fine day and marrying an heiress. She knew, too, the danger, in her situation, of attaching herself to a young man of whom she was rather too fond . . .

It is always an easy matter for a woman to get a man to ask her questions. Riri manœuvred in such a way as to lead Roger Lagarde to ask:

"What is the matter with you just now? I find you changed."

Reticently, she replied:

"There is something that is worrying me."

"You don't want to tell me what it is?"

"What would be the use?" Riri said.

"Oh, come now," Roger Lagarde said tenderly, "don't you think of me as a friend—just a little?"

"Very well, then," Riri answered, speaking very rapidly, "there's someone asking to marry me—since you want to know everything!"

"Oh, so that's why you are not as you used to be!"

He seemed overwhelmed, and indeed he was so, by the seeming likelihood that his devotion during the past three months would count for nothing now that this offer had been made. Circumstances were getting beyond his control. With his heart rent in anguish, and torn by vague, ill-defined jealousy, he asked her:

"Do you like this man?"

Riri Jumier would not give him a direct reply.

"I have to consider the prospects," she said.

"Are they very splendid?" Roger Lagarde asked, his distress even still more acute.

"Oh, quite good," Riri said. "And it means a safe future for me. What is a lone woman to do with her life? She can never be sure of getting proper consideration and respect, and no support she may be given is ever disinterested."

"So it isn't a love match that you are thinking of?" Roger Lagarde asked her, following up the idea that was in his mind.

"A marriage of convenience is not always the worst kind. When there is a solid affection, you know . . ."

"Yes—if one is not in love with someone else. As for me, I can only say that I should be quite incapable now of going in for a marriage of that kind, even if it meant a big fortune. You can guess why?"

This question did not seem to arouse Riri's curiosity, for she replied:

"For a man it's not the same thing at all. Men are independent in life. But we poor women, if we let our hearts rule our heads, nine times out of ten it's all up with us. I made that stupid mistake myself once. So I know what I am talking about."

"I can see that you have suffered," Roger Lagarde said to her. "But haven't you forgotten that sorrow now?"

"Yes," Riri answered, with straightforward candour, and looking him squarely in the face. "But I'm afraid to start out on another adventure of the same kind. I don't trust sentiment! Here I have an opportunity of marrying under favourable conditions, and a man who is a good worthy creature, while I myself have a cool head about it all. . . . What would you do in my place?"

"If I were in your place," cried Roger Lagarde, who had now completely lost his self-possession, "I should agree to a quite different suggestion. Supposing I asked you to marry me?"

These words were the climax of feelings which had been growing daily in intensity, and he could not have done other than utter them. Roger Lagarde, who had been awaiting for three months past the moment at which he would clasp Riri in his arms, was now quite incapable of giving her up. He felt that throughout the length and breadth of Grenoble there could not be found another young woman so desirable, so elegant as she, with such an even temperament, with an interior so charming as hers, so well adapted to love-making and the pleasures of home life. After all, for a young engineer whose future was still by no means assured, a pretty person like Riri Jumier, with money of her own, a small car and a charming flat, was not such a bad match! This was the reasoning born of his desire. In reality Roger Lagarde was feeling that it was beyond his power to continue to spend his nights alone while an insignificant piece of brickwork, as fragile as a convention, was all that lay between himself and Riri and he was imagining her in the bewitching postures of sleep or dreams, like a Titian *Venus* or the *Maja nue* of Goya.

"Are you speaking seriously?" Riri asked.

"Can you doubt it?" Roger Lagarde replied, thinking that, having spoken of marriage, he was now at long last free to hold the young woman in close embrace. She made no protest, nor did she withhold her lips nor the full charming curves of her breast. Her store of heroic virtue was now exhausted, and she had not the heart to keep at arm's length the first man who offered her marriage. Let the future take care of itself! The present was tempting indeed . . .

That night they made trial of life conjugal to the last degree, with the impetuous ardour of long-pent-up passion.

Three years had now gone by during which Lucie Euffe, having vanished from Grenoble, had been living with Bruno Spaniente in lawful wedlock, at Nice. A false picture of the marriage had been drawn by the Euffes, who had represented it as a romantic, touching, and highly suitable match. When the inevitable had come to pass, Edmond had set a rumour afloat to the effect that his sister was making a love match and leaving for the Colonies with her husband, a young man with very small means but of good education and with fine prospects. In view of Mlle. Euffe's personal appearance, people were a trifle surprised by the news, but declared without exception that they were "very pleased for that nice Lucie's sake, who had so well deserved her happiness." Then, as it takes so short a time for people to grow accustomed to doing without former friends, inquiries relating to the young woman who had now disappeared from Grenoble soon became limited to those which a minimum of politeness demanded. The tone of voice in which these questions were asked made it quite evident that the circumstances and fate of the elder of the Euffe young ladies were a matter that was rarely if ever in people's minds.

There was nothing for it but to swallow the insult! The Euffes of Sassenage had ceased going to Nice, or only went through the town in a car and driving at considerable speed. When on the Riviera, at Juan, or Cannes, they kept their eyes open in order to avoid running suddenly into the Spaniente couple, with whom they wished to have no dealings whatever except by correspondence, and that limited to what was strictly necessary, such as New Year's greetings and business matters. For Edmond had succeeded in retaining his sister's capital for the Silken Net, having made the sacrifice—the only member of his family to do so—of attending the marriage ceremony. One may disapprove of a marriage, but that is no reason for placing a firm's progress in jeopardy, or running the risk of seeing a large proportion of the shares pass into the hands of strangers. Furthermore, Edmond declared, to manage her capital for her was a service of which that misguided young woman stood definitely in need. Without his supervision and care she might very possibly have been robbed, or, having a big sum of ready money at her disposal, might see her fortune frittered away by the dangerous Spaniente. It was bad enough in all conscience that this man should be beating her. (Claire would believe nothing but that Lucie was being thus treated by her "stableboy," saying that in a marriage of that kind it was all that could be expected.)

Lucie, happily, had no desire to return to Grenoble, which contained nothing for her but memories of past humiliations, while at Nice she was living in great comfort, at a villa at Cimiez, in a beautiful climate. Contrary to the assertions of her own family, she was far from being unhappy.

There was nothing ill-natured or unkind about Bruno. He was indeed quite an agreeable companion, never making difficulties so long as there was no further question of work. Apart from that of idleness, he had no overmastering needs, his exploits being mostly verbal and his activities limited to gesture that stopped short of action. Delighted at being a man of independent means who need have no anxiety for the future, he allowed himself to be tended and admired by Lucie and never snubbed or rebuffed her.

Lucie was by no means anxious that Bruno should have a profession, as this would give him independence and relegate herself to a place of secondary importance. What she wanted was to remain a daily necessity to him. Nevertheless she wished to see him with an occupation, some absorbing hobby, which would save him from complete idleness, association with some rather fishy companions, and the temptations which the Riviera offers. She turned his attention to tennis, a fashionable game. It would be Bruno's best means, while at the same time enjoying himself, of attaining some little celebrity in circles where physical dexterity and skill is of greater importance than good birth. And he possessed a natural aptitude for such things.

Having formerly been employed as a ball boy, Bruno actually had in his mind's eye the strokes and movements of champions, and, by a spirit of imitation, possessed all the rudiments of the technique. Almost since the days of his childhood he had been able properly to appreciate a fine smash, a grand drive, a solid backhand, a decisive volley. As a lad he had handled a racquet during the hours at which the courts were not let. He was supple, naturally quick on his feet, and could cover the court at great speed. He was now a rich man and could afford to pay for lessons, practise all the year round in sunshine, play with different partners and make rapid progress. He soon acquired a complete game, and was a particularly wily player. A well-fed and idle man, he had powers of resistance that often disheartened his adversary and gave him victory. He cultivated a special stroke, a short backhand played at a very sharp angle across the court, which gained him points. It was then that he realized all the advantages of a good backhand. He preserved and worked hard at this stroke. He learnt to take a perfect stance, to strike without undue haste, but resolutely and with determination. It was thus that he acquired a lightning backhand stroke, very difficult to return on account of its speed, and which made the ball shoot when it touched the ground. This backhand became his principal weapon, his most precise and accurate attacking stroke. It took his opponents by surprise, the backhand being universally regarded as the weakest stroke and a player's left as his more vulnerable side.

Bruno became quite a personage on the tennis courts, a man who had his supporters and admirers. Bets were made on his chances and his future as a player, and this was done the more enthusiastically in that he was generous in standing drinks, after the baths and dressing. Having become a regular player in tournaments, he passed easily from third to second string, where he had a good place. He went off to play matches at Monte Carlo, Cannes, Juan-les-Pins, Marseilles, accompanied on every occasion by Lucie, who saw that his sweaters, white trousers, and tennis shirts were all in good condition. His supporters maintained that he might go further still if he could get more punch into his forehand. He might even reach the first string, and perhaps be seeded among the first twenty players in France. It must be added that this was perhaps Lucie's ambition rather than Bruno's. The latter was perfectly happy on the courts, returning the ball for two or three hours on end, and accepting victory or defeat with the same fine equanimity.

It had now become evident to all who knew him that Bruno Spaniente had wished for nothing better than to lead a straight, honest life with all his time at his own disposal. The headstrong behaviour of Lucie having provided him with the means, he became a highly presentable sporting gentleman, who looked very well in tennis clothes. Content with his lot, he showed his gratitude to Lucie by giving her a child. The neighbourhood of the tennis courts on which his father so greatly distinguished himself was the scene of this boy's first footsteps. Bruno announced that his son would have a racquet in his hand at an early age and would become a great champion.

The trouble for the Euffes was precisely the reputation which Bruno had now acquired, with his name appearing in the sporting news. There were even some papers in which his photograph was reproduced. In one of these photographs a careful examination had enabled people to recognize Lucie in the background, enjoying a share in her husband's glory.

"The poor creature's looks have not improved!" Claire said.

This was a falsehood; there was some improvement in Lucie's appearance; she had put on flesh and looked calm and peaceful. But Claire thought that to advertise herself in this way showed a want of discretion that was in the worst possible taste. To let himself be forgotten was the least that the usurper of several of the Euffe millions should have done. They were terrified lest the undesirable relation should come and show himself off at Grenoble, and gather fresh laurels at Lesdiguières. But Bruno had ceased to give a thought to Grenoble. Moreover he was by no means anxious to reappear in places where he might have been known as a servant of the Euffes, standing by the door of a saloon car. He too had begun his ascent of the social ladder. It was now his turn to think of making his son a well-brought-up, well-mannered boy, a worthy offshoot of a good French bourgeois stock, who would never be handicapped in days to come by any reference to his origin. This child would even be able later on to afford a chauffeur himself. Bruno would then teach him the necessary caution and discernment in choosing the man. There are certain adventures which should not become traditional in families, in the same way as it is undesirable that all the instincts of mothers should be transmitted to their daughters.

He was expecting a daughter. Lucie was now awaiting a second confinement. Bruno was by no means displeased that there should be a further addition to his family to strengthen the bonds which united him to the Euffes of the Silken Net. It had the further advantage that he would not have Lucie continually dogging his footsteps. There are exceedingly pretty players at the courts, and Lucie viewed the prospect of her husband playing numbers of mixed doubles matches with a very unfavour-

206

able eye. It was all very well to say that where sport is concerned the relations between men and girls are exclusively of the friendly type—she didn't trust them all the same! Above all she did not want Bruno to jeopardize his tennis for the sake of some frivolous little creature who looked nice in her shorts. He had a good ranking. He might go farther still.

12. MOTHER AND SON Edmond Euffe was losing his hair and acquiring a weighty importance in life. With a full and varied experience behind him, and enriched thereby, he would henceforth be in a better position to lay down definite and final rules for the conduct of · his life and start the decisive phase of his career. His fortieth year was giving him an inner firmness and stability of which he had never hitherto been conscious. He had at last obtained a clear and definite picture of his inmost self, knew its needs, and made indulgent concessions to it which he kept secret, in order that he might give to others a picture of himself corresponding to what he imagined to be their conception of dignity, intelligence, and worth—in a word, of a man destined by his merits to develop on noble lines. It is only at the cost of some concealment of our true feelings, some control of the attitudes we adopt, that we human beings can make an impression on others, just as one poses for a photograph in profile or three-quarter face, after numerous experiments before one's mirror in an attempt to appear at what we personally conceive to be our best. A collection of appetites and desires, of selfish motives and empty pride, by which our actions are sometimes determined, should never be allowed to appear on the surface except under a disguise of maxims and principles to which no one could take exception. In the same way that we are concerned to display our physical frame to advantage by means of toilet and dress, so should we protect our minds and hearts with the armour of a high moral standard and only let them be seen in gala dress. Edmond Euffe was arriving at the most important period of maturity, that of full development, when the individual, now free from the impulsiveness and hesitations of youth, should know what he wants, whither he is going, and what he looks to life to give him.

He was looking at a picture of himself, with a vista of years ahead, still in the same places as in former days, and in a setting from which he had never long been absent. This was for him an occasion for some serious reflection on his past life, and for taking stock of the importance of the progress he had made. Some of the town's residents who had formerly inspired him with respect or with fear were now becoming old men. Edmond could see by the way they looked at him that they were thinking of him as a man in an established position, a man of ability and strength, whose privileges of taking wide action and making final decisions they could no longer question. Edmond belonged to the generation which held the reins of power, that which, for a period of about twenty years, assumes the leadership and takes control of human affairs. He was conscious of having acquired an outlook that was powerfully realistic, in a wide sense of that term, and of having become a useful and effective servant of the community. He was feeling that his authority had increased, and that, having superseded his father, he had ceased to be "old Euffe's son" and had become the elder M. Euffe, head of the family, director of a great firm, owner of a fine country house, and an important person in Grenoble. The distance which separated him from a man like M. Philibert Mivois was tending to diminish; and in any case M. Mivois, upon whom age had now laid a heavy hand, was becoming an old driveller in his dotage. He was now sustained by memories of the power he had wielded in days gone by, but henceforth he would belong to the generation which was about to hand over to others, after being the repository of manners and customs which would soon disappear forever.

It had been a fixed principle with the late M. Constant Euffe that there is no substitute for the supervision of the director himself. Even during the last years of his life, when pleasure and self-indulgence were taking up too much of his time, the director of the Silken Net never missed a day in visiting his offices or one of his branch establishments or warehouses. His supervision was exercised by means of surprise visits, which were made in every direction, in order that no one might be tempted to drift into the fatal habits of slackening off in his work or of waste, either of which, sooner or later, will wreck any business concern.

Egged on by his wife, whose chief concern was her circle of acquaintance and who despised catering, Edmond had wished to free himself from the shackles of business. But whenever he relaxed control, he was conscious of the disadvantages of relying exclusively on subordinates, people whose fortunes and interests are not at stake. As director and head of the business, he found himself in this embarrassing dilemma—whether to immerse himself completely in grocery and give up all his social engagements, or let the Silken Net take its own course, and sacrifice a proportion of his income. The thought of having to make such sacrifice was, however, quite enough to re-establish his habit of unremitting attention to the business. He had made a study of new systems of supervision devised for the avoidance of wastage. For where vast quantities of goods are being handled and a very large staff employed, wastage may spread like an epidemic of disease and grow to ruinous proportions. Edmond had come to realize that it is essential that the head of a big business should be available and on the spot. Any negligence on the part of the management becomes a costly matter, for it is multiplied by similar shortcomings on the part of subordinates. Furthermore, in the wholesale catering business there is a speculative side which calls for the closest attention, a concentration of all a man's faculties. The right moment has to be chosen for the purchase of wines, sugar, jams, dried vegetables, tinned fish, et cetera, the current prices of which are affected by the weather, the harvest, the price of manures, imports, and many other things.

For these reasons Edmond came sedulously to his office in the Avenue d'Alsace-Lorraine. And he did so the more willingly in that Claire, with her picture shows, lectures, musical parties, and social gossip and news items from Paris, was a continual nuisance, besides compelling him to visit people whose refinement was unquestionable but whose company he did not invariably enjoy. In his own house at Sassenage, among his wife's guests, nearly all of whom were friends of the Bargès family, he cut a sorry figure.

It was in the Avenue d'Alsace-Lorraine that Edmond was able to recover himself, give his own personality free play, and do a little thinking on his own account. There were now some fresh anxieties, new matters needing attention, that were occupying his mind owing to the way in which current events were shaping. And a disturbing outlook it was!

M. Constant Euffe, continually on the lookout for opportunities of making friends in all parties, had kept steadily aloof from politics. "After all," he used to say, "a man's stomach has got one opinion only, and that is, that it should get good food at a cheap rate. Anybody who can gain the good will of stomachs is bound to make friends." Edmond wondered whether he had the right to reason in so summary a fashion, and he doubted it. His father had been a man of the 1900 period, and between 1914 and 1918 was at the zenith of his commercial glory. (The Silken Net, by instituting a special line of goods known as "The Parcel for the Front," had made some very big profits. These parcels, of which there were six different varieties, were sewn up and weighed in advance, and the shops undertook their dispatch on behalf of the families.

Subscriptions could be taken out for a weekly, fortnightly, or monthly parcel. There were also parcels made up, on request, containing Balaklava helmets, gloves, socks, et cetera. There were many housewives who appreciated these facilities, which saved them the trouble of looking for paper and string and going to the post office. Further, these packages, which later on were marked "The Soldier's Silken Net," contained articles of good quality only and were always punctually dispatched. Dauphiné soldiers used to write from the front asking for their "Silken Net.")

Edmond Euffe was taking the helm in other times—anxious, troubled times, stirred by deep undercurrents of social unrest—and one could feel, as he himself thought, a dreadful surge and swell of appetites and covetous desire, in every class of society. Money was becoming unstable. Taxation was growing continually more severe. The future—the immediate future—was darkened by the prospect of elections which might have an unfortunate result.

In the opinion of Edmond Euffe, who read treatises on economics, the truth of the matter was that the progress of mechanical invention was setting up new problems which were now calling for solution. The world was entering upon an age of machinery and mass production. It was a bad thing that the different steps taken to meet changing conditions should be nullified one by one by the action of the proletariat in strikes and disturbances, simply because the employers had failed to forestall the inevitable difficulties in the process of adaptation. The system of contracts put the body of employers in a very thankless position. Edmond was an advocate of different methods, and an advocate who was all the more convinced in view of the fact that a wages increase meant an increase in the purchasing power of the workers, who made up a large proportion of his customers. He defended these methods before the Employers' Federation of Dauphiné, in which he was now taking an important place. His suggestions were being carefully considered, that is to say, they had divided the federation into two factions, almost equal in numbers, which, without coming to any decision, were bickering over the question whether they should take the initiative or await events.

"If we make offers," one side urged, "we shall put ourselves in a position of inferiority. It will be said that we are making them because we cannot do otherwise—because we are afraid."

"If we don't make offers," the others replied, "we shall get no thanks for yielding when a time comes that we have to do so. It is not so much the making over of a few sums of money that we have to fear, as a constant and ever-increasing enmity between employers and employed."

"Vain imaginings!" said some.

"Dangerous obstinacy!" said the others.

"We can make some concessions without any danger to our own interests. For in actual fact it is the consumer who pays."

"We shall always be called exploiters, whatever we do!"

Edmond spoke in favour of the American method commended by Ford:

"If you pay the workman on a scale which enables him to become an important consumer, his money will contribute to prosperity by adding to the volume of trade."

"Oh no," he was told. "If you raise the workman's wages to any very material extent, you will turn him into a member of the lower middle class. But it is a well-known fact that while the workman spends all he earns, the French lower middle classes have only one idea in their heads —to economize, to save for the future, and they spend nothing."

"But surely you will educate him, this modern workman!"

"The more you educate him, the more he will want to be your equal. And the more difficult he will be to control."

"But these social questions can't be left indefinitely as a battleground for conflicting opinions!"

"Can you stop wealth being regarded as a challenge?"

No progress was being made in these matters. But so far as discussing them went, Edmond was becoming stronger in dialectical argument and debate and acquiring a certain eloquence together with precision. He was also searching for further knowledge and material for argument, and for this purpose was reading more than hitherto. It occurred to him that these activities might lead to something other than his place in the Employers' Federation. (The expenses of an election would be a mere trifle to him.) He unburdened himself on the subject to Claire, who expressed warm approval of his idea. Nothing could please her more than to see her husband holding some public office, which would greatly add to the importance and influence of her receptions and social gatherings.

"The trouble is," Edmond said to her, "that I have no chance of success as a Conservative, with the present trend of opinion as it is, here in Grenoble. The clever thing would be to get myself put up as a radical candidate—or even a socialist one."

"Socialist?" Claire asked. "And what about your religious views?"

"Socialism is not incompatible with Catholicism, far from it. And in my opinion a few moderate men are just what is needed among the socialists. If there are nothing but genuine socialists in their party, their programme becomes a far more pernicious one than it would be otherwise. And it flatters those people to have a few millionaires amongst them. And in any case it is becoming more and more the fashion for rich men to join the parties of the Left. It is a case of doing what is expedient—and of being broad-minded."

"And how will you approach these people?"

"I could offer a certain sum of money for the party funds. But I should want someone to act as an intermediary for me. I should rely on your friends for that. This would be essentially an occasion for turning to them for help."

"Tell me," Claire said, "you are not thinking of becoming a freemason?"

"No," Edmond replied, "I don't expect I shall go so far as that. But anyhow, taking it all in all, the whole question boils down to this: does one stand for Parliament in order to be elected or to be turned down?"

"To be elected, obviously," said Claire. "It would be absurd, in your position, to be beaten."

"That is just what I think," Edmond said. "To say nothing of the fact that my election would be an excellent advertisement for the Silken Net."

"On the whole, you would dislike standing as a Conservative candidate?" Claire asked him.

"Oh, by no means," Edmond replied, "I shouldn't dislike it at all! The only thing I should dislike would be getting beaten. Indeed it would be as a man of the Right that I should come forward if I saw a fairly good chance for myself on that side. But I don't see any. You will agree, too, that I am justified in relying on my own customers to vote for me, even if I had to go so far as to reduce my prices during the election period. Now my customers' political sympathies are all of the Left, like those of most people of small means who think that they will have nothing to lose by political developments of a certain kind."

"You aren't afraid that people may rather disapprove of you in certain circles among our friends?" Claire asked him.

"Not a bit of it—if I'm elected! In any case, it will be a victory for us employers. And so far as that is concerned, the Conservative people will have plenty of requests to make to me, and you may be sure they won't fail to do so."

Leaving his ambitions out of account, it may be said that Edmond's life was organized comfortably and on stable and well-balanced lines. For some years past he had devoted a half day several times a week to the dark-haired Irma Moufeton, manageress of his branch establishment at Voiron. Occasionally, too, this kindly and attractive woman accompanied him semi-officially on one or other of his journeys. In her he had come in contact with a rich feminine nature, a woman whose manners and behaviour were distinguished by their sincerity and their complete freedom from affectation of any kind. This simplicity drew him to her, and was a refreshment after time spent in a home where he must always be on his best behaviour and exposed to the cold and rather contemptuous gaze of Claire, of the Bargès family, and her reminders of his humble origin. In Irma's eyes he was an important person, a real gentleman, and he had no need whatever to stand on ceremony with that kindly creature, with her warm, impulsive bursts of feeling and her fervent sighs. At Sassenage, Edmond had a stately, pompous home in which his position was somewhat similar to that of chamberlain to a cold, ironic empress. And at Voiron he had another home —one which rejoiced his heart and appealed to his senses (those Euffe instincts which his father had bequeathed to him), and where he found caresses, devotion, admiration, and disinterested unselfishness. Irma enjoyed herself at the shop and did not wish to stop doing a little work, saying: "It amuses me when you are away to watch all the people coming in and going out. What should I do if I were to shut myself up, all alone, waiting for you? Because I shall never, never advise you to leave your wife and children like some women would do in my place. It would break my heart to think of those little ones."

Her requirements in the way of money were on a very moderate scale, so much so that Edmond·frequently offered her money without any request from her. So touched was she by a present that it brought tears to her eyes. In order to have her nearer to him, the director of the Silken Net would have liked to install this excellent friend at Grenoble. But she refused, fearing tittle-tattle, and knowing how greatly a man in the public eye is exposed to the danger of indiscretions and evil tongues. At Voiron her happiness was enjoyed in humble circumstances, but it was protected and safe.

"We have been happy and undisturbed up till now. I'm afraid of upsetting everything."

"But it's just this," Edmond said, "that with you so far away there is something I miss."

"Oh, I daresay," she said, "but still, we never get everything we should like in our lives. You have a wife with fine manners, a splendid house, children, and all the high society in Grenoble goes to visit you. But I, who am left alone ... Oh well, I'm quite content."

"Yes, but I want something more."

"Too much!" Irma said. "And then, if you saw me too often you would get tired. I too get weary of waiting for you. But that's my pleasure. If I had you always by me I shouldn't have my heart racing like it does on the days when you are coming. And then when I hear your car drawing up! I should know its sound among a thousand."

Edmond Euffe had thus reached a period of his life which gave him some real satisfaction, when he might perhaps have been on the eve of venturing on some big undertakings. But a new family complication supervened, causing him anxiety and demanding his attention and care.

It came about that a peculiar change took place in Mme. Euffe, the mother. At first no notice was taken of it, each member of the family being busy on his or her own account, and this state of affairs continued until one fine day the Euffe children found themselves faced by a situation which had fully developed, and were asking themselves every few weeks: "What on earth has happened to Mother?" The worthy and respectable old lady had undergone a strange renewal of her youth, accompanied by a state of emotional excitement, all of which, amid the everyday life of Grenoble, shed a glamour of the oddest kind. Clémentine was suddenly taking her revenge for sixty-five years of semi-obliteration and silence, by means of an unexpected and mysterious physiological transformation, the effects of which extended to the functioning of her brain, which hitherto had been discreet almost to the point of nonexistence. Consulted by Edmond, the good Dr. Lavigerie diagnosed a failure of the internal-secretions glands to maintain their synchronism, which had brought about a disturbance in the blending of the hormones produced by those same glands, particularly the sub-renal and the thyroid, while the deterioration of the ovaries was bringing a growth of hair to Mme. Euffe's chin that would have done credit to an old army veteran. The doctor advised taking a blood test with a view to a thorough and methodical examination of the case. (He had a theory that, as human beings are bisexual in origin, cases of a sudden upward thrust of the repressed sex may sometimes occur. He further maintained that there are numbers of cases where the predominance of the recognized sex is insufficiently characterized, with the result that there are indications of femininity in men and masculinity in women. He also declared that a law of complementaries was often responsible for the mutual attraction of the sexes on the lines of the questions here referred to, which are so little understood.) But Clémentine refused to be examined, the new turbulence of her blood causing her to suspect evil intentions on the part of every male being, doctors included. . . .

The hairy growth gave the good lady an energy which made her forget the humiliations of the past and drove her to wild and foolish behaviour. At the same time the blotchiness of her skin, which had previously been limited to her cheeks, spread to such an extent as to give it a smooth and even colour, more harmonious perhaps, but startling nevertheless, that suggested a confirmed and inveterate imbiber of whisky. Her flesh grew hard and firm and took on an appearance of parchment, while her features acquired those severe and finely chiselled outlines that denote a strong and determined disposition. This naturally lymphatic person became turbulent and restless. Even her voice changed. Having been flat and colourless, with halting speech, it became high-pitched and shrill, with nasal inflexions that carried self-assertiveness with them. As this excellent person had been a little deaf for a few years past, she would start making preposterous remarks in a loud voice, punctuated by bursts of sneering and derisive laughter and sly, roguish looks, giving everybody to understand that she had at long last come to realize that humanity is made up of scoundrels and fools, the worst of whom were in her own immediate circle of friends.

Poor Clémentine's revival of youth as evidenced by the clothes she wore was a terrible business; she paraded the town in an anachronistic display of furbelows and flounces, glass beads and bugles, brooches, flowered silks and shawls, all of which greatly astonished the inhabitants. At the same time she plunged into some reckless extravagance. This alarmed her family, especially Edmond, who supervised her expenditure. And it was this in particular that drew his attention to the changes that had come about in his dear old parent.

Then there came another blow, a still more terrible one. The truth had to be faced: Clémentine was smelling outrageously of rum, to such an extent indeed that the emanations from her grandmotherly kisses were a surprise even to her son's children. She had acquired a taste for strong drink at the time of M. Euffe's death. Her sorrow had disappeared but her taste for rum had increased. It was this beverage that was responsible for certain gay and lively antics of hers, for the way the widow had of displaying keen amusement, shared by no one else, over things which she alone could see and understand; it was doubtless rum that brought about her mad demonstrations of mischievous delight, her sudden bursts of uncontrollable and roguish laughter so out of keeping with her age, as though this boisterous and irrepressible dame had nothing else to do but play tricks on her contemporaries. When these attacks were at their worst, Clémentine, having decked herself out in a fashion which delayed the date of her birth by some twenty-five years, had a mania for going out and making a round of calls upon other widows, quiet old ladies who made no attempt to conceal their actual age. These visits made a sensation.

There was one person, and one only, who was delighted at this change, and this was the widow of General de Sainte-Foy, who was completely undismayed by displays of eccentricity. On the contrary, she saw in the new Clémentine an aide-de-camp in whose company she could carry on her good work and even intensify her feminine campaign.

But Edmond was extremely upset by his mother's becoming so turbulent, so gaudy in appearance, and so much addicted to rum.

"It's a disaster," he said to Dr. Lavigerie.

"Oh, by no means," the doctor replied. With his mind concentrated on glandular secretions, he was becoming enthusiastic over the widow's strange case. "I am wondering," he said, "whether your mother's remarkable development will not open up new horizons for medicine."

"What do you mean, Doctor?"

"Would it not be a wonderful thing if a certain condition of the glandular secretions—the causes of which we shall investigate later on —were able to give back a state of adolescence, or something like it, to an organism that has grown old? Now matter sustains the spirit, which disappears when matter decays. If, then, one could improve the condition of matter, it is probable that one would delay the coming, not only of death, but of spiritual decline."

"But you're not going to tell me that my mother's extraordinary behaviour has put her on a higher spiritual level?"

"No, but it may be that her previous spiritual condition was such as to make her insufficiently prepared to receive an increase of physical vigour. In any case, it is always interesting to observe what disturbances may be brought about, in a person whose spiritual condition is below the average, by an additional supply of physical strength. The great discoveries in medicine have been made from cases where there are clearly defined pathological states, not when the conditions are healthy and normal. Speaking from a doctor's point of view, your mother is more interesting at the present time than she has ever been in her life."

"You don't think it would be a good thing to put her in a mental home?"

"She is not asking for this?"

216

"No."

"Then I don't think you would have any right to do so. We should have to wait till she became so incoherent as to leave no room for doubt. It may be that she has an unconscious sexual repression which was latent in her and is only now appearing. Was your mother not cold when she was younger?"

"Now, look here, Doctor . . ."

"You don't like my asking you that question? All right, my dear chap, I respect your reticence where your mother is concerned. But you will understand that when I ask questions I have nothing but the patient, and his or her interests, in mind."

"I quite understand, Doctor. But your question goes back to a time when there were certain things I didn't understand."

"Very well, then, let us allow your mother's condition to develop as it may, and just quietly wait for a crisis, if there is to be one."

"But could the crisis not be staved off?"

"My dear fellow, if medicine could prevent things happening, what might it not accomplish! It observes and takes note—and often without understanding. But it so happens that I personally have a taste for trying to understand. That is why I talk to you at such length about certain things."

"Doctor, one word more. Do you think that my mother will become insane, or fall into her dotage?"

"Well, well," said the doctor amiably, "I can give you two alternative prospects, and the chances of either happening are about equal. Either her excited condition will grow steadily worse or she will break up completely. . . . There is actually a third alternative—that her immoderate behaviour will continue, with a picturesque side to it, excessive and noisy if you like, but on the whole likable and not unattractive. If that happens, you will not be able to prevent her from mixing in society and enjoying herself in that way. One sometimes sees people happy over a long period in a disordered mental condition, and getting pleasure out of it."

"Really?" said Edmond, dismayed at hearing this. "But there's the rum, Doctor . . ."

"Oh," said the doctor, "the organisms of people who take to alcohol late in life can keep up a prolonged resistance to it."

"How do you account for my mother, who was sobriety itself, taking to strong drink now, and rum in particular?"

"That is one of the features of her case that are so fascinating. Did she not have ancestors who were navigators and spent much time in the South Seas?"

"I seem to have heard that my great-grandfather on my mother's side was in the merchant service and knocked about the world a lot before he settled down and married."

"Very well, then," the doctor said, rubbing his hands, "this taking too much rum is a throwback to the great-grandfather! It's a mistake to suppose that a man's tastes are only transmitted to the boys of the family. Hereditary traits reappear in whom they will and at the moment they choose. You will find that out for yourself one day."

"Perhaps," Edmond said, as he made a mental comparison between his appetite for Irma Moufeton and the ardent feelings that bound the late M. Euffe to Riri Jumier. "Man is a strange animal."

"You may well say so," the doctor agreed. "And he will still continue to astonish us. I am always in raptures over him."

The fact that the mother of a man who was nourishing political ambitions was making herself conspicuous in the town by her eccentric behaviour was creating an embarrassing situation. It was obviously necessary to make an attempt to keep this behaviour within limits, by finding some vigilant person to supervise and walk alongside Mme. Euffe, with her bursts of mocking laughter. Edmond decided to engage a lady companion who would accompany his mother wherever she went. But the difficulty was to discover this rara avis, who should be a person of about the widow's own age, in a position to give every guarantee of a high moral standard, good education, and an unselfish outlook. One could not turn to people with very humble qualifications, to those sources from which the obscurer type of servant is recruited. It seemed preferable to make one's search among persons who had perhaps fallen from some previous high estate, or who at least had known better times. Edmond set to work in this matter, making inquiries in all directions, from Irma Moufeton to the widow of General de Sainte-Foy; and he also called in the aid of a few old ladies with a passion for good works.

A maiden lady of fifty-five summers was procured for the Euffes, Caroline Tupier by name, who had spent many years of humiliation and flattery in middle-class circles, whence she had drawn her subsistence, after reverses of fortune. She had been ruined by an infamous brother and abandoned by a fiancé who was merely a fortune hunter. Having spent thirty years in polishing up the account of her misfortunes, she had made a moving story out of them. The old ladies in the happy possession of independent means were entranced; for its harrowing episodes enabled them the better to appreciate their own security and good fortune. And so it was that Caroline Tupier had excellent references in her possession when she arrived to introduce herself to Edmond and offer him, together with her own personal experience of misfortune, promises of devotion to a poor lady who sometimes raved and talked drivelling nonsense.

The danger was that Mme. Euffe, who had grown extremely stubborn, might refuse to adapt herself to a bodyguard so austere and forbidding in appearance as Caroline Tupier. But it came as a delightful surprise to the family when, shortly afterwards, they observed that the two ladies got on wonderfully together and seemed inseparable.

After several months had gone by Edmond discovered the explanation of this perfect harmony when one day he chanced to meet Mme. Euffe and her inseparable lady companion. Mme. Euffe's cheeks were a lovely garnet red, and the natural accompaniment of a reckless, devil-may-care display of high spirits which, in a public street, was distinctly unfortunate. It was not difficult to attribute the lady's gaiety and the colour of her face to rum. Edmond looked severely at Caroline Tupier in order to draw her attention to his mother's condition and obtain the necessary explanation. But the lady companion's complexion was itself no less highly coloured than Mme. Euffe's; her laughter was even more strident, her balance less assured; and as for her breath, its fragrance was no more nor less than that of an old cask. These ladies had a common passion for alcohol; hence their mutual understanding. Caroline Tupier drank more than her mistress, who had sometimes to support her lady companion who, when the occasion arose, rendered her a similar service.

Caroline Tupier was dismissed, and a further search had to be undertaken. Inquiries were made at the Anti-alcoholic League, which supplied a widow who limped, was on a milk diet, and wanted two hours off every day for her prayers. She went to Mass every morning, took an hour in the afternoon for telling her beads. and went back to the church in the evening. Unfortunately this edifying person stole sugar, coffee, Italian pastry, and, generally speaking, everything eatable that was kept in cupboards—not to mention small sums of money. She also had to be dismissed. Mme. Euffe was giving great trouble.

"None of this would have happened," Claire said, "if that crazy creature Lucie had done her duty. She should have stayed with her mother and looked after her for the rest of her life! What is the use of having plain daughters if they desert you like the others!"

"But Lucie wanted to work out her own life," Edmond said.

"Work out her own life!" Claire exclaimed, with a mocking laugh. "You're talking like the lower orders who won't keep to their own proper station. It is just because the common people have been taught that famous 'right to work out one's own life' that one can't get any servants nowadays. And now you are wanting to be a socialist member of Parliament!"

"Oh, socialist—it's not that I care about," Edmond said. "I should like to be a member, that's all."

"And in order to be a member you are prepared to break away from your own party!"

"From my party, my party! Well, the fact is that they are at a great disadvantage. They wish to safeguard their money and have nothing to promise to their constituents. The people on the Left, on the other hand. can promise the electors our money, which doesn't belong to them. It gives them an enormous pull over us."

"Still," Claire said, "the men of our party stand for order and stability."

"But the populace doesn't demand order. In any case, taking it all round, they've got it already, and they take it for granted. What they are clamouring for are advantages, privileges. We must wait till the Left grows rich, and then the Right will have an effective programme for elections—to tempt the electors with the fortunes of their political opponents."

"Then does all your politics dangle round this question of money and wealth?"

"Goodness me, one talks a lot, but really I don't see that there is much else at stake beyond this—you take or you keep. So the Left starts out armed with an active and practically unlimited programme, while the programme of the Right, which is merely passive, has no interest for the masses."

"Tell me now," Claire asked him one day, "why is it that you are so bent on becoming a member?"

"Well. it seems to me that in my position it is rather my duty to take some part in the business of running the country. And I might become a Minister one day. . . ."

The elections came on. At the last moment Edmond hesitated and stood as a candidate with moderate views. A socialist was elected. This setback embittered him. The standard of living had fallen, and the effects of the crisis were felt in his business. It was all very well to say that people must always eat, but nevertheless the turnover in the branch establishments of the Silken Net was going down, with no corresponding diminution in the general expenses. Privations and hardships were becoming a necessity: and they had to be accepted by everybody, without the propertied class having to bear the whole cost of the reforms. Edmond was of opinion that the country was in need of profound changes, of some strong, energetic leadership and firm control. The more thought he gave to the subject, the less displeasing to him did the conception of dictatorship become. This conception, which had been tried out in some of the European nations, had given good results. Furthermore, a dictator could not fail to call upon the services of capable men, of men who had recently come into prominence, and there would be no need for these men to expose themselves to the baseness and scurvy tricks of electioneering.

13. SUNSHINE OVER THE ALPS

Arriving in England at the age of twenty, Germain Euffe was captivated by the immensity and variety of London, captivated by the English countryside, with all its greenness, and its imposing and stately country houses in their framing of beautiful trees. He was charmed by the golf and the tennis, and by the way in which those games are played over there, with their delicate insistence on the requirements of fair play. And lastly, he was delighted by the English ways of life, which allow of so liberal a measure of freedom, by giving a wide interpretation to the conception of independence which, with them, involves none of the indiscretions of French provincial life. The Englishman uses his egotism in a way that is the most comfortable for himself and the least embarrassing for other people, since it leads him never to ask questions and never to be surprised at anything.

But this particular manifestation of egotism, which results in the egotist's being very self-centred, cuts right across the need of the Latin races to tell everything that is in their minds to some third person. There are limits to self-revelation to overstep which surprise and shock the British, who are not in the least curious about your feelings. When a French boy has just had an adventure of the kind which had brought together and then separated Flavie and Germain, his friends soon know all about it. Germain was dying to talk about Flavie, to show her photograph, to hear people saying to him that she, if anyone, must be a woman who could inspire a great passion. But apart from the difficulty of telling his story in a language of which he knew little, Germain realized that it would fail to interest his new companions. Their politeness was beyond reproach, but it was irresponsive and restrained, and no one seemed in the least anxious to learn a great deal about the young Frenchman. He was admitted to British homes that he might taste British pleasures in their own calm and stolid way, and enjoy their comfort and their ways of life, but he had no authority to go beyond the bounds of British reserve in all matters relating to private life, even by speaking of his own. There are things in England which are not done. It is on the impossibility of doing them that a particular element in British life and the liberalism which proceeds from it are based. But apart from the necessity for this reserve, Germain could take, with young and charming English girls, liberties which a French girl could not have allowed without compromising herself seriously and losing the respect of all her friends. But this very daring behaviour was all one with the British refusal to become interested in other people's lives and actions, everyone being of sufficient stature to know what he should do and shoulder the responsibility for doing it. It seemed to Germain that this point of view had its compensations, of which he took advantage by indulging in a few pleasant flirtations. English girls have some charming moments of surrender, which they know how to check at the right moment, but what they do concede is more than worth while. Germain became fascinated by this pleasant dalliance, which was of a kind quite new to him and proved a great assistance to him in his study of the English language, in which he made play with the tenderest tones of voice.

In spite of all this, he had his days of homesickness and depression, and the terrible English Sundays bored him to death. It was boredom that made him buy some books. He made discoveries of Shakespeare, Byron, Shelley, and the English novelists. Within quite a short space of time he could read the different authors in the original text and do so in the surroundings of a completely English atmosphere. He set out to do a great deal of reading, to discover aspects of the world and life in general through the medium of English literature. Because it was foreign, this literature struck him as being original and he was deeply moved by it. A further reason why it so touched him was that his discovery went hand in hand with that of the pretty Margaret Swales, with whom he was in love.

As often happens as a sequel to an all-absorbing love, Germain was in search, among other women, of a woman of Flavie Lacail's type. He believed that he had found her in Margaret Swales, an English girl with dark hair and far from angular. It is at the same time possible that the likeness between Flavie and Margaret was not very noticeable. The latter was younger, with a more slender figure, and the mystery of her personality was less striking than in the case of a young woman of thirty with a full knowledge of her own feminine temperament and character, which have left their mark upon her. The pretty Margaret stood hesitating and uncertain on the threshold of her own life, not knowing to what extent she was influenced by her ambitions, her senses, or her dreams. She was still taking as her guide those vague myths that occupy a young girl's mind and are related to such things as the colour of the beloved's eyes, the elegance of his figure, the quality of his voice. In any event she was too thoroughly English to behave incautiously with a young man from the Continent, though she thought Germain's fair hair and skin delightful and that there was some strange charm about him that was lacking in the young men of her own race.

Through Margaret Swales, Germain learned the infinite resources of the English kiss, and certain ways of remaining virginal, diabolically disturbing, which the charming creature had. For at the very moment when, dizzied by romantic setting, moonlight, and lovers' sighs, another girl would have lost her head, this delicious daughter of Albion kept the marriage contract steadily in view and protected herself against the contingency of a final surrender no less carefully than the men of her island would protect the approaches to the Suez Canal. At the same time, she always managed, as a girl with an eye to the main chance, to get all she could out of her acquiescences thus grudgingly given. But she had the faculty, too, of emerging from these skirmishes, which left her somewhat dishevelled, with the appearance of the proverbial child wife, like Dora in *David Copperfield*.

These sweet encounters, mingled with the poetry of an English evening that is born of Shakespearean parks and hills, peopled by witches and fairies, threw Germain completely off his balance. He returned in haste to Grenoble to announce to Edmond that he was engaged to be married and to ask him to speed the attainment of his happiness by helping him with his marriage to the most dazzling and tenderest "miss" that the world had ever known.

"I think you must be ill," Edmond said to him coldly. "In the first place, to marry at your age is a piece of stupidity. But to marry a foreigner would be sheer madness."

"Oh," Germain said, "I speak English fluently now, and Margaret is learning French. We can understand each other perfectly."

"You young idiot!" Edmond said to him. "One never understands a woman of another race perfectly. It's hard enough to understand a woman of one's own country!"

"But how can you judge without knowing Margaret? I can assure you that we have the same tastes in sport, literature, painting, music."

"Good heavens!" Edmond exclaimed. "Just because she has some opinions of her own on painting and literature and music, this English girl of yours, then it's all up with you!"

"But Claire has opinions on those things, hasn't she?"

"Yes," Edmond said, with his face suddenly clouded.

"Yes, she has. Anyhow, that's her business. But you're not going to compare Claire, who represents a very large and important local business, with your young lady—what is she anyway? Is she rich, your English girl? Of course you haven't the slightest idea. Do you suppose by chance that an Englishwoman, if she had everything she needed in her own country, would come and live on the Continent just for love of you?"

"I assure you that you are wrong," Germain said. "If only you knew Margaret . . . In any case, why shouldn't she love me?"

"She may love you, but only as an English girl loves. In the same way that the English can't colonize without their minds being fixed on petrol and diamonds. She loves you as a convenience."

"I repeat, Edmond, that you don't know her and that you would be astonished if you saw her. And you know that it's quite enough for me to love a woman for you to find her hateful. The first time it was Flavie. Now it's Margaret."

"You must agree that Flavie was impossible after the scandal, when you were contemplating making her into something more than an ordinary mistress. But look here now, if I had to choose between two pieces of foolishness, I would rather you married someone like Flavie Lacail. She comes from Domène, from our own valleys. But an English girl—it's the height of folly! Come now, there are plenty of girls in Grenoble or Lyon who would do for you all right, if you really feel you must get married."

"I don't feel that at all," Germain said. "But I can't live without Margaret."

"Oh, very well, then, now we're starting all over again! You couldn't live without Flavie, and you are getting on without her magnificently. And now it's the young lady from London who has become indispensable to you. You are behaving like a child."

"I love her!" Germain said.

"Have it your own way, then!" Edmond replied. "But what with

224

your English girl and Lucie's Bruno, it looks like our descendants being a pretty mixed lot! If Father were to see this . . ."

"Oh, you're wrong there. Father had nothing to say against the English."

"But I have nothing against the English either!" Edmond exclaimed. "In their own country they are charming. There are very pretty Englishwomen, exceedingly pleasant to look at, to meet at tea or at tennis-parties. But when one is a Frenchman, one doesn't land one's family with an English girl. Those people are meant to keep to themselves. You have only to see the way they behave to know that."

"But you must distinguish between the men and the women. The women are much more adaptable."

"I don't think so for a moment," Edmond said. "The English never adapt themselves, neither the men nor the women. It's you who have to do the adapting. That is their great strength. But I myself prefer not to be up against it."

There was no help for it. Germain married his Margaret, who was certainly a most attractive girl, with an air of childish innocence about her. But beneath that outward appearance one could detect the vigorous and determined temperament of a young woman copiously nourished on underdone roast beef, eggs, smoke-cured pork, haddock, fruit and vegetables, cakes and butter, puddings, baked-custard tarts, and jam. That appearance further concealed an unshakable egotism, solidly based upon a firm conviction of the superiority of everything English, with Shakespeare and the Home Fleet at the pinnacle of all those glories.

Germain had known Margaret during a time of holiday, with a continuous round of excursions, picnics, boating parties on the Thames, or perhaps a short stay in a hotel with a few friends; when the only prospect was one of happy enjoyment with complete freedom from any tiresome restraint. It was a case always of being with friends for pleasure's sake alone—carefree pleasure, safe from interruption. It was ideal. But our ordinary, everyday lives have a different aspect altogether, with their worries over questions of ways and means, housekeeping, cooking, maintenance and supervision. Germain soon grew weary of having an interior which was beginning to resemble that of a boardinghouse, with everything thrown down here, there, and everywhere, in a hurly-burly of the continual comings and goings of this person and that. Margaret expected to be waited upon without trouble to herself, even in the thick of both wastage and confusion. She had no conception of any responsibilities other than those which affected her own health or mood, and thought of nothing but these and her exercise, her sports and games, her hours of rest, her visits to art galleries and museums, and the usual tea parties. She seemed to have no idea whatever that this particular design for living might have consequential effects upon the spirits and state of mind of her companion. Incidentally, women found her a pleasant friend; she never expected them to put themselves out for her any more than she did for them.

Claire was no less of an egotist than Margaret, and for this reason the two sisters-in-law might have got on well together, might have met on the common ground of their belief in the pre-eminence of their own sex. But Claire's egotism was essentially French and based on the little vanities and precautions common to her class. Margaret's brand of egotism took no account of these, ignoring them with the calm confidence natural to a girl belonging to the race for which the vast populations of world-wide Dominions are working. She was living at Grenoble in the same way as she would have lived at Singapore or in India, and giving people the impression that she regarded a French family as a sort of club at which she spent her leisure hours. She did not begin to understand French motives and points of view, or found them paltry and absurd. Her indifference was no less extreme, and it was unshakable. She exasperated Claire, but lost not a whit of her own serenity, being merely astonished at the French mania for having a finger in other people's pies.

To save himself from having to admit that he had made a mistake, Germain stood up for Margaret, and did his utmost to display a cheerful countenance to the members of his family. As long as he kept up this attitude everyone, without saying it in so many words, made considerable efforts to let him see that his marriage had been a first-class blunder. But everyone also discovered excellent qualities in that nice little Margaret, together with a host of excuses for her, when eighteen months later Germain, coming round to his family's way of thinking, declared that he had had enough and more than enough of it and that at all costs he must get a divorce. Claire herself, while detesting Margaret, put loyalty to her own sex above every other consideration. She could not endure a woman's being dismissed, and would only recognize divorce if the husband were the guilty party. Furthermore, Margaret, simply on account of her failure to fall in with French manners and customs, was an important person in the Euffe family, whom she was constantly supplying with themes for conversation and criticism. If she were no longer there, the others would be left without the standard of comparison by means of which the superiority of the French family, the French woman, French customs, French orderliness and method,

French politeness, good manners, and wit were being constantly displayed. Never at any time before this young Englishwoman had come amongst them had the Euffes been so pleased with themselves, so proud of their refinement, of their high degree of courtesy and of tolerance. They were coming to regard themselves for good and all as altruistic people.

Germain yielded to the arguments they put forward and agreed to exercise his soul in patience for a little while longer. In point of fact he was rather proud of being the only young man in Grenoble to have married an English girl. Margaret could not do without England and had to make a stay there every year, like a colonial who returns to the mother country. She came back newly soaked each time in the manners and outlook of her own land and filled with fresh English prejudice which, with strength revived, came into collision with French prejudice and for a month or two gave a fresh fillip to people's interest in Germain's marriage to a foreign girl.

As soon as the cold weather arrived Margaret departed for winter sports, after which she put in some time in the South, at Cannes or St. Raphael, where English people abound. She had the Englishwoman's faculty of living alone, with cigarettes, books, bridge, and a minimum of conversation. She surprised the French women by her ways of behaving like a man, for whom tobacco, alcoholic drinks, and the frequenting of bars is of primary importance. She thought of marriage as celibacy with a man to share it. When Germain came to see her, she received him as though he were a pleasant companion for a hotel life, but still by no means indispensable.

From the day when it was proved that Germain had ceased to take any interest in his wife and was openly unfaithful to her, dear Margaret was taken under her wing by Claire who, ceasing to criticize her, now began to show her pity. Margaret as little wished for pity as she did for blame. But there was no question of that in the sympathy she received. The Euffe family had now taken charge of the foreign girl and were adopting a moral and generous attitude towards her, saying that after all the poor child had been handicapped by the strange way in which she had been brought up and that one could hardly reproach her for this. Margaret was undeniably pretty, and there was something rather quaint about her prettiness. Claire was beginning to speak with satisfaction of her "English sister-in-law who might have come straight out of a novel by Meredith or Huxley, with a very original personality." It was a peculiarity of Claire's that everything with which she came in contact acquired thereby a stamp of originality, rarity, and social brilliance. In her hands Margaret acquired the reputation of being a rather strange, unusual kind of young woman, of gentle birth, with many relations among the "gentry" of London.

Germain, who was now breaking away from Margaret, met Flavie Lacail once more—which in a town like Grenoble was inevitable. His former mistress had the same glamour as of old, and it was not hard to see that the fires of passion were still smouldering within her. Her rich, abundant masses had lost none of their firmness. Germain was deeply stirred when his eyes fell once more upon that lovely bosom which had given him delight when he was but nineteen years old. It was certainly true that since then he had enjoyed, through Margaret, the joys of romance. But those joys had barely gone beyond the preliminary stages of love. Margaret married was far indeed from having fulfilled the promise of Margaret in England, that girl of mystery, with her background of bright, gay cottages and old Gothic mansions shrouded in curtains of ancient trees, and her feelings expressed in a delicious farrago of would-be French. At such times as his thoughts dwelt upon pleasure of a certain kind, he would say to himself that he knew nothing that could be compared with Flavie when she gave him the bold, resourceful experience of her thirty years of life and all the treasures it contained. He saw, from the look she gave him, that her passion for him was still intact, that she was still thinking of him as one whom she could never forget.

He decided to see her again from time to time. for their meetings would no longer involve the same risks as they had before. Further, he no longer feared, protected as he was by his marriage, that Flavie would be more than a whim or fancy in his life; and one is not fired at by the same individual on more than one occasion. They met in secret. They found that some coldness had crept into their embraces, and this was somewhat slow to depart. Their mutual enjoyment and pleasure were revived when Flavie uttered her sweet endearments as of old, her deep, repeated cries of delight and joy. But the old fires had burned low, at least in Germain, who had lost his former illusions. He needed the stimulus of romance, which henceforth would be lacking in this affair. His nervous, irresolute, complicated nature was requiring from one and the same being Flavie's own voluptuousness together with the poetry of the Margaret with her English setting and his own first avowals of love.

At the age of twenty-five Germain was faced with the fact that his life, so far as his deeper feelings were concerned, was a failure, that his family life was disordered and adrift. With his thoughts now directed to the future, he returned to his plan for divorce, and marriage to some healthy

Grenoble girl, so that he might have children and a properly run house. He thought that by these means he would be able to adjust his life and restore its true balance. He unbosomed himself to Edmond, who replied:

"That is how you should have started in the first instance. I did everything I could to spare you the English episode, which was bound to end badly. Then I advised you to keep Margaret, so as to give her a chance, and allow yourself time to get a little older. But you are quite free to do as you wish."

The divorce took place. Sixteen months later Germain married Marie-Thérèse Marousson, who had every appearance of possessing good solid *bourgeois* qualities and would bring him a fairly good dowry. She lost no time in presenting him with twins. Then she became again *enceinte.* Then again. She was a doleful, whining creature, rather overwhelmed by the frequency of her confinements. Everything in the house was secondary to the infants, who turned it into a howling nursery, in the midst of which Marie-Thérèse, easygoing, languid, and flabby, kept smiling at all the cries and catastrophes, in a little world of damp napkins, bibs, breakages, diarrhœa, and measles. She had given up all attempts at looking smart and well dressed, and spent whole days in a dressing gown, exhausted with nursing.

Germain began to miss the romance of Margaret and the sensual delight which Flavie Lacail had given him. In this disordered state of his feelings he occupied himself in an unsuccessful attempt to think out a few rules of conduct which later on he might instil into his children and teach them how to live. Sometimes he said to himself that he had taken a wrong direction, contrary to his real nature—that of an artist, he thought it was. During the romantic period of his life (the English period) he had toyed with the idea of writing. He was keeping a few poems written during that time and reproaching himself for not having persevered in this direction. But it was too late now. Marie-Thérèse was expecting another child. He himself was harnessed to the Silken Net, where he was in charge of the deliveries section. Life was keeping around his neck the iron collar of obligations and duties. He was too honest to evade them.

But there was one part of himself—the best, perhaps—that was remaining unsatisfied. He was conscious of aspirations which were failing to find an outlet. Some portion of his being, which he was hesitating to call his soul, was finding it impossible to expand in the company of that good creature Marie-Thérèse, so prolific, so unconcerned, who was allowing her figure, as she did everything else around her, to go to rack and ruin, in a house where the carpets were becoming little swamps owing to the babies, whose incontinence was looked upon with rather too indulgent an eye.

Germain embarked on the task of carving out for himself a life of the mind, to be kept well apart from the clamour and confusion created in the flat by his offspring. He shut himself up in a room which no one else was allowed to enter. He bought a rhyming dictionary and applied himself in secret to a study of the art of poetry. His previous poems had frequently transgressed the rules of prosody. He wished to start at the beginning and master the form, before tackling the sources of inspiration with a large I.

Nevertheless he wrote with difficulty, though he was conscious that his mind was teeming with things to express. These things were sparkling, fairylike, in some rose-pink, misty region far away. But no sooner did his pen begin to set them down on paper than they became deplorably commonplace. The nymphs and water sprites were changed into witches and old women in their dotage.

Germain understood that one cannot write poems as one drafts commercial letters. What is required is a state of trance favourable to inspiration; a man must be transformed into a visionary. Poets have their stimulants, sometimes their drugs. Germain provided himself with a cupboard well stocked with drinks and bought himself an excellent assortment of pipes. Before setting to work he would fill a pipe methodically and light it with care. After that there was nothing like a good glass of some old liqueur mingling its own aroma with that of the tobacco smoke, while the latter was coiling itself in and out of one's iridescent dreams. Germain would pour himself out a glass of armagnac or old brandy and sip it slowly. Then he would become immersed in an anthology and thus find himself on a level with the poets. After that there would be a second glass of some liqueur, with more to follow, and fresh pipes. . . .

But it was in vain that he awaited that moment when he would be writing at the dictation of the angels, with blithe and nimble pen flying over the paper with never an erasure, and leaving thereon, with playful ease, gems of inspiration and ideas of genius. For he had always imagined that inspiration was like that—a divine facility granted to the artist for a few brief moments and raising him far above ordinary men (the only difficulty being to discover the rules, which differ in each individual case, favouring a state of receptivity). Make trial as he would of every kind of liqueur and every pattern of pipe, still his muse remained a sleepyhead, an idler and a lazybones. Fountain pen in hand, he would sit dazed and vacant with a sheet of paper before him and his head buzzing with a noisy din of words elusive and hard to catch, which he could never bring to heel and put in order. He might succeed in building up an octosyllable or an alexandrine. But after that it was the devil's own job to fit out a second line to go beneath it. He would moil and toil for hours, making little scribbles on his sheet of paper, and these in turn made him lose the thread of his ideas. Where, then, did the secret lie? What is so baffling in art is the lack of apparent means. He would take up the anthologies once more, and read a passage like this:

> Ah! que le temps vienne
> Où les cœurs s'éprennent!

Or again:

> Mon Dieu, mon Dieu, la vie est là
> Simple et tranquille
> Cette paisible rumeur-là
> Vient de la ville.

And farther on:

> Mon beau navire ô ma mémoire
> Avons-nous assez navigué
> Dans une onde mauvaise à boire
> Avons-nous assez divagué
> De la belle aube au triste soir.

You will never get people to believe that you have to take your head in both hands to think out little things like that, which look mere trifles. But they are incredibly difficult. And the simpler they look—almost childish perhaps—the harder they are! That was what Germain Euffe discovered every evening. And he went to bed late with a touch of headache and his mouth clammy from having drunk too much armagnac and smoked too many pipes, after slipping his paper into a drawer which he then carefully locked.

He tried his hand at poems of a simple and homely type, and produced the following, with which he was decidedly pleased, having worked hard at it and polished it throughout three successive evenings.

> Humble leeks and pineapple,
> Mackerel, sardines,
> Tunny fish or butter,
> Spinach, cheese, and beans.
> Beverages of every kind,
> Fruit, brioches, or cake,
> Summer salads, winter soups,
> All of these you take
> Away with you—now don't forget!—
> From the famous SILKEN NET.

"Dear me," he said to himself, "I must show that to Bob. He's always on the lookout for slogans for our advertising. We could have some advertisements in rhyme in the *Dauphiné Gazette* and so give them a definite literary flavour. Yes, I'll speak to him about it tomorrow."

Bob de Bazair was now presiding over the destinies of the Silken Net as a third partner with his two brothers-in-law. It seemed to him that this collaboration, which incidentally enabled all the family assets to be kept together, was not without its humorous side. It also had the advantage of making supervision easier at a time when those who were directing the business had no wish to work from twelve to fourteen hours a day as M. Constant Euffe had done in his prime, when he was building up the fortunes of his firm. But Bob, not wishing to be mixed up in the haggling over prices of groceries, had taken over the publicity side of the business, which demands a resourceful, inspiriting and persuasive turn of mind. He had people working under his orders, perfecting continually changing methods of advertisement and of tapping fresh sources of custom. Upon this work of management he spent about two hours a day only, for he hit upon the most marvellous ideas when out walking, or devoting his time to other forms of activity.

Acting in accordance with the programme which he had always had in mind, he had gained a footing in important societies of which, with the help of his aristocratic name, he had contrived to become a member of the executive committees. He had little or no difficulty in making money by this means, and was continually increasing the range of his business connections and acquaintances, which was beginning to extend beyond the limits of Grenoble itself. It was his opinion that the descendants of aristocrats should not adopt a standoffish attitude in a democratic community, however deplorable the latter may be, but should get all they could out of it. And in justice to democracy it must be admitted that it does continue to pay aristocrats a tribute of admiration and make some efforts—by means, at least, of its limited liability companies and the dowries of its young women—to give them back some of the privileges of which it formerly deprived them. Bob de Bazair had soon come to realize the advantages to be obtained through the possession of a title borne with dignity and adroitly kept to the fore.

Life, thought Bob, after much taking stock of what he saw around him, is simply a question of material organization. It is far less a matter of living in order to do something or other than it is of doing something in order to live—and to live as pleasantly as one can. (Things might be better, but that is how they are!) In any case it is by no means easy to know how to live pleasantly, and few there are who succeed in doing so. And as for living harmoniously, elegantly, with a certain lordly detachment, that is more difficult still. (To succeed in that, an innate conviction of being perfectly well able to live in some quite different way is probably necessary.) Bob had watched Germain Euffe floundering about in marital experiment, with touching but misplaced and clumsy faith, without finding any of that pleasure and satisfaction which would have been his just due. He saw Edmond belittled and shrinking under the cold patronage of his wife, only to acquire in Grenoble circles an importance of a rather laughable kind. He watched people striking attitudes, pretending to be other than they really were, with one man trying to hide his weakness, another his fear, another his covetousness or his lust, another his disgust with himself. He listened to people talking of courage, of duty, of unselfishness, while nearly every one of them, governed by fear, with only the most witless conception of where their own interests really lay, refused to take the very slightest of risks or sacrifice one jot or tittle of their fine programmes. It made him smile from pity.

This is what he felt—that all our actions that are wholehearted and sincere arise out of a deep-seated feeling of ease and freedom. To live as he was living now, without bragging but free from all false constraint, gave him joy and gladness every day. He had come to regard his own pleasure almost in the light of a duty, thinking that there was no better occupation, that perhaps there never would be a better, in a mediocre and basely greedy world. But he knew quite well that he had within him a reserve of strength which would enable him to face up to any adventure, to any danger, to any upheaval of whatsoever kind it might be; that he was well able to look death itself in the face, without trembling before it overtook him. That inner strength of his, when he was in repose, was hidden by a mask of listlessness and indifference, but it was there none the less. He was nothing if not the descendant of a few stout and vigorous adventurers, who in their own day had gone the pace, and died with a word of defiance on their lips. He felt that he too could meet death as befitted a man of his noble line; and this seemed to him to make all things easy, to atone for everything.

(He was to die—alone of those inhabitants of Grenoble of whom we have written here—in battle on the fourteenth of May, 1940, in Belgium, as a lieutenant in command of an advanced section of his company. He died in the radiance of a lovely spring morning, in which until the moment of his death he had taken keen delight; he died without having seen the war as anything but a kind of thrilling Valkyries ride in which he felt, in every fibre of his being, more ease and freedom than he had ever known before. And yet, for twenty-four hours past, he had been saying to himself: "It looks as though this show is going to crash. You'd think that a whole bunch of Captain Bidons were running it!" But no fear had gripped him, no panic touched him. Despite the shilly-shallying of warriors and the wavering uncertainty of the situation, he for his part had the pleasurable satisfaction of feeling, just at the critical moment, the old imperturbable calm of the de Bazairs settling within him, with the knowledge that he had a firm hold of those secret portions of his being which in others may give way altogether, but which in him were grouping themselves in a pile of trusty weapons. When the deadly burst of machine-gun fire caught him, Bob de Bazair was wondering at the incipient fury of battle being accompanied by the scent of flowers and the radiance of a lovely morning taken unawares. He was smiling with pleasure at this. The smile still stayed upon his lips in death, for death did not come to him as a shattering. He knew nothing of the tense moment of apprehension, the terror lest suddenly the world be blotted out. His death was a smooth and easy ending to his story, and it left his memory free from any recollection of him other than as a young man with an abundance of youthful grace, of charm and daring.)

But we are in 1935. No one is thinking of the death of Bob de Bazair, and he less than anyone. If tremendous and sinister events are looming ahead, they are still in shadow, and the whole world averts its eyes from those signs which may mar its peace of mind and alarm the selfish rich. It seems as though life were flowing in one vast stream of happiness and bliss, a stream that is growing ever wider. Between Paris, Cannes, Lyon, Grenoble, Annecy, Mégève, and Chamonix, Bob comes and goes ceaselessly, at the steering wheel of powerful cars; he is in universal request; everywhere he is received with open arms. He makes money, and spends it, with amazing facility. He squanders it right royally, taking it wherever he finds it, without being overscrupulous. His lack of scruples is redeemed by the complete absence of any sordid motive. Money to him is but a game, counters which he takes from the automatic machines of destiny, only to gamble with them elsewhere. His strength lies in his being capable of ruining himself and then starting again, as he says, from zero. The goddess of Chance likes these people who will force a situation, these tightrope walkers, these young lords who save the face of a century notable for middle-class domination and mean and petty greed. Bob de Bazair is never ruined. On the contrary, the higher the stakes for which he plays, the more readily does Fate crown with success his instincts as gambler or gentleman of fortune. A strange epoch it is—one in which nothing is deserved and everything is obtained. There are days when Bob is sick to death of this effortless drawing of winning numbers. Then he carves himself another slice of life, as it were a second helping of roast beef, and so—on with the good work! When one sees those wealthy profiteers with their ugly mugs, it would be too stupid altogether not to go one better than those wretched people—not to ride them down as they deserve. You must take your period as you find it; it isn't every century that can offer you crusades, romantic wars, epic adventure . . .

Such was Bob de Bazair, at the threshold of his maturity. He had decided to get all the amusement he could out of everything. And he was still getting it when that morning he returned to Germain his little poem of the previous day:

"I didn't know you had this talent. One ought to be able to make use of that little thing. It's really very good. Do you think you could give me the stuff for a publicity campaign carried on by means of these rhymed couplets, to appear at certain intervals?"

"Yes, I think I could," Germain replied. "But I should have to be given some short notice each time. I only want to supply things with a real literary flavour in them. By the way, it would be nice of you not to mention this to Edmond. I would rather he didn't know that these little poems were written by me."

"I quite understand," Bob said. "I won't let anyone into the secret. Is Marie-Thérèse well?"

"Yes. I left her on all fours in the drawing room, with the children. And Alberte?"

"Alberte is in splendid form, thanks very much. Are you coming to tennis this afternoon? The season will soon be over. We ought to get in a few more days' play."

"Who will be staying at the office?"

"Edmond will certainly be here. He went to Voiron yesterday to see his Irma. We can hand the firm over to him today. Will you come?"

"I am not in form."

"Look here," said Bob, "there's something wrong with you! Overdoing the intellectual work, perhaps?"

"The intellectual work is a wholesome distraction for me. I get a queer sort of feeling. I think about life . . ."

"You should live without thinking. Anything else?"

"It will soon be ten years since Father died. After his death, all of us, and you too by your marriage, became the Euffe heirs, the heirs of a man who had succeeded in working his way up by his own efforts. It was then our turn to feel ourselves full of plans and possibilities. Will you tell me what good all that has done us?"

"You really are much too complex in the way you think!" Bob said. "How can you be happy if you live like that? You are Germain Euffe, a lucky heir, and don't forget it."

"Yes, but the thing is that I should have liked to do better, to distinguish myself in something or other, even if it meant a big effort on my part. I should like to begin all over again. I don't know if you follow me?"

"Oh, perfectly, perfectly!" Bob said. "Ideas like that have sometimes flashed across my mind too. When it happens, what I do is to drive three hundred miles at an average of sixty, or I play poker all night, or I get through a flask of whisky. You see, old chap, we have to make the best of a bad job. I was reading the other day that there are nearly two milliards of human beings on this planet. Each of us is lost in this huge mass. Some people emerge, but they are few and far between. You can't yourself choose to be one of them. That is decided quite apart from any will of our own."

"Then the Euffe family—the Euffe heirs—what does that mean?"

"My poor old chap, it's simply a bourgeois label—nothing more. Why should it count for so much, after all? Each of us has his own little personal history, which is worth just about the same as other people's little histories, a little more or a little less, as the case may be. Let us make the best of it."

"You're discouraging," Germain said.

"I don't think so. But you yourself need more courage. And you are too complex. Are you free for lunch?"

"I could telephone."

"Then please do. We will lunch together. I shouldn't like to leave you in a state of mind like that—you, the most worried and anxious of the Euffe heirs!"

One cannot nowadays speak of Grenoble and of the life in that town without taking account of Edgar Lapérine, even if to some people he may appear prejudiced. We shall now give the reader yet another specimen of the style of this isolated and lonely philosopher. There can be no doubt that Lapérine was a great lover of Nature, to whom he often confided his secret thoughts. There are passages in his books which remind one of the tender effusions of Henri Beyle in speaking of Claix and Montbonnot. But Lapérine's reactions to the scenery around Grenoble

236

were peculiar to himself. He has described them in the following passage:

"Nature, when she takes it upon herself to be grandiose, awe-inspiring, becomes, for us human beings, overpowering. She dominates us—from the heights of her inaccessible and solitary places, and from the depths of a mysterious age-old past, in which her origins are buried. This is strongly felt at Grenoble, where the eye is confronted on every side by gigantic piles of earth and rock, at the summit of which a silence now reigns which harbours memories of the splitting, crashing noises, the roar and din of the great ice age. At the foot of the St.-Eynard and of the Belledonne peaks, a man is but a speck in the depths of an abyss. The primeval devastation which prevails in the approaches to the Lautaret and the Galibier gives an impression of a vast immensity that is impassable, impregnable, and casts us back, in all our insignificance, to the depths of the valleys, where the houses in our towns seem scarcely more important than the huts of prehistoric times. Up there, so far above us, is the Unchanging, the Immutable, beyond our reach, in the rugged outlines, the heights and hollows of the naked rock, where it would seem that the judges of the world are seated. Man may look upon this grandeur, may carry daring to the point of desecrating, half in fear, some solitary haunts among those lofty heights; but he will have quickly to leave them to their own proud isolation, where destinies are wrought whose accomplishment will take five hundred thousand years. I have never come down from those mountains without feeling as though dizzied from contemplation of the infinite, and my return to the town always made it seem in some ways a horribly mean and paltry place."

These impressions and feelings are worth noting. Anyone, however, who prefers to be happy will do better not to be influenced by the gloomy disenchantment of Lapérine. The native of Grenoble has a nature with charm, variety, and a certain sweetness in it, despite its rough corners and its tremendous fluctuations of mood. It can give you joy and encourage you to live.

In this cheerful frame of mind were those of Grenoble's inhabitants whom we know. Dismissing all painful thoughts from their minds, they were allowing the seasons of the year, each of which brings back its own form of pleasure and enchantment, to have their full effect upon them. All of them were appreciating these pleasures, even Claire Euffe, whose mood in springtime underwent a thawing process, whose manner became less stilted and strained, and whose determination to be in the fashionable "swim" took on a less rigid, more sociable turn; even Edmond, who on account of his stiff, uncompromising appearance and the

237

coldness of his oratory, which were reacting unfavourably on the electors, was experiencing political setbacks; even Clémentine, who, when the sap was rising everywhere and having certain effects on her endocrine glands, had a recrudescence of her previous activities, even though the poor lady, whose head had now taken to tremulous shaking, was accustomed to sink at intervals into a state of torpor, despite her doses of rum; even Germain who, by admirable perseverance and tenacity sustained by armagnac brandy, was maintaining himself in an atmosphere in which he came near to mastering the ryhthms of the greatest poets; even Félix Lacail who, forgetting that fleeting visit of Freddy Glowes to his own home, had taken up once more the methodical training of a fervent devotee of cycle touring, and having regained that strength of leg that he had enjoyed of old, was making records on the runs to the Lautaret and the Porte passes; even the widow of General de Sainte-Foy, a sort of cuirassier in corsets, as formidably corpulent as ever, as fully prepared to lead troops of maidens to assaults on the god of love, and whose activities were resembling those cavalry charges at the period of our fourteenth of July, when military display is at the height of its glory; even the good Dr. Lavigerie who, now that the right time of year had come, was visiting those places where humanity displays itself in sweaters and shorts, that he might give his patients treatment of the true Socratic blend, in the form of philosophical maxims and harmonious discourse; even M. Philibert Mivois, who had the full use of his faculties at brief moments only, since the breaking of a blood vessel in his brain had given him a slight facial paralysis, accompanied by stammering.

Even in the case of Lucie Spaniente and Riri Jumier, each permanently settled at a long distance from Grenoble, impressions and recollections of the town were often in their minds. They remembered the light falling in patches upon the summits and slopes of the mountains, a strange and dazzling brightness in which the valleys were bathed, the fragrance of mountain air in Grenoble itself, something indefinable but none the less unique which made up the atmosphere of one's native town, so different from all others. These recollections did not provoke any actual longing to revisit all this, but they brought with them remembrances of some vague, ill-defined feelings of tenderness, and of physical well-being which could not be felt in quite the same way in any other place. The freshness of the morning air in the Place Grenette, the vista of the wide avenues of Grenoble, which carries the eye upwards to aerial heights that seem to overhang the roofs, the russet splendours of autumn in the valley of the Grésivaudan, the tunnel of green leaves along the tree-lined walks of Pont-de-Claix, the songs of birds in the undergrowth ot Green Island, the flower-bedecked terraces of Bouquéron—all this made up a store of memories with which the remembrance of their youth and its first illusions went hand in hand.

There was one being, among all those whose acquaintance we have made, who had remained faithful throughout to the character and nature of the town where she was born, which was the continual source of her balance and her strength. This was Alberte de Bazair. Her life was going forward on lines of such happiness as to give her a power of radiating joy so great that all jealousies were disarmed, and that no one could speak of her otherwise than as "that charming Alberte." This unanimity of praise exasperated her sister-in-law, the lady of the manor of Sassenage. "She is certainly a nice creature and quite pretty," Claire said, "but I don't think she is particularly intelligent, and I wonder why it is that everyone is always smiling at her." Intelligent or not, Alberte had a natural gift for bringing people pleasure, for creating an atmosphere of peace around her; she had a simple, openhearted grace and charm, in which nevertheless there was a touch of mystery. There was friendliness in her eyes when she looked at you; but you felt that there was something deep down within her that you could never hope to reach, some hidden source of serenity and of joys profound. She was a pretty woman of about thirty years of age, with health and happiness in full bloom and mother of three fine children, three boys, Robert, Gontran, and Stanislas, aged eight, six and five respectively, three real little de Bazairs in character, appearance, and manners. All three resembled their father, which gave Alberte yet another reason for loving them dearly when she looked at them. For she had still but one admiration. one motive, one passion which came before all others—Bob, at whom, ten years later, she would gaze as fervently as in the early days. Grenoble she found magnificent, the different seasons held brilliance and sweetness for her: she could not prefer any one to any other. Her life was still a marvellous dream. She never ceased to wonder that it was she who had been chosen as the means of preserving unbroken the line of the de Bazairs, and that the blood of the family had acquired, in her own person, sufficient strength to transmit to the young generation the foreheads, chins, lips, and oval faces which one saw in their ancestors, in their portraits at Champagnier.

At Champagnier she lived within a setting of mute princesses who, in their portraits of semi-state, smiled down at her in the dim light of gilded drawing rooms. Long and earnestly she would gaze at these women of olden times—lovely women, disturbing to look at, their brilliance a trifle dimmed amid the silence of the many years gone by. At them she gazed, not from pride because she was their successor, but to ask them to tell her how to resemble them as nearly as possible, so that in days to come she may be worthy to follow them and take her place in the gallery wherein de Bazairs of future times may speak of her to each other as the sweet and tender Countess Alberte, the devoted wife of Bob de Bazair. For her children she had a kind of respect and admiration, not because they were her sons, but because, thanks be to Bob, they would be young nobleman. She wished them to be worthy of their name, worthy of her own fidelity and attachment to the family cause. Her children enchanted her, because she was sweet enough to attribute to their father every point of charm, or perfection, that she discovered in them. The warmth and fervour of her love were keeping her very young, and her sincerity and goodwill were touching to behold. Her senses were still stirred at times in the presence of him whom she loved and she would blush; so great was her adoration that she hardly dared to look at him; she was as shy as she had been in days past at Green Island. This complete happiness gave her a radiance which at the same time was quiet and serious, and it was this that had won her the friendship of the old count.

The count's declining years were being spent in contempt of the times in which he was then living. He could see nothing but absurdity in human beings who no longer recognized the supremacy of cavalry officers of noble birth, people who set greater value on a motorcar than a thoroughbred. The old squireen displayed a countenance that was thin but still kept its old distinction, with an eaglelike profile, and eyes which maintained a hard, fixed stare beneath their bushy eyebrows. He spent whole days when he scarcely uttered a word, wandering in the park, stick in hand, and chewing his cigars, from which he drew puffs of smoke which he blew vigorously from his lips as though they were sarcastic remarks addressed to the fool of a doctor who would have liked to deny him his tobacco. He still wore gaiters and riding breeches, which were a challenge. He took but little notice of his grandchildren, thinking of them as doomed to work of little or no distinction, in a world which held less and less interest as time went on. His own son interested him very little more, though by his marriage Bob had saved what remained of the family inheritance, the castle and a few estates, and had given a fresh store of life and energy to their line. The old man was accustomed to come out at times and sit down by Alberte; and for her alone he would evoke memories of the past, to which she listened with gentle gravity, because he was Bob's father and she honoured this man, who was the link in the chain which had given her her own place in the line of the de Bazairs. She loved the grim and malevolent old man who was always railing against the iniquities of the present age. She felt that she procured him a little peace, so that he even gave her an occasional smile, with which no one now but she was favoured, and which once must have had great charm. With that smile could be seen the last dying gleams of youth in the bitter old face. There was something in her father-in-law's different expressions that reminded her of Bob: and she wondered whether he would become like his father someday. But that thought held no fears for her: him too she would be well able to soothe. Even as she talked—so gently—to the count, she felt as though she were speaking to a Bob grown old. She was studying, as a beginner, the part she would have to play later on. Bob had confided to her that the de Bazairs often turned out to be unbearable as they grew old, refusing to submit to the loss of their former energy and fire, to resign them-selves to remaining inactive and worn out while the lives of others flowed by in a steady stream. She smiled as she heard this; never, for her, could Bob become unbearable. But a time would come when she would be in-dispensable to him, far more so than now. On this she based her expec-tation of happiness to come. Sometimes she would enjoy herself in imagining that Bob would then resemble the count, that he would have the same proud, sarcastic look, while her children would be like Bob as he was at the present day: in this way she would always have him to look at—at every stage of her life. She conceived of old age as a time of great happiness, because Bob would be seated near her, and for longer hours than ever before. She knew that she would love him always, with a love which, if needs be, would ask for nothing in return, provided only that he came back to her and that she would know, from the expression in his eyes, that in her alone he found peace and rest.

But with all this Alberte remained loyal and faithful to the Euffes, paying honour to the memory of her father, who was resting in the St.-Roch cemetery, in the peace and calm of rose-pink dawns and evenings with skies of fading blue. She was associating him with the glory of the de Bazairs and devising a legend about him for her children to hear. She would bring her boys to the graveside and there they would all talk together of this man now buried in oblivion, who had bequeathed some of his own features and instincts to the young de Bazairs. In these visits there was nothing sad or gloomy, no feeling of an irksome duty. Alberte chose lovely days for making them and dressed the boys as though for a party; and off they would go in the car, bearing flowers with them and chatting merrily on the way.

"Good morning, Daddy," she would say as they arrived. "I've brought the children for you to see how they have grown. We all think of you such a lot."

She liked the dead to be thought of as nice friendly spirits, with nothing in the least terrifying about them, but the sort of people to make you feel sorry that you hadn't known them.

"What was Granddad like?" Robert, the eldest boy, asked one day.

"He was ever so kind. He would have loved you."

"Was it a long time ago that he died?"

"Yes," Alberte said, "a long, long time ago. Before all of you were born."

"Was he like Grandie?" (This was the count.)

"No," Alberte said, "not at all. But I have always been told that I was very like him."

The children were amazed to think that an old man could possibly be like a pretty young woman. They thought their mother lovely and were proud of her when they met their young friends.

"Why did he die, Granddad?"

"Because he had worked very hard all his life. He had worked very hard so that we should have everything we wanted. We ought all of us to be very grateful to him."

"Is he in heaven?"

"Oh yes, certainly," Alberte said. She did not believe that the part played in former days by Riri Jumier could be an obstacle to the attainment of heavenly bliss when a man had been such a good kind father as hers.

She believed that men will be judged by the quality of their thoughts and feelings and the sincerity of their actions, and that there are no major sins other than envy, hatred, cupidity, and meanness. It is only minds in torment and haunted by blasphemous thoughts that have imagined a God of terror. Alberte's God, He who was her protection and of whom she taught her children, deserved full well the name of father, of a rather overindulgent father if needs be. On the face of the almighty Judge she could clearly see a smile like that which the founder of the Silken Net used once to give her when he turned to his favourite daughter.

Sometimes, too, it came about that Alberte would go alone to visit the Virgin of the Church of St.-Laurent. It was a pilgrimage to the place whither she used to come with the hopes and prayers of her young girlhood. The Virgin was still there, in her magic serenity, holding the Child of redemption in her arms. Alberte could smile at her with her own experience as a mother. She did not come with a request, but to return thanks in joy and wonder that everything should have come to pass as she had wished, should be so like the substance of her dreams.

"I am happy," Alberte would say, "very, very happy. . . . How kind you have been to me!"

Waiting at the door for her was her small car which she drove herself from Champagnier to Grenoble to do her shopping. She took her place at the steering wheel and started off, after a rapid glance at her list of purchases to be made. Yes, she was happy, happy . . . And how simple it was! But was it really possible that ten years had already gone by since those first meetings at Green Island. . . . Ten years already!

Another year had gone by. Once more Grenoble was at the threshold of the luminous seasons, of those long days of spring and summer with their scents of flowers and fields. For some days past the town had rediscovered its lovely sky, an unbroken, infinite expanse of azure blue. At the Lesdiguières tennis club the courts with their rose-pink soil were being rolled. The flower beds were adorning themselves with a trimming of bright colours. The tree-lined walks of Pont-de-Claix were putting on their garments of foliage, and verdure was appearing on the mountain slopes. Overcoats and wraps had been discarded, and all the townsfolk were feeling the comfort and well-being of the return of warm weather. Although this warmth was still a little deceptive and there was a sharp tang in the air, there was a temptation to sit down on the benches in Victor-Hugo and Verdun squares and, while looking upwards at the perfect blue of the sky, to take deep breaths of the air which had been purified on the mountain tops and still bore the chill and freshness of the snow.

In the Rue Turenne a woman was daydreaming at her window, the same woman and the same window as ten years ago. Her thoughts, a little weary now, were revolving around the same theme as in those days when, at this same window, she indulged in vague and shadowy hopes. But hope had died, and regret now taken its place. Perhaps, to sustain her courage, she was dreaming of those old illusions. She was forty years of age, and was conscious of the same strength and firmness of frame and torment of desire. She was wondering whether anything would happen before the time came for her to live that same life which she had seen her mother live when, with all her woman's tasks of love and motherhood completed, she had become a fretful, peevish old creature, with her ingrained habits and her cats. When once they have reached this last stage of their earthly lives, human beings grow unconscious of their shrivelled selfishness, so distressing to behold—and this is in some ways a mercy for them. But what is difficult is the crossing of the gap which divides the latest of the years in which illusions are still possible from those years when neglect and loneliness become the lot of aged people.

From her window Flavie Lacail was gazing at the mountains whose beauty almost rent the heart. The great currents of air which swept along the avenues bore with them whiffs of penetrating fragrance. Nature was at one of those points of extreme magnificence which she attains on a few days only in the year. Flavie was in a state of languor which amounted almost to indisposition. She looked down, vaguely, at the pavement below. She remembered . . . In her mind's eye she saw M. Euffe once more, at full length on his stretcher in the chemist's shop, at the point of death. Germain too she saw, at the age of nineteen, with his blushes and his awkwardness that were so charming. She thrilled at the remembrance of her first surrender. Next she saw the blood flowing from a face she loved so well. Lastly, she thought of the dark night of years which had spread its pall over her, those years whose length had dragged out so wearily in the company of a man whose flabbiness and general mediocrity she knew too well.

At that moment a scent of lilac reached her nostrils, and a voice behind her which made her start, so exactly did the words and intonation chime in with her secret thoughts, was heard saying:

"Many happy returns, Flavie! It's me, your old Pampan."

She turned round and saw Pamphile Garambois, quite close to her. He was holding out a bunch of flowers as in the old days.

"Who is it that's faithful?" he said. "Who is it that hasn't forgotten?"

"Thank you," she said mechanically as she took the flowers.

"Shan't I get my reward someday?" Pamphile asked.

"Ah, my poor friend," Flavie said, "if you only knew . . ."

She did not know what she herself meant by those words. Except, perhaps, that this obstinate man with greying hair, whom once she had hated, represented the only possibility of adventure now left to her. After all, it was to him that she had indirectly owed the happy periods of her life.

"What about a kiss?" Pamphile asked. "On a day like today!"

"All right, then," said Flavie, offering her cheek.

"Flavie," Pamphile said, when the kiss had been given, "you know what I offered you once? I am still ready to keep my word."

"My poor old Pampan, you would be making a very bad bargain!"

They stood at the window, with their elbows on the sill, side by side. Flavie suddenly broke out into a burst of rather hysterical laughter, with a cracked sound in her voice.

"What's the matter with you?" Pamphile asked.

"I'm thinking of the vase again," Flavie said. "Plouf, it went—down there in the street! Today is the anniversary."

"That's true," said Pamphile. "Right bang onto his head! Poor old Euffe, all the same!"

Flavie was thinking sadly that the ugliness of Pamphile Carambois had not grown less with the passage of the years. Nevertheless this man's fidelity was the sole blessing that she would have from now henceforth. She said to herself that she would have done better to leave everything years ago and begin her life afresh, no matter with whom, no matter how . . . But it was too late.

The sun was shining over the Alps, scattering all the mist and leaving only springtime purity. Grenoble was flooded with beautiful light, in which the pretty cyclist girls were riding gaily, displaying their white legs within the circles of their flying skirts.

"Poor old Daddy Euffe!" Flavie repeated with a sigh, while she was not quite sure whether this funeral oration concerned an old man who had been violently laid low or her own disillusionment and vain searching for someone to love in order to make life possible.

How heavy is an empty heart to bear! And Freddy Glowes, who had died prematurely at the height of his fame, had disappeared from the screen. Feminine search for a fresh idol to worship and admire had completely failed.

14. A PHONEY WAR "There is one pleasant thing at least about this war, and that is, that one can now get general servants and charwomen. These girls are less unreasonable than they were before."

"Yes, I have heard that too. The servant problem is becoming less and less difficult, so it appears. Maids are turning up without even being asked to. And wages are lower."

"How do you account for this, my dear?"

"Since their men have been mobilized, the women of the poorer classes are having to shift for themselves, or at the very least to find some way of making a bit extra."

"This war is a sad business, there's no doubt of that. But perhaps it was the only way to get things straight. It will put people in their place. And frankly, they needed it."

"In any case, as far as servants go, my feeling is that one should make some sort of compromise, and bring wages down . . . These girls were getting above themselves, expecting too much altogether."

"It's the same as for the workmen. You're not satisfied? Very well, then, into the army you go! And why, I ask you, should one pay the men working in the factories while the others at the front, who are in danger, get hardly anything at all? It isn't just!"

"Yes, it's high time for a little more justice to be done. We badly need some firmness and discipline in France."

"The military people will be making themselves felt. Courtmartials, martial law, and all that sort of thing! It may be the best way of getting rid of the tub thumpers and their crowd for good and all."

"Let us only hope you are right!"

At the beginning of November 1939 the weather was still mild. Save for a brief interlude of cold in October, the spell of autumn sunshine had remained almost unbroken. The valleys around Grenoble were still, at this late season, displaying brilliant tints of russet and gold. At White Terraces, Claire Euffe was entertaining women friends in a drawing room on the ground floor in which a log fire was crackling. Through the wide bay windows one could see the mountains with slopes still green. These ladies were speaking of the war, which had not yet lost its feeling of novelty and of purposeless inactivity. The whole district was stirred and restless with military movements on a large scale. Even at Sassenage the quartermaster general's department had set up offices in a country house. Artillery was quartered there, as also at Neuray, Veurey, Fontaine, and Seyssinet. There were some light tanks (actually the little Renault tanks of the previous war) at Seyssins, and infantry units at Eichirolles, Champagnier, and High and Low Jarrie. There were still more troops at Fure, Tullins, Voreppe, and La Monta. Engineer units occupied different centres in the Grésivaudan valley. Work for national defence was being carried on in the factories at Pont-de-Claix. The headquarters of the army of the Alps was set up at Uriage. Even in Grenoble itself all branches and all ranks of the army were to be seen, and the peaked cap held sway; on the pavements in front of the cafés it was almost universal. One feature of the war was entirely without precedent, the plunging of part of Europe into darkness owing to the fear of attacks from the air: the effects of the shock to people's minds caused by the terrible blasting of Warsaw had not yet died away. At Grenoble the blackout was very strict. The only compensation for the lack of any form of shelter was a great profusion of whistles and cries of "Lights out!"

In the drawing room the conversation pursued its course.

246

"Tell me, Claire, have you good news of Edmond?"

"Yes, excellent," Claire said. "He is at Lyon now. He telephones nearly every day."

"How is it that he didn't stay at Grenoble?"

"Oh, but he's only about seventy miles away, a couple of hours' journey by road. He has just got his fourth band as senior administrative officer on the quartermaster general's staff. They sent him to Lyon to run something or other, I don't know what. With his exact mind and his experience of management, it was thought he could do some very valuable work."

"Indeed, I am not surprised! And besides, with all the people you know, he would easily be able to get himself recalled to Grenoble if he felt like it."

"Yes, no doubt. . . . But for the moment he likes being at Lyon. It takes him out of himself a bit. Besides, you know Edmond. He says that a man in his position must do his duty and set a good example."

"Oh, yes, he's splendid in that way. It would be a good thing if a lot of other Frenchmen were as good as he is at sticking to their principles. Do you see him occasionally?"

"Every week. Either I go to Lyon or he comes here. He has a car and chauffeur entirely at his disposal. And Edmond is very anxious not to lose sight of the Silken Net. A man can serve his country without sacrificing his own interests entirely."

"His brother Germain is taking over the management for the time being?"

"Yes, that became necessary as Edmond was keen on being in uniform. He was bent on getting that fourth band."

"A major. just fancy! Delightful."

"Yes, isn't it? And it really wouldn't be worth while—so he said—working hard as he does in peacetime and then not persevere and do his best now. Between you and me, there may be a wee bit of childishness about it; uniform rather suits these gentlemen, you know. It makes them look younger."

"He must be splendid in it!"

"It does add to his appearance, it certainly does. But joking apart, I think he really did want to place himself and his abilities at the country's disposal. The only trouble has been his having to hand over the Silken Net to Germain. You know what he's like, Germain? Charming, of course, but . . ."

"Oh, yes, charming."

"Well, the fact is that he needs Edmond to prompt him. He is really not up to the work when he's quite alone. Too often he doesn't know his own mind, he's too much of a dreamer . . . too poetical!"

"Poor Germain! That's his sentimental side. . . . And what about your de Bazair brother-in-law?"

"He is on the Belgian frontier. We should have liked to keep him at Grenoble, to work with Germain; we had the means of doing so. But he wouldn't hear of it. He's a reckless, daredevil fellow, like all the de Bazairs. And as he says himself: 'Noblesse oblige!' "

"Oh, but that's splendid!"

"Yes, and he wanted to see the war at close quarters. He says he's delighted to be where he is, 'in the front seat,' as he wrote—in case anything happens."

"But will anything happen?"

"Opinions differ a good deal about that."

"What does your husband think?"

"He had an opportunity of a talk with the general on the subject. The general thinks that the chief danger is that of air raids interfering badly with our mobilization. What has been so clever on our part, in his opinion, is the having taken advantage of the war in Poland to get our armies together. Now that our dispositions have been satisfactorily made, the general thinks we can face up to anything that may come along, whatever it may be."

"And we have the Maginot Line! We're told that it's impassable . . ."

"It must be a marvel!"

"This time we shall avoid the mistakes we made in 1914—Charleroi, the retreat . . ."

"Yes, everyone thinks so."

"And Italy? What is Italy going to do?"

"She is in a state of paralysis, so I've been told! She won't budge, you'll see. And it's almost a pity for us. The general thinks so too. He says that if Italy had marched with Germany, we should have a battlefield all ready made. It appears that the great strategic difficulty is to find a field of battle, avoiding the fortifications. If Italy had marched against us we should immediately have crossed the Alps. We should have attacked Germany on a more weakly defended front—the South."

"Oh, I say, that would have been magnificent!"

"But wouldn't it have meant a great many more casualties?"

"Ah yes, it might! And our G.H.Q. are supposed to be planning an entirely defensive war. As little bloodshed as possible. One can't blame them . . ."

248

"No, of course not . . . still . . . it doesn't do to be too timid, in war!"

"That reminds me that we have a friend who has just come back from Paris, a man who spends a lot of time in government and military circles, knows people in Daladier's cabinet, and is in touch with General Georges headquarters staff and all that sort of thing. He says there are two different schools of thought, the people who favour an offensive policy, and the others. It's Gamelin who is putting on the brake, holding himself in reserve, in agreement with Daladier."

"I heard something of that kind . . ."

"These people are saying that if we don't attack, seeing that the Germans on their side have no interest in doing so, the war will never end."

"People are saying that Gamelin is influenced by the British idea—economic war. It seems that the Germans have very little petrol. That's where we shall get them. Blockade along the whole line."

"There is the Russian petrol . . ."

"But do you know that there is a huge army being got together in Syria, under Weygand's command? Why in Syria?"

"People are wondering . . . Well, we shall see."

"Yes, we shall see. . . . And we have plenty of time. The English are said to be preparing for a three years' war."

"That's pretty brave of them, I must say! Good heavens, think of this horrible blackout lasting three years! I might get used to everything else. But this darkness, never! Grenoble at night is becoming impossible."

"But, my dear, you have to think of air raids. You know what happened at Warsaw!"

"But you are not going to compare France to Poland! We have resources which those people hadn't got at all. We have better people in command, a better organization. And besides, if what I was told is true . . ."

"What was that?"

"I shouldn't like to give away a military secret . . . Well anyhow, this is what it was. It appears that there are three batteries of 75s defending Grenoble, to say nothing of machine guns in all the barracks. And I was given the opinion of a man with technical knowledge. It seems that Grenoble, in its circle of mountains, is practically impossible to attack. The planes, having made their dive, would find it too difficult to gain height again so as to escape."

"In any case, if they drop bombs on us, we shall do the same on them!"

"Yes, so we shall!"

"And if we've gone to war, it means that we have all we need to carry it on."

"Not a doubt about it!"

"You haven't heard that the military people are anxious in any way?"

"No, indeed I have not, my dear. And everybody is thinking how wonderfully the mobilization has gone."

"Yes, hasn't it? I really have a sort of feeling that France has pulled herself together. We can get servants again, at less than three hundred francs a month. It may be only a detail, this . . . But it goes to prove that everyone has got back to his proper place. There has been a real change at last!"

People were finding themselves compelled to settle down anywhere and everywhere in this war without battles, a "humanitarian" war waged by instalments of statistics and propaganda. Everyone was basing his arrangements on the probability of a long duration. Many officers on the reserve were appreciating their escape from family duties and the humdrum of their ordinary everyday existence. Far from their wives, and provided with cars and petrol, they were ordering themselves new uniforms to replace those which they had used for their periods of service and were now out of date. They were living in messes which were gay and noisy with songs and jokes and laughter. In the barracks, where the usual routine was being temporarily upset by the mobilization, the young recruits were arriving. The words "military service" were once more occupying their minds as they had in time of peace. Only the offices concerned with questions of manpower were in full swing, identifying, classifying, indexing, filing masses of men scattered over the whole country.

The chief source of worry for headquarters staffs was the problem of winter quarters for troops stationed in the valleys. It was suddenly realized that barns, coach houses, and stables, which had been good enough on the whole during the fine autumn weather, would be quite insufficient protection for the men from the rigours of the winter season. It became a matter of urgency to fit up adequate quarters by means of beams and scantling, oilcloth, tarred felt, straw, stoves, palliasses, et cetera. An engineer officer, Lieutenant Roger Lagarde (the husband of Riri Jumier), whom circumstances had brought back to Grenoble, was commissioned to draw up a schedule of the requirements of each unit, and by his own personal efforts to co-ordinate the work of the officers on the quartermaster general's staff, the staff of the Engineers, and those in charge of military stores, three organizations which rarely saw eye to eye, threw responsibilities on to each other's shoulders, and steadily refused to make necessary decisions.

In the men's quarters everything was primitive and wretchedly inadequate. There was lack of corrugated iron, cement, plaster, and tools. The military stores branch had at their disposal, for all purposes, a beggarly total of one hundred and ninety-five stoves which were allotted to "rooms with fires," where the men of a section or detachment would come and warm themselves in turn.

There were still shortages of blankets, boots, et cetera. The equipment of the larger units had cleared out the warehouses and shops. There was a shortage of hutments, a shortage of guns, and of other arms and munitions for instruction. To the people lacking these things the same answer was given as is always given in France in such circumstances: "Do the best you can!" For the time being the men defended themselves against the cold by building up ramparts consisting of bundles of straw, and obtained a semblance of comfort by means of odds and ends filched and patched up. The war machine was badly in need of adjustment and polish.

Scarcely had he finished with the business of winter quarters than Lieutenant Lagarde was sent off on a mission to M——. He had to hasten the carrying out of certain works, such as "building D," in the courtyard of a requisitioned factory. A bitter dispute was in progress between the Medical Service and the military authority over a hospital barracks—a dispute which was the byword of the district. A large barracks, evacuated at the time of the mobilization, was to be turned into a hospital. The Medical Service took possession of the building and began the work of conversion. They took away the shelves for packs, the arms racks and the bedsteads. They stopped up the holes in brick partitions, disinfected, knocked down dividing walls in order to prepare operating theatres, and gave everything a coat of paint. Then it was suddenly noticed that there was nowhere to put the young recruits who were to arrive shortly. The military authority decided to restore the hospital, now in process of installation, to its normal use as a barracks . . . on the understanding that when, a few months hence, other quarters would be ready for the new recruits, the barracks could then be used as a hospital. Anger and wrath on the part of the Medical Service. But its protests fell on deaf ears: hammering into the newly distempered walls was begun and the shelves for packs, the arms racks, and the bedsteads were fixed once more in their old places. In the meantime the Medical Service had refused to give way. Entrenched in a remote section of the buildings, with a wholesale and energetic display of spite and ill will they set out to hamper the work in process, hiding ladders and tools, which had then to be borrowed from building yards two or three miles away. Roger Lagarde was instructed to put these matters to rights, even though it meant intervening between two parties in violent and unyielding opposition. But those engaged in sabotaging the work were displaying infinitely greater zeal and cunning than those responsible for hastening it forward. Roger Lagarde observed this and decided to let things take their course. This clash was not a really serious matter. The other works in progress were jogging along, and with the shortage of labour, tools and materials, it was no one's business to alter their pace. Lieutenant Lagarde struck up an acquaintance, at the hotel, with officers of the Air Force and parachutists. But the Air Force officers had orders to fly as little as possible in order to economize in material, which was extremely scanty. Among these officers was a squadron leader, a very pleasant person to meet and a man of great determination, who had had some narrow escapes from fatal accidents in flying. Roger asked him what part aviation would play in this war. The squadron leader did not think that it would be a preponderant one.

"Even over towns?"

"Even over towns," the squadron leader said. "Look what happened in Spain. Madrid, when you come to think of it, suffered very little."

The squadron leader confessed that he had never flown at more than one hundred and seventy miles an hour. He knew nothing of the characteristics of our latest machines. He seemed quite unconvinced that the new speeds would make any great difference to the uses of aviation, which, so far as he was concerned, were limited to observation and spotting for artillery, and reconnaissance in depth over enemy territory. It seemed to Roger Lagarde that this squadron leader was expressing opinions prevalent in military aviation circles. He was recalled to Grenoble and entrusted with other special jobs.

Winter arrived suddenly in mid-December, severe wintry weather, freezing mains, fountains, gutters in the town, and ponds and puddles in the country. There were heavy falls of snow, and a dangerous thin coating of ice on the roads; the night skies were arctic in appearance, with brilliant starlight, and the winds in the valleys blew as though across the Russian steppes, like dashing charges of Cossack cavalry. People were firmly ensconced in comparative warmth indoors, with shutters and curtains carefully closed in a flawless blackout which resembled a night in the Middle Ages with the constables of the watch going the rounds. The cafés were more crowded than ever with soldiers, for whom the carefree pleasure of the moment was the order of the day. But those same soldiers were citizens who, except for the hours thus spent, had the citizen's customary cares and discontents, kept far away as they were from their rightful avocations. The war was failing to give them that element of the picturesque which they had expected. Many were declaring that they were tired of it.

Pamphile Garambois's cinema was always full. The Silken Net's branch establishments were as busy as they could be. The restaurants in Grenoble, large and small, had several services at every meal. The numbers of requisitioned motorcars, of which skiddings and collisions were responsible for a considerable massacre, were vast on all the roads. People were beginning to murmur that too many men had been mobilized for this stagnant conflict. From the depots and from the front many men were being withdrawn who had been detailed for special work, and preferred to return home. Certain people who were eager to have done with the war were demanding that the fighting should be hurried forward. Others, more prudent, were in favour of lying low and waiting— waiting till this somnolent war should end of itself—should die of inanition in an atmosphere of ridicule. The epithet "odd" was making its appearance. Casual love affairs were filling idle hours. There was dancing in the public bars.

In January 1940, Edmond Euffe, taking advantage of a visit to Grenoble, went to Varce where he owned a property. There were troops quartered in the buildings, and he feared the possibility of damage. He stayed on at Varce until later than he had intended, and did not start back to Grenoble till after nightfall, though he was due again at Lyon on the following morning. As he got into his car he said to his military chauffeur: "I'm in rather a hurry"—a rash remark to make to a boy already too inclined to drive with a dangerous lack of ordinary caution. But at night, in a car with the windows tightly closed (it was very cold), he was unconscious of the speed at which they were travelling.

On the five-mile stretch which separates Pont-de-Claix from Grenoble, the chauffeur accelerated. He had good visibility on a wide and perfectly straight road, and felt that he was protected by his lights. He took no account of the hidden dangers of a road with an uneven surface. Travelling at about seventy miles an hour, he came to a section covered with a thin coating of ice, felt the car swerving, turned the steering wheel too strongly, put on his brakes, and lost direction. The car left the roadway, capsized, and was hurled into a ditch. Edmond Euffe was killed on the spot. The chauffeur escaped with scratches.

It was one of those stupid military accidents of the same kind as a certain number of others which had already occurred owing to fast cars having been entrusted to inexperienced drivers. Several officers had been killed in this way.

The war was not sufficiently active to prevent this tragedy from attracting considerable attention at Grenoble, where it made some stir. This was now the second occasion on which the man at the head of the Silken Net had been struck down by a fatal accident. People were saying that Edmond Euffe, driven by a soldier and killed in uniform, had died on active service and laid down his life for his country, while his fortune might have enabled him to escape certain obligations. A great crowd of military people attended the funeral, including the general himself, who was bearing in mind that the dead man was a person of consequence. All the rank and fashion of Grenoble were present, with solemn and rapt expressions, which seemed to say: "See what the war does. . . . Each one of us has to make his sacrifice, whatever his job or to whatever class he belongs!"

Lucie came from Nice. Though many years had passed since she had last been seen, her presence was noticed, but many people did not recognize her. It could hardly be said that her appearance had improved. Her face was spoilt by her blotchy complexion, as her mother's had been before her. But as a strong, self-confident lady, whose life was working out in normal fashion, there was an air of calm satisfaction about her. She was accompanied by her eldest son, aged thirteen, whose presence was helpful from the point of view of family reconciliation. He was a healthy-looking boy, with a wide-awake appearance, and very well dressed.

On the whole the funeral, despite the war which had disorganized so many things and scattered people in all directions, was a notable and striking event. It was a consolation for Claire—who made a theatrical display of grief—to be surrounded by sympathy, expressed in the warmest possible manner, from her fashionable friends. Mourning suited her, gave her character. In certain circles she was regarded as the first war widow. People said to her "you poor dear" in tones full of earnestness and compassion and of esteem for her proud dignity and great courage in the tragedy that had befallen her.

At the end of February the weather suddenly cleared. The ice and snow melted. March opened magnificently, warm and with brilliant sunshine. At that time Bob took leave from the front to go to Paris, where Alberte went to join him.

Paris was splendid ("so brave and jaunty" was its description in the newspapers) with its adornment of fresh green trees and verdure, its skies all spick and span, its assembly of gold braid and gaily bedizened chests. How graceful were the women as they made their way along the Champs Elysées, with admiring glances cast in their direction and their background of the sky of tender blue which ringed the Arc de Triomphe within a halo of loveliness. What laughing, lively crowds in all the restaurants and public places! What carefree jauntiness and unconcern! To Bob de Bazair, as they were dining at a restaurant, surrounded by gay lights and lovely frocks, friends of his were saying to him: "We have never been out so much in our lives!" Others were saying, with a note of surprise in their voices:

"Do you really enjoy it, that life at the front? But the place where everything is happening is Paris. Paris is the only place to be in, in a war like this! Get yourself posted here. Would you like us to see about it for you? We know . . ." mentioning people of note.

"No, no, thanks very much."

"You are an astonishing person! Everyone is bestirring himself at the moment so as to get a good job. The time will come when it's too late. You may be sorry then."

Bob de Bazair saw men specially well informed, of whom there were so many in Paris. They told him:

"Nothing will happen this year because the English are not ready. The clash will come next year."

"Is everyone quite happy about it?"

"Oh yes. The only thing that is really worrying those at the head of affairs is having to keep inactive troops under arms."

"And what about the air?"

"We are feeling perfectly safe now. We have models under way that definitely outclass the German machines. However, there is one snag, and it comes from the army. There is supposed, unfortunately, to be disagreement between Gamelin and General Georges. Georges' idea is—and there are many people who agree with him—that we ought to have made a determined attack in September, got our teeth into the Siegfried Line, and entered Germany—to have taken advantage of the war in Poland for doing this. Gamelin refused to take it on. Do you know what they have christened him? 'The Eiderdown,' or 'Joffre without the Marne.' He's a man who never reacts at all."

"But he's supposed to be intelligent?"

"It's a staff officer's intelligence. But he's not a big enough man for a very high command. That at least is what is being murmured in certain exalted circles."

"Then how about the big push?"

"You need not expect it this year. The opportunity has been let slip. Now we've got to wait for the English. Always supposing . . . always supposing that the Germans don't think up some other plan first. Time is working against them—and they know it. If they tried to make peace after Poland—well, they had their reasons for doing so."

Alberte's eyes were fixed on Bob with a look that was grave and charged with meaning, a look that was in itself an unspoken prayer with some such words as these: "As you are being given the opportunity, why not come back here and get away from the danger, for my sake and the children's? As it would be quite understood . . . As very nice people are advising you to do it; as they do it themselves . . ." But his own laughter forestalled any such words, prevented their being ever uttered. He replied:

"There is only one excuse for pleasure at the present time, and that is, that your own life should be in danger. For me at least this Paris which, thinking it is sheltered and safe, has gone on the spree, has a bad smell. There are too many people here who are taking cover, hiding, shall we say, and making money. The front, with its huts, its encampments, and its mud, has better style."

Alberte managed to repress her sorrow, and she admired him. Despite her apprehensions she was proud that he had taken this attitude and was committing himself heart and soul to this task, that his actions were those of a true de Bazair. She thought him very handsome in uniform, handsomer than ever. He was wearing one of the earliest *Croix de guerre*.

They spent the last evening together, and during its course, in a gay and charming way he repeated several times: "I've always had luck, impudent luck, luck I didn't deserve! And then you know, my little Albe, I am not going to miss such an opportunity as this to escape from grocery. Not that I'm ashamed of grocery, but really, it didn't quite satisfy the needs of a whole lifetime!"

She went with him to the station—to his carriage. She was pale and sad, but tried to hide it. She knew that he would never give way, and her love had always been guided by the principle—his will be done! She knew that she wished with all her soul and all her strength to tear him from that place, that horrible place where killing was done. But she knew also that she would never have dared, that she would have been ashamed to ask him not to return there, to ask him for something which he would have considered a weakness, an act of cowardice, a humiliation. Until the last moment of all she continued to smile at him; she smiled at the carriage door from which he had been leaning, at the train which was bearing him away . . .

But when that train had disappeared, an icy chill gripped her heart; she felt shattered, panic-stricken. . .   From that moment onwards she knew that she had to get ready. . . . In her mind's eye she saw those friends to whom she told her secrets, the pretty countesses long since dead, those of Champagnier, mysterious and sad, the Countess Ghislaine, the Countess Aurora, the Countess Marie-Edmée, the Countess Speranza, the Countess Violaine, all those who, in the dust of years and the sadness of autumn days, had waited for de Bazairs who never came back. She knew that her own time had come, and that the Countess Alberte, in the gallery of portraits, would have her own look, no less than the others, as of some hidden, inconsolable grief. . . .

She left the station, weeping and stumbling in the sombre darkness of this night of war. Over and again, in her despair, she kept repeating these words: "I commit him to your care, I commit him to your care!" She was addressing her protectress, the Virgin of St.-Laurent. . . . But while making this appeal she failed to recall the familiar features. The Lady of Heaven remained hidden in the unfathomable blackout, as though she too had taken fright at all the threats and horrors summed up in that small word—war.

15. VOREPPE CRIES HALT—AND LIFE GOES ON

On the tenth of May, 1940, in the morning, the Prefecture at Grenoble learned of the German attack on Belgium, Luxembourg, and the Netherlands. News was further received of an event which carried a more immediate threat to Grenoble itself—the German raid on the aerodrome at Bron, near Lyon. A message conveying this news was taken to the home of a friend of Edmond Euffe, Major S——, who had arrived the day before on leave and was on Gamelin's staff. He had asked that a warning might be sent him in the event of any serious developments. From the prefect's office Major S—— telephoned direct to his operational headquarters, which would be acting as a signal box for the battle which was then beginning. He received a precise reply to the effect that "All's well. Everything proceeding according to plan." Fortified by this encouraging reply, he reassured everybody. Then, as he still had a little time to spare before catching his train, the conversation was continued. With a map spread out before them, they discussed the various possibilities of enemy movements. Someone spoke of the Sedan gap. On this point the major was very emphatic.

"If they debouch there, we shall be ready for them! I know for certain that we are on the lookout for them at that point."

"Is there a trap being set for them in that district?"

The major smiled, with the air of a man who could tell far more than he does.

"I can only repeat: 'So far as Sedan is concerned you have nothing to fear.' I will go even further, and say, 'If they show up there, so much the better.' "

This assurance brought encouragement. Everyone did his best to keep calm, to show no sign of anxiety, but there was much hidden anguish and many a heavy heart, so improbable had it seemed that an actual attack came within what they had conceived to be the very limited range of the enemy's capacity. French propaganda had just issued a pamphlet entitled *King Petrol* and published an expensively produced album of photographs of France at war, and the general tone of the official reports had been continuously very optimistic.

In Grenoble, one saw faces pale with anxiety, and people whose gestures betrayed their nervousness. Our armies had already set out for Belgium.

"This time," people were saying, "it's up to us."

The word Sedan appeared in print, but was quickly superseded by the actual course of events—thus causing much embarrassment to Félix Lacail who, while engaged in spreading abroad rumours current at the Prefecture, had assumed the role of prophet and announced to all his friends: "The big showdown will be at Sedan. You'll see what we've got up our sleeves for them in that corner there!" The communiqué of the nineteenth of May gave out that the Germans were already at Guise and Landrecies. On the twenty-first came news of the fall of Amiens and of Arras. France was being stricken by a new Charleroi, and still more brutally than on the earlier occasion. It was distressing to have to admit that neither experience nor foresight had been sufficient to spare us these troubles. And now there was something abnormal taking place, which gave much food for thought: one saw combatant soldiers filtering back to the interior, non-commissioned officers and men, who had let everything go and taken to flight. These men looked haggard and drawn, and a little embarrassed, and could make only incoherent unintelligible remarks, the gist of which appeared to be that the war was a terrifying business and that the whole thing was

258

a mystery. Nevertheless all these men who had fallen back bore with them papers which were quite in order and had been issued to them by some unknown authorities, as though to quit the field of battle had become a normal occurrence. There were rumours, repeated in whispers (people were afraid of being denounced), of panic and rout. Boulogne . . . Calais . . . Dunkirk. Two alternative possibilities, only, seemed now to be left—a miracle, or collapse. Prediction had become a matter of choice between them.

Claire Euffe arranged for the delivery at Sassenage—over and above what she had already accumulated—of half a ton of sugar, and of oil, soap, and tinned and preserved foods in the same proportion. She bought in various shops quantities of cloth and woven materials, silk stockings, gloves, wool, et cetera. She ordered thirty tons of coal. She advised all the people in her own circle to take similar precautions.

"Now that Edmond is not here," she was saying, "I have to see to everything, and I must take all the responsibility. What would happen to us if I were to go and lose my head! This is going to be a long war, and Sassenage may become a place of refuge."

It very soon became obvious that she bore these cares lightly and that she loved the responsibility they entailed. Her egotistical nature was manifested in her adoption on all occasions of an extremely firm line of conduct, which at the same time showed practical ability and clear judgment.

Germain Euffe was far from possessing this admirable firmness. Under stress of the emotions aroused in him by our reverses, this highly susceptible person talked of enlisting. The family grew uneasy at hearing the director of the Silken Net discussing abandonment of a firm with a capital of several million francs which constituted the assets of his own immediate relations, in order to go off and secure a very tardy initiation in the use of arms. However, they had in reality but little fear that he would actually put his plan into execution; they knew what a timorous, and also erratic, person he was. But as he was always in pursuit of some will-o'-the-wisp or other, this fanciful young visionary was fully capable of leaving the firm entirely in the lurch at the very moment when he had some vital decisions to make: for it is always at the time of great catastrophes that fortunes are made and unmade. Claire Euffe, always a capable woman, sent the widow of General de Sainte-Foy to see him; she was a lady of whom he stood in terror.

"Well," she said to him in her loud and metallic voice, "what is this I hear? You're wanting to play the knight-errant, are you? With seven children and a spineless lump of a wife on your hands? Are you going

off your head, Germain? Don't you think that things are bad enough already?"

"But one shouldn't worry about making money at a time like this.
What I want is to do my duty."

"Your duty, my friend, is to stay where you are. And where did you
get hold of that idea—that the war should stop people from making
money? Just you look around a bit!"

"Exactly—just what I do," Germain said. "And because my heart is
in the right place . . ."

"Oh, leave your heart alone, Germain!" the general's widow com-
manded him. "It has made you do quite enough stupid idiotic things
already. And as for the war, there are men—specialists—who have been
given the job of running it. You'll be telling me that they have a
funny way of doing so, perhaps. Well, so they have. but it doesn't altogether surprise me. I have seen generals at close quarters—having married one. If they are all of the same stamp as my old man, I can tell you
straightway that it's all up with us. But that makes no difference to your
duty, which is to feed people. Whatever happens, people will always
have to eat, though they don't deserve to. You have enlisted in grocery.
Stay there!"

"Might I mention, madame, that I have never liked that occupation?"

"Heavens alive," the general's widow cried out, "do you think we
have been put into this world to do what we like? Do you imagine that
I have ever liked being a woman? But Nature has enrolled me among
the women, just as circumstances have pushed you into grocery. Your
temperament is a sight too sensitive! What I ought to have had was
a beard and biceps and all the rest of it. I ought to have had command
of artillery, of armies—the whole bag of tricks. And I'll bet my bottom
dollar that if I'd been there, those gentlemen facing us would have
come a cropper on the Meuse! Your sex are a pitiful lot!"

The speed of approaching disaster was now overwhelming. A poli-
tician, an important man in the Department, had said: "I do not believe
in miracles." Events were crowding in each other's train. Labour for
the repair of damage caused by the enemy was arriving everywhere too
late.

On the morning of Monday the seventeenth of June, the work of
shoring up the cellars of the Prefecture with beams and sandbags was
put in hand. On the upper floors, as had been done in the Ministries,
cupboards and filing cabinets were emptied of their contents and ar-
chives turned topsy-turvy; then all the papers were taken down in
the courtyard to be burnt. Throughout the district there was a frantic

succession of arrests of suspects, of spies, parachutists, and members of the Fifth Column—genuine or otherwise. Grenoble was crammed with people who had been forced back, soldiers and civilians alike. The blare of loud-speakers was like the ringing of a knell.

On the nineteenth of June, at about half-past three in the afternoon, several officials, with Félix Lacail amongst them, carrying files under their arms, were assembled in the prefect's room. The telephone rang and the meeting was interrupted. The prefect grabbed the receiver. When he replaced it he was somewhat pale.

"Gentlemen," he said, "Prefect Bollaert has bid me farewell. The Germans are entering Lyon at this moment. They will be at the Prefecture of the Rhone within the next few minutes."

"It will be our turn soon . . ."

"I understand that the military people want to put up a fight."

"Put up a fight—it's about time they did!"

"Nine miles from Grenoble. At Voreppe."

The village of Voreppe, standing on high ground, looks down upon a narrow section of the Isère valley, between the mountain group of the Grande Chartreuse and the last of the rocky heights of the Vercors. This situation had been responsible for its choice as a point of resistance for the checking of the German columns coming from the north, which could have taken the army of the Alps in the rear. The topography of the place made it a suitable one for the purpose of defence, particularly in view of the very limited armament at our disposal, which consisted of no more than one anti-tank 25 and a few guns, 47s, 65s and 75s. With these, a few hundred men only, of various arms. (There were plenty of men in the depots, but no weapons for them.)

There was a rumour of fighting at Voreppe, and of the Germans having been held up there. This was a fact. A few enemy tanks had been dispersed by the artillery, on the morning of the twenty-third of June. On the same day a second column of tanks, caught unawares by the fire of the 75s, was diverted. In order to deal with this unexpected resistance the Germans massed some heavy artillery in the Rives-Moirans-Voiron area. On the twenty-fourth of June this artillery concentrated its fire on Voreppe and sent a few shells into the outskirts of Grenoble. Then came a surprise.

At White Terraces, where Marie-Thérèse Euffe and her seven children had taken refuge, there was heard during the afternoon of the twenty-fourth a series of violent explosions at very short intervals, which seemed to be coming from the Sassenage valley. They were the first rounds to be fired by twelve French guns, eight 105s and four 155s, which had been hastily brought up at the last moment and were firing on the German parks and batteries. These batteries they silenced, thereby saving Voreppe, and possibly Grenoble itself, from a murderous bombardment.

Marie-Thérèse and her seven children were extremely frightened. But Claire, as she always did, displayed great firmness; she expressed herself as being utterly determined, if the Germans should arrive, not to hand over her house, furniture and provisions to them. Her domineering nature made her continually conscious of what she believed to be her due, and caused her to feel that even in war, a fate which might befall people of small account could never overtake a woman like herself, Claire Euffe, née Bargès, a lady of the manor and one of the leading feminine personalities of Grenoble. "I don't allow that!" she was accustomed to say. She would never admit the possibility of the war causing some interruption of the respect and consideration which were accorded her by all those with whom she came in contact. She would never admit that a French defeat could touch her in so far as her private interests were concerned. She was already preparing to receive the conquerors with a haughty air that would put those people in their place.

But the conquerors never appeared, having failed to reach Grenoble when the armistice arrived. Thanks for this were due to the men who fought at the village of Voreppe and a few pieces of artillery in the valley of Sassenage.

Two women whom sorrow had already brought together, and was now doing so once more. One of these more upset than the other, weeping: Irma Moufeton, solitary, ashamed. The other, Alberte, deathly pale ever since she had known of the death of Bob de Bazair at the front, but having certain things around her to rescue and sustain her, with her duties and the mission with which she was entrusted still—the care of Champagnier, ancient background and storehouse of family tradition, and the preservation of the long line of the de Bazairs in the person of her three children, her three sons who were playing in the park and whose voices she could hear.

Some months previously, in great distress after Edmond's violent death, Irma Moufeton, remembering Alberte, her lover's favourite sister, and her lovely face, had come to see her; she had come as a humble woman in deep distress, a woman who could have no rightful share in any family mourning of the Euffes, though truly it was she herself who was the widow, could widowhood have been measured in terms of desolation and a breaking heart. She knew that Bob de Bazair was absent, and this gave her more courage; and she came neither to beg nor to reproach, nor had she any intention of emerging from the position of obscurity to which she had resigned herself from the beginning. She had wished no more than to avail herself of a precious opportunity of being able to talk of Edmond, with Alberte as her listener. For this purpose an excuse was available in a life insurance of three hundred thousand francs, of which sum she now found herself in possession by virtue of certain arrangements made by the dead man (who had thereby faithfully followed a good example set by his father). She came to ask—though there was no question of this being the case—whether those arrangements would encroach upon the rights of Edmond's children. She may have been prepared, if only to be received at times in the Euffe family circle and earn their esteem and that of the society in which they moved, to forgo a portion of that sum of money.

Alberte made no such demands upon her. Just as in days past, with daughterly devotion, she had seen no harm in the part played by Riri Jumier in her father's life, so now she saw none in that which Irma Moufeton had played in her brother's. For years past she had known Claire for a cold, contemptuous, and selfish woman. In Alberte's eyes, sincerity and disinterestedness were factors which outweighed all others. That she herself had been sincere in her love without infringing the social code, she felt was due to her own good fortune. She had no strictures to make on people who commit those acts of impulse which the world calls stupid because self-interest has no part in them. She knew instinctively that Irma Moufeton was a good woman, faithful and devoted, who had given Edmond some true happiness, perhaps the most he had enjoyed. This woman in tears gave her knowledge of a whole side of Edmond's life of which the Euffes and their friends were ignorant. This hidden portion of his existence showed him in an entirely different light from that in which his own family had known him. In that life, his stiff and formal dignity as an employer and head of the family, as a giver of instructions and advice, had disappeared altogether. In his romance at Voiron there was an informal, free-and-easy element as well as a touch of the drawing-room ballad, all of which vanished into thin air when confronted with the pomp and display of White Terraces, with bridge, golf, and worship of the goddess Fashion. (Irma Moufeton and he used to play piquet or dominoes together.) But this only made Edmond appear the more human, more understandable. In this hidden phase of a man's life, a humble and unpretentious one, Alberte was in some way reminded of her father's

263

smile in days gone by, of his humming of a tune as he made a hasty exit after the evening meal, with some business appointment as his excuse. . . .

In a particularly indulgent frame of mind, due to Bob's absence and the ever-present danger which made that absence weigh heavy on her heart, Alberte received Irma Moufeton in a natural, easy manner which could only encourage her. She allowed her to come again from time to time. She felt that she was doing a good deed in receiving and listening to Irma, as it were a pious duty carried out in memory of her brother, because that memory would be better, more genuinely honoured in this way than it could be at Sassenage, where Claire, a completely self-centred woman, never spoke of Edmond without laying particular stress (in her usual theatrical manner) on her own sufferings in this calamity. Alberte had already had proof of how quickly the dead are forgotten. If the good, kindly Irma's heart was a little storehouse of loyal and faithful memories, those tender feelings could hardly be discouraged . . .

And now that it was Bob's wife whose turn had come to be stricken, Irma Moufeton, at Champagnier, was shedding tears for Alberte's grievous loss as well as for her own—for Alberte, to whom she was feeling deeply grateful for having welcomed her to the home of one born an Euffe, and cared nothing for the fact that her sorrow had no sanction of the law.

She would have devoted herself unreservedly to the family. In so doing she would be making atonement for having deprived others, owing to certain arrangements previously made, of money which was in reality theirs. She was genuinely distressed by the cruel blow which Alberte had sustained.

"It is fortunate indeed," she said to her by way of consolation, "that you have your three children, three lovely children who are so like their father!"

"Yes," Alberte said, with her thoughts far distant, replying mechanically and with no conception of the meaning of the words her lips were uttering, "yes, I have three children."

"And you have a family round you!"

"Yes," Alberte repeated, "a family . . ." as she vaguely wondered "What family?" knowing full well that there was no compensation anywhere . . .

"And you have your father-in-law, the count!"

"Yes," Alberte said, "I have him. . . ."

It was he who in point of fact was her chief support and consolation, this tall, grim old man obsessed by feelings of passionate indigna-

264

tion expressed in fits of cursing and derisive laughter; but an aristocrat through and through. He had for her an affection which contained a full measure of the subtle delicacy and tact of a man who had always been an adept at talking to a woman, whether he treated her as a princess or a light-o'-love. With Alberte he recovered his old faculty for displaying exquisite behaviour. Since Bob's death he had been surrounding her with every care and attention, quietly, unostentatiously, and without overwhelming her with too many words of comfort and consolation. He seemed to be thanking her for bearing unaided and alone the full weight of the family fortunes, at that point in their history which was the connecting link between the past, of which he himself was the representative, and the future as represented by his three grandchildren. In these he was beginning to take more interest. One of them was very like what he had been in his own childhood. In this boy he recognized the de Bazair characteristics which he himself possessed—fire, boldness, and impudence.

After long resistance, the aging count had at length resigned himself to growing old. For him the world was moving farther and farther away, was being blotted out by the fog of his own indifference. From a past which had seen charges of cavalry, love affairs with rich and lovely women, duels, nights of gambling, alarums and excursions and adventures of every kind, all that he now had left was one horse growing old in the stables, three boisterous grandsons who were afraid of him, and this daughter-in-law, grown pale, a true staunch woman such as the de Bazairs had always needed, courageous, loyal—and rich. A woman, also, who could suffer and endure, for all of them were doomed to suffer in due time, those women who placed their fate in de Bazair hands, tender creatures set apart for glorious sacrifice. This one at least was privileged in that she had been spared from suffering as a wife. Henceforth she would suffer for the honour of the family name which, faithful to the legend which at Champagnier held firm sway, she would continue to bear until her death. That this legend was now perhaps out of date mattered nothing. The hour had come for the tender, loving Countess Alberte to suffer in silence and apart, displaying to the world a proud and noble countenance, and upholding the old motto of the family coat of arms: "Love supports me."

It was for all these reasons that the old count, chewing a cigar no longer alight, would come and prowl about in the room where Alberte, with eyes that looked as though she were walking in her sleep, pondered and brooded over her heart-rending loss, in a solitude surrounded by the songs of birds, children's cries, the rustling of leafy trees, flowers on balconies and reflections in still waters—a thousand different things of such sweetness that they pierced the heart, while de Bazairs of days long past looked down at her with thoughtful gaze, silent in their frames upon the walls, where they watched the spectacle of life in these latter days, themselves a rich storehouse of secrets they would never betray, sphinxes of an unfathomable past. . . . There were times when the count, half unconsciously so it seemed, would stroke Alberte's hair with his wasted old hand, without speaking, or muttering some little words over and over again, inaudibly, like the little sounds one makes to soothe a troubled child. His consciousness of what has been destroyed and lost was becoming more vivid with advancing years. He felt that the lightning of destruction had fallen upon his line, and that instead of striking the old branch at the top of the tree, it had blasted a strong and flourishing bough, his son; whose wife was still an integral, living bough, this Alberte with the fine eyes and Madonnalike oval face, who had appealed to him ever since the earliest days of their acquaintance. He was conscious of her having received a blow that struck at the roots of her life's work, in the same way that war—always war!—when it had struck him in the hip twenty-six years before had destroyed the best parts of himself, the horseman and the warrior. He knew that time is needed—sometimes much time—to recover from these severe, these fundamental amputations. . . . Bodies must grow old, their strength and vigour diminish, before they can resign themselves to . . One has to reach a stage of narrow egotism, a vegetative, self-centred, aimless life . . .

"Come now, Albe," he asked her one day, in rather a grumbling tone of voice and without looking at her, "if you had to live your life over again, would you have it different?"

"No, no . . ." she murmured, with tears rolling silently down her cheeks, like drops of rain on chrysanthemums. . . .

"Very well, then," he said to her, "be proud! Do you think that the lady of Sassenage (a derisive reference to Claire) has so very much to regret and to weep for? Carry your head high, Albe! And think of Bob. Full of vigour and zest he was on that lovely morning when he met his death, facing north, which is the proud way for every Frenchman, with no thought but of victory, and a smile on his lips until he died, as they told you. No moaning, no pain and suffering for him. He was physically at his best—no hint or sign of decay in that young frame. He had never had to submit to pity—not from a living soul. Be proud, Albe! Let him be your inspiration—and your pride."

How right he was, the old nobleman, for all his bitterness! That

266

thought of pride—what better support could Alberte have? And as for the rest—that undercurrent of rebellion in a young and vigorous body—perhaps that too would be stilled, some day. . . .

This question was touched upon at White Terraces, where certain friends of the Euffes were discussing Alberte and thinking of her in the light of a heroine of romance who had met her Prince Charming in the gardens of Green Island.

"It is quite certain," Claire announced decisively, "that Alberte can not marry again. *On account of the title!*"

Claire was incapable of seeing any further than the title, which she envied. Some of her sister-in-law's feelings were a closed book to her. It was beyond her comprehension that Alberte should regard a life of love and marriage as finished for ever, so far as she herself was concerned, simply in deference to a certain principle of the de Bazairs, and to uphold a certain greatness and dignity inspired by the family name—qualities of which the title was a fitting adornment, but not essential to them, not their essence. She knew nothing of the mystery of those fond and gentle Countesses long since dead, with their heavy hearts and sorrowful eyes, who had told Alberte their secrets, at Champagnier. . . .

"Goodness gracious," Claire said spitefully to two or three of her special friends, "that little countess who's risen from grocery . . ."

She had been saying things like this for a long while past, and it was a mean and wretched thing to do. The fact was that she was impressed by Alberte who, for all her outward simplicity, drew self-confidence in plenty from sources of which this offshoot of the Bargès family was entirely ignorant. Yes, indeed she had become a true de Bazair, had this daughter of Constant Euffe, that rough diamond, that simple man! And this she had done without affectation, effortlessly, and with no selfish motive nor deep-laid scheme. Even as a widow she remained beneath the spell, with all its charm, which the de Bazairs had cast upon her, who was now guardian of a tradition to be handed on to her three children. It was better, therefore, so Claire thought, to be pleasant to her when they met, and have the satisfaction of being able to say: "My sister-in-law Countess de Bazair," when introducing her to friends. In the same way it would be flattering for Edmond's children to have de Bazair cousins. Sassenage must not become estranged from Champagnier.

This business—the war—being now provisionally settled, it was becoming an urgent matter to provide for the future of the Silken Net, which had been robbed of the firm's two best brains, Edmond Euffe and Bob de Bazair. For this purpose little reliance could be placed on Germain, "the incompetent member of the family." A number of people, besides Claire herself, and her two children, were interested in the Silken Net's future: Madame Constant Euffe, still living ("and frankly one wonders why!"); Germain, his wife, and their seven children; Alberte de Bazair and her three boys; Lucie and her husband, and their three children. Until such time as George Euffe, Claire's eldest child, should be of an age to enter the business (of which, by virtue of seniority, he would have the largest share, ousting his cousins up to the limit of what was practicable) it would have to be run on sound and competent lines. It could therefore not be left solely in the hands of Germain, a dangerously fanciful person, nor could it be entrusted to strangers brought in from outside. Claire, after giving the matter some thought, felt that with her determined nature she might very well become capable within a short space of time of exercising some supervision over the Silken Net. A small executive committee would have to be formed. Apart from Germain, the only man now left in the family was that queer fish, that low fellow—Bruno Spaniente. Still, a young man who had contrived to get round Lucie, and then managed his affairs very cleverly, could hardly be a fool. . . . Might he, perhaps, be really of some use? But first of all, what had happened to him, what had he been doing in the war?

With her masterful character and her speed in coming to a decision, Claire Euffe took the bull by the horns and promptly went off to Nice, where she rang at Lucie Spaniente's door and found her alone. She addressed her without hesitation by her Christian name as in the old days, and by adopting a natural manner wiped out the long severance of their relations.

"Oh," she said, "how prettily you have arranged everything! And what a nice house! Are those photographs of your children? Why, they're splendid! And how well they look! Really, my dear Lucie, you have shown both taste and character in the way you've managed things. I congratulate you and it makes me happy to see it. Sincerely happy!"

Though under no illusions where her sister-in-law was concerned, Lucie was powerless to prevent Claire from speaking to her in a tone of voice which made her feelings of satisfaction and of self-importance only too evident. Claire was far too accustomed to having docile and amenable listeners, entirely at her service and disposal. She wielded a weapon against which there seemed to be no defence—a firm belief that her wit, her education, and her social gifts were unsurpassed. So strong was this conviction—so radiant—that she ended by making others share it with her.

She said that the death of the head of the family had been a cruel bereavement for them all, and that it had resulted in many changes. Interspersing her questions with favourable comments and praise, she learned all she wanted to know. Bruno Spaniente who, as he grew older, was devoting less time to games, had bought a garage. This had turned out to be a fortunate move on his part. Thanks to this garage he had succeeded in getting himself mobilized for special service locally, because his workshops carried out the repairs for a military car park.

Before her visit was over, Claire saw entering the room a kind of sporting gentleman with decidedly handsome features and whose manners were by no means bad. His appearance and demeanour were perhaps rather those of an impresario or a gentleman attending a race meeting, but this was what suited him best. He was full of the Southern geniality and good nature; you felt that he would promise anything you asked, and do so effusively; and that with all this there was guile and cunning in the man. Further, he was the kind of person whom nothing surprises. On seeing Claire, whom he had not met for years past, he showed no trace of astonishment.

"Hullo!" he said, with his Southern accent. "Why, it's that nice Claire! And how goes it?"

It was no part of Claire's purpose to give full powers to Bruno; her intention was rather to make use of him, should the occasion arise, as a counterweight to decisions made by Germain. She was contemplating the formation of a triumvirate for the management of the Silken Net, with herself occupying a place between the two brothers-in-law. After all, the fortune of the Bargès family had had its beginnings in old Grandmother Bargès, a remarkable woman who died at the age of eighty-seven and had always driven everybody at the sword's point. As there now appeared to be some necessity for it, Claire summoned her own heredity to the rescue, and felt confident of discovering within herself some of those qualities which had belonged to her masterful grandmamma. In these ways the rights and interests of the Euffe heirs would be protected by the interested persons themselves.

It was pleasant and amusing for Bruno Spaniente that this proud Euffe family, which had treated him as an intruder, should now be coming to him with a favour to ask. It was pleasant and amusing to be making a triumphal return to Grenoble, on a footing of equality with the members of a social sphere with which he had previously been in contact when standing at the door of a motorcar, with a chauffeur's peaked cap upon his head. . . . His children would be on the same social level as their cousins, born of highly respectable bourgeois marriages which had met with universal approval. It made him laugh to think of himself addressing as "Mother" that dear old lady, a little off her head and a tippler of no mean accomplishment, poor Mother Euffe, who, on the advice of the widow of General de Sainte-Foy, had once given him the sack.

Bruno might perhaps have succumbed to the temptation to remain at Nice and not desert his beloved Mediterranean. But there was now a question of duty, the duty for the carrying out of which he had made himself responsible when he rose in the social scale, a family duty to which he must devote himself for his children's sake. This imperative duty was summed up in a single expression, an expression resplendent in the vastness of all that it implied and the hereditary promise it contained; an expression which already had the strength of a tradition, and stood for all that is honest, fair, and upright in catering; an expression which, by the inspiration of a man now in his grave, had become a symbol of lasting strength and power, around which, some jealousies and vanity notwithstanding, all his descendants stood grouped in close array; an expression more powerful than the family itself, whose motto, in a sense, it formed: the Silken Net.

Claire's decision to form a triumvirate of management which would include her Southern brother-in-law was destined to prove an excellent one in the situation that had now arisen. The resistance at Voreppe was the beginning of what would be, from every point of view, a new stage of the war. Claire foresaw this, and she refused to give way to the feelings of confusion and dismay by which at that time so many of the weaker vessels were being overcome. She kept entirely separate in her mind the unhappy position in which France was now placed, and her own, which was that of a great lady and mistress of a large country house. While the Vichy government were speaking of "misfortune" and "calamity," Claire maintained a rigorous attitude of mind, excluding the people of her own class from all responsibility for the catastrophe. She did, however, make direct references to those whom she regarded as the responsible persons, declaring that all those people who had been at the head of affairs up till now should be shot without further ado. Did the matter call for any discussion at all, and why all this fuss? Did the facts not speak for themselves, and were they not deadly? Then let all that riffraff be swept away, those despicable wretches who had wanted war and declared it, at the instigation of that treacherous country, England.

"In any case," said Claire, to whose utterances much attention was paid, "I am not particularly surprised at what is happening to us. I felt it coming. And my poor Edmond shared my opinion. He was very pessimistic as regards the future."

"It remains to be seen," old M. Mivois said quietly, "whether all that is happening now is a good thing for us, or not."

"Well, at any rate, it's the Republic that will go down to history as responsible for the defeat," another of the guests at White Terraces remarked.

"The Republic is hard hit! So hard that it will never recover. We certainly shan't be sorry to see the last of it."

"This seems to be a unique opportunity for getting rid of a distinct tendency to mob rule."

"And, dear lady, you didn't see that thrilling entry of the Germans into Lyon? The order, the discipline, the marvellous equipment . . ."

"All the things we so badly needed ourselves!"

"And their correctness, their wonderful bearing! All that sort of thing had vanished, in France."

"Nobody ever kept to his proper station in life."

"And no one wanted to do a stroke of work."

"Don't you think they were sublime, those words of the Marshal: *The spirit of enjoyment has got the better of the spirit of sacrifice. Our defeat is due to the cessation of effort. I invite you to a moral and intellectual revival.*' "

"It's as lovely as a Greek statue!"

"And how true it all is!"

"When you come to think of it, didn't the people need this lesson? They see now how badly they have been led. And let us have the courage to say so!"

"Yes indeed, let us!"

It was discussions of this nature that were taking place among Claire's circle of friends. And it was because that lady had a strong character, and was convinced of her own superiority and sure of being a privileged person, that she very soon perceived a silver lining to the cloud of catastrophe—from a moral and social point of view. The national collapse would bring with it an opportunity for the restoration of authority over the common herd, the main body of the population still in a dazed condition and on the brink of destitution. Nothing could be saved from the national wreck without a strengthening of the position of the body of employers, who would obviously be a mainstay of the new regime. Those employers, who only yesterday were being bullied to grant unthinkable concessions, would now at last be enabled to restore the law and order which were their due.

It was with these thoughts in her mind that, when the question arose of giving back to the country, in its service and for its good, some of the élite and flower of its population, Claire deliberately sided with Vichy. Of that élite, she had always claimed to be an embodiment.

"What a pity," she would say, "that Edmond is no longer here! With his knowledge of economic questions, he would have been just the kind of man that is needed for reorganizing France." Agreement with these remarks was all the heartier because it was known how great was the influence which this resolute woman had exercised over her husband. It was indeed generally recognized that Claire, with her talent for conducting a *salon* and for skilful plotting, would have been invaluable to a man engaged in public business.

Her widowhood having robbed her of those great opportunities, Claire concentrated all her efforts upon the Silken Net. In no way handicapped by the enfeebling effects of a tender and sympathetic nature, she was a magnificent business woman, with clear-cut views and an unfaltering will. In short, it was she who was the real head and leader of the family, a task which could be assigned neither to Alberte, insufficiently interested and too much a countess, nor to the crazy Lucie, nor to Germain, a mixture of hesitations and dreams.

Though not openly discussed, there were differences of outlook and opinion among the members of the family. The de Bazairs, at Champagnier, were professed adherents of de Gaulle. The only reason for this was given by Alberte in these words: "If Bob were still alive, I am certain that he would not have agreed to the armistice, and would have gone off to fight." She kept alive in her children's hearts the sure knowledge of their father's heroism—a legacy which every son of the de Bazairs could all but claim as his due. In the boys' eyes there often shone a steely defiant light. In their warlike games they had revived the word "Boche," which the frequenters of White Terraces had banished from their vocabulary as being vulgar and out of place.

Germain's eyes also were turned in the direction of London. As sentiment was the mainspring of all his thoughts and actions, it is probable that memories of the pretty Margaret were not unconnected with his present outlook and convictions, and that equally responsible for them were recollections of English parties, English poets, English tennis and golf, English downs and meadows, the empty boredom of English Sundays, certain characters in Shakespeare and Dickens—in short, a whole medley of unfamiliar customs, new sights and sounds, of idle thoughts and daydreams, by which his youth had been enthralled. Sometimes he wondered whether he should go to the rescue of France and make for

Africa or the English coast at Dover. For the grocery business only filled him with horror. But his plans met with no better fate than his poems which he never finished, and his love affairs which fell short, always, of the sublime. He was one of those who stand upon the seashore and watch the ships while they sail away into the distance. His life was compounded of disillusions and habits. The disillusions were now bidding him depart. But the habits, which were stronger and more comfortable, were holding him fast in a place where he hated to be.

His was the cast of mind that is only too ready to believe that all is lost. A future of setbacks and disaster would not have been altogether distasteful to him: he would have made it an excuse for his own surrender, for ceasing from all further effort. Even the smiles of the fat, good-natured Marie-Thérèse failed to restore his courage and faith. It must here be said that that plump, inert materfamilias did in fact take all the poetry out of his life. There she would sit in state, cheerful and happy and only half conscious of her surroundings, in the midst of a brood of squalling children, continuously handling babies' napkins, feeding bottles, and other appliances, or spooning gruel into some little wide-open mouth. Languidly and with no trace of ill temper, she would call out an occasional word of reproach to a dishevelled little band of children who, having transformed the house into a miniature battlefield with bridgeheads and points of resistance, fought devastating engagements with a miscellaneous collection of projectiles. Mirrors, vases, candelabra came crashing to the floor amid the din of counterattacks. Every evening on his return to his home Germain Euffe found it strewn with wreckage and turned topsy-turvy as though it had been searched. In the midst of this devastation Marie-Thérèse, with the calm composure of a woman whose numerous confinements are easy and who has come to rather more than full bloom, would be giving not a thought to the tumult of a Europe at war and would say to him placidly: "The children have been enjoying themselves like anything." One could have hit the fat creature! But later, with her fine ample frame which despite its plumpness was as firm as ever; with all her sighs, which only hid a smile, she recovered charms to which Germain was still ready to succumb. In every duty that fell to her to carry out, Marie-Thérèse showed the same liberality, the same good will; an air of pleasure in which there was a touch of plaintiveness; and complete sincerity. The curves of her figure were certainly unrestrained, extremely unfashionable, and such as would be inadmissible in any woman but a lawful wife and mother of a large family. Such curves, which no man would have chosen for his own, prevented her from looking well dressed. But they still brought Germain pleasure, and

273

their possession gave him a feeling of power which, for a man lacking in stability and whose constitution was rather frail, was a tonic and a consolation. And so their lives went on. And still the children came. And Germain felt himself bound more and more to the Silken Net, though as a merchant he was lamentably incompetent. He avenged himself for his enslavement by adopting a policy so liberal that it cost the firm dear. He made it a point of honour to buy his stocks without any bargaining over prices and to sell at a profit so small as to be completely safe from criticism on moral grounds. But the dividends suffered thereby. It was to put a stop to all this that Claire went to Nice to seek out Bruno Spaniente.

Bruno was indeed a heaven-sent man, in that he had no hesitation in shouldering the rough-and-tumble responsibilities which neither Claire, on account of her social position, nor Germain, with his unpractical idealism and fanciful nature, would have dared to take. The way in which he picked up the ins and outs of catering was remarkable, and very soon, by dint of business methods involving subtleties not far removed from dishonest trading, he showed himself to be a man of the same stamp and abilities as M. Constant Euffe, the founder of the firm. So far, at least, as results were concerned. For his ways of working were quite different, and derived rather from a Southern love of experiment than from any fixed method. He was a past master in the art of addressing a comparative stranger in the most familiar way, slapping him on the shoulder and making a great display of sincerity just suited to the occasion, with an abundant flow of words and a touch of pathos where required, and good nature always to the fore. The fact was that he had not got the same rigid conception of what constitutes a lie as those who live in the north of France. In his opinion it was not by diligence and hard work that money was made, but rather by tricks and dodges and artfulness and guile, and a certain elasticity where promises and undertakings are concerned. A power to convince others, and to make himself liked, seemed to radiate from him: Claire herself took his "Hullo, fair lady!" and "I say, sister . . ." without being shocked, astonishingly familiar though these methods of addressing her were. He won Alberte's heart by flattering remarks about her sons, whom he compared with young princes. He pleased Marie-Thérèse by sprawling on the carpet with her little urchins and leading them in an attack on cupboards and such pieces of furniture as were still serviceable. He bewitched Germain by saying to him: "You're a brainy young man, aren't you? Very well then, brother-in-law, just you leave mustard to me and get on with that literature of yours. You'll be making the family famous."

With Claire's agreement and approval, he overthrew the Euffe principles as laid down by the late Constant Euffe, which Edmond had faithfully followed. The running of the firm had been based upon a rule of steady and regular sale, which was constantly checked. Bruno adopted the reverse policy, that of restricting supply, and at a time when demand was continually increasing. He was one of the first men to foresee that France would be depleted of all the material means of life. He secretly stocked thousands of tins of sardines, margarine, chocolate, and preserved foods of various kinds, together with bottles of vintage wines, old brandy, cocktails, et cetera. The less he sold, the more he bought, carrying off everything on which he could lay hands. Rising prices had no fears for him, for he believed that it would be long before they began to swing back once more. He rented new warehouses and arranged for the transport of tons of goods to White Terraces, Bouquéron, Montbonnot, and the various flats occupied by the members of the family. He predicted that a day would come when he would sell everything at ten to twenty times its present purchase price. He foretold a despotic reign of human appetite, a dictatorship of provision merchants, a supremacy of food; he prophesied that the holders of "key products" would always find means of obtaining petrol, safe-conducts, apartments, boots and shoes, wearing apparel, fuel, tobacco, and everything that makes life happy and pleasant and warm. Whatever the outcome of the nation's ordeal, the Euffes, thanks to the Silken Net, would be in a good position when they emerged. The German defeat in the Battle of Britain enabled him to prophesy a long and exhausting war: from the commercial point of view it was exactly what he desired.

There was another way in which the family's position was altogether a good one, in that it had a footing in both camps. Alberte and Germain were siding with the resistance movement. Bruno, however, was among the first to be enrolled in the Pétain Legion. Not that he had political views of any kind. But the wearing of the badge assured him of certain advantages, with great freedom of action, and, as he himself said, "It's all to the good of the customers." His enjoyment of priority in the purchase of important stocks, his being able to procure extra lorries, with special authority (withheld from rival firms) to send them where he wished—these privileges were doubtless due to the backing he received from the Committee of the Legion, a few important members of which, thanks to the Silken Net, had as much sugar, coffee, butter, spirits, and even *foie gras* as they wanted. In addition to these gentlemen, there were some carefully selected officials and civil servants who were liberally supplied. Bruno had the run of the Prefecture and the Town Hall, where the secretaries and typists, upon whom he showered small presents, made him welcome. And as for the inspectors of the Vichy Economic Control Commission, all of whom were friends of his, their lives were a round of feasting.

Side by side with all this, Bruno arranged some magnificent dinner parties which became widely known, and at which the guests, egged on by their consciousness of the prevailing dearth of food and the emaciated condition of Frenchmen in a state of destitution, gorged themselves to the point of repletion. These gluttonous parties were occasions for the cementing of various friendships and hatching of plots which had very considerable ramifications throughout the economic system of France. Bruno's guests would exclaim gaily: "What are people complaining about? Aren't we living just as we used to do?"

Little by little Claire, whose principles of management were derived from the Bargès-Chouin, the leading family among the great employers of labour in the district, found herself flirting with collaboration. Now she knew, so she said, "Their" behaviour was correct, one could work with "them." That there was a lot that was good in the German orderliness and method was beyond all question. And M. Bargès, her father, generally supposed to be a cunning old fox, was saying to all and sundry: "As long as they are here, everyone will be kept up to the mark."

The Silken Net dividends were above suspicion. But Bruno kept at his disposal a secret fund which enabled him to handle certain transactions which would hardly bear the light of day. This fund contained sums of money the total of which finally came to exceed that of the turnover appearing in the firm's books. Bruno might be seen walking along quite casually and carrying a big leather portfolio stuffed to bursting point with five-thousand-franc notes. He was known to be a man who would bring off a deal *sub rosa* of a million francs cash down for goods which later would be travelling, duly camouflaged, in government lorries. It was merely a question of arrangement with the Youth Camps and other state organizations. Everyone profited handsomely by these transactions—except the Treasury. But it was a leading slogan in black-market circles—who ruled the whole situation: "Only the—— pay taxes." That was being said openly.

From the special profits which were his own perquisite, Bruno deducted and set aside a certain portion. With this he bought a country house and a fine estate, with furniture, china, and pictures; he took a share in a hotel and a cinema, and wallowed in golden louis and twenty-dollar pieces. Francs by the million came his way with a steady and easy flow. And the different grades of the community were plain for all to see: at the top were those who could consume a thousand francs' worth of food at a meal; below them came the remainder, the ordinary miscellaneous crowd of the thin and insufficiently fed. Considerable efforts had been made to find some way of restoring eminent people to the positions they should occupy. This saying was very much to the point: "Tell me what you eat, I will tell you the sort of man you are."

Were not the men of genuine ability—the men with the most fertile brains of that period—those who knew how to escape from the clutches of the Exchequer, and from all supervision and control, and build up enormous fortunes? Bruno did not doubt that they were. He felt a giant, full of boldness and strength, copiously supplied as he was with food and drink, clad in good soft woollen garments, with his feet in comfortable and watertight shoes and his body at ease in silken underwear: he was indeed magnificently provided with this world's goods, as compared with the penury which was now the lot of those others, mere imbeciles and fools. Professors, intellectuals, artists, officials, all came to pay him court, because they were hungry, poor devils! Beggars, the learned and the humble alike, invaded his offices in a constant stream, and called him saviour. Bruno acknowledged this tribute of praise with a few pounds of chocolate, preserved food, or fats. For him, a mere trifle!

One afternoon in the spring, at about five o'clock, he was at the Shady Nook, at the extremity of Green Island. (Through his good offices this establishment had an ample stock of provisions.) Bruno had a great fondness for this spot, which reminded him of the past, of the early stages of his promotion to the comparatively safe and settled existence of a member of the middle classes. He had driven there with a companion, a young person with captivating eyes. He had ordered, in a private room, a meal which included foie gras, cold chicken, Gruyère cheese, preserves, and champagne. The pretty girl gazed at this luxurious fare with amazement and gratitude. She ate greedily, and Bruno was continually refilling her plate.

"Carry on, sweetie, eat away. And there'll be just as much for you tomorrow if you'd like it."

Her name was Lucette. She had grace and charm and a natural distinction. But for the time being she could think of nothing but the satisfaction of hunger and was holding a leg of chicken to her lips and devouring it till the bone was stripped and bare, with a voracity like that of an animal but which was by no means unpleasant to watch. She had greasy fingers, and her eyes were glistening with her greed. She was too absorbed to think of protecting herself from the idle caresses of Bruno, who was seated beside her.

"Aren't you eating anything, then?"

"I'm tired of eating," Bruno replied. "And I'm getting shamefully fat."

"Well, you are a lucky man!"

She drank deep and then fell upon the remainder of the chicken, tearing off the breast with her fine strong teeth. Her lipstick was forming a red coating which stained the lower portion of her face. Bruno's hand was laid upon a firm hip that was soft and smooth to the touch, and now gaining the warmth which copious nourishment brings. He felt the young woman taking on a new lease of life.

"Well, my beauty, you were hungry!"

"Should I be here if I hadn't been hungry? It's hunger that rules the world today. Don't you think that's vile?"

"Vile?"

Framed by the open window, through a gap in the fresh green foliage he caught sight of the flowery slopes of the Grésivaudan, looking just as they did in former days when he used to come here with Lucie. . . . The air was all a-quiver with rays of sunshine. The scent of lilac was floating in from somewhere hard by. He had with him a hundred thousand francs, which he could spend that very day if he felt so inclined, without accounting for it to anybody. In a world dismembered and out of joint, a world in which beauty and talent went hungry, he had food at his disposal. He felt as though, for the moment, he were one of that world's great potentates.

His hand slid along Lucette's arm until it came in contact with a young bosom elastic and warm. He bent over his companion, over the scented nape of her neck, without her pausing for one moment in her attack on a thick slice of Gruyère. And hiding his flushed face in the soft embrace of her hair, he replied:

"All the same, these are splendid times. For an heir of the Euffes— absolutely 'splendid!"

Of the Euffes, Alberte was the only one who had been really stricken. But the family needed a hero, and Bob de Bazair had filled that need. He had left behind him a countess and titled children. This was all to the good.

He kissed the perfumed neck, murmuring as he did so:

"Have some more to eat. Don't bother about me."

But Lucette asked him, as she made inroads on the jam:

"What do you do with yourself? What are you?"

"What, me?"

His eyes fell upon the pretty girl before him, the iced champagne, the flowers in a vase, his gold cigarette case which lay on the tablecloth, the fine material of his suit, his magnificent morocco-leather portfolio in which he was carrying so many bundles of notes.

"Well," he said, "if you want to know, I'm a winner! Started from scratch, and look at me now . . ."

At that moment a fearsome explosion shook every hole and corner of the town. It felt as though everything was in imminent danger of collapsing in ruin. During the profound silence which followed, it was surprising to observe the sun still shining in the heavens and the mountain heights unmoved. The sounds of firing were heard in the distance, and the rattle of machine guns.

"Ah," cried Bruno, who had been startled, "there's no peace now! Why can't they leave us alone!"

He was thinking of his money, on which he was relying for protection from every danger. But the terrible struggle of the Resistance was about to be intensified at Grenoble and disrupt the whole town. Just as in 1940 the fighting had been brought to a dead stop at Voreppe, so now in the neighbourhood of Voreppe a seething undercurrent of murderous clandestine warfare was destined to begin. There were hidden arms at Champagnier. Robert de Bazair, who was not quite seventeen, was already beseeching his mother to let him go and join the maquis. Alberte refused to give him permission, as this seemed clearly right, but did so with a feeling of horror which was all the greater because in her heart she knew that one day she would give her consent as she thought of Bob, of whom her eldest son was the living image. For it was a law of the de Bazairs that when there is danger ahead, they must go to meet it. She must resign herself to this. Claire, her sister-in-law, was a selfish and conceited woman who would always take sides straightway with those whom she regarded as the Righteous and the Just. Bruno was a profiteer and a man who could tide over any difficulty. But the de Bazairs were noblemen. It is a privilege for which a high price must be paid, when circumstances require it.

On the following day reinforcements of the Gestapo arrived at Grenoble. Arrests and reprisals were beginning.

Bruno departed on a well-timed journey. His attention had been drawn to some interesting stocks at Lyon and he had been told of a few excellent places off the beaten track, in the department of the Ain, where one lived like a prince, at a thousand francs a day.

While in that part of the country it was borne in upon him that there were immense sums of money for which he could be called to account, and it occurred to him accordingly that it would be a clever move on his part to make over a good round sum to the Resistance. To do this at the right moment, neither too soon nor too late, was a somewhat ticklish problem.

He set out to give the matter the most careful thought, following all the official statements and the wireless news. It was becoming more necessary than ever to play a cautious game and to be in a good position in case the landings should take place. He himself would have preferred a patched-up peace which would leave everyone undisturbed so far as occupations and incomes were concerned. But who could tell how the whole business would end? It would be best to have guarantees from both sides. . . .

He felt confident that for himself there were still fine times ahead. "Catering," he said, "has a bigger future than ever." That blessed old Daddy Euffe, now dead and gone, had shown amazing perspicacity when he chose it as his career! Bruno, who was supplying the black market on a big scale, was the true representative of the commercial descendants of the founder of the Silken Net—by his exclusive and wholehearted devotion to His Majesty the Human Stomach, god of war and peace alike.

"If Germain can claim credit for writing rhymes. Claire for being a swell society lady, and Alberte a countess, who've they got to thank for it? Yours truly!"

He was now at the head of that mighty combination, the Euffe Heirs —a man raised by circumstances to a high level of wealth and power.

Printed in the United Kingdom
by Lightning Source UK Ltd.
117671UKS00001B/229